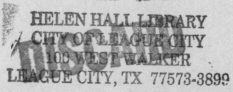

"Vel[...] [...] [...]he decade's great
Ame[...] [...]r latest historical
novel is an incredible acco[...] . . . awesome . . . filled
with action. Anyone who enjoys Native American historical
fiction should try Ms. Munn, who is obviously second to none."
—*The Midwest Book Review*

"Vella Munn creates superior historical romances set among
native Americans, mostly in the years before white encroach-
ment eroded their traditional culture. *Blackfeet Season* is a
story of political and spiritual intrigue, a romance whose soul
is rooted in the connections between the spiritual and the
mundane." —*Oregon Statesman Journal*

"Brims with adventure, emotion and detail."
—*Eugene Register-Guard* on *Spirit of the Eagle*

"Readers will be immediately drawn into this stirring novel . . .
a powerful, exciting read."
—*Romantic Times* on *Daughter of the Mountain*

"A beautiful love story; sensitive, hard-hitting on the emotions." —Catherine Anderson on *The River's Daughter*

By Vella Munn from Tom Doherty Associates

VELLA MUNN

SOUL OF THE SACRED EARTH

A TOM DOHERTY ASSOCIATES BOOK
NEW YORK

SOUL OF THE SACRED EARTH

Copyright © 2000 by Vella Munn

A Forge Book
Published by Tom Doherty Associates, LLC
175 Fifth Avenue
New York, NY 10010

www.tor.com

Forge® is a registered trademark of Tom Doherty Associates, LLC.

ISBN: 0-812-57066-9
Library of Congress Catalog Card Number: 00-023934

First edition: May 2000
First mass market edition: May 2001

Printed in the United States of America

0 9 8 7 6 5 4 3 2 1

My friends, you are my lifeline, my sanity,
   inspiration, and the core of my creativity.
Pat, Tallie, Mary Lou—thank you for being part of
   my life.
Mother, Dick, Hank, and Ryan, I love you.
Julian, Grandma is rich because of you.
   Your kisses and zerbicks are everything.
And, Lance, you touched my heart.

Author's Musings

Soul of the Sacred Earth began whispering to me the first time I visited Arizona. I'm the product of a Northwest forest upbringing and am nourished by evergreens and mountains, not great sweeps of land and forever skies. Still, I wanted to learn everything I could about the people who originally settled in that water-starved country.

Back home, I began my research, or maybe the truth is that the past took hold and led me where it wanted. I learned of the Hopi, who call themselves People Of Peace, and the more aggressive Navajo. The two tribes fought and traded and shared the same rocks, sand, and hardy grasses. They had unique belief systems, legends, and creation stories, yet they were tolerant of each other's differences—unlike the Spanish.

Although it has no place in this story, I'd like to share a bit of my most recent trip to Arizona. With me were my mother and husband, both wise enough to give me space and silence when I'm absorbing an environment I want to incorporate into a book. In late October, we traveled through

Navajo land and into the Hopi reservation, often not encountering other travelers for miles. My ultimate goal was Oraibi—Rock Place On High to the Hopi—possibly the oldest continuously occupied settlement in the United States.

Cameras aren't allowed at Oraibi, so I would have to depend on my senses to record it as I walked around the ancient, crumbling buildings. Old men with graying braids stared at me and collarless dogs silently tailed me as I followed narrow dirt streets. Eventually, I came to the edge of the mesa and looked down, down to the sweeping valley far below where Hopi farmers once tended the precious corn that was both food and an integral part of their religious ceremonies. Directly below me was a ledge, and on that an ageless kiva, or ceremonial chamber. As much as it fascinated me, I was an outsider and had no right or wish to disturb the precious structure. The memory would be enough.

The sky went on and on, as did the land, untouched and unspoiled. Proud and defiant. Only the wind spoke to me that day, and I understood—the earth endures.

Vella Munn

1

"Stand fast!" Vincente de Zaldivar ordered the half-frozen men around him. His breath puffed white in the frigid air, and he shivered inside his heavy armor. "Fire and fire again. We are God's soldiers! The heathens will not prevail!"

"But—"

"Silence!" Cold, anger, hunger, and weariness spurred his words. "Our enemies must be defeated! My brother's death *will* be avenged!" He glared at the filthy soldier, a youth barely old enough to have left his mother's side. "Look at what we have accomplished." He pointed up at the mesa-top Keres pueblo known as the Sky City and its nearly one thousand heathen residents. "Our weapons have created great holes in the stone walls and will continue to do so. Lead and powder and cannonballs will stand the day, not arrows and stones."

Almost before he'd finished speaking, a large rock hurled

from high overhead landed less than a foot away, causing him to jump back. His boots crunched on the ice that coated the vast and worthless land. If any of the men under him noticed his sudden fright, they were wise enough not to acknowledge it. That the primitive savages had thus far resisted the best the Spanish army could mount was unacceptable. The heathens' time of regret and his of vengeance was coming, and when it did . . .

At the insistence of his uncle, Captain General Don Juan de Oñate, the Indians had been told—not once, not twice, but three times—to lay down their arms and submit to the authority of the King our Lord. Beyond that, they'd been commanded to surrender those responsible for the uprising so they could be dealt with justly.

Pacing because anger and frustration made inactivity impossible and because the frigid, relentless wind in this barren and Godless place cut through everything, Vincente recalled his instructions. If God was so merciful as to grant a victory—and surely He would—he, Vincente, was charged with arresting young and old alike and punishing all those of fighting age in any way he deemed prudent, as a warning to all savages living in the Crown's newly claimed kingdom.

"Those you execute you will expose to public view," his uncle had concluded. "And if you should want to show leniency, you must do everything possible to make the Indians believe you do so at the request of the friars, so they will see that the friars are their benefactors and protectors, so they will come to love and esteem them, and to fear us."

Fear the Spanish army, yes!

"Where is Tomas?" he demanded, looking around for the tame Mexican Indian who'd come here nine years ago with the colonizer Gaspar Castano de Sosa and spoke some of the Pueblo language. When the short, stocky creature hurried up to him, clutching his ragged blankets around him, Vincente ordered him to once again address the savages.

"Remind them that we have been sent here by the most powerful king and ruler in the world, that they *must* meekly render obedience and vassalage to that king and the Christian God, that we serve God our Lord and will bring about the salvation of their souls but are also committed to bringing them to justice," he told Tomas. "Remind them that many of their number have fallen under our weapons and more will do so if they do not surrender and place themselves under my care."

"They will not listen."

"They will!" Was he surrounded by dullards? "Tell them to count their dead. Remind them that we have already been here two days and nights and will not leave. Order them to look into the eyes of their women and children and ask themselves if they are willing to risk those lives as well."

Tomas continued to look skeptical, but he was obviously intelligent enough not to argue with his better. At no small risk to his own life, Tomas once again plodded to the base of the large, sharp bluff upon which the Sky City had been built.

Vincente paid little attention to Tomas's bellowed, halting words; nor did he care whether the Indian's command of the heathens' language was adequate to the task. What mattered to Vincente was that at his order, his men had ceased their firing so his brother's killers could hear everything that was being said to them.

Silence followed Tomas's incomprehensible speech, but finally someone called out from the pueblo high above.

"What did they say?" he demanded of Tomas.

"That—that they will die before they surrender."

As the frozen afternoon beat on, Vincente put the next phase of his plan into action. Not yet thirty, he'd already led some sixty men onto the plains in an attempt to capture and domesticate buffalo. Although the plan had failed, he'd learned how to command. Now, covered by heavy musket and cannon fire, a number of his handpicked soldiers managed to scramble up the four hundred feet of narrow stairway from the plains to the mesa top, where two hundred interconnected houses had been built.

The first Spanish explorers to see the Sky City had proclaimed it the greatest stronghold ever seen, and it had been, in part because its residents kept it fortified with rocks that they rolled down on any attackers. In addition, the pueblo had been well stocked with maize, beans, and turkeys. Still, at first the Keres had not been seen as a warlike people.

Years later, when the now dead Juan de Zaldivar and his thirty fellow soldiers had reached the pueblo, they found that Vincente's uncle's troops had departed only a few days before, taking large quantities of the Indians' blankets, clothing, and food with them and leaving the Keres with barely enough for their own needs in the middle of winter. The natives' refusal to surrender what little warmth and food remained had enraged Juan and led to his death at the hands of the equally determined Indians. Now, relentless retaliatory fighting led by Vincente had depleted the natives' rock supply.

At Vincente's order, the first soldiers to reach the pueblo had immediately set fire to the roofs of the stone houses, forcing the Indian defenders, most of whom had no arrows left, to retreat deep into the honeycombed structures. More and more soldiers, hauling a small cannon up with them, joined their companions as their fleeing foes crowded into kivas. Instead of risking ambush within the dimly lit religious and ceremonial chambers, the soldiers fired lead and everything they could load into the cannon at the walls, crumbling what had taken thousands of hands many years to construct.

Vincente was standing before the largest hole when the first plea for mercy reached him. Although he hadn't brought Tomas with him, it didn't matter—there was no mistaking the pitiful cries of women and children.

"Surrender!" he ordered, using one of the handful of Keres words he'd bothered to learn. "Surrender!"

Silence flowed on the heels of his command, seeming to freeze as solidly as the earth that lay under the winter snow. He drew in the acrid stench of charred wood and flesh. Then a small shadow filled the nearby opening created by lead and powder. Vincente lifted his bloodied sword. The shadow shrank back, and this time when he ordered surrender, the single bellowed word echoed against stone.

A woman clutching a baby to her breast was the first to emerge. Vincente's fingers ached to send the sword in a swift, wide arch that would separate the woman's body from her head, but instead of avenging his late brother, he stepped back, allowing her to pass. Another woman was directly behind the first, and after that came a number of children. It pleased him that they were all ash-covered from the fires, coughing, their eyes streaming tears. Smoke would not, he vowed, be their only reason for crying.

It had never occurred to the heathens that their reliance on a single access to their mesa-top settlement might one day trap them. Vincente, his hunger and exhaustion forgotten, took full advantage by forcing them to descend the torturous path, one at a time, into the waiting and ungentle arms of his men.

Many of the captives tried to buy his forgiveness by presenting him with gifts of food, blankets, and robes as they filed past, but he disdained all offerings. The heathens' stench was all but unbearable, the look in their eyes reminding him of curs seeking forgiveness from an angry master.

"We are in a wild land peopled by godless savages," his uncle had said not long after the expedition—consisting of a hundred loaded wagons, more than seven thousand animals, and many troops in addition to one hundred and thirty Spanish families—started moving along the west bank of the Rio Grande little more than half a year ago. "Those brave souls who came before us succeeded because they met hostility with might. The savages must come to understand that their arrows and knives are no match against war horses and muskets. Better a number die now than for us and those who depend on us for protection to live in fear."

Vincente could not have agreed more.

Fear could render a man stupid; Vincente knew that. Now, as the sun slid toward the west and shrouded the tiled fields, sharp rocks, red cliffs, narrow valleys, lava mounds, and rugged native grasses that made up this wild land, he learned that whatever limited intellect the Indians might have once possessed had deserted them. Otherwise, certainly they would have seen the futility in trying to hide. However, as the line of men, women, and children, many of them wounded, continued down the twisting path, it became clear that hundreds more remained hidden in the dark chambers that made up their miserable homes.

When he ordered his men to go find them, he was met with protest. The heathens might be armed and waiting to attack. Wasn't it better simply to set fire to every stick of wood in the pueblo, thus giving the Indians the option of either surrendering or burning to death? Vincente contemplated that, but his sword hadn't yet tasted enough blood, and the need for revenge burned within him.

"You defy me?" he demanded of his troops. "You are afraid of women and children? Infants?"

"No!"

"Of the men perhaps? You, the king's soldiers, believe yourselves inferior to those who can barely walk erect?"

"No!"

"You doubt God's hand in this? His demand for might and justice?"

"No!"

The denial was still echoing around him when the first soldier pushed his way into the nearest chamber, a dagger in one hand, rapier in the other. He was followed, antlike, by his companions, and although Vincente remained outside with what there was of the sun on his back and his stomach rumbling, his ears soon told him that his men had found their prey.

The Indians came out singly or in small groups, cowering before the soldiers or wrestled to the surface by superior strength. Vincente allowed the first resistor, a crone of a woman, to scrabble past him, but when she was followed by a tall man with a side wound that streamed blood, he lunged at the savage, burying his sword to the hilt in the yielding flesh.

More Indians emerged, their cries pounding in his head. He permitted none to pass; instead, he dispatched them one by one until the smell of blood filled him and he couldn't move for the bodies piled around him.

This was for his brother!

His arms and shoulders ached. His head became a drumbeat of pain and exhilaration, and he killed and killed again as if he'd been born to this one task. Arms, legs, and heads flew. Other soldiers followed his lead, their prayers to a vengeful god lending them strength.

Panting, his legs trembling, Vincente finally took note of the dying light. From his vantage point high above the endless, godless land, it seemed as if he could see forever. If the great explorer Francisco Vasquez de Coronado had been able to stand here and look out almost sixty years earlier, perhaps he wouldn't have continued his futile search for the legendary Seven Cities Of Gold.

"Set fire to it all!" Vincente cried. His throat rasped, bringing tears to his eyes.

As night sought to sweep over the plains, mesa, and pueblo of Acoma, it was kept at bay by red, clawing flames. If any insects were about, whatever sound they made was lost in the screams of dying Keres.

February 12, 1599

Competition had been fierce among those seeking a contract for the colonization of the land north of New Spain, which some now called Mexico. Although a number of the contenders had been compelled by religious zeal, others coveted the appointment because they had heard tales of gold and silver. Despite the earlier debacle of the expedition led by Gaspar Castano de Sosa, which saw him eventually imprisoned for what the Crown determined were grave injustices against the natives, there had been no shortage of applicants for the position.

Don Juan de Oñate of Zacatecas was a man of enormous wealth and distinguished lineage with more than twenty years of experience fighting and pacifying Mexican Indians. His wife was Dona Isabel de Tolosa, and her lineage was impeccable: her grandfather had been Cortes and her great grandfather Montezuma; her father was a renowned conquistador and mine owner.

Oñate's contract with the Crown made him in almost every sense a dictator. As governor and captain general, he was the colony's highest judicial officer, with the power of settling all decisions in civil and criminal cases. Most importantly, he presented himself as a devout Catholic, his image winning him favor with the Church's highest officials.

On this day, some three weeks after the burning of the Sky City and the killing of more than eight hundred Indians, the remaining five hundred Keres, plus a handful from different tribes, stood at the village of Santo Domingo awaiting their fate.

With his nephew, Vincente, at his elbow, Oñate strode forward. His eyes swept dispassionately over the wounded remnants of a people that had once provided him and his men with food, clothing, and shelter. He spoke through Tomas.

"Responsibility for meting out punishment has been granted me both by the Crown and by God. I could set you free, but if I did, you might rise up against us again, and I will not, cannot allow that to happen. After much deliberation, I have determined that nothing will be served by more deaths. Instead, the men among you will serve as an example of the Crown's power. All males over the age of twenty-five years will give twenty years of personal servitude to the Crown. In addition, they each will have one foot cut off." Vincente grunted almost soundlessly; crippled, the men would be harmless.

Groans and sobs followed the translation of Oñate's announcement, and he waited out the irritating sound.

"Furthermore, all males between twelve and twenty-five are sentenced to twenty years of servitude, save for the two Hopi and one Navajo Indian who were among those apprehended. They will have their right hands cut off and be set free to convey news of this punishment to their people."

A single sound, a curse perhaps, briefly stopped him.

"I am a just man and as such I declare that all children under twelve are free and innocent of the offenses their parents carry. I place the girls under the care and guidance of our father commissary, Fray Alonso Martinez, asking him to distribute them in this kingdom or elsewhere so they may attain the knowledge of God and salvation of their souls.

"Boys of tender age are entrusted to my nephew in order that they may attain the same goal."

His still-young features impassive, Vincente nodded.

"Finally, the old men and women as well as those disabled in the war are to be entrusted to the Apaches of the province of Querechos to be utilized as it pleases the wild Indians."

When he was done, Oñate nodded to his soldiers, who began grabbing adult male prisoners and hauling them toward the large stone he'd selected as the mutilation site. If only the rest of the kingdom's heathens could see the stricken looks or hear the pitiful cries! If they heard, then no Spanish man, woman, or child need ever fear the kind of death Juan had suffered.

"Begin," he ordered the massive man who waited, axe uplifted, beside the stone.

2

Summer, 1628, Hopi Land, Black Mesa

According to Navajo legend, when the First People lived in the Fifth World, they made their homes near rivers and springs or the Place of Emergence because the only water was there; but after clouds were formed, rain fell on the mountain and in valleys and people could travel wherever they wanted to gather the seeds, berries, and nuts they needed for life. The valleys and mesas turned green with grasses and bright with flowering shrubs.

As the Dineh began to divide into families and clans and made ready to move to different places, First Woman turned to the Bird People for wisdom on how to build houses. Eagle, who lived on the crest of Blue Mountain, showed them his nest made from sticks, poles, twigs, spruce trees, and feathers from his breast. Although Eagle's nest wasn't warm enough for the winter months, First Woman proclaimed that all should follow his plan so the First People's homes would be round like the sun.

After Eagle left, Mrs. Oriole showed First Woman her willow bark, marsh grass, and milkweed pod fuzz nest. Hosteen Woodpecker tried to convince First People to peck their homes into the side of a tree trunk, but although First Woman declared that the Dineh couldn't live in hollow logs, she decided they would use the sound he made to call people to council meetings and summon help.

Cliff Swallow took the First People to his bluff-top home made from adobe mud and grass. Some said they couldn't live so far from the ground but thanked Swallow for showing them how to make adobe plaster. Others, however, said they didn't mind building ladders. They became the Cliff House People or Cliff Dwellers.

Those still looking for a home studied the work of the Water People such as Hosteen Muskrat, Hosteen Mink, and Hosteen Otter as well as the dwellings made by Beaver People, Mrs. Caterpillar, Spider Woman, and finally Ant People whose homes were partly underground and partly on ground level, all covered with earth. When First People saw the roof opening with its hidden doorway facing the east to greet the morning sun, the circular floor in the shape of the sun and full moon, and the storage rooms, they knew they'd found a place that couldn't blow away and that the rain couldn't harm, one that would be cool in summer and warm in winter.

The Navajo warrior named Cougar, whose mother and thus he were members of the White Shell clan, had repeated the familiar legend to himself as he made his way to the windswept, low bluff that provided a view of the Hopi pueblo Oraibi. The legend, he had hoped, would keep his mind clean and pure, but now he cleared his thoughts of everything except why he'd come here. Even the chants and songs a tribal singer had given him for strength and courage would have to wait. Otherwise, he might die.

Naked except for a doeskin over his privates and moccasins, Cougar clutched his stone knife in his powerful right hand, alert for a glimpse of those who'd recently come here, those he already hated. Around his shoulder, he'd wound the rope he hoped to use to lead away one of their horses.

A horse!

For a moment, the dream of sitting astride one of the powerful animals pushed aside caution. As a boy, he'd occasionally seen them from a distance, the sight filling him with awe and envy and even disbelief, but a horse wasn't for an untried youth, and even the bravest warrior seldom risked getting close enough to the animals' masters—men who called themselves Spanish soldiers—to touch, let alone steal, one.

His grandfather had warned that the soldiers would kill to protect their prized possessions, and Cougar believed Drums No More. However, he was a man now and, along with many other braves, believed that if his people were to survive the impact of the newcomers, they must fight with the weapons of these new enemies. Besides, horses made the Dineh swift. Strong.

A slow, deep breath to calm his heart's pounding, a testing of his long, firm legs, a quick hand over his broad, dark chest, and he was on the move again, bent low. His hair was caught against his skull with a length of hide, but he still felt its movement along the sides of his neck. This morning he'd drunk as much as his belly could hold, and if he had to wait until tomorrow or even beyond that to drink again, so be it. Neither would he heed the need for sleep or food.

It was summer, the land dry and hard. He felt heat through his moccasins and sweat ran from him, but he'd lived through enough seasons that he trusted the Holy People to again bless the land with precious rain.

His legs propelled him effortlessly past endless nothing, around the countless rocks that grew from the earth, into a dry wash and back up again. A prairie dog poked its head out of its underground home and regarded him with a child's curiosity. Lifting his hand, he acknowledged the small creature. Further on he spotted a crow and honored its existence as well. What he'd thought was a small root poking up from the earth revealed itself as a lizard, but it scrambled away on a blur of tiny legs before he could greet it.

New sounds came to him now that he was close to Oraibi, not the dangerous clank and clatter of armor and fire-spewing weapons, but the soft chewing of many horses. Stopping, he dropped to his knees behind a piñon bush and peered through its branches.

The wind shifted and he caught the horses' scent, which was rich and alive like the smell of buffalo, deer, or antelope. Horses had more meat over their bones than even a healthy, spring-fed doe, and from many days of watching as they and their owners made their way to the sacred Hopi village, he knew how strong they were, and how swift.

He would ride one of them! Claim it as his own! The soldiers would try to kill him, but to be Navajo meant to take what one needed. If he died today, he would begin his journey to the underworld where those who'd died before him, including his wife, waited. It was good.

Oraibi had been built atop a broad, high mesa, and as always, the sight of the great rock city snagged his breath. He would never understand why the Hopi chose to live their lives in one place and so close to each other, robbed of the ability to move where and when the gods told them to, but he could admire what they'd created. It was said that Oraibi had been here forever. It belonged to the land, stone set in stone, gray like summer-dead grasses.

In order to reach the farming and hunting lands that lay below the many-roomed structure, the Hopi climbed down several hundred of feet of steep cliff, aided for part of the journey by ladders. Tending the sparse corn and other crops, which somehow found life in the thin earth and deeply buried, precious moisture, meant traveling long distances and exposing themselves to attack, but it wasn't for a Navajo to question the way of those who called themselves People of Peace.

Closer, closer he moved, his body nearly one with the earth. The Hopi, many wearing cotton shirts and leggings, trudged from valley floor up to Oraibi and back down again. He kept his distance from them.

Cougar searched the land. A warrior who'd recently come here to trade had told him of the Spanish. The soldiers had set up camp in the open. One, perhaps their leader, slept nearby and yet separate, along with two slaves. There was another, a brown-clothed man called a padre, who had erected a small shelter made of blankets and sticks at the base of the mesa, mere feet from a well-trod path. At least one soldier was always near him, making Cougar wonder whether the man was afraid of being alone or if he had something the soldiers wanted.

Someone coughed, the sound close. Motionless and ready to fight, he glanced to his right, but it was only an old woman, her face like cracked clay. If she'd spotted him, she might have cried out, but perhaps her eyes were failing her, for she trudged past. Cougar started forward again.

The newcomers' many sheep, although loose, grazed under the watchful eye of a mounted soldier. The horses, more than he could count, were contained within a large stick-and-rope barrier. Deer grew fat because they were free to roam endlessly for food; shouldn't the Spanish have learned from the wisdom of deer and allowed the horses the same freedom? Perhaps, he pondered as he waited for his ears and eyes and nose to bring him wisdom, the Spanish knew of no other way than to make prisoners of everything that came within their grasp.

And perhaps—this thought brought a brief smile to his lips—the Spanish feared as well as hated his people, who had once wandered the earth but had long ago found peace in Dinehtah, The Land. If they did, then they were not as stupid as they appeared.

No, not stupid. A man who hacks the hand off a helpless and unarmed man is dangerous. Grizzly dangerous. Cougar's mouth went dry at the memory of what his grandfather had endured years ago at the Sky City and would continue to endure as long as Drums No More drew breath.

Although Cougar hated crawling on his belly like a snake, only someone who keeps his head lower than the surrounding growth can hope to move unseen toward his enemy. Despite his efforts, the dry grass protested as he wriggled past.

He prayed to First Man that the sounds of the wind and of the grazing, sometimes whinnying horses would hide the soft rustle, but if it didn't, he still had his knife, now gripped between his teeth. The hot midday sun beat down on his exposed back and insects crawled onto and over him, causing his flesh to twitch. He blinked only rarely, his gaze fixed on the solitary soldier sitting near the horse corral.

Last night he'd imagined his knife cutting through the leather gate fastening, so that not only the horse he chose could escape, but also many others. It was too bad more of his people weren't here to help, but his namesake was a solitary hunter and, today, so was he, because that had been the shaman Storm Wind's wisdom.

Closer, closer, his progress was measured in one muscle pull at a time. His elbows were being rubbed raw by the ground and his knees burned.

Drums No More would be proud.

Voices flowed over him. He was no stranger to the language of the Hopi, having learned it when his parents had given shelter to a Hopi youth through a long, cold winter and he and the boy had become friends. Today, though, the words tangled like spider webs in his mind and he felt no need to separate them. The conversations, like the sound of horses, made what he was doing easier.

He was watching several children at play when he spotted another soldier, this one's body held prisoner within a hard, shining suit. This tall man was the one who slept separate from the others. He walked with long, sweeping steps, a bull elk striding unafraid. He appeared several years older than the rest and his mouth was set in a strong, unsmiling line. His eyes moved constantly, first taking in the path leading up to Oraibi, then looking into the distance where several Hopi men were using sticks to loosen the ground around their corn, then at the horses. When the soldier's eyes settled on the shelter where the padre was staying, his spine straightened, and he clenched his fingers.

The other soldiers had removed their heavy metal head coverings, but this one still wore his. Sweat streamed out from under it. Perhaps the Spanish adorned themselves in elaborate costumes, as Apaches did during their rituals, to ward off illness or evil powers. If that was so, then a Spanish ritual must last many moons. There was another possibility. The metal the soldiers covered themselves with was too thick and hard for an arrow to pierce, and those who feared attack lived in a state of constant readiness.

Looking around, Cougar saw that two young Hopi women were climbing down the ladder, one just now reaching the ground. Straightening, the maiden tugged on her dress so the hem covered her knees. Her eyes fell on the helmeted soldier, and she pulled her arms close to her body as if trying to make less of herself. The soldier's back was to her; it would be an easy matter for her to rush at him and bury a knife in him.

The earth has been laid down, the earth has been laid down. The earth has been laid down, it has been made. The earth spirit has been laid down. It is covered over with the growing things, it has been laid down. The earth has been laid down, it has been made.

The sweat lodge song flowed through Cougar, strengthening and centering him, leaving him empty of everything except what it was to be one of the Earth People. After another look at the helmeted soldier's back, he rose. He would have preferred to remain close to the ground, but countless feet had trampled what little grass grew here, and there was nothing for him to hide behind.

He was far enough away from the soldiers that any sound he might make wouldn't carry. True, he might be spotted because he wore less clothing than most Hopi men, but, he told himself, the Spanish didn't have eagles' eyes. As long as he walked slowly, his head down, and as long as the dry painting's magic remained with him, he would be safe.

A rangy dog woke from its nap and ambled toward the horse corral. For a long time, the soldier sitting near the gate paid the dog no mind, but finally the animal slunk close enough that it could have stretched out its muzzle and touched the man. The man turned first his head and then his upper body toward the dog. Whatever he said caused the dog's ears to swing forward.

Whether the man offered the dog something to eat or chased it away was of no concern to Cougar, who stood on the opposite side of the corral, but it occurred to him that perhaps the creature was a diversion sent by First Man. He took advantage of the distraction by dropping to his knees and rolling under the lowest stretch of rope, then quickly stood and, with his back to the horses, assessed his world. Soldier and dog were nearly one now, the man's hand extended toward the animal, panting dog's eyes locked on those fingers.

Slowly, like a snake uncoiling, Cougar faced the horses. Barely aware of what he was doing, he took the rope off his shoulder and tried to remember what he'd been told and observed about the creatures. They placidly submitted to a man's weight on their back, but the slightest thing, like a wind-borne feather, could startle them. They were curious and shy, but sometimes bold. Lacking the wisdom of deer and antelope, they would probably starve or die of thirst if left alone on the plains. Most of all they were strength and speed.

He'd never been this close to one before, hadn't realized they were this tall or that their feet were solid like rocks, or that they could sleep standing up, which many appeared to be doing on this long, hot day. The soldiers put strange contraptions on their backs and used loops that hung down the animals' sides to assist them in mounting, but none of these horses were so encumbered. That—

Movement to his right snagged his breath and made him tighten his muscles the way his namesake did just before charging its prey. What had caught his attention wasn't a rabbit or fawn but an approaching red-brown horse with long, pale hair on the back of its neck. Glancing under its belly, he determined that it was female. It moved like a dancer ruled by rapid drumbeats, the prancing letting him know it was young. He wasn't sure what a female horse should be called, so he thought of it as a doe.

"Thank you, Nandza' gai," he whispered, and touched the leather bag around his neck.

It still seemed wondrous that the horse doe hadn't run away, still more magical that it actually extended its head toward him. Driven by curiosity, he reached out and touched the black nose. He was surprised to find it soft, the creature's damp breath warm and gentle on his flesh. The horse took yet another step closer, and he fought not to draw away. Now its head was so close and low that he could look deep into eyes large like a night-darkened lake.

"Do you not fear me?" he asked. "I am called Cougar, a warrior, a hunter. A doe should fear a cougar."

By way of answer, the horse pressed her head against his chest and pushed, nearly knocking him off balance. He was glad no one could hear his quick intake of breath or know his heart no longer beat in rhythm.

"No," he laughed. "You do not fear me."

There were questions he wanted to ask the horse and messages he needed to give it. Most of all, he wished he knew how he was going to get onto the high, broad back, but before he could fully turn his mind to that, he heard a low growl. Alarmed, he pressed the palm of his hand along the underside of the horse's neck where a vein pulsed, and listened. The growl wasn't repeated, but he still felt its echo inside him. There were so many horses between him and the soldier that he could no longer see the man or the dog. Although he told himself that no one had spoken of the Spanish being able to change form or fly, he couldn't be sure. Nandza' gai might have sent the dog to the soldier as a distraction, but that didn't mean he dared cease being cautious.

"I want you to come with me," he whispered to the horse. "My people need you and others of your kind. Please, tell me how this thing will be done."

By way of answer, the doe bared strong teeth and reached for the rope dangling from his fingers. Feeling foolish, he shook out the length and looped it over the animal's neck just behind the ears, as he'd seen soldiers do. The doe laid back both ears, but only for a heartbeat before letting her head sag forward as if bored. He felt more sure of himself now that he had a way of leading the gods'-given gift, but he still didn't know how he would get her beyond the soldiers.

A horse squealed nearby. On his toes, he looked around, but his vision was limited by the many large bodies. The sound might have been one of those senseless things the creatures did, but he didn't dare allow himself to be lulled by the thought. He wrapped his fingers around the long, pale neck hair and pulled, testing its strength.

His legs must have known what he needed to do because he first crouched slightly, then sprang up and onto the broad, warm back with its twitching skin. He briefly hung there with his belly pressed against the hard ridge of bone, then scooted around so he now straddled the doe's back. His legs felt stretched far apart, vulnerable because he no longer had earth under him and he was too high off the ground, but others had done this thing, and so could he.

His mind bounced from one question to another. What if the horse started to run and he couldn't stop her; what if he fell off and those rock-hoofs connected with his arms or legs or head; how was he going to go from being a prisoner inside the corral to racing to safety?

Another sound, this one human—and loud—sent lightning coursing through him. Although he couldn't see who had yelled, he knew he'd been spotted.

"Pray for me, Grandfather!" he cried.

Then he pressed his legs and heels into the horse's side and leaned low along her back to make as small a target as possible. He bellowed. Great muscles gathered under him, tightened, exploded into action.

He exploded with her, a leaf trapped in a torrent of water. His fingers were knotted in her hair, his legs locked around her. He wanted this! Loved this!

She became a lizard, twisting first one way and then the other as she pushed through the other horses. Ahead of him waited the rope-and-stick enclosure. The guard, who'd been crouched before the dog, jumped to his feet, started to aim with his weapon. The dog shied to one side—the same direction as the soldier. The two then crashed into each other and the soldier was upended.

"Fly! Fly!"

3

The mare's hind legs scraped the top rope, but her jump was still a thing of beauty, like the flight of a bird. From where she stood next to her sister, Morning Butterfly took note of the rider's nearly waist-length hair and naked chest and knew he wasn't Hopi.

"Navajo," she breathed, then hurried forward, wondering whether the soldiers would pursue him.

The guard who'd been stationed at the corral fired after the fleeing Navajo, but although the sharp sound forced a gasp from the horse, he didn't hit his target. Cursing loud enough to be heard despite the nervous prancing of the horses and the muttering Hopi, the Spaniard sprinted toward his own mount. The scraggly-tailed horse shied away, nearly causing the soldier to lose his balance. Righting himself, he struck the frightened animal on the face.

"No!" Morning Butterfly gasped, and would have broken into a run if her sister hadn't grabbed her arm.

"Do not—please, do not cause them to turn their anger on you," Singer Of Songs begged.

"I—he should not . . ."

As the leader of the Spanish troops strode toward the other man, his hard head covering and uniform catching the sun and throwing it back at her, she let her words fall away.

Although the newcomers had been here no more than three days and nights, she knew not to call attention to herself. Instead, she joined the handful of other Hopi watching the strangers. It seemed foolish of the Spaniards to be arguing while their enemy raced away, but it wasn't for her to understand the ways and thinking of those she wished she'd never laid eyes on.

"Sister?" Singer Of Songs tugged on her arm. "You believe he was Navajo?"

"Yes."

"But what if the Spanish think he is Hopi? Will they punish us?"

"I do not know."

"But perhaps you can find out." That came from a nearby brave.

Several older women, two young children, and a healer nodded encouragement as she walked slowly closer to the soldiers, her sister just behind her. Being surrounded by her people, Morning Butterfly told herself, would keep her safe and inconspicuous. However, that wasn't her only concern. Summer solstice with its Niman ceremony hadn't yet arrived, which meant the kachinas of the Hopi now lived on earth, not in the World Below as they had done each winter since the beginning of time. She wished they'd gone to their other living place, because while there, kachinas—spirits of the invisible forces of life—were safer than when they assumed material form and inhabited the bodies of humans.

Her bare feet scraped the ground under the blue-and-brown long cotton skirt her uncle had woven for her, allowing her to feel the contact throughout her body. Outsiders with killing weapons and horses, and a deep-voiced Spaniard dressed entirely in brown who called himself a man of God had come to her homeland, and now Oraibi sounded, smelled, and looked different, but it was still her people's land.

Would always be Tuwanasavi—Center of the Universe.

She was close enough to hear what the men were saying. At first the words made no sense, but after a deep breath that brought her the familiar scent of sun-ripening corn and the strange, pungent smell of sheep and horses, she was able to concentrate.

"Do not ask me to go out there alone, please, Captain," the soldier who'd fired his musket was saying. "I would rather take a beating than risk being killed—or worse—by a savage. A heathen."

"Did I say anything about you being alone?" the helmeted man questioned. "If you had had your mind on your responsibilities instead of allowing your full belly to rule you, this would not have happened."

"Not my belly, sir," the soldier muttered, his eyes downcast and his hands crossed over his heart. "If it hadn't been for that miserable cur, that savage would be dead."

The other—Morning Butterfly had heard soldiers refer to him as Captain Lopez de Leiva—didn't respond. Instead, he strode closer to the corral and stared at the milling horses. A lean, wary man with black eyes that seemed to miss nothing, he reminded Morning Butterfly of an antelope.

"We are in a wild land." He seemed to be talking to himself. "I do not know what I must do in order to make those under me aware of that simple fact. One moment of inattention, a single wandering thought may be the last one."

"Sir, what did you say?"

"Logic. Reality," he replied, without looking at the undernourished and bedraggled soldier. "If a single savage believes he can take what he wants, if he gets away with it, others will attempt the same thing."

"I will be ready for them the next time. I promise."

That made Captain Lopez laugh, a quick harsh sound with no joy in it.

"There will not be a next time." His gaze swept over the gathered Hopi. It seemed to Morning Butterfly that his eyes held on her over-long, and she wondered if she should have told her mother not to arrange her hair in the squash blossom that said she was a woman of marriageable age—but how would a man like him know the meaning of the thick coils on either side of her head?

Neither could he guess she understood his every word.

"Not a next time, Captain?" the soldier repeated. "I . . . ah . . ."

"I will do the speaking, understand! What is your name? It escapes me at the moment."

"Pablo. Pablo Sh—"

"Listen to me, Pablo. From now on there will be *no* laxity." The words, each one separated from the other, put her in mind of drumbeats. "How many times have I warned you of the Navajo?"

"Navajo? But—"

"Do you think a Hopi did that?" the captain asked as she breathed a sigh of relief. "Ha! They are too intimidated to attempt such a thing. However, if one Navajo believes he can steal from us, so will the rest of that heathen band. Your order, your only order, was to guard the horses, was it not?"

"Yes Captain, but—"

"I would be within my rights to order you to turn over your musket, would I not?"

"Yes, but—"

"Then you would no longer be a member of the Crown's forces, would you?"

"No."

"Alone and unarmed in the middle of a godless land surrounded by murdering Navajo, is that true?"

"Yes."

Captain Lopez pursed his almost nonexistent lips. "I do not need to say more, do I?"

The man's head sagged even lower. "No, Captain."

"The next time one of the savages attempts to make off with one of the Crown's horses, you will do whatever it takes to assure that he fails, will you not?"

"Yes, Captain." He spoke without looking up. "But—but what if the whole tribe attacks?"

"Your stupidity has made that my responsibility. I simply

wished to impress upon you the consequences of your action. These *creatures* understand force and precious little else. If we are to remain in control, they must never question or challenge that force."

As a young man, Morning Butterfly's father's uncle had been at the Sky City of the Keres when the Spanish had destroyed it. The soldiers had killed hundreds and mutilated an uncounted number of warriors, One Hand among them.

One Hand might have died if it hadn't been for the compassion of the now dead Aztec Indian Tomas, who'd been brought north by the Spanish. In the aftermath of the bloodbath, Tomas had helped One Hand return home, then he'd lived out his days at Oraibi, teaching those who cared to learn what he knew of the Spanish language. Included among his attentive pupils had been the child Morning Butterfly.

Now she could carry Captain Lopez's words to her people.

"I do not wish to hear this, Captain. It is your duty to assure that the infidels submit to the Crown's orders regarding the Christianizing of this land. It is mine to carry the Lord's word to them."

"Fray Angelico, I am well aware of our respective duties and will never shrink from mine. My sole purpose in speaking to you today was to warn you that the Navajo have just proven themselves most bold. I cannot be responsible for your safety if you venture beyond range of our weapons."

Captain Lopez de Leiva was at least six inches taller than Fray Angelico. As a result, the forty-three-year-old Franciscan friar had to tilt his head up in order to meet the soldier's eyes. That was bad enough; added to this, the sandals he'd worn during the long walk north from Santa Fe had barely survived the journey and were held together with strips of cloth torn from the hem of his robe. He wasn't ashamed of the way he looked—Franciscans lived to obey God's word and minister to the godless, not to concern themselves with the material world—but the sandals had caused a number of blisters, and he would give a great deal to be able to sit down, even on the hard, nearly lifeless earth. However, if he did, the captain might see that as a sign of weakness.

"I travel where the Lord commands me to go, Captain," he replied, his voice deliberately low so the soldier had to lean forward to hear. "If I receive a sign that He wants me to devote myself to converting the Navajo, I will do so."

"Then you will die."

Captain Lopez spoke too frequently of death and danger, and Fray Angelico would have told him so if there weren't more important matters to discuss. Balancing himself as best as he could on his swollen feet, he pointed up at the great gray mass that was Oraibi.

Today the sky was a soft blue and as such provided a striking contrast to the multi-roomed stone-and-mud structures and the red-brown sandstone that made up the broad mesa on which the village had been built. The mesa itself extended some six hundred feet above the plains. On the north side the slope was relatively gentle, but for reasons he might never understand, most of the meager farmland was south of the pueblo. The Hopi didn't seem to mind scrambling up and down the steep incline with trails cut into crevices and breaks in the red-brown sandstone, but he hated making the exhausting journey. In fact, he wouldn't have come back down this afternoon if the majority of the Hopi men hadn't been out on the desert, tending to their corn, beans, and squash. Well, perhaps that wasn't the only reason he'd left the pueblo, he admitted to himself as a shudder touched his sparse frame.

"I have made my decision," he said.

"Decision?" Captain Lopez's jaw remained clenched.

"The mission will be built at Oraibi itself."

"What? You cannot be serious."

"Indeed, I am." He shifted his weight, the unwise movement causing a stab of pain to run up his legs. With an effort, he kept his features immobile. "I have given the matter a great deal of thought and prayer; the Lord sent the answer to me this morning in a glorious vision."

He waited for the captain to prompt him to continue. When he didn't, Angelico stifled his irritation and went on anyway. "After my waking prayers, I made the climb to Oraibi at first light, thinking to gather as many as could hear my voice for morning mass, but the heathens were already intent on their day's tasks. Some of the men travel so far to reach their plots that they are compelled to remain away overnight, so they would have missed my blessing anyway."

"Yes, yes."

So the captain was impatient. Good. "Their pueblo is the center of these peoples' existence. If I am to minister to their religious needs, I must be accessible to them."

"How do you propose to carry the necessary materials up there? The wagons would never survive the journey."

"The Hopi erected their crude structures there; they are capable of following my directions in creating a church worthy of our Lord. Captain Lopez, with faith, all things are possible."

"Faith does not put strength in a man's back."

"You mock God?"

Although the captain gave a dismissive wave, his eyes took on a nervous cast, once again giving Angelico proof that the ways of the Lord were wondrous indeed since even those whose faith was imperfect crumbled like dead leaves when faced with the consequences of invoking His wrath.

"I am relieved to hear that, Captain," he said with just a touch of compassion. "If I believed you capable of ridicule, I would feel compelled to pray for you."

"Father, you and I are not charged with the same responsibilities," Captain Lopez stated. "What your plans are, I readily admit, are not my concern."

That was because the hard military man had allowed himself to be drawn off the path of righteousness carved by a vengeful God. "I am sorry for you," Angelico whispered.

A shrug of the lean shoulders under the heavy uniform was the captain's only reaction. "Today," he said, "I concern myself with determining what steps must be taken to assure the Navajo won't steal more horses or the sheep which the Crown saw fit to add to the bountiful provisions it provided for this colony. What I do not want, what I truly wish you would reconsider, is your insistence on this ill-conceived church."

"Ill conceived? Why do you think I am here? My mission—"

"Father, the Crown charged me with doing everything within my power to claim this land for Spain, and to that end I have the governor's generous backing in addition to what my wife's father has provided. The king and his ministers have declared that the Church be given primary responsibility for taming the savages. Yes, yes, I know," he went on when Angelico tried to speak. "You call it baptism, not taming. Nonetheless . . ."

He looked around distractedly, then continued. "I have only seven men under my command. If the mission is built on the mesa, I will be compelled to charge my men with guarding it."

"That is indeed your responsibility."

"And as a consequence, I will not have adequate manpower to oversee the Hopi while they work to provide the State with its due, or the needed presence to keep the Navajo at bay."

"Captain, if I am to succeed in the Lord's work, I *must* position the church so it overshadows the barbaric sites to which the heathens, in their ignorance, attach religious significance."

"If I am to succeed, Father, I must have freedom of movement. I will not have that if I am forced to station my men at Oraibi."

"Do not call it Oraibi! The mission will be named for Francis Bernadone, patron saint of the Franciscans. By the time the church is complete, the Hopi will have forgotten that what stands on the mesa was ever known by any other name."

"Perhaps."

Perhaps? "Once they have been baptized, they will sing praise to the Lord as they go about their work with willing hearts."

"You think so?"

Closing his eyes, Angelico lifted his arms to the heavens. His feet still throbbed and he sweated under his loose robe, but although the thought of the enormous task exhausted him, he'd never felt more convinced of the necessity of what he had to do than at this moment, or more compelled to devote his every breath to the work that had been his calling since early childhood. He was surrounded by heathens whose souls, if they had them, would spend eternity in hell unless he guided them to the light.

With God's direction, he would succeed!

The padre was a fool. Worse than that, he was so deeply buried in religious fanaticism that he couldn't see the truth.

Teeth clenched against the chafing caused by his uniform, Lopez left Fray Angelico standing alone. His only thought was to put an end to the useless argument, thus giving himself time to marshal the facts needed to change the padre's mind. When he'd first seen the church wagon laden with paintings of saints, silver and gold ornaments, a life-size statue of Christ, heavy bronze church bells, altar supplies, wall hangings depicting religious events, and the fifteen-foot-high ornately carved wooden cross that Fray Angelico intended to take with him into Hopi land, he'd resigned himself to assuming responsibility for these, in his mind, unnecessary religious trappings. However, for the padre to be so misguided as to believe that logs for the proposed church could be hauled here from Kisiwu or the even more distant San Francisco mountains and then wrestled up the mesa . . .

Thinking to ask the padre how he intended to convince the savages they should build something to worship a Christian god when they already had what they needed for their pagan ceremonies, he whirled back around, but although his armor clanked and clattered, Fray Angelico paid him no attention. Instead, the padre stared up at Oraibi. Because his back was to him, Lopez couldn't see his expression, but the little man held his body so stiffly that it looked in danger of snapping.

He hates it up there.

Smiling to himself, he continued his appraisal of Fray Angelico. There were times when the padre's features were so serene, so at peace that Lopez actually envied him and wondered if blind service to the Lord could indeed make one oblivious of the body's needs and discomforts; could blind one to danger. The padre had walked the entire way from Santa Fe, and although his feet were in pitiful condition, he barely limped. He ate sparingly and cared little how food was prepared; if his groin stirred at the sight of so many females after weeks of being surrounded by ill-smelling men, he gave no sign.

Still, some unsettling wind had blown through the padre's world. Lopez reluctantly admitted to himself that he had felt the same wind.

Fray Angelico had stopped his gawking and was heading toward a group of children who'd been studying the horses, as they and the adult Hopi so often did. As he drew closer to the children, the padre said something to them, but Lopez couldn't hear the words and didn't care. What interested him was how the children reacted.

Fray Angelico was shuffling and speaking, looking like a small, gray mouse. Although this wasn't the first time the padre had approached a group of Hopi, they gawked openmouthed at him—no wonder, since none of the savages could possibly understand a word of Spanish. The largest, a boy who would soon be old enough to be pressed into worthwhile service, stood sentry-like at the front. From a few steps away, the padre reached out as if to touch the boy's head, but the boy jerked back. After a moment's hesitation, the padre turned his attention to a much smaller girl, naked as the day she'd been born. Like the boy, she too tried to shy away, but other children were so close around that she couldn't.

When Fray Angelico rested his hand on her head, she dug her toes into the ground and gnawed on her lower lip. Instead of coming to her defense, the largest boy scurried away. He was immediately followed by the others, leaving the little girl alone with the padre.

"Be not afraid, my child, my lamb," Fray Angelico said, his voice carrying. "Feel. Feel. The Lord our God moves within my hands. I offer His blessing to you, welcome you into the light and entreat you to spread word of this wondrous moment to the others."

Still biting her lip, the girl whimpered.

"You will soon know the joy of service to the Lord. All of you will," the padre continued. "To give your lives in service—ah, child, how can I make you understand how rich your souls will become?"

The only way the padre could hope to make the Hopi understand was to learn enough of their language to allow him to communicate with them, something that was of little concern to Lopez.

"You will be baptized. Brought into the light of the Lord. Learn God's commandments. Turn from your heathen ways and be free of the devil's clutches."

They don't know who the devil is, Father. How are you going to tell them about that?

"Heaven waits for you and all of your people. I am the instrument for that journey. How willingly I accept that task. How joyously!"

Weary of the padre's ranting, Lopez turned away. As he did, his gaze caught on one of his soldiers, a man who'd had the audacity to call himself Madariaga de Oñate. From what he'd been able to gather, Madariaga had somehow convinced Governor Felipe de Zotylo that he was more than what he obviously was—a mestizo, a bastard born of a Spanish father and Indian mother. His lies about his parentage had ended when Lopez informed him that as Captain General Don Juan de Oñate's grandson, *he,* Lopez, spoke with authority about the great man's family.

No one named Madariaga, particularly not a mestizo, could have Oñate blood flowing in his veins. Madariaga had briefly questioned Lopez's parentage but he'd calmly, sharply pointed out that his mother was Don Juan de Oñate's daughter.

It was indeed fitting that he, Lopez, should be engaged in the same task his grandfather had given himself in 1598 when he'd taken possession of all the kingdoms and provinces of this new land in the name of King Philip. His grandfather had subdued the Keres and taught hordes of Indians the meaning of fear. He, Lopez, would subdue the Hopi and Navajo—and then devote himself to finding the mineral wealth that had eluded his ancestor and every other explorer to come here.

Nothing would stand in his way! Nothing!

4

The hogan where Cougar lived with his parents, two younger brothers, sister, and grandfather had been built on a rise overlooking a dry gully. Cougar's grandfather had advocated erecting the conical-shaped structure in a nearby valley closer to the other hogans which made up the small Navajo village, but Cougar's father had had a spirit-dream directing him to the safest place for his family.

Cougar, who'd done much of the work of covering timbers and poles with bark and dirt, had grown up with Drums No More's cautions and had given them due weight, but he also believed in the wisdom of his father's spirits.

Although light remained in the sky when he reached the hogan, the sun had set and a blessed coolness had begun to touch the land. On any other day he would have given thanks to the sun for a few hours of rest from the heat, but he was unable to think of anything except how quickly a horse—*his* horse—could travel. A journey that had always taken two days and nights had been completed in less than half that time.

"I return," he cried. "My family, come see what I brought with me."

The words sounded boastful, and he quickly gave thanks to the Holy People who'd made his accomplishment possible.

His sister, the youngest in the family with a mere eight winters behind her, was the first to emerge. Gray Eyes crowed with delight, but although Cougar encouraged her to touch the horse, she shook her head. His brothers, however, began running their hands up and down the animal's legs while arguing who would mount her first. Cougar's mother shook her head in disbelief while his father, Walks Swiftly, gawked and then ordered his middle son to hurry to the nearby hogans to spread the news.

Drums No More had been slow to join the others. Although his eyes remained fixed on Cougar, he said nothing until Cougar dismounted and walked over to him.

"Have you no words for me, Grandfather?" Cougar asked. "You knew what I hoped to do today and said you would offer a prayer for me. Be happy; your prayer for my safety was answered."

"My prayer or your determination."

"You think I was wrong to do this?"

Instead of answering, Drums No More stepped toward the horse much as a wary antelope approaches water. His dark eyes, so often somber, glistened with interest and excitement. Still, Cougar waited for the full weight of the older man's reaction. By now, Gray Eyes had gotten over her initial fear and was running her fingers through the horse's tail.

"Be careful," Drums No More warned. "If she kicks you—"

"She will not," Cougar interrupted, and then lowered his gaze because he would never intentionally contradict anything his elders said. "If one is careful and speaks gently, a horse is as safe to be around as a small bird."

"You know this? What is it, Cougar? You have suddenly been blessed with knowledge about horses?"

"No. I did not mean . . ." His family was watching, listening. "Grandfather, I did this thing today because of you. For you." *And for all our people, because I believe horses will change everything for the Navajo.* He pointed at the animal, who looked about to fall asleep. "It came to me that her name should be Four Legs, but if you wish to give her another, that is your right."

He started to reach for his grandfather, then stopped himself because the arm without a hand at the end of it was closest to him and Drums No More never wanted to be touched there.

"This is my gift to you. The newcomers took from you; it is only right that, finally, you have something from them."

"He put it down. He put it down. First Man put down the sweat house. On the edge of the hole where they came up, He put down the Son of the She Dark. He built it of valuable soft materials. Everlasting and peaceful, he put it there. He put it there."

As the oldest Navajo inside the sweat lodge, it was Drums No More's right to sing the Sweat Bath Song. Cougar tried to lose himself in the familiar words, to absorb the rhythm of his grandfather's voice and become one with the other men who shared the tripod-shaped structure with him, but the combination of his long, stressful day and heat from the hot rocks was stealing his strength.

His grandfather had said nothing when he told him that Four Legs was his, but Drums No More had always been slow to reveal his thoughts.

"We are here because much has happened today which must be discussed," Cougar's father said once the beginning ritual was over. "Everyone knows what my son has done. It has always been said that horses are a gift from the spirits. At first I questioned that because the Spanish brought them to Dinehtah and the Spanish do not give homage to the Holy People; but life is a journey, and the way one walks is never clear before each step is taken. No matter how many prayers and rituals a man performs, he can never be sure he has done them as First Man ordered. I now say horses were sent by

First Man as a test. If a warrior is brave and his heart pure, First Man will know and reward him. My first-born son is such a man."

Rising, Cougar stepped to the middle of the dark room and acknowledged his elders by inclining his head toward them. Surrounded by his people, deeply aware of how much a part of him they were, he began his story by detailing how he'd prepared himself with prayers, songs, and a sand painting. Then he said:

"There are seven soldiers and their leader and one brown-caped man. Two Indians sleep near the leader, but I did not try to speak to them. I think they may be Aztec slaves from the way they dress and act. The soldiers brought with them a great many sheep, weapons, food, blankets, tools, and other things I do not recognize. The horses . . ." Closing his eyes, he envisioned the crowded corral. "Their numbers are beyond my counting. They are healthy, strong. And wondrous to ride."

As he expected, that drew excited responses. "You were not afraid?" someone asked.

"At first, yes," he admitted. "Then my thoughts were on how I could escape without being shot."

"Tell us," a brave near his age asked, "would you go back again?"

"Yes."

"Why?"

"Because I walk with the Holy Ones in my heart and even if something about my preparation is incomplete, the reward is worth the risk."

That, obviously, was what the assembled men wanted to hear. Although there'd been a great deal of talk about wanting to see everything the newcomers had brought with them, Cougar had been the first to travel to Oraibi. It wasn't that the others were afraid, but a man who practices caution in the face of danger lives to see another morning.

The Navajo were raiders; it had always been their way to take from other tribes. But the Spanish fought with strange, deadly weapons, covered themselves in armor, and their horses allowed them to travel faster than the swiftest man could run. The wisdom of the past hadn't told the Navajo how to deal with this new and dangerous force.

"It is our way to discuss something at length before a decision is made," Walks Swiftly said. "Unlike the Apache, we are not ruled by chiefs, which is the way it should be. How can one man have the wisdom to say what is right for everyone? My son has proven that it is possible for a Navajo to take ownership of a horse, but one is not enough."

No one disagreed, and as the evening wore on, it became clear that each man had pondered how much his life would change if he had a horse. However, there was danger in taking what the Spanish claimed as their own.

"This is what I say we must decide tonight," Walks Swiftly said when it was once again his turn to speak. "It is the way of the Navajo to make use of Dinehtah's gifts, to not stay long in any place, because if we did, Dinehtah would be stripped bare. If the Spanish had not come, I would be for moving elsewhere before winter, but my thoughts have changed. We would be foolish not to take the soldiers' possessions for ourselves."

Cougar agreed, but he was content to let the others talk. He wasn't surprised when no one objected to remaining near Oraibi. In truth, he wanted nothing more than to take possession of another horse. Gradually, however, he became aware that his grandfather, whom he was sitting next to, was shaking his head.

"What is it?" he asked. "You think we are wrong?"

Drums No More wiped sweat off his forehead with his left hand and then, groaning a little with the effort, stood. When he held up his mutilated arm, all eyes were on him.

"Look at this," he began. "Look and remember the lesson it represents. I hear the excitement as each man speaks of taking horses, and yes, ownership of them will make us powerful. But a warrior does not try to take a kill from a cougar. I say the Spanish are cougars. They will not easily give up what is theirs. There will be fighting. War."

"We fear no one."

Once again Drums No More thrust out his stump, silencing the young brave who'd spoken. "Would a Hopi do this? No! Would even an Apache? No! The Spanish are different from our old enemies. If we anger the Spanish, their need for revenge will know no end. Even our children will feel their wrath."

"My father," Walks Swiftly said, "I do not put words in your mouth; I would never do such a thing, but what I hear—do you say we should slink off like wounded animals?"

"Do not speak to me of wounds! I am Navajo, and my heart beats strong and brave. But . . ." he briefly stared at the ground, ". . . I speak for caution."

By the time Cougar entered his hogan, his mind ached with the weight of everything he'd said and heard, particularly his grandfather's contribution. He was too tired to think any more. However, as he'd expected, his mother wanted to know what had been discussed, and because his father and grandfather hadn't yet returned, the task fell to him.

"There will be more sweat-talks," he said. "No decision has been made."

"Hm. Tell me, should I begin to make ready to move to a winter place?"

"No. Not yet."

"Ha! That is what I thought." She uncrossed and recrossed her legs. "I am of two minds about this. The thought of having a horse to carry my burdens—ah, that would be wonderful. However, Spanish weapons can kill from a great distance."

"The men will be careful."

"Men." She snorted. "They will think with their fists and muscle. With their penises."

"If they did not, the Navajo would have nothing; they would not even be."

"If it was not for women, Navajo men would starve."

They'd had this conversation before, the same one she had

with her husband. If he hadn't been so weary, he would have enjoyed the good-natured bantering.

"As long as you are alive, Mother, I will not starve," he pointed out.

"It should be your wife preparing food for you, not me."

"I will find another."

"I know you will." Leaning forward, she took his hand and pressed it to her breast. "I do not wish to open your heart-wound, my son, but it is natural for me to want to see you with a wife, to watch her belly swell with my grandchildren. To hear you laugh with a woman."

"I will. Someday."

"But not if your days are filled with horse taking. Ah, Cougar, if only we knew what tomorrows will bring."

He wasn't sure he wanted that. When he'd left his mother's hogan and gone to live with his wife, he'd thought he would spend the rest of his life sleeping with Sweet Water, but they'd only been married two moons when she began having headaches. Shortly after, her sight had started to fail. Although the shaman had created several dry paintings and the entire family had prayed, Sweet Water hadn't recovered. Instead, she'd grown weak, her body often convulsed, and finally she no longer recognized him.

Wondering if he'd done something to offend a ghost or *chindi*, he'd been torn between his desire to remain with Sweet Water and the fear that his presence would threaten her health even more. When she died in her mother's arms, he'd been elsewhere; he would have broken taboo by being near his mother-in-law.

Sweet Water's parents had quickly prepared her body and buried her lest the ghost of an Earth Surface Person who had died should return and seek revenge. Sweet Water now lived below the earth's surface, in the afterworld to the north—the direction of evil. He was glad her ancestors had been there to ease her four-day journey to the afterworld, but whenever he thought about where she'd gone and what her life without him was like, he couldn't sleep.

"Give me more time," he told his mother. "My mourning is not finished."

"I know you loved her, but she has been gone since last winter and you walk in today."

"Today I captured and brought home a horse," he told her. "And now I am weary. Tomorrow . . ." He yawned. "Tomorrow I will look to the future."

"A future with a wife in it?"

Perhaps, if the newcomers do not change too much about Dinehtah.

Most Hopi clothing was made by men from the wild cotton that grew throughout their land. The men each had several costumes for the numerous religious ceremonies. However, when they went about the work of caring for their crops, their clothing was less elaborate. Women covered themselves with sleeveless dresses tied on one shoulder. In winter, they added shirts or blankets in addition to moccasins. Unless a woman wanted to proclaim her marriageable state, she usually wore two braids, while men tended to catch their long hair in a single knot at the nape of their necks.

Fray Angelico had noted, in the course of studying those for whose spiritual well-being he was responsible, that their clothing, almost without exception, was clean and well tended. He'd taken it upon himself to study such things as divisions of labor, diet, and the regard given children and the elderly, but he still had a great deal to learn. Most of all, he wondered what kept them here when they could have gone to where there was more water and less heat. Something held them to the area, but what?

Today, however, the question didn't concern him. All that did was God's glory, God's message, God's orders to him.

"Do you believe in Christ Jesus, the Son of God?" he asked in Spanish. "Who was born of the Virgin Mary, and was crucified under Pontius Pilate, and was dead and buried, and rose again the third day, alive from the dead, and ascended into heaven, and sat at the right hand of the Father, and will come to judge the living and the dead?"

A black-eyed boy stared up at Fray Angelico, a sheep-like expression on his face.

"Do you believe in the Holy Spirit, in the Holy Church, and the resurrection of the body?"

Angelico rested his hand on the boy's head and prayed the youth would say something—anything. Just the same, he gave thanks to God for presenting him with his first convert, and for the sharp wind that cut a little of the afternoon's heat.

Although the Hopi whom he'd managed to gather around him made no attempt to join him in prayer, surely some good came out of their hearing the holy words. The question of whether a padre should learn the native language in order to minister to the people had been discussed for nearly a hundred years, starting when Fray Marcos de Niza accompanied the explorer Don Francisco Vasquez de Coronado into country never before seen by civilized man, but Angelico, like most of his Franciscan brothers, believed in the unity of Catholicism and Spanish. God spoke in a single voice, all who were brought to him would learn that voice—and eventually Latin as well.

It bothered Angelico that Captain Lopez insisted he had more important things to do than attend this baptism. After all, only a single horse out of a herd of nearly eighty had been stolen two days ago. It wasn't as if there was any danger that the Navajo would attack in mass, not with just one horse among them while the soldiers had a cannon and muskets at their disposal.

"Most righteous God." He spoke as loudly as his dry throat would allow. "Look down on this poor creature and take him into Your heart. Spread Your wisdom and word among the unsaved and make this day a celebration of You."

He kicked the boy's knees out from under him and then kept him sprawled on the ground by placing his foot on the back of the boy's neck.

The padre had intended to shut his eyes as he lifted his face to the heavens, but before he could, a distant bird caught his attention. He didn't know whether it was a hawk or an eagle or maybe something indigenous to the desert, and couldn't understand how it could go about its life's work oblivious to the parching heat.

Under his foot, the boy squirmed. Careful to keep his features peaceful, Angelico pressed a little harder. He would have immersed the child in water if there'd been enough. As it was, he'd had only a few spoonsful to sprinkle on the boy's head, and that had evaporated almost immediately.

"Hear me, my children," he said, although of course the ignorant Hopi couldn't understand. "This one is most blessed among you. From now on, he will serve a new master and great joy will be his. Joy which all of you will receive as soon as you have been saved from your heathen ways."

A faint grating sound returned him to his surroundings. Except for the plants the Hopi labored over so diligently, the land was lifeless, barren, godless. He'd failed his God by not conducting this baptism at Oraibi and yet . . .

Father, with my entire being I believe in Your love and direction. You are the God almighty, maker of all things, both visible and invisible. My life has been in service to You and I joyously give what life remains in that celebration. But the devil's strength is strong here. I feel it whenever I am near the savages' underground sites where they worship their false gods and thus . . . thus . . .

The devil will not win!

Where was that infernal racket coming from? Tilting his head to one side, he determined that the sound was human, as close to human speech as the Hopi were capable of, anyway. Someone was chanting.

"Silence!"

The Indians jumped back, then eased forward again. "Do you not understand?" he demanded. "You risk the Lord's wrath by interfering in this baptism."

A woman, her head lowered, stepped in front of the others and held out her hands, indicating the child on the ground. When the boy again tried to wriggle free, Angelico pulled him to his feet and held him against him. The woman squeaked something incomprehensible, the sound letting him know it wasn't her that he'd heard. In fact, the accursed chanting continued.

Chanting.

Sweat that had nothing to do with the day's heat ran down the small of his back, and he fought to suppress a shudder. He'd heard the sound before and would have immediately recognized it if he hadn't been otherwise occupied. Still holding onto the boy, he turned so he was no longer looking directly into the sun, and studied his surroundings. A trio of young women was directly ahead of him. Behind them stood someone wearing a mask that resembled nothing he had ever seen before. The chanting came from the mask wearer.

Another shiver wracked him. He opened his mouth to speak but let it close because no matter how simply he expressed himself, he wouldn't be understood. If only his fellow priest Fray Joseph were here, but the old man had died before the journey was two weeks old.

The mask wearer shuffled toward Angelico, his dark feet kicking up small puffs of dirt. It took both of his hands to keep the wood-and-feather mask in place, but the wearer seemed oblivious to any discomfort. His words were strung together, sharp like rock grating against rock, sometimes low and almost pleasant but mostly an insult to the ears.

Angelico made note of the black, white, and red colors decorating the mask; an inverted triangle of a mouth; tiny, dark eyes; and, most alarming, what looked like horns sticking out of the side of the head. The wearer—a man, the padre determined after noting that except for the mask, he wore only a loincloth—turned his head this way and that as if challenging anyone to risk being gored by the white-tipped horns.

From what he'd gathered from the writings of the first Franciscans to reach the new land, the Indians believed in a multitude of devil-gods. This must be a depiction of one of them, perhaps the most powerful and dangerous the Hopi, in their ignorance, worshiped.

With the resisting boy clutched in front of him, Angelico backed away, then forced himself to stand his ground as he prayed. *You are holy, Lord, the only God, and Your deeds are wonderful. You are strong. You are great. You are the Most High. You are Almighty.*

His throat closed and he struggled to breathe. "How misguided you all are to give homage to anything except the Lord God!" he screamed. "This is the road to hell and eternal damnation. Come to me. Beg for forgiveness and understanding. I will show you the true way, the only way!" *You are my protector, my guardian and defender. You are my courage, my haven and hope.*

"Fight the devil! Cast him out and be saved!"

He watched the Indians closely, searching for any signs of belief. He was stunned—surely that hadn't been comprehension in the eyes of one of the young women. The masked figure continued to approach, and Angelico released the boy. For a moment he was tempted to begin the boy's education or to identify the woman he had just seen, but the Hopi still advanced. Trying to look dignified rather than afraid, Angelico moved away quickly.

The boy, on the verge of tears and yet wanting to appear brave, stood with his hands by his side as his mother embraced him. She wiped him from head to foot with her skirt and then released him to play.

The boy's uncle, a member of the Marau society, removed his Ahote mask. Ahote, a singer of sacred songs, was a benevolent kachina, but the uncle had guessed the padre didn't know that and would be frightened the way small children were the first time they witnessed the winter Powamu ceremony to celebrate the fall harvest.

"Are you sure what you did was wise?" the boy's mother, Slow Runner, asked him as Morning Butterfly joined them. "You wore your costume when it was not a kachina ceremony. The gods may be displeased."

"The gods will understand," Morning Butterfly ventured. "It should please them to see that a wooden mask frightens the newcomers."

"Perhaps," Slow Runner muttered. "I do not like it that

the padre took my son and made him do things he did not want to."

"Should we expect anything different?" said Nose Too Long, eldest son of the village's senior chief.

"I wish they would go away." Slow Runner stared at the departing padre. "I pray they will want nothing from us and will go elsewhere, that they will not do to us as was done to the Keres at the Sky City."

Among the Hopi, the men were the leaders, but as several braves came to stand beside Nose Too Long, Morning Butterfly felt she had to speak.

"The padre's words made little sense to me," she admitted. "The words themselves had meaning, but put together they were nonsense." After thinking about it for a moment, she said she thought the padre had performed a religious ceremony because he'd used the words "lord" and "god." He'd obviously wanted some response from the boy, and when he hadn't gotten it, he'd become agitated.

"He is different from the soldiers, and there are no others like him," she said. "Perhaps he is lonely and wants us to join him in what he does."

"That will never be," another brave insisted. "To be Hopi is to be one of the People, nothing else."

"But if we are forced to . . ." Slow Runner clamped a hand over her mouth. "I do not want this thing! I want back what we were before they came."

"Not everything that comes from the newcomers is bad," Nose Too Long pointed out. "We knew about sheep and horses, but now that they are here, I see how valuable they are. I want to take the sheep fur and turn it into clothing. Perhaps we will find it is better than cotton."

"That cannot be," Slow Runner retorted. "Cotton is a gift from Mother Earth."

The debate over whether the good might outweigh the bad in respect to the newcomers' possessions continued, but Morning Butterfly didn't try to contribute, and the padre was far enough away that he couldn't overhear.

It seemed that he'd looked at her more than he had the others. The soldiers were like that, staring at her until she wanted to run, but it was her understanding that a padre wasn't like other men. She wasn't as tall as she would have liked to be and no matter how much she ate, she remained thin, but maybe the strangers liked to sleep with skinny women.

No, she would never willingly give herself to one of them.

Nose Too Long's father, Chief Cold Morning, hadn't been around while the padre forced the boy to do his bidding, but he was here now, his thick hair wind-tangled and his eyes narrow with concern.

"The men must talk," he declared. "It is time for decisions to be made."

"Decisions?" Morning Butterfly wasn't afraid of Cold Morning—no Hopi woman feared a Hopi man—but she'd recently been a child, while Cold Morning had been a leader for many, many seasons.

"The Keres who survived were forced to become a thing called Christians. Many of their children were stolen and never seen again. My father and grandfather prayed the Spanish would go back to where they came from, but they have not. Instead, they traveled further north and are now in Hopi land. I do not want to see my people bow before them."

"I must try to put more meaning to the padre's words," she said. "His and the soldiers'. Otherwise, we may never know what we must about them."

Chief Cold Morning nodded. "My thoughts are the same, Morning Butterfly. But I do not want to ask such a thing of you because I am afraid the soldiers may try to rape you. You are not the only one who understands their language. Your whole family does. I will speak to your father.

"No. My father is not well and my mother spends her time caring for him. I do not want them burdened any more than they already are."

Cold Morning started to nod, then went still, his gaze fixed on the padre. Fray Angelico had turned around and was shuffling toward them. He'd tucked his hands into the loose sleeves of his robe.

"What is going on here?" the padre demanded. "If you so much as raise a fist against me, I will insist you be punished." He jerked his head toward the military compound in emphasis. "The Lord's work *will* be done, and your heathen souls *will* be saved, all of them!"

The chief glanced at Morning Butterfly, who struggled to keep her features impassive although she ached to translate.

"I keep reminding myself that you are children," the padre continued. "That it is my duty to show you the way to the light. The task seems daunting, but I *will* prevail. Understand! I will baptize all of you, show you how to fear the Lord our God."

Fear?

"Do you think I want to punish anyone? Of course not. Mine is a merciful God, but I will never turn from my task. I am beholden to the patrons who financed my trip here, powerful and wealthy men determined to make this godless country safe. If you insist on remaining heathens, you will suffer the consequences. Do you understand me? Do you?"

Despite herself, Morning Butterfly flinched at his anger. When she did, the padre's gray eyes met hers, then he whirled and moved off swiftly.

She was beautiful. Whether the girl was a virgin or not wasn't something Fray Angelico concerned himself with. Nakedness was so common among the heathens, especially among the children who showed no shame at exposing themselves, that he couldn't imagine that keeping oneself pure mattered to them.

They would learn the error of their ways! Repent and—

His right thigh muscle cramped, forcing him to stop and try to rub the knot out of it. He tried to distract himself from the discomfort by taking in his surroundings, but Oraibi dominated everything. Was there no way the accursed thing wouldn't mock him . . .

The pain in his thigh eased, allowing him to think beyond

it. He could have started walking again, but it was easier to remain where he was, to continue to massage the muscle, the front of his leg, higher, to brush against the organ that had swollen while he looked at the Hopi woman. If anyone saw what he was doing, what had happened to him—

A sob clogged his throat and he dropped his hand. He was a priest, a man of God. Why, after all these years, was he being tested by temptations of the flesh?

The woman was responsible. She and whatever devils she and her people worshiped.

5

A few wispy clouds danced above the horizon, but Cougar paid them little mind as he and five other Navajo warriors crept toward Oraibi. The journey had begun with a song to Nandza'gai, daylight, and Chahalgel, darkness, to insure a safe raid. Armed with knives and ropes, their intention was to steal as many horses as they could. Although his companions wanted to strike as soon as possible, Cougar had successfully argued that they should wait until evening so they could take advantage of darkness. He remembered what the corral looked like, he'd explained, and promised to guide the others safely to the herd.

Now the sun had begun its downward journey and they were crouched behind a rise, looking out and up at the proud mesa where ancient Hopi had ended their long search for a home. He wasn't afraid to be here, but neither did he allow himself to be lulled into thinking that earlier success and a song had adequately prepared him for what he was about to do. If the gods were pleased with him, he would continue to live; if he'd done something to displease them, he would join his wife in the afterworld. In truth, death-thoughts had stalked him since the decision to raid had been made, not that he'd speak of them to anyone.

"There are too many horses," Blue Corn Eater said. "I do not understand why they brought so many with them. The sparse grass here will not feed them all, and there is not enough water."

Cougar nodded agreement. From where they were, he could see three sand-covered plots with their deep-planted and widely spaced still-green corn stalks. Although he had no interest in farming, he admired the Hopi's ability to make anything grow on their few little bits of land not covered with rocks or too steep. The corn, squash, beans, and tobacco plants gentled the landscape and spoke softly of life.

"The Hopi are slow to take up weapons," he said, "but I cannot believe they will continue to allow the newcomers to take so much of what their springs offer."

"Perhaps they are afraid to speak."

"Perhaps." For a moment he was distracted by the memory of the sound of the musket that had been fired at him. "But there are hundreds of Hopi, while the soldiers number only a few." He shrugged. "I do not understand the Hopi. I never will."

"Nor they us." Blue Corn Eater wiped an ant off his leg, then did the same to one crawling over Cougar's instep. "When this day is over, and I have learned how to ride a horse, you and I will race. Your legs may be longer, but I will capture the swifter animal."

"You think so?" Cougar jabbed playfully at his cousin. "With your poor eyesight, you will probably come away with a sheep."

"Never, although it would be good to have sheep. Because your warrior skills are so poor, I have decided I will put you to work guarding my herd and harvesting their wool. Perhaps the women can teach you how to turn it into something useful."

"Ha! When the sheep see you, their hearts will stop. All you will be left with is rotting carcasses and buzzards."

The easy banter continued, with the other Navajo men adding their own jokes. More than once Cougar reminded himself to be content to sit and keep insects off him until dark, but he'd always hated inactivity. As a young boy, he'd ranged so far that his parents had feared he'd get lost. While others his age were content to sit and listen to the tales of Coyote the Troublemaker, the Hero Twins, and how the People came to Dinehtah, his restless muscles had insisted on turning the legends into plays, with him acting all the parts. He loved to run and hunt, measuring success not just in a kill, but in matching twists and turns with a rabbit or slipping close enough to an antelope to look into its eyes.

At long last, the setting sun filled the sky with red and orange brilliance that reluctantly faded to deep purple and then black. The warriors sent streams of urine to the ground and, after a quick prayer to the Hero Twins, they left their hiding place. Although comforted by their presence, Cougar concentrated on the task ahead of them, and the danger.

"You are my brother tonight," he told Blue Corn Eater. "We will walk together like the Hero Twins and if there is trouble, we will know the other is there."

"Good." All humor had been stripped from Blue Corn Eater's voice. "There is none I would rather have beside me."

When he'd first seen the Spaniards' dogs, which were much larger than those belonging to the Hopi, Cougar had been concerned they'd warn their masters if anyone tried to get close, but the creatures seemed more interested in filling their bellies, and their barking was sudden and senseless. Hopefully if they howled now, the soldiers wouldn't take note.

A few Hopi sometimes remained near their gardens at night, but the majority returned to Oraibi and in any case they were no threat. The soldiers, however, slept on the desert floor and took turns guarding the horses. For reasons that baffled him, they positioned themselves near the gate, which made it easy for him and the others to slip around to the far side and slide under the bottom strand of rope.

Summer's heat hadn't yet left the earth, but the soldiers

had already lit a fire and all but the single guard were sitting on their blankets around it, their heads bent in what he assumed to be prayer because they sing-songed in unison. They'd brought two laden wagons with them. One was near the padre's shelter while the other—leaning brokenly on a shattered wheel—might have carried the soldiers' belongings.

He saw the wisdom in the Spaniards' selection of a lifted ridge of land which allowed them a view of much of their surroundings, and yet he wondered why they hadn't chosen a nearby wash with a fine layer of sand to provide cushioning for their beds. Obviously they didn't care that their blankets, spare clothing, cooking utensils, weapons, and personal leather chests were exposed to view. They'd made no attempt to build permanent structures, but although he hoped it meant they didn't plan to remain here, he knew better than to believe that. From where they were, he couldn't see the leader's sleeping place.

"Let the horses know you are here," Cougar whispered once they were all inside the corral. "That way you will not frighten them."

"They fear us?" Blue Corn Eater asked. "But they are much larger than us."

Later, hopefully, they'd have the opportunity to discuss the ways of horses, but now all that mattered was taking them. Letting his silence speak for him, Cougar began inching toward the nearest animal. A few stars were already out, making it possible for him to see shapes and shadows. His heart pounded and he had trouble controlling his breathing, wondered why he felt this way when he'd spiritually prepared himself for what he was doing. Death wasn't a fearful thing.

A nearby horse stomped the ground, startling him. He sensed alarm from the rest of the herd and vowed to remain calm and show no fear. Humming the Door Path song, he slowly stood and touched the horse's shoulder with gentle fingers, wincing when its flesh danced. He wasn't sure his companions could see what he was doing, but their senses were tuned to his, so hopefully their hearts would know.

"I have come to you," he whispered to the horse. "Come because I am Navajo. You will go with me, you and others of your kind, and you will learn what it is to become Navajo."

When the animal stopped sucking in noisy breaths and extended its neck to sniff him, he shook out the rope over his arm and slipped it into the horse's mouth before looping it around the lower jaw. Another Navajo—he couldn't be sure who it was—had taken his lead and now stood beside the horse he'd just secured. He had tried to convince his companions to each mount a horse and then to lead as many away as possible, but only Blue Corn Eater had thought he could do that. The rest pointed out that someone who has never ridden can't be expected to handle more than a single animal. Cougar, however, had worked with Four Legs daily and hoped he could follow the soldiers' example of controlling a number of horses at once.

Intent on placing ropes around the necks of as many as he thought he could handle, he could only pray that his companions would be ready to leave when he was. He'd secured three in addition to the one he intended to ride when he sensed a presence behind him. He whirled, then let out a sigh of relief when he realized it was Blue Corn Eater.

"We have been here too long," his cousin whispered. "My ears and eyes and heart tell me this is not a safe place."

"I agree." To give weight to his words, he clutched the ropes in his left hand, grabbed the nearest horse's mane with his right, and vaulted onto its back. Then he glanced around, relieved because he could make out the forms of his fellow warriors, each standing near a horse.

"Now!" he whispered harshly. "Now we ride!"

Digging his heels into his mount's flank, he urged it on. At the same time, he yanked on the lead ropes. His plan, formulated last night when he couldn't sleep, had been to gallop at the flimsy looking gate instead of trying to clear it. In daylight, the horse would probably see the barrier and stop before hitting it, but now hopefully they'd focus on his orders, not where they were going.

"Ride!" he yelled. A couple of horses squealed, half burying his cry under theirs.

He loved the power and speed, muscles under his legs! Most of all he loved what he and his fellow warriors were doing to the Spanish. He couldn't die tonight! No Navajo could!

The corral was so small that the horses could barely move about in it. As a result, he reached the gate before his mount reached a full gallop. Seeing the rope obstacle, he ground his heels and knees into the horse and prayed for forgiveness.

For an instant the ropes held, forcing the horse to shift its weight to its rear legs. Then, as despair surged through Cougar, the resistance was gone and his mount half ran, half stumbled to freedom. Although it was impossible to tell how many others were following his lead, he felt as if he'd become part of a river of horses. The arm holding onto the lead ropes was nearly wrenched from its socket, but he refused to let go.

The soldiers were all on their feet now, two running into each other, the others reaching for their weapons. Blood red glinted off the muskets. Letting instinct take over, Cougar stretched low along the length of his horse's back so he would present as small a target as possible. He wished he knew how long it took the soldiers to load and how accurate they were.

Most of all, he prayed for First Man to ride with him.

Someone bellowed, snagging his attention. A man was running toward him, his musket aimed at his chest. Almost without thinking, he jerked his mount's head toward his enemy, using the animal as a shield. The galloping horse snorted and tried to avoid the soldier, but it was too late. Screaming, the man fell backward, defenseless against sharp hooves.

"So be it!" Cougar shouted. "Yes, the Dineh are mighty!" He'd barely gotten the words out when an explosion of

sound filled his ears. It was immediately followed by another. And then another.

Blue Corn Eater, young, strong, and courageous, jerked
upright and then, before Cougar could catch him, fell off his
horse and lay still. Cougar's horse took him racing past his
cousin, forcing him to yank on the jaw rope, but even as he
struggled to stop his mount, he knew he couldn't do anything because the soldiers had already surrounded Blue
Corn Eater.

Be dead, he prayed. *Safe from their cruelty.*

Morning Butterfly was on her way to the mesa to help her
mother settle her father in for the night when she heard the
commotion. For a frightful moment, she thought the soldiers
were shooting at her; then she looked over her shoulder and
understood. Her sister, who was ahead of her, spun around.
They watched in silence as the horses scattered, many running
in all directions but those with riders galloping one after
another into the darkness.

She prayed the Navajo—it had to be them—would succeed with their raid, but although most of the soldiers
seemed to have no idea what to do, one ran after the fleeing
raiders, then stopped and aimed his musket. The horrible
sound echoed and echoed, was still alive when a Navajo top-
pled off his horse and plunged to the ground.

"They shot him!" Singer of Songs gasped. "They have
killed him."

"Maybe he is only wounded."

"Pray he is dead. Otherwise the Spanish will make him
wish he were."

Her sister was right. Singer of Songs insisted they learn
everything they could about the attack—and the soldiers' reaction—so Morning Butterfly joined the knot of curious,
wary Hopi who'd gathered near the corral. The fallen
Navajo lay face down in the dirt, toes pointed in. One soldier
and then another kicked him in the side and head, but he remained motionless. It was clear to Morning Butterfly that he

was beyond life. Not so the ill-clad soldier who writhed on the ground nearby.

To a man, the soldiers insisted on going after the Navajo, but Captain Lopez angrily pointed out that nothing could be accomplished at night.

"We will have our revenge," he announced. After glaring at the Navajo's body, he knelt beside the injured Spaniard. If the captain was aware of his growing Hopi audience, he gave no indication. Instead, he directed his attention to his gathered men. "But I will not risk any of your lives. When we go after them, we will be prepared, and there will be no doubt of the outcome."

Morning Butterfly had no doubt he wouldn't let the raid go unpunished.

Although she wasn't close enough to see the full extent of the fallen soldier's injuries, others were, and the details quickly spread. The man hadn't been wounded by a Navajo arrow but had been trampled by the stampeding horses and was possibly dying. Someone spread out a blanket and he was moved onto it. The captain didn't touch the writhing man. Instead, he spoke to the padre who stood nearby. Morning Butterfly could not hear his words, but the padre's reply was clear.

"I intend to pray for his soul," he said. "This child is devout in his devotion to the Lord; certainly I would never refuse him last rites."

"Last rites?" the injured man bleated. "Captain, I ain't dying. Oh God, God . . . please do not let me die!"

The captain's dark glare was a fearful thing as he straightened, his eyes raking over the audience.

"He needs to be cleaned up," he said, speaking to no one in particular. "Until I can see the extent of his injuries, speculation of any kind is useless."

He glanced at Morning Butterfly, looked away, then focused on her again. With a shock, she realized she'd isolated herself from her companions. Before she could react, he grabbed her and hauled her roughly to his side, then forced her to look down at the whimpering man.

"How do I make you savages understand?" he demanded. "I want you to do what you can to make him comfortable. That is all. Surely you are capable of that simple thing."

"Captain, I don't want her touchin' me. If she has a knife on her—"

"Good point."

While gripping her arm so tightly that it began to go numb, the captain ran his hand over her, lingering on her breasts, forcing his fingers between her legs. She'd never been treated like this, and rage and disbelief warred within her. If he fell upon her now, would anyone try to stop him?

"She is clean, Pablo," he announced. "Probably not *clean,* because who knows what vile diseases they carry, but at least she will not finish what the Navajo tried to do."

"Lord, I beseech—you are certain?"

"You question me?" Captain Lopez showed his teeth. "Do you think I chose her at random? No. My thought is that if you respond to her as a man responds to a woman, we will both know you are going to live." He chuckled. "In fact, I encourage you to put all your energy into getting well because if you succeed, she is your reward."

Horrified, Morning Butterfly renewed her efforts to free herself, but although the captain cursed when she tried to scratch him, he refused to let go. Most of the Hopi had drawn back, but Singer Of Songs remained where she was, her hands clamped into fists. Taking note of her, the captain ordered another of his soldiers to seize her as well.

"Do you understand now?" Lopez demanded of Morning Butterfly as the soldier snaked a rope over Singer Of Songs, trapping her arms at her sides. "Do as I order or she will suffer the consequences."

"Captain, I protest." The padre cleared his throat and his voice shook, not with fear but determination. "The Church's dictates on such matters are inflexible. There will be no taking advantage of the native women within the shadows of a church."

"Your church is not yet built, Padre. Besides, this is a military matter, not a religious one, and the lives and productivity of each of my men is my priority." He glanced at the dead Navajo. "Burn his body. Burn it so there will be no misunderstanding my contempt for the savages."

The man called Pablo had at least one broken rib and the flesh around it had been torn open, probably by a hoof. Despite the poor lighting, Morning Butterfly located sore places all over his body. He groaned and prayed every time she touched him, so she did that as little as possible. Still, focusing on him helped distract her, at least a little, from the stench of burning flesh.

She and Pablo had been left alone, the other Hopi having been forced back at sword point, the padre disappearing into the night once he'd finished praying over the injured man. His repeated words about the son of god, salvation, ascending to the heavens, the holy spirit, and judging the living and dead had made little sense to her, but they'd obviously comforted the man called Pablo.

The captain, after assuring himself there was enough of a fire to consume a human body, had hauled Singer Of Songs off with him, and until Morning Butterfly knew whether her sister was all right, she'd do as she had been ordered. She left Pablo only long enough to get some water, which she used to clean his bleeding wounds. She didn't know whether the heat pulsing through her was due to what remained of the sun's gift, the captain's cruelty, her distaste of what she was doing, or fear for her sister.

Pablo felt warm to the touch, yet he shivered.

"You will live," she whispered in Hopi. "But your body does not know and that is why you shake. Be calm. Calm. There is nothing to fear."

Pablo stopped praying and stared up at her. Although she didn't want to feel anything for him, didn't want to think of him as a human being, she could not help herself—could not keep from offering comfort.

"Hear not my words," she continued, "but the truth in their sound. I speak to you as a mother does to a crying child. An infant may not understand what is being said to him, but he is comforted by the sound."

He took a long deep breath, held it, then let it out in a sigh. "Mary, Mother of God, ever Virgin," he whispered.

"Listen to your body," she continued once he was finished, her face close to his. "If you heed it, it will tell you the truth. Muscles and bone speak to the head and blood carries those messages from one part to another."

"I do not understand," he said in Spanish.

"It does not matter." It amused her that she could answer him without his knowing. "Perhaps if you spend your life here, the time will come when you see into the heart of a Hopi. Perhaps."

The night creatures had found their voices; uncounted numbers and varieties of insects now sang their endless songs. The child she'd once been used to fall asleep to their lullabies, but although she longed to lay down and rest, she didn't dare. She didn't want to think about what might be taking place between the captain and her sister. Singer Of Songs, whose woman's bleeding time had begun just this spring, still cared little that the men of their tribe smiled at her, but if the Spanish could chop the hands off helpless prisoners, they were capable of raping a maiden.

"Sister," she whispered. "Please, make little of yourself. Remain silent and still so you will not touch his mind. Please."

"I cannot do everything at once, Padre," Captain Lopez retorted. "I am sorry if you believe I am remiss in not anticipating that the Navajo would attack, but—"

"Not attack," Fray Angelico corrected. Obviously not caring that the three-sided brush structure Lopez had had his servants erect the day after their arrival constituted the captain's private domicile, the padre had walked right in and now stood less than three feet away in the cramped space. "I do not believe their intention was to kill anyone. The heathen thieves were after horses—and they succeeded."

The padre had quickly become the bane of his existence, Lopez admitted. Didn't the single-minded celibate realize he had more important things to do than carry on useless arguments? At least, he acknowledged as he reassured himself that the Hopi girl wasn't trying to slip away, he'd managed to put off Angelico long enough to direct his men to stand guard around the remaining horses. As for his servants, they'd wisely faded into the night. Fear of the Navajo would keep them close enough.

"They succeeded because *you* insisted I concern myself with *your* agenda. You cannot deny that I have attempted to accommodate you in every possible way, but tonight serves as an unfortunate reminder of what my priorities must be. My men's safety *must* come first! That, and assuring that no more horses are lost."

"The Lord's work precedes everything else," Angelico said as Lopez contemplated having to tell both his father-in-law and the governor that the large herd he'd argued so strongly for had been decreased nearly by half. "That is why I came to you, even though I should at this moment be ministering to Pablo's soul. I beseech you, do not abandon me while you search for the thieves."

"Damnation! The Lord's work will never be done if you are not alive to do it."

"Whether I am the one to convert the savages or the task falls to another of my brothers does not matter," Fray Angelico insisted. "If I give my life in service to God, my benefactors will lend their support to my successor. The Lord's work *will* be done."

"I am busy, Father," Lopez retorted, "with responsibilities far beyond your comprehension. Why do you think I acted swiftly and decisively tonight, putting fire to the Navajo carcass? So there will be no doubt of my determination to punish."

"The stench—"

"Hopefully will carry for leagues. Father, you proclaimed where you want the church built and I agreed to force the Hopi's cooperation." He'd been standing with his arm draped over the young woman's shoulder, now he pulled her hard against his side. "What I do with the rest of my time is not your concern."

Fray Angelico's attention shifted to the Hopi who'd been forced off balance and was trying to right herself while not touching Lopez.

"You cannot—I protest!"

"Protest all you want, Father. Convert the savages until there are none left, but do not attempt to control me." He turned her so she now faced him, and pulled her forward until his pelvis ground into her belly. "I am a soldier, Padre. A man with needs and priorities." She flung her head back, unwittingly exposing her throat. He nipped it, chuckling when she gasped.

"You cannot—the Lord—"

"Understands a soldier's needs. Women, female savages, were placed here to accommodate us. Tonight I accept the gift."

"You are married."

Something cold circled Lopez's throat, but he fought it off. "That is not your concern."

"Your father-in-law—"

"Shut up! Get out!" The padre fled in the face of Lopez's anger.

The man smelled of sweat, smoke and something her nostrils had never tasted. As he yanked her dress over her head, fear threatened to bury Singer Of Songs, but she fought to take herself from what was being done to her. She'd begun her day by asking her father to tell her of his most successful deer hunt. She had heard the tale many times before, but talking about the days when he had joined the other men in providing food for his family helped him forget that now his legs supported him for only a few minutes at a time. Both she and Morning Butterfly took care to praise him for what he'd once accomplished and never mentioned that their mother's youngest brother was the one who now filled the family's cooking bowls with meat. What hurt almost as much as seeing her father hobble around was the look in her mother's eyes, the sorrow and—

Pain!

The man had forced her legs apart and was on top of her, forcing his penis into her. The women had told her that her first time might hurt, but that it would be all right because pleasure—

. No pleasure! Only revulsion and searing pain and cries held back by clenched teeth and her fingers digging into the earth and silent sobs.

She paid no attention to his muttered words of surprise.

6

Fray Angelico's burning branch illuminated enough of his surroundings that he easily made his way back to where he'd left Pablo. A merciful God might allow the young man to live, but because God's ways were mysterious, even to him, he made no attempt to bargain for Pablo's life. Instead, he turned that decision—like everything else—over to his maker.

Angelico had been barely nine when his parents took him to a Franciscan monastery and charged the monks with responsibility for his religious education; if he'd been consulted in the matter, he didn't remember. Less than a year later, along with others of the order, he'd boarded a ship bound for New Spain. The knowledge that he might never see his family or homeland again cast him into a depression that hadn't lifted until the journey was over and, like the others, he began the barefoot walk from Veracruz to Mexico City. Being on shipboard hadn't lifted the cloak of melancholy and fear, but the sights, sounds, and smells of an untamed and heathen world had, and despite his tender age, he'd known he was playing his own small part in history.

As the years passed, he forgot the sound of his mother's voice and embraced, wholly, the evangelical crusade set forth by the Twelve Apostles. A true believer with every breath he took, he'd accepted a life of poverty and committed himself to the salvation of the "baby birds," or Indians, living in the new land. These children, under his care and love, learned to fear and praise God, and although their souls were so primitive they must be denied the sacraments of Communion and Extreme Unction, he never doubted they could be molded to fit into the Christian community.

God in his mysterious wisdom had sent him to work first among the Tarascans of Patzcuaro, then the Aztecs living at Tepeyae, and finally to Santa Fe, where a great Franciscan mission was being built. He had been spreading the Word there when, to his great joy, he was selected to help the conversion of the Hopi savages to the north.

If he had any doubts—not fears, surely—it was because this would be his first true involvement with the military, and from the moment he'd met Captain Lopez, Angelico had known that the man's strong personality would test his own. They were nothing alike, not with Lopez's challenging nature when it came to religious matters, and yet . . .

"Pablo," he called out when he reached the unfortunate. "God walks among us tonight. Feel His glory and take your strength from Him."

"Father?"

The soldier was weak—there was no doubt of that—but Angelico had witnessed many deaths during his years of ministering to Indians, and Pablo's voice gave no indication of impending death. When he stepped close, flames illuminated both the prone figure and the Hopi woman charged with caring for him. If his gaze remained overlong on her, it was, Angelico told himself, because he wanted to assure himself that she was worthy of the task. As he dropped to his knees beside Pablo, she backed away, nearly disappearing into the night.

"Pray with me, my child," he told Pablo. "The Lord is our God, the Lord alone. For us there is one God, the Father, from whom are all things and for whom we exist, and one Lord, Jesus Christ, through whom are all things and through whom we exist."

In a halting voice, Pablo repeated the prayer. Then: "Padre, are you ever afraid here?"

"Afraid?"

"I—this is my first post. My dream had been to become like you, dedicated to a lifetime of service to God, but . . ."

"But what my son?"

Pablo took a long time answering. "If I tell you, you will hate me."

"I hate no one."

The young man briefly gripped his hand, then released it as if ashamed of the contact. "I am incapable of purity of faith because I am not pure of blood."

For a moment Angelico thought Pablo was trying to tell him he was Negro or a mestizo, but he wasn't dark enough to be a Negro and a bastard mestizo couldn't possibly aspire to a religious life.

"Jewish," he guessed. "You are Jewish?"

"Not me!" Pablo sounded both angry and defensive. "But my grandfather was, and no matter how devoutly I embrace the true faith, I will never be accepted."

That was true. Nevertheless, the right or wrongness of the situation was of little concern to Angelico, the son of Catholics who saw placing the boy in the priesthood as the ultimate proof of their faith.

"We are all God's children here," he told Pablo. After all, the man was wounded and still might die.

"I want to believe that." Pablo whimpered, then began again. "But we are so far from any church, so—"

"I will build one, soon."

"I know." His voice trailed off. "But even then, will I truly feel God's embrace or . . . or will the devil's hold on the savages remain as strong as it is now? Will . . . will we be safe?"

* * *

The land was Morning Butterfly's mother, her father, her ancestors. She'd grown up believing that simple truth, and as night gripped her, she took comfort from the rocks and dirt beneath her feet. Her thoughts whirled in one direction and then the other like a winter-driven wind, and when fear for her sister threatened to drive her mad, she focused on the earth. She prayed her sister could do the same.

The First World was Tokpela, endless space. Even before that was Taiowa the Creator. There was no beginning, no end, no shape, simply the great void where Taiowa dwelled.

Taiowa's first creation was Sotuknang, and Taiowa said to him, "I have created you, the first power and instrument, as a person, to carry out my plan for life in endless space. I am your Uncle. You are my Nephew. Go now and lay out those universes in proper order so they may work harmoniously with one another according to my plan."

Lost in the Creation Story, Morning Butterfly was slow to make sense of what she heard. Her eyes took in the first message as Singer Of Songs emerged from the shadows, then she heard her sister's cry and ran to her.

"What is it?" she gasped as she enveloped Singer Of Songs.

The injured soldier snored nearby; except for him, they had this space to themselves. Instead of answering, Singer Of Songs sagged.

"He hurt you?"

"Yes."

"Took you?"

"Yes."

The awful truth of how her sister had lost her innocence felt like a knife to her heart. Crying, she stroked Singer Of Songs' thick hair.

"And then he let you go?" she asked. "He had no more use for you?"

"I—I did not want to, but I cried out when he entered me, and I think he knew I had never been with a man. After that—after that he became almost gentle, and when he was done, he told me to leave."

"Why would he care that you are—were a virgin?"

"I do not know. I wish—I wish today had not happened."

"We are People of Peace," Morning Butterfly whispered around the knot in her throat. "Peace will sustain you. You and I belong to the Sun Clan, which takes its name from that which feeds this land. Sotuknang, nephew of the Creator, brought the sun into being even before the living things; that truth makes Sun Clan members endless."

"Morning Butterfly, I want to go home."

Of course she did. Shielding Singer Of Songs from Pablo, she glanced down at him and then dismissed the young man from her thoughts. If the captain punished her for deserting her patient, so be it.

Singer Of Songs needed help making her way up to Oraibi, and even when she finally was standing on the ground their ancestors had claimed for the Hopi, she didn't seem to know where she was. Gently, Morning Butterfly reminded her.

"Look around you," she encouraged. "Here the Hopi are as one, each with their own task and responsibility, all important."

Morning Butterfly reminded her sister of the countless, intricate baskets the women made, sitting on rooftops so they could watch and visit as they worked.

"I hear your words, my sister," Singer Of Songs whispered as dawn combed her hair with golden highlights. "But I cannot take them into my heart today."

"Why?"

"I am ashamed. I do not want our parents . . ."

"They will understand. No one will say this was your fault."

"You do not?"

"You are a young woman, not a warrior."

"I wish I was!"

Encouraged by her sister's show of spirit, she said, "Maybe

you wish you were one of the Navajo who caused the soldier to be injured."

"If that were so, I would be far away now. On horseback. You will stay with me?"

"I will never leave you," Morning Butterfly promised.

Just the same, as they made their way up the short ladder leading to their pueblo's roof entry, her thoughts went to the Navajo. Her sister would still be a virgin if the raiders hadn't come. The Navajo were free to roam as far as their newly captured horses could carry them, while she couldn't go any further than her legs took her.

She might hate and fear the Navajo, but that didn't mean she couldn't envy them.

Morning Butterfly and Singer Of Songs' older brothers lived in their wives' homes at the other side of Oraibi. Although they would have to be told about what had been done to their sister, Morning Butterfly was glad her mother hadn't insisted on doing so this morning. It was enough that her parents and her father's uncle, who lived with them, were staring at Singer Of Songs.

Their mother, as befitted her status as owner of the house, was the first to speak. "When my daughters did not come home last night, I could not sleep for my fear," Roadrunner said. "I told myself they might have gone to another house to talk about the raid and fallen asleep there, but my mother's heart found no peace in that, not after I heard what had been done to the dead Navajo." She shuddered.

As briefly as possible, Morning Butterfly told them how she'd spent the night. No one asked about the soldier's condition. Neither, thankfully, did they press Singer Of Songs for details of her rape. Morning Butterfly prayed that being in the single room with its clay floor, adobe walls, and brush, grass, and mud ceiling would bring her sister comfort.

"Does this captain know who you are?" Roadrunner asked Singer Of Songs.

"I pray not. It was dark and I left when he fell asleep."

"Praise Sotuknang that you were able to. Perhaps he will not know where to look for you."

"Perhaps." Singer Of Songs, who'd slumped to her knees, stared at the ground.

Roadrunner bent and kissed the top of her youngest child's head. "That is what I pray. If you remain here, you will be safe and your voice in song will gladden my heart as it always has."

"But I cannot. You need me to gather more rabbit brush and sumac twigs so we can make new baskets."

"That can wait."

But not for long, Morning Butterfly admitted to herself. Roadrunner had once been skilled at basket making, but age had slowed and twisted her fingers. Recently, probably because her mind had been on her husband's poor health, she'd dropped two large clay bowls painted red, brown, and black, shattering them.

Their father cleared his throat. Deer Ears had little in the way of wisdom to pass on to his daughters but he was deeply troubled by what had happened. He would soon retire to his clan's kiva, where he intended to pray. Morning Butterfly wondered if Roadrunner or Singer Of Songs would ask him to say nothing to the other men he was bound to meet there, but they didn't.

She'd been in the kiva of course, once to help repair the roof and for a number of ceremonies, but the underground council, workshop, and ceremonial structure was for men; what they said and did there remained mostly mystery, steeped in tradition and belief.

"Will you ask for a Council of Chiefs?" her father's uncle asked, speaking for the first time.

"I do not know. I must speak to Wanderer before I do anything else."

Wanderer was a member of the Bear Clan, the first Hopi clan to reach the Third Mesa. Wanderer's age and position within the clan made him the village's senior chief and as such he would preside over a Council of Chiefs. Morning

Butterfly wished she knew more about the chief's thoughts and beliefs, but a man entrusted with the tribe's sacred objects doesn't share of himself with a young woman.

"I will go with you," One Hand said. He was a quiet man who moved so slowly that sometimes Morning Butterfly wondered if he'd fallen asleep while on his feet. As a young child, she'd often stared at the scarred stump where a hand should be but had been afraid to ask about it. She'd learned of what he'd endured at Acoma from the Aztec Tomas—and from One Hand's nightmares. Awake, her father's uncle never spoke of those days.

One Hand had been married when the invaders chopped off his hand. His young wife, terrified by his dreams, had tearfully asked him to leave. Weak and silent, he'd returned to the pueblo of his birth, taking Tomas with him. One Hand couldn't join the other men when they hunted, and although he maintained a small garden, he needed Tomas's help to tend it. After the Aztec's death, he had come to live with Morning Butterfly's parents.

Deer Ears, supporting himself by gripping One Hand's shoulder, stopped with a foot on the ladder's bottom rung. His eyes swept over his wife and daughters, lingering on Singer Of Songs, but when he spoke, it was to One Hand. "While in kiva, I will speak a father's words and thoughts. I take pride in having fed and clothed all my children, and I love them."

"I know you do," One Hand said.

"Do you? You are not a father." He ducked his head, signifying he hadn't intended to speak harshly. "The way you have walked your life has been hard; I acknowledge that. I know you will speak of that life, but I do not want those to be the only words the men hear."

"I know you, Deer Ears," One Hand responded. "You are a man of action. A brave man. Not always a wise man."

"A sick man," Deer Ears reminded him. "One who can no longer draw a bow as he once did."

"Yes, but what you cannot do for yourself you may convince others to do."

One Hand was right, thought Morning Butterfly; her father spoke of the peaceful way as did everyone, and yet he'd never allowed his family to be wronged. Once, when a longer than usual drought had jeopardized the corn harvest, Deer Ears had refused to share the water from the underground spring on his land. Another time, he'd been so vocal in his objection to his oldest son's romantic interest that the young man had changed his mind about participating in a *dumaiya*, which would have drawn the girl into his blanket with him for the night and maybe resulted in a pregnancy and thus a marriage. Now, Morning Butterfly guessed One Hand was afraid his nephew would speak of exacting revenge.

Her father shrugged at One Hand but said nothing, and the two left together, one old man assisting the other. Her mother continued to touch Singer Of Songs' head, but the younger woman gave no indication that she was aware of the contact. She seemed to be staring at nothing and yet her eyes were bright and focused.

"I hate them!" she blurted. "The soldiers and their leader, even the one who calls himself a man of God! I wish they were all dead!"

Only a few slats of daylight made their way into the kiva. As a result, One Hand couldn't look into Deer Ears' eyes and know what was in his nephew's heart. As he'd expected, Deer Ears had wasted no time telling the assembled men about the attack on his youngest daughter; for once he seemed to have forgotten his unsteady legs. Although everyone had muttered disbelief and sympathy, they waited for Wanderer to speak.

Wanderer, who was so old no one alive remembered his parents, stood and stamped his feet.

"I do this to call upon Siliomomo," he explained. "Siliomomo who was born of a Hopi girl near Singer Of Songs' age and Antelope-Spirit."

"Siliomomo?" Deer Ears questioned. "But he was not a kachina?"

"No, he was not," Wanderer agreed. "It has come to me

that the Hopi are faced with something they never have experienced before. Our old ways may not help us.

"Kachinas have life-and-death influence over the Hopi and bring rain and other gifts to us. They stand at the center of our beliefs, yes, but they are good and gentle when there is nothing good or gentle about the Spanish."

Wanderer closed his eyes and walked over to the shrine-shelf that held a large number of kachina dolls. After touching each in turn, he faced his audience.

"I feel their love and concern, their fear for us."

"Fear? No!"

"If we do not speak of a thing, does that mean it does not exist? My thoughts are still like mist. For it to fully show itself to me—and to the rest of you whose wisdom I respect— I believe we must start with the legend."

At Wanderer's suggestion, One Hand nodded and began the tale.

"Before the Hopi settled here, one of the migrating clans lived near Canyon de Chelly. Famine visited them. One day when a girl like Singer Of Songs was out gathering the wild grain *noona*, she was visited by a strange and powerful man who told her not to fear him. He fed her meat and she shared her bed of soft branches with him. They were not intimate, and yet she became pregnant. When the boy-child was born, they named him Siliomomo because they were of the Sawungwa Clan, but although *sawungwa* means yucca fruit plant, he was one with the animals.

"The time came when Siliomomo went in search of his father. His father came to him and took him to a kiva where he stamped his foot. Inside the kiva, he met people who turned into the animals of the earth. His father was Antelope. Antelope taught him about his magic power so he could always feed his people, and after he had done that, Siliomomo took his prayer sticks to the kiva to honor the gift he had been given.

"The spirit people came to Siliomomo's clan village and shared their spirit powers with the people, but although the spirit people live in kivas, they are not kachinas. There is more," he said with a glance at Wanderer. "Do you wish me to continue?"

"Later. First, I turn to everyone and ask if my thoughts carry weight and if we should begin ceremonies so the truth of my thoughts might be borne out."

"What is that?" One Hand asked.

"The Hopi walk the Road of Peace and our kachinas do no harm, but is it possible that I think of Siliomomo and the spirit people because death and bad things have come to Oraibi and the spirit people taught Siliomomo how to kill?"

"But only animals, so his people would not starve!" One Hand exclaimed.

"Yes," Wanderer agreed. "And yet is it possible that killing animals was only part of the spirit people's wisdom?"

"Blue Corn Eater did not keep his mind pure and that is why he was killed."

"He is dead—if he is—because a soldier's ball pierced him."

"But it would not have if he had been walking the way of a Navajo."

Cougar didn't agree with his grandfather, but he didn't want to waste his energy or cause disharmony by arguing. The trip back to the Navajo village had taken nearly as long as if they'd been on foot, because none of the men knew how to lead horses, and learning how to ride had taken its own time. Besides, they'd been slowed by grief and shock.

Cougar had managed to grab the horse Blue Corn Eater had been riding and had turned it over to Blue Corn Eater's family—the only thing he could do for these people he loved. Because they didn't have the young man's body, they'd killed the horse which might have been the last living thing the young warrior touched. They were digging a large grave and hoped to have the body in the ground before dark.

Blue Corn Eater's spirit, if he indeed had died, might be angry at not being properly disposed of, and instead of traveling along a mountain trail as it should, might remain as an angry ghost—a *chindi*. That was what he and his grandfather should be talking about, not what Blue Corn Eater might have done to bring about his death.

"I agree with Drums No More," the elderly singer Wolf Stalker said. He left his study of the newly acquired horses and joined the knot of men gathered around Cougar and his grandfather. "Ritual has been broken and we are at risk. A sing must be performed to bring us back in harmony with the earth. Besides, we must do certain things to insure our safety."

Cougar nodded because he felt like a leaf tossed about by an angry wind, a man who has lost his way and needs to find it again. If Sweet Water were still alive, he could have expelled his energy inside his wife and fallen asleep with his head on her breast; but he couldn't.

As a respected singer, Wolf Stalker could announce a sing whenever he wanted. He climbed onto a rock and called to Estanatelehi, Changing Woman, who created human beings and was one with the Earth, Sun, First Man, First Woman, and the Hero Twins.

"The Universe is orderly," Wolf Stalker said as Cougar sat near him, determined to give himself up to the truth, to still his fear of reprisal. "It is both good and evil. So are the Holy People, and we stand in respect of them. Today we call on Yeis, the force of nature, and the Helpers who show the Holy People and us the way to each other. The Helpers have come to me with their wisdom and tell me to conduct a *hatal*."

A *hatal* or holy chant could take the rest of the day and into the night, but if that was what it took for Wolf Stalker and Drums No More—and himself—to feel at peace again, so be it.

"The First World was an island," Wolf Stalker continued, "surrounded by oceans, and there lived the first beings. Although they are called people, they were not people as we now know them, but insects. They were twelve in number: Dragon Flies, Black Ants, Red Ants, Black Beetles, Red Beetles, Yellow Beetles, White-Faced Beetles, Dung Beetles, Hard Beetles, Locusts, Bats, and White Locusts."

The Insect People had lived near the borders of three

streams in the middle of the First World. The First World's surface was red; white arose in the east and was considered day, while the yellow of the west was evening. The four chiefs, or gods, lived in surrounding oceans and became angry with the Insect People because they'd committed adultery. Cougar couldn't remember when he hadn't known that, but he held onto every word as if it was the first time he'd heard them. He couldn't imagine wanting to share another brave's woman, or that a woman would leave her husband for him. He'd had a wife and he'd loved her. Giving himself to another . . .

Although his eyes were open, he didn't try to focus on his surroundings. Instead, he felt himself traveling back to Oraibi. He and his fellow braves were gone from Oraibi, except for Blue Corn Eater, who'd been left at the mercy of the Spanish. The others were safe and had succeeded at what they'd set out to accomplish. That should be the end of it, and yet the Spanish might be filled with the need for revenge and try to find the Navajo.

The Hopi. He couldn't understand why they allowed themselves to be treated like sheep. Surely the soldiers were angry. They might take out their frustration on a Hopi.

More than frustration, Cougar acknowledged as Wolf Stalker droned on. The Spanish hadn't brought any women with them, but even if they had, would that stop them from raping the Peaceful Ones?

I am sorry. If what my people did brought shame and pain to a Hopi woman, I wish you to know I did not want that.

Singer Of Songs had finally fallen asleep, and from the sound of her parents' breathing, Morning Butterfly knew they had, too. It had taken One Hand longer to surrender to the night, but that was usual. A man who fears his sleeping thoughts fights them.

Morning Butterfly sat in the darkened pueblo and tried not to think about what had happened to the way of life she'd always known. The seasons of her people's lives had taken her from spring to summer to fall and into winter and she'd entered wholeheartedly into the rhythm. Now that rhythm was gone.

Tomorrow she'd insist that Singer Of Songs go with her while she looked at the corn in her family's garden. They would walk far from wherever the soldiers were and run from them if necessary. They would look for butterflies and other winged creatures, maybe teasing each other about who could find the most, and Singer Of Songs would smile again.

When Morning Butterfly least expected it, when she was certain she had her emotions under control, the anger she'd felt—not just at the soldiers but at the Navajo as well—returned. She didn't question her feelings toward the Spanish, but why had her heart hardened against the Navajo? It couldn't be that she envied their boldness, their freedom.

Although she doubted she could fall asleep, she'd started to stretch out on the ground when One Hand moaned. Practiced in the ways of dealing with his nightmares, she hurried to his side, knelt, and whispered into his ear.

"You are not alone, old man. Walk in today with me and leave the past behind. Think not of what happened when you were a youth. Instead, put your thoughts on preparations for *Niman*. The time for the kachinas' return to the World Below approaches and you and the other men will spend your nights in the kivas, smoking, praying, making prayer sticks, decorating your kachina masks, and practicing your songs."

"No no no."

"Hush. Hush. Spit on the past. Embrace the future. Think with me. Which kachina will be chosen for Niman? It can be any but I say it will be Hemis, the Far Away Kachina. What better one than that which carries the symbols of rain and a bountiful harvest?"

"Go . . . no. No."

"Hush. Hush and be at peace. Think of Hemis with its white dots signifying rain, the blues and yellows for the sun and clouds."

"H-mm."

"Yes, yes, you see it, do you not?"

One Hand's legs spasmed.

"Do you wish to dance? Maybe you want to be one of the men chosen to gather the sacred spruce Hemis requires? Your legs are strong enough for the long journey. Remember that, your legs are healthy."

Once again the old man's body twitched. She started to press closer to him, then stopped as his breathing settled. His nightmares never lasted long, and most times she was able to dismiss them and fall asleep herself, but not tonight. Instead, she sat beside him, thinking of the horror and pain he'd experienced. No wonder he'd hidden from the soldiers and padre ever since they arrived. No wonder he begged his people to do nothing to incur their wrath.

But she wasn't One Hand. *Kachinas, spirit people, hear the thunder of my anger. Let me know that your thunder is the same. Show the Hopi how to make their own thunder.*

The Navajo sing didn't end until near dawn, but although his body ached with fatigue, Cougar knew he couldn't sleep. Instead, as Wolf Stalker indicated he wanted something to eat, Cougar got to his feet and faced the assembled warriors. They looked up at him through red-rimmed eyes.

"Wolf Stalker, thank you. I have been embraced by The Way Of The Rainbow which guides us in everything. I will always mourn the loss of Blue Corn Eater and will ask what I might have done to prevent this thing from happening, but that is not all. The thought that now consumes me is whether the taking of horses has placed our people in danger."

His statement was met with nods of agreement.

"Would you rather we had not raided?" Wolf Stalker asked.

"No! Horses will change a great deal about the Navajo and those changes will be good. But the only way we will feel safe from revenge is if the soldiers are gone."

"Gone? You speak nonsense."

"No, I do not." Then, although his head ached with weariness and his belly rumbled, he laid out his plan. According to the stories Drums No More told of when the first Spanish came to Dinehtah, the conquistadors had been searching for something that the tribes knew did not exist in something called the Seven Cities Of Gold.

"Has this foolish dream died? I say no, because otherwise, why would the soldiers be here? What is at Oraibi for them? Nothing. I believe they brought so many horses because they plan to travel great distances, because they believe they will need the animals to carry the treasures they hope to find."

He paused, struggling to comprehend what possible use the Spanish could have for the rocks they called gold and turquoise. "It is not for us to understand their thoughts or what is important to them. What matters is that we make use of their greed."

"How?"

"We must fill their thoughts with dreams of becoming rich so they will go to where they believe that richness lies."

Several of the older warriors gave him a skeptical look, but no one called him foolish. Instead, they listened respectfully while he laid out the details of his plan. Finally, only one aspect of the plan remained to be decided—who would carry the lie of a vast, hidden treasure to the Spanish.

"You," Wolf Stalker said decisively. "Because you have twice been among them without being killed or hurt."

"I do not know their language," Cougar pointed out as a knot he refused to call fear tightened in his chest.

"But some of the Hopi do. You must get one to translate for you."

7

The Hopi's elaborate masks and kachinas were the work of the devil, of that Fray Angelico had no doubt. The question was how to free the ignorant savages from the devil's control, witnessed by such abominations as piles of buzzard feathers, gourd rattles and vessels, pipes and tobacco pouches, carved and painted sticks, even cornmeal—which wasn't eaten but presented with great ceremony to some unseen deity.

The day would come—soon, if he was diligent in going about the Lord's work—when he could command the savages to destroy these pagan representations and follow him into the light of true belief, but until he'd baptized the entire Hopi population and thus begun the salvation of their souls, he knew better than to risk alienating them.

That was why he'd chosen this spot at Oraibi, near their "religious" center, for his first pueblo-wide sermon; nothing else he could do would make more of an impact on the poor, ignorant creatures. Still, although he'd spent the night praying for courage and direction, he was careful to keep his back to the kiva and say nothing about the ten or more Hopi men who'd come to mass wearing fearsome-looking masks and carrying feathers, pipes, or staffs decorated to look like lightning bolts.

Captain Lopez was here along with his soldiers; even Pablo had managed to drag himself up here for the blessing. Another young soldier, Madariaga de Oñate, stood beside Pablo, and the two occasionally whispered to each other in the easy way of friends. Angelico knew them to be equally devout, but it wasn't their eagerness to devote themselves to God's service that had briefly snagged his attention. It was the thought that, in his entire life, he'd never had a true friend. A man who lives for and through his maker shouldn't concern himself with anything else, and yet he couldn't deny the small stab of envy.

The military men stood apart from the savages, and although he'd made it clear that mass was no place for the carrying of weapons, they were all armed—no doubt because the captain had ordered it so. Given the recent unfortunate experience with the Navajo, he saw a certain logic in the order, but still, the captain's disregard for Church doctrine was something he could hardly ignore. In fact, if Lopez committed another sin such as the one he had committed with the Hopi woman, he would have no choice but to inform not just Captain Lopez's father-in-law, but the territorial governor as well.

A breeze nearly as hot as the winds of hell plastered his robe to his body. If only he could remove his hood—but there was no way he was going to go bareheaded. The savages, for reasons he didn't understand but for which he was grateful, accorded anyone in uniform or costume a measure of respect, and he was determined to capture that respect today.

"We adore You, O Lord Jesus Christ, in this Church and all the Churches of the world," he began. "And we bless You, because, by Your Holy Cross You have redeemed the world."

Pablo, Madariaga, and the others bowed their heads and crossed themselves. So did Lopez, but not until the others had begun. As for the Hopi—

"Yet for us there is one God, the Father, from whom are all things and for whom we exist, and one Lord, Jesus Christ, through whom are all things and through whom we exist."

Through whom we exist. Touched by the simple power of those words, he turned his face to the heavens, and if his voice filled with tears as he thanked God for this opportunity to spread His word, so be it. Embraced by God's glory, he took in the assembled Hopi. He suspected that not every member of the tribe had been induced to attend services, but certainly the majority had been suitably impressed by the military presence. Either that or their so-called holy men had predicted that whatever spirits they worshiped would strike the padre dead, and they all wanted to see that.

They would be disappointed! Sorely disappointed and disillusioned with their religious leaders.

He'd begun to bow his head again when his attention was drawn to a young woman standing in the midst of a group of elderly women. At first he didn't know why she'd caught his eye, but then he recognized her as the one who'd been called upon to care for Pablo.

"Lord," his voice echoed off the nearby stone walls, "Lord, look down on this multitude and see that a miracle has been wrought. We are gathered here in worship and humility. Although many of us are ignorant of You and Your teachings, You have seen fit to send me, your servant, to spread the Word. Stand over us today and all our todays and guide us from darkness into the light."

An infant whimpered, but he ignored it. "If, in Your wisdom, You wish the gathered to understand the glories that will become theirs once they are believers, I pray their hearts and minds will open today, that—"

He swayed, and quickly spread his legs for balance. What had happened? He looked around, but no one else appeared the slightest bit alarmed. If there'd been an earth tremor, certainly he couldn't be the only one affected.

"This land may be new to You, oh Lord, for this is the first time You have been asked to spread Your word here, but—"

Once again the ground—or something—shuddered, stopping him in mid-sentence. Pulling his hands free of the long sleeves, he reached out for support, but it wasn't offered. The adult Hopi stared unemotionally but the children, at least those who were brave enough to peek out from behind their mothers' skirts, gaped openmouthed at him. He'd intended to direct much of the sermon at them since a child's mind was more malleable and the devil hadn't, he prayed, had time to corrupt them, but now he could barely remember what he'd been going to say.

"God's glory is upon us," he intoned. "I placed all my confidence in God, and He saw me safely here. There can be no doubt that my mission was meant to be, that—"

Was that the wind? Cold fingers slid down his spine, clamped onto his belly, touched his heart. Afraid he might pass out, he struggled to clear his vision, but the sudden mist refused to lift. Occasionally he drank enough wine to become lightheaded, but although this sensation reminded him of that, he didn't feel at all relaxed.

"Captain?" His voice no longer echoed but squeaked like that of a frightened mouse.

Lord God, what—

"No! Devil, I cast you out!"

The effort of speaking sent his head to splitting, but he refused to be silent. "I am God's servant. I will continue! I will, and my words will free us all. This place—this place will become Yours, oh Lord. The dark forces are cast out, now, never to return, never . . ."

Hearing his own voice calmed him, but although he'd always believed in the power of prayer, today he couldn't quite find peace in it. Instead it seemed that he'd faced a test; he couldn't say whether he'd passed or failed, just that it wasn't over.

Cougar would have preferred to lose himself in the knots of Hopi gathered around the padre, but he needed to stand out. He hadn't intended to enter Oraibi, since standing on the isolated mesa made him feel trapped, but for reasons he couldn't comprehend, the villagers—and, most importantly, the soldiers—had gathered here. Most of the Hopi men were shirtless in deference to the hot day. Since he, too, wore nothing from the waist up except for the large turquoise necklace that covered much of his chest, he should blend in until it was time for him to speak.

Forcing himself to relax, he turned his attention to the Hopi; hopefully, one or more of them had learned a little Spanish. He noted the dull look of incomprehension, the slackening interest, but here and there, mostly among the older Hopi, someone was paying attention, occasionally nodding or shaking their heads. He would have to—

Whatever he'd been thinking died as he took a second look at a young woman surrounded by others old enough to be her mother or even grandmother. Her eyes never left the padre, and yet he sensed she was also aware of the soldiers. She gave no outward sign of her reaction to what the padre was saying beyond a change of color in her large, expressive eyes. Those eyes said she was taking measure of the small man, perhaps looking for strengths and weaknesses in him, listening to his tone of voice but more importantly, his choice of words. At one point, the padre stretched his arms toward the sky and fairly screamed something that put Cougar in mind of the sound circling vultures made. The woman—her squash-blossom hairdo told him she was un-married—leaned toward one of her companions and whispered. Then she did the same with another, this time eliciting a shake of the head.

She understands.

Cougar licked his dry lips and reassured himself that he hadn't lost the bag containing the highly polished green rocks that he'd brought with him. He was still convinced his plan was a worthy one, but he hated being here. Hated feeling so vulnerable.

Whatever the padre was doing went on and on. Sometimes he spoke with his eyes open, but occasionally he grew weary, closed them, and nodded as if falling asleep. For the most part he stood, but at least four times he dropped to his knees and remained there while continuing that ear-hurting chant of his. He indicated he wanted the Hopi to kneel when he did, but although a handful of those closest to the soldiers followed suit when the military men knelt, most simply watched. Someday, maybe, he'd ask the young woman the meaning of the padre's words—and her reaction to them.

But for now . . .

Someone was staring at her. Alarmed, Morning Butterfly looked around. At first all she saw were the faces of her people. She was afraid one of the soldiers had come close, but they were still standing off by themselves. She grew aware that the staring came from her right. Slowly she turned in that direction.

There. Part and yet not part of the gathering stood a man. An outsider would think him Hopi, but not only didn't she recognize him, he carried himself in the way of the Navajo, bold and aggressive. His eyes held on her, and he nodded. When her mouth parted involuntarily, he covered his lips with a finger. Despite her shock, she nodded. After a moment, he jerked his head, indicating he wanted her to come stand beside him. Much as she hated it, she couldn't ignore his unspoken message.

Leaving her companions and making her way to him took a long time because she didn't want to draw attention to herself. Fortunately, a number of Hopi children had become restless and their relatives were engaged in trying to make them remain quiet.

Finally, for the first time in her life, she stood close enough to a Navajo to touch him. His necklace was magnificent, its clusters of small turquoise pieces within silver of Zuni design.

"I am called Cougar," he whispered in Hopi. "You are . . ."

"Morning Butterfly. How is it you speak the language of the Peaceful Ones?"

"When I was a child, my parents came across a Hopi with a broken leg. It was winter and the boy stayed with us until spring. He and I became like brothers."

She acknowledged his explanation with a brief nod, then looked at the padre to make sure he still held the majority's attention.

"What are you doing here?" she asked.

"I must speak to the newcomers."

"No!" Fortunately, her fear of the soldiers was enough that even in shock, she kept her voice low. "Navajo wounded one of them. They hate you."

"I know. My cousin was shot during the raid. He—I wanted to come back for him, but I did not dare. He—is he alive?"

"No," she whispered. Then: "The captain had his body burned."

"Atch, no. His death spirit . . ." His mouth drawn into a hard line, he continued to take in his surroundings, putting her in mind of a deer watching wolves.

"You say you wish to speak to them. What if they do to you as they did to your cousin?"

His eyes narrowed, but if he was afraid, he didn't show it. "Then our spirits will be joined. We may become *chindi* together."

"Chindi?"

"It does not matter now. You speak their language."

She'd been right to think of him as bold and aggressive. Yes, his tall, muscular body was so taut that she thought he might fly apart, but she couldn't imagine him running from danger. He smelled of earth and grass, of the wind even, and she envied him without knowing why.

"Yes," she told him. "How did you know?"

"I watched you. Saw the truth in your eyes."

The padre looked as if he was going to kneel again, but instead he tucked his hands up in his long sleeves, bent his head and stared at his feet. Earlier, when he'd first stood near an abandoned *sipapu* or Hole Of Emergence inside a kiva, he'd acted as if he was in the grip of an angry spirit, and she'd hoped his heart would stop beating, but he'd managed to calm himself. She should concentrate on what he was saying, but it no longer mattered.

"I am not the only one who understands their words, at least some of them," she explained. "I do not want the newcomers to know." Then whispering low in her throat, she told him what had happened to her sister after the Navajo raid.

"She would still be an innocent if not for what you and others of your tribe did. The captain became like a puma after his man was wounded. His rage and frustration—there was nowhere for it to go except in a sexual way. Rape."

"Do not say that. It is not the truth."

"Not!"

"Do you really believe the soldiers would have gone forever not touching a woman? I apologize to you for having to care for that man. That thing was my doing, but the Navajo did not turn the newcomers into dogs in heat."

Needing to sort out her thoughts, she tried to concentrate on her surroundings and renew herself in the familiar, but his presence made that impossible. Her family occasionally traded with the Navajo, and she'd watched Hopi and Navajo men together and concluded that physically they were little different one from the other. What set Hopi and Navajo apart was what went on inside them.

"Morning Butterfly?"

"What?" If only he would go away!

"You say you do not want the newcomers to know you understand them, but if you are ever to be rid of them, you must do as I ask."

"What do you want to say to the soldiers?"

"Not want, but must." Moving as little as possible, he reached inside the bag around his waist and pulled out several chunks of green rock. "Emeralds," he said.

"Ha! They are worthless rocks that have been polished until their color shows. Only your necklace has any value."

"But the soldiers do not know that. They will look at them and go in search of more—leave Oraibi."

"You can promise that?"

"We must try. Otherwise they may be here forever."

The service ended then. The padre clapped his hands and

indicated to the soldiers that he wanted them to walk among the Hopi, forcing them to bow their heads.

Both Cougar and Morning Butterfly joined what he assumed was some kind of prayer, and although doing so didn't seem to bother her, it was all he could do to submit. He kept his eyes open, his attention drawn to the nearest sacred Hopi place they called a kiva. The Hopi youth his family had cared for had described them to him, and he'd been fascinated by descriptions of kachinas and the role the meeting places and spirit-figures played in pueblo life. He wished there was time to ask Morning Butterfly about the *sipapu* and why it had frightened the padre.

"Now," he whispered to her when the Spanish god-man finally stopped talking.

"I am afraid."

Of drawing attention to herself? Of course she was, he admitted, regretting what he'd asked of her. Still, she hadn't refused. After briefly meeting his eyes, she walked toward the padre, head high and graceful, and began to speak.

After a moment, the padre called out something that caused the captain to look his way and then settle his gaze on Morning Butterfly. Still, she remained where she was, putting Cougar in awe of her courage. After shifting his musket from one shoulder to the other, the captain approached her. Morning Butterfly said something to the captain, then pointed at Cougar.

"Come," she ordered in Hopi. "They know you are Navajo and that you wish to show them something. They now also know the truth about me." He heard the regret in her voice.

"You blame me for that?"

"There is no time for blame, Cougar."

As he closed the distance between himself and the Spanish, he sensed many eyes on him. Oraibi was like an anthill, alive with Hopi, and he didn't belong—he and the newcomers. It seemed to Cougar that Morning Butterfly positioned herself so she was closer to him than to the padre or the soldier, but that might only be a trick of his mind.

The captain said something and Morning Butterfly sucked

in a deep breath, her eyes alive with concern. "He says he will kill you."

"If he does, he will never have what first brought his kind here." The sun was on fire and yet he felt cold. "Tell him that."

She looked a heartbeat away from running; yet she stood her ground, speaking slowly in Spanish. She concentrated on the captain's reply.

"He wants you to speak to me and for me to repeat exactly what you say," she translated. "Then he will decide what is to be done with you."

Feeling like a deer who has fallen into a man-dug trap, Cougar struggled to remain in control. "Perhaps the captain will believe I am lying to him, that we both are."

"Perhaps."

Because the Hopi were a slow-moving people with the patience to coax life from the hard ground, he'd wondered if their thinking was simple like an animal's but now he knew better. As everyone stared, Cougar kept his attention on Morning Butterfly and prayed he'd been wise in trusting her.

The longer she spoke, the more like flowing water her unfamiliar words became. The uniformed man stopped her several times to ask questions, and when she replied, she kept her eyes level on the man who had the power of life and death.

"He is much taken with your necklace but it is the emeralds he demands to see," she said at last.

"Does he believe they *are* emeralds?"

"His eyes say he wants to, but he is cautious and suspicious."

As well he should be, Cougar thought as he held out his carefully selected collection of rocks. The sun buried a little of itself in the glittering surfaces and the soldier's face took on the look of a hungry predator.

Captain Lopez wasn't the only one to draw closer. As he snatched the stones from Cougar, the other soldiers gathered around, along with Fray Angelico.

"Emeralds," Lopez said, savoring the way the word felt on

his tongue. "Not gold. Emeralds." He watched the Navajo out of the corner of his eye, looking for some sign of deceit, a subtle twitch that would give away the savage's pathetic attempt at a lie, but his features remained impassive.

"They're that all right, Captain," Madariaga announced. He all but licked his lips. "I've seen them on royalty, but never close up like this."

Ignoring the irritating impostor, Lopez asked the Hopi woman to repeat where the Navajo had found them.

"At the edge of the great canyon," she said. "Within its walls lie uncounted stones of great value."

"Hm." He'd heard of the canyon all right, thanks to the writings of the colonist Pedro de Castaneda, who'd been part of one of the first expeditions. In August of 1540, Captain Garcia Lopez de Cardenas and twenty-five men under him had been the first explorers to set eyes on the massive cut into the earth. Three of their party had attempted the descent to the river at the bottom, but failed. If the canyon was as large as Castaneda had recorded, he might spend the rest of his life searching for the exact origin point of the precious stones he held in his hand. "And why do you say he's willing to tell me this?" he asked suspiciously.

"Because he fears your wrath."

That might be the most intelligent thing he'd heard since coming here. According to the woman, this Navajo hadn't been with those who'd stolen the horses. When he'd heard about the theft, he'd consulted his so-called spirits and they'd warned him that Spanish soldiers wouldn't allow the atrocity to go unpunished. Scared down to his bones, the brave had decided to try to atone by "paying" for the horses with emeralds.

Pay? Not too bloody likely!

"Seize him!" Lopez ordered.

Several of his men stood rooted like damnable beasts of burden, but Madariaga and another sprang at the Navajo and wrestled him to the ground despite his struggles. Madariaga held a knife to his throat and even nicked the dark flesh. The savage bared his teeth in a low growl.

"Be careful!" Lopez warned as he stood over the still-struggling captive. "I do not want him injured!"

"But he's a thief. All of them Navajo are."

He'd never argue with that, but he'd be a hundred kinds of a fool if he silenced the blazing-eyed bastard before forcing him to reveal *exactly* where the emeralds had come from. Once Madariaga had tied the Navajo's arms behind him and looped a rope around his neck, the savage stopped struggling, proving he was gifted with enough intellect to understand when he was outmanned. Still, he growled defiantly.

The Hopi stood as close as they dared, muttering in that infernal language of theirs. Although it didn't appear a one of them carried so much as a cooking knife, Lopez knew he'd be a fool if he allowed himself to be lulled into a sense of safety. Besides, this damnable place made his flesh crawl.

"Get him out of here. And make sure the Hopi stay where they are, all except for the female. Wait." Striding forward, he yanked the necklace off his captive's chest. Why not? It wasn't as if the savage would need it in hell.

Morning Butterfly. That was her name.

Feeling invisible, Fray Angelico had followed Captain Lopez, the prisoner, and the soldiers off the mesa. In truth, he was enormously relieved to no longer be anywhere near the kivas and the strange sensations he'd felt during mass. He hadn't forgotten the hungry look in the captain's eyes as Lopez stared at the emeralds, but that wasn't what mattered. When the captain asked the Hopi maiden her name, she'd first replied with something incomprehensible in her own language and then, stumbling a little over the Spanish words, told him "Morning Butterfly."

Hearing that, he'd been reminded of the small, white butterflies flitting around the multitude of flowers that grew in the well-tended gardens of the Franciscan monastery in Tepeaca. He'd spent many hours meditating and praying there, waiting for the Lord to show him the direction his life should take. It had never occurred to him that those delicate creatures might give their names, their whispered perfection, to a native woman.

Captain Lopez forced the Navajo to kneel before him. Then Fray Angelico watched him take Morning Butterfly's arm and squeeze it as he insisted she get the Navajo to reveal exactly where he'd found the precious stones. If the captain hurt her—

Angelico sucked in what he could of the too-hot air and struggled to find something, anything to concentrate on. His blurred vision finally settled on the captive who, he had to admit, wasn't groveling before his captors, despite his humble position.

"So he wants to know if I am going to kill him, does he?" the captain was saying to Morning Butterfly. "I command you to tell him he has no soul and when all the blood's been run out of his miserable hide, that will be the end of him."

The end of him. Without a soul. Springing forward, Angelico clapped his hands on the Navajo's head and quickly, inadequately baptized him.

"What are you doing?" Lopez demanded. "Padre, this is *not* your concern."

"But it is! I was sent here to take charge of the savages' souls, to save them for the Lord God."

"Now is hardly the time for a religious ceremony. You had your opportunity earlier, and I dare say you took full advantage of it."

"But there were no baptisms."

"Why not?"

The explanation was too complex, too deeply rooted in his distaste, distrust, and, yes, his fear of Oraibi—not that he would ever confess those things to the captain.

"The Lord is selective in His instructions to me," he said instead, "as to when to lead the natives into the light of salvation. He did not see fit to have me do so this morning, but He does now."

Captain Lopez's features were still dark with anger. "I warn you, Padre. Do *not* interfere in military matters."

"Military and religious concerns are not separate. You

tend to your responsibilities, and I tend to mine which, I do not believe I need to point out, are of at least equal weight."

Lopez glared down at the captive, whose athletic frame looked capable of bursting his bonds. "If you think you now have jurisdiction over him, you are mistaken. The miserable beast does not know what you have done."

"But the Lord does. And so do your men. Are you going to murder someone who has just received God's blessing?"

A muscle jumped in the captain's jaw. "I warn you—not until he has told me everything, but then—yes."

Morning Butterfly had stood unmoving throughout the exchange, but as the captain issued his warning, Angelico heard her draw in a shocked breath. For reasons that escaped his comprehension, she didn't want the Navajo to die.

No, he amended. He did understand. She was a compassionate creature after all, fully alive, her heart beating, breasts rising and falling, beautiful dark eyes—

"Padre?"

Angelico forced his attention off Morning Butterfly, and if a small, forbidden part of him continued to be aware of her—and it was—that was his burden.

"Question the Navajo," he told Lopez. "But I order you in front of your men, do not kill someone who is now under my guidance and protection. If you do, as God is my witness, I will bring the Church's influence to bear and have you relieved of your post."

8

Cougar's head pounded and his wrists ached. Beyond that, fury and fear warred inside him, making it nearly impossible for him to concentrate on what was going on. It might have been easier if he'd understood what was being said, but the soldier and padre threw words without meaning at each other.

Before he could ask Morning Butterfly to translate or ask why the padre had clamped his hands over his head and spoken in a sing-song tone, the captain stalked over to her and twisted her arm behind her, causing her to double over. The padre sprang forward and fastened a hand on the captain's wrist, but the captain only laughed at him.

The two were speaking again, the captain's words like thunder, the padre's voice higher and yet equally hard.

"What is it?" Cougar demanded of Morning Butterfly. "What are they saying?"

The captain had relaxed his grip on her, allowing her to straighten but not letting her go. Tears glinted in her eyes.

"Fray Angelico baptized you and placed you under his

protection. The captain says the padre must choose between your safety and mine."

"Baptize?"

"Do not ask me to explain. I do not fully understand, but it means a great deal to him."

She'd barely finished when the captain spun her around and, after shoving his face close to hers, again spoke in that drumbeat way of his. She trembled slightly but didn't try to back away. Despite his frustration at not understanding what his enemies were saying, Cougar forced himself to concentrate on their bodies' language.

He'd heard that a man who devoted his life to the spirit the Spanish called God turned his back on earthly concerns, lived in prayer, and knew nothing of a man's needs for a woman, but that was clearly wrong, because Fray Angelico's now hot eyes remained fixed on Morning Butterfly, and he'd positioned his hand so that he covered his manhood.

Cougar wasn't the only one who noticed; the captain smirked at the sheltering hand and when he pointed, his laugh was harsh. Cheeks flaming, the padre shook his head so vigorously that Cougar wondered if he might snap his neck. Then, although surely his strength didn't equal the soldier's, the padre tried to shove him away from Morning Butterfly. That earned him a barrage of words from the captain.

"What did he say?" Cougar demanded.

"That the padre should allow me to be killed so he will not be tempted."

Mindless of his bonds, Cougar surged forward and used his shoulder to force himself among those he hated. A couple of the soldiers grabbed him, but not until he'd made his presence known, not before he'd been assaulted by their smell and strength. After calling up courage from deep inside him, he demanded to be told why he'd been made prisoner when he'd come offering jewels to appease the soldiers' anger.

"I will tell them where to find the stones, lead them there," he told Morning Butterfly, his tone as calm as he could manage.

"No!"

"Yes. Morning Butterfly, please, tell them."

Comprehension dawned in her eyes. "But you will not do that thing, will you?" she asked. "You wish my lie to grow until it encompasses both of us and maybe all of my people."

"We have no choice. Would you rather they stay until you are an old woman, until they fill your womb with their seed and you give birth to a daughter who is then forced to become their bed slave?"

"Do not say that!"

"My silence will not change anything. Can you call me a liar? Can you?"

"I hate you! Wish they had killed you!"

Before he could respond, she turned her attention to the others. Although her voice trembled and she looked a heartbeat from bolting, when she spoke, she kept her head high and proud. From the captain's response, it was clear he didn't know whether to believe her, but whatever it was he said, she didn't back away. She'd become a storm, whipped by wind and lightning, perhaps creating those forces. After a conversation that seemed to go on forever, she turned back to Cougar.

"He has decided to go to the great canyon and will take you and me with him," she said. "You have what you want."

"*You?* Why?"

"That is the only way he will know your words."

"I do not want you to be part of this," he told her, self-loathing riding with his words.

"Neither do I, but it is too late for that. I hate you, Cougar. Take my words into you and know they are the truth."

From where she stood, Morning Butterfly couldn't see the Navajo. The sun pressed down on the top of her head and thirst had dried her throat. There was a song in the wind, but she couldn't search for its meaning because her thoughts trapped her, turned her this way and that, offered no way out. Fray Angelico knelt nearby, his voice part and yet not part of the wind. If she looked behind her, she might have a better understanding of what was happening this afternoon, but comprehension wouldn't change anything.

The padre had insisted on having her with him, that was her reality.

That Cougar had been forced to stay with Captain Lopez was his.

Although she fought the memory, her mind insisted on replaying what had happened earlier in the day. Whether she'd spoken from the bottom of her heart when she'd told Cougar she hated him she couldn't say; maybe she'd never know.

She had learned that the soldier was more powerful than the man of God, at least today; certainly he was stronger, and never without a weapon. Despite that, Captain Lopez walked softly around the padre, and when Fray Angelico announced he would seek God's guidance about the wisdom of seeking jewels instead of setting up a church, the captain hadn't objected. He'd also promised to obey the padre's order that he do nothing to harm the Navajo, at least not now.

But later?

"Padre?" she ventured when he fell silent.

"What, my child?"

"If I ask something of you, will you give me an answer?"

He was a long time responding, and she sensed it had never occurred to him that a Hopi might be capable of carrying on a conversation with him.

"Will you?" she repeated.

"I . . . of course my child."

She wasn't his child. "Why did you come here?"

His mouth sagged, and he stared so intently that she felt as if she'd been burned. "You have to ask? It is not clear?"

"You want the Hopi to become something different from what they have always been. That I understand, but I do not know why. We have always—"

"Misguided. Taken down the wrong path by the devil."

"The devil? Where is he? I have never seen him."

"You cannot possibly understand. You are a simple people, children in need of guidance. I can teach you to follow His teachings. To fear His wrath and seek the light. It may be impossible for you to comprehend any more than that. Maybe . . ." He started to hold out his hand toward her, then stopped and stared at it for a long time before shoving it into the folds of his robe.

"Morning Butterfly, the captain said certain things about me—about certain desires."

"Yes."

His body jerked and he clutched the heavy necklace he always wore and often prayed over. "The devils' influence is everywhere, perhaps tempting me more than most because he knows I would never shrink from the battle. Temptation is a lifelong assault upon a man's devotion to his Lord and must—"

"Do you wish me dead so you will not be tempted?"

"What? My God, no! My child, the captain was wrong. What happened earlier was a function of the flesh. I turn that all too human flesh over to my lord and—"

"Let the Navajo go," she interrupted. "Make the captain release him."

"He is your enemy."

"The Navajo are not enemies of the Hopi."

"Ha! They are raiders!"

That was the way of the Navajo; couldn't the padre understand that? How much easier things had been before she and this man had begun talking to each other. Seeking distance from him, she tried to see where Cougar had been taken. The padre began praying again.

"She is a child, my Lord. Only a child. I need guidance from You, to be shown how my path should be walked. To atone for the sin of lust."

She'd worked hard to increase her knowledge of the newcomers' language, but although she'd heard the padre use the word sin a number of times, she didn't know what he was talking about. Now he spoke of something called lust.

If only the newcomers would leave! If only her people could go back to what they'd always been!

When she stepped back, the padre ordered her to remain where she was, then closed his eyes and went back to speaking to the blue sky.

Captain Lopez had tied Cougar's hands behind him and made the warrior helpless. He might be dead, dying.

The Spanish must fear the night, Cougar thought as he watched the soldiers gather around a campfire not far from where he'd been left, his feet now tied with the same rope that held his hands. He'd never known anything except freedom, and being unable to move terrified him. If he hadn't forced himself to concentrate on what he'd come here to accomplish, he might have allowed that fear to show. Still, fighting the emotion exhausted him.

Stop!

Think of the soldiers' fear!

Laugh at them for trying to hide from the night! Refuse to let your thoughts go to what was done to Blue Corn Eater's body.

Fighting off that image, he took what comfort he could from the fact that he was far enough away from the gathered soldiers that he couldn't hear more than a faint murmur of voices. Night hid him from their hate-filled eyes. Night was his friend, his companion, a sheltering blanket. Within its folds he became one with the past and was embraced by his ancestors. As long as he walked the path—

"Cougar?"

At the sudden sound, his heart seemed to crash against his chest. Panting, he waited for its beat to return to normal. Only then did he understand that the voice belonged to a woman.

"Morning Butterfly?"

"Yes. You—you are all right?"

His shoulders throbbed from the position they'd been forced into and the ropes had rubbed some of the flesh from his wrists. "Who is with you?" he asked, angry at the darkness the soldiers feared.

"No one. Have you been hurt?"

She stood behind him and no matter how he strained, he couldn't see her. Giving up, he concentrated on her tone. She reminded him of a wild animal that has sensed danger yet stays where it is until it understands that danger.

"No," he told her. "Not hurt. What are you doing here?"

"I do not . . . I . . . are you alone?"

"Yes." He'd been lying on his side because that was how he'd been positioned when his legs were confined. Now he struggled to sit up, the effort causing his body to scream out in pain. "The padre," he whispered when he trusted himself to speak. "You have been with him?"

"For a long time, while he prayed. I thought it would never end."

"That is all he did? Pray?"

"Yes."

"He did not take you?"

She sucked in a deep breath. "No, he is not like Captain Lopez. Cougar, it is not safe for you to remain here. You *must* leave."

He would have laughed if he hadn't been concerned that someone might hear. Whispering harshly, he reminded her of why he'd come here, his determination to get the soldiers to leave so his people could take more horses—and be safe.

"You do not know what the Spanish are capable of. Their cruelty is—"

"I do know," he interrupted as an image of what had been done years ago to Drums No More and more recently to Blue Corn Eater filled his mind. Despite himself, he shivered.

"Then you should want nothing to do with them."

"To be Navajo is to be part of a whole. What happens to me is a little thing if it means my people are protected."

"He *will* kill you."

"Perhaps

"Not perhaps. Some of our holy men say the soldiers are kachinas, not good ones who bring rain, protect life, and see that our crops succeed, but evil. They do not spend seasons deep in their land with the other spirits, but remain here, untouched by sacred cornmeal from the Powamu chief as should be. They are different, evil."

She'd used several words that meant nothing to him, but he couldn't dismiss their intensity. The Navajo didn't believe in kachinas, but he was on Hopi land.

"It is not for you or me to understand what is in the hearts, minds, and souls of the newcomers."

"No," she agreed. "Cougar, go back to your people. Tonight."

"I cannot."

"Because you made a promise to them? Ha! I take your promise and step on it."

Someone laughed in the distance, reminding him of how much a voice could carry.

"I will say this to you one time," she continued, softly, before he could warn her. "It does not matter whether you believe me, or whether my words mean anything to you; in this thing, I will have my way."

He sensed her coming closer.

"You say you are ready to die as long as your people benefit from your sacrifice, but this is not between Navajo and Spanish. The Hopi, too, have become part of it."

He'd been wrong; he didn't hate the night after all. How could he when darkness made it possible for him and Morning Butterfly to be together like this, for him to learn of her beliefs and courage?

"Yes, they have." He sighed. "And because of that, you should thank the Navajo for wanting to take the Spanish far from you."

"Thank?" she echoed. "And if a Hopi dies in this, will I thank you for that? Do not speak, Cougar. It is my turn. It was your plan to lead the Spanish to the great canyon, was it? Perhaps it was your thought to stay with them until they were far from Oraibi and then slip away while other Navajo came here and stole their horses. Yes, that would be a Navajo's plan."

"You make it sound like a foolish thing."

"Because it is."

Before he could do more than open his mouth to object, he felt something hard and sharp touch his side. He jumped but, trussed, was unable to move away.

"A knife." She explained the obvious. "Like the Spanish would use on the Hopi."

"The Hopi? But—"

"If you get the Spanish to leave with you, the time will come when they will know they have been deceived. Their anger will be like a winter wind, and they will seek revenge."

The knife no longer pressed against his flesh, but he'd already dismissed it as he concentrated on her. He'd known her to be courageous from the moment he'd become aware of her, but now he admired her in a way he'd never guessed was possible, a way he didn't want.

"Will they seek to punish the Navajo?" she continued. "No! You will be gone, as will the other Navajo braves. The Spanish do not know where you live, and even if they found that place, your people would already have fled. But the Hopi are not birds—it is not our way to spend our lives moving from one place to the other. Oraibi is our home, our life; because of that we are vulnerable."

The soldiers were talking loudly, their voices like dirt that rolls over the land when the wind has it in its grip. He hated them. Hated what she was saying.

"Tell me, Cougar. How many Hopi will the soldiers kill before they are satisfied?"

Her question slammed into him, but before he'd made full sense of it, he felt her hand on his chest, then moving over his hip, down his leg, finally reaching his bound ankles. She slid the knife under the ropes and began cutting, her breathing coming fast and hard. Once she'd freed his legs, she attacked the bindings on his hands. When, at last, his arms were no longer trapped behind him, it was all he could do not to cry out from the pain.

"Go!" she ordered. "Now!"

"What about you?"

"Go!"

"Your safety—"

"If you do not leave, I will call them and they will kill you."

"Damnation!"

Fray Angelico winced at Captain Lopez's bellow but hurried toward the sound. Because the captain held a flaming torch, he easily saw what had caused the man's anger. As it had been getting dark, Lopez had ordered the captured Navajo to be placed near the soldiers' encampment, but the savage was no longer there. Several short pieces of rope lay on the ground. Lopez kicked at them, then repeated his oath.

"Who allowed this?" he insisted. "Who was supposed to be guarding him?"

It came as no surprise when no one claimed responsibility. Instead, the gathered soldiers seemed inordinately glad to have a man of God in their midst.

"Was it you, Padre?" The captain strode toward him, stopping when they were only inches apart. "Is this how you defy me, by letting the savage go?"

"No," he blurted, then regretted having said anything, because if Lopez believed him, there was only one other logical culprit. "Captain, you have no jurisdiction over me. What I do is my concern and the Lord's, not yours."

"Do not test my patience. The churches you and the rest of your order are determined to erect will never come about without a military presence. I cannot believe—cannot believe . . ."

Captain Lopez fisted his hand and shoved it under Angelico's chin. Refusing to back down, Angelico reached for the pectoral cross around his neck and held it up, defying the military man to ignore what it symbolized. The soldiers, obviously torn between loyalties, shuffled from one foot to the other. Only Madariaga stepped forward.

"If you strike me," Angelico said, "your soul will be cast into everlasting hell."

Although the captain continued to glare, a little of the madness left his eyes. "You have no comprehension of my responsibilities. None. Do you have any idea what the possession of emeralds means to me?" He patted his pocket where he'd earlier placed the jewels. "The potential, the opportunities . . . Of course not, because material profit means nothing to you."

"In God's eyes, material goods are of no—"

"Yes, yes, I know." Lopez clamped his fingers against his temple and squeezed. He noticed that Madariaga had positioned himself so he could protect Angelico.

Lopez's lips thinned. "A man in my position has no alternative but to do all he can to better himself. The pressures confronting me make that an absolutely necessity and I vow, I swear, I will succeed. Neither will I allow any opposition. Do you understand me? Do you?"

Angelico made no attempt to silence Lopez, opting to let him vent his rage and hopefully gain a measure of control over his temper. Madariaga retreated, as if sensing how close he'd come to pushing his leader over the edge.

Captain Lopez continued to rant that from now on there would be a clear demarcation between what the Church had a say in and what were solely military duties and obligations, but Angelico barely listened. He would pray for guidance and calm and, if possible, understanding of what drove the captain; but that would have to wait because it was imperative he look for Morning Butterfly.

Unfortunately, the night hid her.

Exhaustion lapped at Morning Butterfly as, finally, she approached her family's home. From the moment she'd freed Cougar, she had wanted to run here, but when she'd heard Captain Lopez's outburst, she'd forced herself to slip as close as possible to where he and the padre were standing so she could hear the argument between them. She hadn't fully understood what they'd said to each other, but when the padre's eyes had searched the night, she'd guessed he'd been looking for her, and now she prayed he wouldn't come here to try and find her. Oraibi was Hopi, not Catholic, and the padre had to know that, he *had* to.

It would be dawn before long, and she wanted to spend as

much of the day as possible with her sister. It didn't matter
whether they went in search of bowl-making materials or
stayed with other maidens; the important thing was to give
Singer Of Songs a reason to laugh—and for Morning Butterfly to try to make sense of her thoughts, of what she'd
done. She'd told Cougar she didn't care whether he lived or
died, and yet . . .

"Finally," a voice whispered from the shadows. "Finally
you are home."

Recovering from her shock, she concentrated on locating
her father's uncle among the shadows. "You had a nightmare?" she asked One Hand. "I am sorry I was not—"

"No, I was not sleeping. Come here, child. Walk with me
for a minute."

Although she wasn't sure how much longer her legs
would hold her, she matched the old man's pace as he made
his practiced way among the many separate stone structures.
The flat rocks the Hopi used to build their homes were like
the earth, slow to accept the sun's heat and equally slow to
let go of coolness.

"The Spanish now know you speak their language," One
Hand said. "It should not be."

"You stayed in the pueblo during what the padre calls
mass, did you not? How did you know?"

"As long as the Spanish are here, I remain hidden from
their eyes," he agreed. "It does not matter who first told me,
all tongues spoke of little else."

"Yes, I imagine they did."

He stopped walking, and she took advantage of the opportunity to sit. It was all she could do to keep her eyes open.

"Morning Butterfly, I fear for your life!"

"One Hand, I—"

"You should have remained silent. What passes between
our captors and a Navajo is not your concern."

The old man's fears flowed over her, nearly overwhelm-
ing her. "I had no choice." As briefly as possible, she told
him why Cougar had approached her. What she didn't tell
the old man was why she'd agreed to speak for him. Though

One Hand would surely understand her irrational hope that Cougar could indeed convince the Spanish to leave, she had no words for the Navajo's control over her.

"What happened to the Navajo?"

"What?"

"Someone freed him. Your father saw him run off."

"Did he?"

"The ropes had been cut. Morning Butterfly, was it you?"

"Yes."

"Because he begged you to help him?"

"No! Never. He . . . he wanted no danger to come to me."

9

Since as governor, Captain Lopez's grandfather General Don Juan de Oñate of Zacatecas had absolute power over everyone under his jurisdiction, he'd been given the authority "to carry out the discovery, pacification, and conquest of the provinces of New Mexico." He'd pursued this goal with zeal while receiving a salary of six thousand gold ducats of Castile and borrowing a like amount from the provincial treasury. His private estate had encompassed some thirty square leagues.

After bloody years of near dictatorship, his majesty King Philip had fined Oñate heavily and confiscated much of his personal wealth. Eventually, Oñate had received a formal pardon because he had, after all, done a great deal to "civilize" the Indians with whom he'd come into contact, but he'd died without regaining the money, land, or jewels that had once made him and his family wealthy.

Lopez, born and raised in Veracruz, the chief port of New Spain, had lived for the days when the fleet from the mother country dropped anchor in the harbor. His father, fortunately skilled in metal working, had been much in demand repairing battered vessels, and Lopez, the only son, had been first called into service assisting him when he was but six. At Huerta de Leiva's side, Lopez had worked long hours in the hot, muggy climate, falling exhausted into bed when Huerta—bitter over the loss of the family's fortune—finally released him. His mother, busy with his four older sisters and daily worship, had been only too happy to abdicate responsibility for the raising of this unexpected child, born when she'd thought her childbearing years were behind her.

When Huerta spoke, which was seldom, it was usually to impress upon Lopez his belief that only hard work mattered. If he neglected his wife and daughters, that was unfortunate but unavoidable, and if there were times when he missed mass because his work was so much in demand, surely God understood. Lopez, unable to sit through long sermons, had been only too willing to forego services in order to assist his father.

He might have become a metal worker himself if his parents hadn't argued over him. His mother had finally insisted that he concentrate on his religious schooling instead of spending all his time out of doors. She had put in a rare appearance at the dock where Huerta plied his trade and announced that she intended to take the boy with her. Equally determined, Huerta had pointed out that Lopez was the only one he trusted to keep the forge coals hot enough, the only one whose eye was keen enough to determine when a support rod was at the correct angle. Twelve years old, naked to the waist and sweating, only inches from the heated coals necessary for bending metal, Lopez had, in a flash of insight, seen two roads open up in front of him. One committed him to a lifetime of working on someone else's ships; the other silenced his inquisitive nature beneath an ocean of religious dogma.

That very day, he had approached a ship's captain and asked to be allowed to accompany him and his crew to prosperous Mexico City. In exchange for the opportunity, he'd said, his father wouldn't charge the captain for the work he had just completed. That was a lie, but his next statement was the truth. He was Don Juan de Oñate's grandson and wanted nothing more in life than to follow in the great man's footsteps, to travel into new land, to explore and conquer, to be a soldier. In urbane Mexico City, where the richest families of New Spain lived, he would make his mark. The captain, impressed by the name, had been willing to accommodate Lopez.

Life in a garrison behind the viceroy's palace had been no easier than working for his father, but he'd made the most of the fact that he was *limpieza de sangra,* pure of blood. Where many of his fellow soldiers were barely literate, he devoted himself to learning, not in the church-run schools but by asking questions, watching and listening, borrowing books, and teaching himself. In due time his facility with reading and figures caught the attention of the viceroy and other royals.

Beginning at age eighteen, in the employ of wealthy land and mine owners, he'd led soldiers into the Mayo and Yaqui valleys of Sonora, where they met only token resistance from the indigenous Indians. He could have become a majordomo or *capataces* for one of those influential men and turned his talent to supervising the work of the defeated Indian laborers, but his dreams lay further north. One of the wealthiest mine owners, Gregorio de Barreto, had been impressed enough with his lineage, intelligence, and aggression that he'd encouraged Lopez to court one of his daughters, and when the so-called romance might have faltered, had presented him with a dowry sizable enough that Lopez had been able to overlook her horse features and hefty hips.

Today, Lopez's thought were far from his less-than-beautiful wife. Instead, he wandered from one Hopi farm plot to the other, not because he cared how the Indians coaxed life from the land, but because his feet needed something to do while he debated his next move. He carried with him the writings of Fray Geronimo de Zarate Salmeron, who'd spent years among the Jemez and served at Zia, Sandia, and Acoma. Fray Geronimo's *Relaciones*, in which the good father detailed the vast treasures to be found in the territory, were, in short, why Lopez had sought his current position—and why he'd believed the captive Navajo's tale about a wealth of emeralds to be found at the great canyon.

Tamping down the excitement that could make him lose his measured judgment, he considered the pros and cons of leading his men on a search for the accursed and dangerous Navajo. If he'd had any confidence that he could find the emeralds on his own, he would already be planning an expedition, but the canyon's vastness made that impossible. His only recourse was to force a savage to serve as guide—and to take along the female Hopi interpreter.

Something akin to a smile touched his lips as he contemplated what other use he might put her to, but it died when he recalled the padre's reaction to her. It might be an interesting exercise in assessing the padre's strength and determination if he were to bed the female, but undoubtedly Angelico would fight for her so-called honor— maybe carrying that fight to Lopez's troops. They were a simple lot, more fearful of their surroundings than he would have preferred, but he'd worked with undisciplined men before, and relished the challenge of turning these into seasoned soldiers. However, they were, down to their core, religious. Knowing that, Fray Angelico would manipulate their deep-rooted and blind devotion to the Church, and he, Lopez, wasn't about to run the risk of losing their loyalty to a man of God. Besides, although he privately questioned many of the Church's dictates, his mother had taught him to fear the Lord's wrath; even now, he wasn't of a mind to test the limits of God's patience.

All right; he wouldn't bed the interpreter, whatever her name was. Besides, he'd found another—

Stopping in mid-stride, he looked around, but although the dry and rolling land was dotted with toiling Hopi, none were close enough for him to make out their features. His observations of the way the savages worked their land had led him to conclude that farming was considered men's work. Whatever the females and children occupied themselves with was conducted for the most part at Oraibi, which meant he'd have to go up there if he hoped to find the virgin he'd bedded the other night.

A virgin.

His first.

"Atse Hastin, First Man, hear me. You live because the Mirage People walked four times around eagle feathers, buckskin, and ears of corn, and the wind turned the white corn into First Man and First Woman. To them were born a boy and a girl who grew to maturity in four days and lived as man and wife. Before it was done, First Man and First Woman had five pairs of twins, and all but one of those had children. Four days after the last pair was born, the gods took First Man and First Woman to the East where they learned many things. They wore Hasteyalti and Hastehogan masks and prayed for all good things such as rain and crops, but while in the East, they also learned the secrets of witchcraft."

Contemplating the awesome power of witchcraft, Cougar fell silent. When Morning Butterfly had set him free and ordered him to leave, he'd wanted to do just that, running like a deer who has escaped a pack of wolves, but he hadn't dared. If he broke a leg in the dark, he might die before any of his people found him. Instead, he'd traveled as fast as his searching feet and eyes could take him, not stopping until his body forced him to rest. Now it was morning, and he was on his way home again.

This land was mother and father. He'd never known anything except day after day after day of no rain, grasses clinging to life in the seemingly barren soil, birds and animals who needed little water and were oblivious to summer's intense heat or winter's cold. He loved hearing the wind's song, being able to see distant horizons, rocks, the occasional canyon, and the equally rare hill. He couldn't imagine the world being any different.

Witches and *chindi* shared this land with the Navajo, but

as long as he walked The Way Of Life, he had nothing to fear from them.

The Way Of Life. Maybe his feet no longer walked that journey because he'd unwittingly endangered a life—a Hopi life.

His throat felt dry, but although he was thirsty, the lack of water was only partially responsible. In preparation for approaching the Spanish, he'd purified himself by focusing on how First Man came into being. He'd believed that recalling the story of how First Man's sons had stopped living with their sister-wives and turned to Mirage People for partners would make him strong.

But something had gone wrong or he wouldn't have been taken prisoner.

Now he was a prisoner no longer—thanks to the Hopi woman.

Moaning, he clamped his hands against the sides of his head. He *had* to go back over everything that had happened, *had* to determine when and how he'd strayed from the path he'd set for himself, but how could he with so much inner turmoil?

Desperate for something, anything to distract himself, he again concentrated on his surroundings. He'd seen fresh deer sign a little while ago, but didn't care enough to determine in which direction the animals had gone. A small gray feather, dusty and bedraggled, held his attention for no more than a heartbeat. He scanned the sky, but if a bird was up there, it was too high overhead for him to see.

The Spanish had come from a place so far away he could barely comprehend its existence. Yes, his ancestors had roamed the earth, but his feet knew little beyond what he could now see in all directions: Dinehtah. As a youth, he'd wondered what it would be like to travel with the speed and endurance of an animal, not to care where he laid his head. He'd been restless then, hungry for something without a name, but the seasons had gentled that restlessness until now nothing meant more than living out his life on this land.

His land! No, not his, because the land had belonged to

the ages, not those who lived and died on it. But the earth, rocks, and grass, the sky and wind were part of him and he part of them, and that was enough.

Had been enough until the strangers arrived.

Were their spirits more powerful than those of the Navajo or Hopi?

Unprepared for the question, he stumbled and nearly fell. Finally he understood what this morning of doubt and question had been about. He'd come to Oraibi and risked his life, not just because he hungered for the strength and speed a horse represented, not just because his people needed horses if they were going to resist and escape the newcomers. . . His plan had been nurtured and nourished with songs and prayers and should have succeeded; it hadn't, not because he hadn't prepared himself spiritually but because. . .

Because, maybe, the Spanish gods were more powerful than those of his people.

Another question struck him. He didn't know much about Hopi beliefs, only that they were ancient and grounded in their own legends. Was it possible that Morning Butterfly was filled with the same doubts and questions? Seeking answers and strength from Hopi spirits?

"Hear me, Morning Butterfly," he said aloud. "Despite the words we spoke to each other, I am glad our paths crossed. It is right that Navajo and Hopi come together in some things. The time may come when we stand face to face and debate what our people must do to rid the land of those who do not belong and seek to change what we have always been."

Movement to his left caught his attention, and for a moment he thought the Hopi maiden had followed him, but then disappointment and something that tasted too much like fear filled him. A wolf stood on a low ridge, its head lifted as if to catch the breeze, so close that he could make out the individual hairs on the dark nose. Wolves belonged here and lived in harmony with the Navajo—but what if this wasn't a true wolf?

Perhaps a *chindi*.

"First Man . . ." After swallowing, he began again. It

would do no good to pray for safety from a *chindi*; only walking the Way Of The Rainbow could protect a man from that danger.

"The beliefs and ways of the Spanish are strange to me. The man who calls himself a padre is a keeper of their religion, just as our singers safeguard what is sacred to us. When I was their prisoner, he did something to me that Morning Butterfly called a baptism. What is that?"

The wolf was still there, not one with its surroundings but set apart, as if the land had rejected it. The creature flowed rather than walked as it faced first the direction of the rising sun and then where Sun went after it was done with its daily journey. Maybe its feet touched rocks and grass, maybe it had no need for them. It howled, long and low and deep.

Then, like the illusion of water on a hot day, it shimmered and was gone. Only the howl's echo remained.

Cougar recoiled and his heart beat furiously. He gasped, then blurted his thoughts. "To be touched by a padre—to be baptized by him—what does that mean? Did it—did it weaken me and make me less Navajo? Open me to *chindi* attack?"

He had to stop these questions! Otherwise his heart and mind might explode.

"First Man, I must know if the creature is a true wolf or maybe—maybe a Spanish *chindi*. It—it could be that." The rest of his thoughts were too horrible for words. The *chindi* of his people was a fearsome force that sometimes took the shape of a wolf and caused disharmony and even death, and if the Spanish religion had the same evil force . . .

He wasn't done with Morning Butterfly after all. She understood their language and lived in their shadow and might have the answer.

Without that answer, he might not survive.

Singer Of Songs crouched over the small fire she was using to heat water. Once it began to simmer, she would drop the tiny yellow flowers she'd collected into it and from that make the yellow dye her father would dip wild cotton into.

Among the Hopi, it had always been a man's job to supply his family's clothing, weaving the various garments from the cotton he'd collected, carded, and spun into cloth. It had never occurred to her to wonder why women were responsible only for dyeing, all she cared was that she had something to do on this hot afternoon.

The padre's bells rang at several points during the day, from dawn until after dark. Although it was possible to avoid responding to the insistent call to prayer, if too few Hopi attended a service, the soldiers would come looking for those who'd remained behind. The latest prayer had been only a short while ago, and if she concentrated on what she was doing, before the next she should be able to present her father with not just yellow dye but orange and green as well. But she did not know whether Deer Ears would be able to work at his loom.

Saddened by thoughts of her father's diminished abilities, she stretched her spine and looked around. In winter, her people worked inside, but once summer afternoons brought shadows to Oraibi, it was more pleasant to do whatever needed doing outside. That had changed some with the coming of the Spanish, but although Singer Of Songs feared she might attract the captain's attention out here, no air moved inside the dark rooms where her father was napping.

A few feet away, her mother sat hunched over her half-finished woven wicker basket. She'd formed its outline with sumac twigs and was adding more supple rabbit-brush branches, the large, intricately designed pot seemingly an extension of her skilled fingers. Through the use of red and yellow dyed fibers she was creating a network of spider-like threads that symbolized the sun's journey.

"I will never have your skill in this," Singer Of Songs told Roadrunner. "No matter how many times I watch you, I do not understand how your fingers know when to weave certain colors and designs together."

"My fingers do what my heart tells them to," Roadrunner said without looking up.

Her mother had told her that before, and although Singer

Of Songs understood that Roadrunner carried the finished product inside her and thus worked instinctively, that knowledge didn't pass the gift onto her.

"My fingers know how to stain themselves different colors, nothing more." She laughed, then sobered. She hadn't felt like laughing in the four days since the captain had raped her.

"Not everyone has the same skill," Roadrunner said.

"I tell myself that, but I still long for your skill. I want to create beauty, not—" she held up her yellow stained fingertips— "not this."

"Your voice is like a bird's. Be thankful for your gift."

"I am."

Sighing, she searched for a way to change the conversation. Usually the village women worked close to one another so they could talk while they went about their tasks, but there wasn't enough shade here to accommodate anyone else. Several children, apparently unaffected by the heat, played tag in one of the streets, their laughter much more familiar than the padre's droning prayers would ever be. Not far away, one of her mother's sisters patted raw piki flat before placing the corn-based staple food into her open-air oven.

"My mouth waters at the smell." Singer Of Songs indicated what her aunt was doing.

"Mine too. It is good that certain things have not changed. My prayer is that the Spanish will not care what we eat."

"Perhaps all they care about is trying to change what we believe."

"Perhaps." Roadrunner briefly fell silent. "I fear what this is doing to your father. It should be enough that he worries about feeding his wife and children. He should not . . ."

Although she continued to hear her mother's voice, Singer Of Songs no longer concentrated on the words. It was a moment before she realized what had caught her attention. The children had stopped running and had fallen silent, as had several of the women.

Singer Of Songs spoke through a mouth as dry as dust. "The soldiers are here."

Barely aware of what she was doing, she scrambled to her knees and started to stand. She prayed the captain wouldn't seek her out again, but the thought faltered as she recognized him.

"This should not be," Roadrunner whispered. "The newcomers walk on land that is not theirs."

"Mother, please."

Whether the captain's attention had been captured by her mother's voice didn't matter, because now Lopez's eyes, alive and searching, registered her presence. He also took in the gray pueblo walls, the naked and unmoving children, the nearest kiva with a ladder extending from the small hole in the solid stone top. What he could see of the mostly underground kiva held his attention the longest. Then he stepped toward her and extended his hand. His eyes told her nothing of what he was thinking.

He wasn't the only soldier to lay claim that day to a Hopi woman.

"Hano, Sichomovi, and Walpi are on the First Mesa and Mishongnovi, Shipaulovi, and Shongopovi on the Second. Hotevilla and Bakavi were also built on the Third Mesa, but Oraibi is the oldest."

Eyes nearly closed, Morning Butterfly listened to the old man with his dark, wrinkled skin and gnarled hands. The kiva of the Bear Clan had been the first built in Oraibi and had four levels, which represented the four stages in man's creation. The depression, or *sipapu*, on the floor represented the Hole of Emergence. As a child, witnessing her first Powamu festival, she'd been so frightened by the masked kachina dancers that she'd believed they'd come from the *sipapu* itself. Now she was older and wise in her people's legends, and understood that Hopi power and strength came from the *sipapu*.

"Oraibi is our people's soul," Sun in the Sky continued while other clan members nodded somber agreement. "The

Hopi may live far from each other because the land so dictates, but there is not one who has not given his heart to Oraibi. I was born here and will die here, and I want the same for my children and grandchildren."

"Yes, yes," those gathered around Sun in the Sky echoed.

Morning Butterfly wanted to do the same but was afraid to add her female voice to the deep male tones. Although the invitation to join the members of the Bear Clan had come this morning from Sun in the Sky himself, she still felt like an outsider. They wanted her to tell them everything she'd learned from listening to the Spanish, but would it be enough?

"Think today of Tuwaqachi, of the Fourth World which is World Complete," Sun in the Sky droned as if speaking to himself. "When the First People reached Tuwaqachi, they were told their emergence was complete, but it was not, because the people still had a great deal to learn. The ancient ones directed them to migrate to the ends of the earth and then return. We have done this. The four migrations are complete and we celebrate the nine yearly ceremonies that insure the Hopi Road of Life. They are held, as they should be, in the kiva, but now . . ."

Barely breathing, Morning Butterfly waited for Sun in the Sky to continue.

"I will speak of that soon," he whispered, "but first I speak of what the kiva represents and why it must remain as it has forever."

Despite herself, her thoughts strayed to Fray Angelico and his insistence on conducting his ceremonies so close to what was sacred to her people. She'd been raised to be gentle and keep only good thoughts, but what he'd done was wrong—wrong!

Equally wrong was the way the soldiers had come up here yesterday, Captain Lopez leaving with Singer Of Songs as if she was a sheep or horse he'd laid claim to, the others leading other women away from their homes.

"Our kivas, which means World Below, are sunk deep into Mother Earth like a womb. The Hopi are born from that womb, surrounded by all that nourishes him. A kiva both touches that which we came from and reaches toward what we are now. It is everything to us. During *Wuwuchim*, the New Fire ceremony, a fire is lit in each kiva's sunken fire pit because life began with fire. The newcomers do not understand that. Instead, they used fire to rid themselves of a Navajo's body. If they saw us during our ceremonies, they would make fun of us."

Either that or order us to stop.

"According to our legends, when Pahana, the Hopi's lost white brother, came, we would welcome his return. Our fathers and grandfathers planned for that time each year on the last day of *Soyal* by marking a line in the sacred stick kept by the Bear Clan. It mattered not to our ancestors when Pahana arrived because they would either meet him at the bottom of Third Mesa if he came when the legends said he would, or at Yellow Rock, Pointed Rock, Cross Fields, or Tawtoma if he was late.

"The newcomer our ancestors thought was Pahana arrived, saying his name was Coronado. Our ancestors greeted him with a line of sacred cornmeal, but their welcome was met with lance and sword and charging horses."

Although Morning Butterfly had heard this story innumerable times, Sun in the Sky's telling chilled her. Coronado couldn't have been Pahana because he and his followers had forced the Hopi to surrender to him. Despite that, the Bear Clan leader had taken Coronado's men to Oraibi and held out his hand, palm up in *nakwach*, the symbol of brotherhood, but the strangers hadn't understood.

At least those early Spaniards hadn't stayed long, leaving to search for gold.

It was different now.

"Morning Butterfly," Sun in the Sky said, distracting her, "I have thought on this for a long time and discussed it with elders of the other clans, and we have come to the same conclusion."

Dismissing the feeling that she didn't belong in this male place, she concentrated on the elder's every word.

"Captain Lopez and Fray Angelico do not speak the same words. Nor are their hearts the same."

"No, they are not," she agreed.

"The soldier is like Coronado, who attacked and murdered many Tiwa at Arenal, and like Captain Oñate, who did the same to the Keres at Acoma." His eyes narrowed. "Your father's uncle was one of those who felt his wrath."

Half sick, she nodded.

"But the men who dress in brown robes and call themselves padres do not kill or mutilate."

Not sure where this was going, she nevertheless nodded again.

"They speak of god—not the gods of the Hopi, but perhaps that does not matter."

Wishing he was talking to anyone except her and that the male members of the Bear Clan weren't all staring at her, she waited him out.

"The padre and soldier do not see with the same eye, do they?"

"No."

"Sometimes they argue."

"Yes."

"What do they disagree about?"

"I do not know everything, but the padre wants the soldiers to stay here with him while the captain speaks of going to the great canyon and trying to find the stones the Navajo called Cougar brought to them."

"What else?"

Shaking herself free of the memory of those moments when it felt as if she and Cougar were the only people in the world, she concentrated on giving the elder as complete an answer as possible.

"The padre wants to baptize all Hopi. To build his church at Oraibi."

Sun in the Sky's weathered features became even more ancient, and tears formed in his eyes. "I pray I will not live to see such a thing."

If you were Navajo, perhaps you would fight.

Other Bear Clan members muttered agreement with Sun in the Sky and several suggested they all put on their kachina costumes, which would help keep their thoughts pure and their hearts good.

"When soldiers have their way with our women, what does the padre say?" the old man asked her.

"He disapproves, but the captain does not listen to him."

"Hm. Prayer brings the Hopi peace. The padre speaks of peace, does he not?"

"He speaks of obedience to his god's law."

That confused Sun in the Sky, but after briefly muttering to himself, he continued. "This is my thought. My decision. The captain is like Coronado and Oñate, incapable of a good heart. I pray the padre is different. Morning Butterfly, I ask you to go to Fray Angelico and look into his heart."

"Me? But—"

Sun in the Sky rocked forward. "I do not want to put this to you, but if the Hopi are to walk in peace, we must know what is in the hearts of the newcomers."

"I know."

"You will do as I—as we ask? If you are afraid—"

"Not afraid, Sun in the Sky," she told him, although she was. "But before I do this thing, I ask for a prayer, to feel surrounded by kachinas and the love of my people."

In unison, the men assured her that they'd already decided on a closing prayer for the meeting, but as she joined the tight circle around the *sipapu,* she was filled not by thoughts of gentle kachinas, but of the other spirit people, the powerful and sometimes angry Siliomono.

10

"I have sinned, my father."

Pablo's confession came as no surprise to Angelico, but before he could encourage him to continue, his equally contrite companion spoke up.

"Weakness of the flesh overcame us, Padre," Madariaga said. "It has been so long since we have tasted human pleasures. The native women are so available, so uninhibited in exposing themselves. Only a saint could . . ."

Despite the somber occasion, Angelico could barely suppress a smile at Madariaga's embarrassment. "I am but a humble servant of God," he explained, "not a saint. And as a human, a man, I understand temptation."

"You have been tempted by the Hopi women?"

"No, not that. Your captain was mistaken earlier." *Lord, please forgive me for this lie. I simply wish to fulfill my role as confessor and advisor for these children.* "My chosen life has taken me beyond such earthly concerns, but I am not blind to what goes on around here. The natives have no shame or modesty. They will, once they have been brought into the fold, but until then—You have come seeking absolution?"

"Yes," the two said in unison, their heads bowed.

The devil's own sun beat down as Angelico and the two soldiers knelt before the wooden cross he'd brought from Santa Fe and had erected during his first full day here. The cross, higher than anything else around, anchored him and served as the setting for the sermons and sporadic baptisms he conducted when not on the mesa. In its shadow, he grounded himself in the belief that had always been the center of his life, felt the Gospel's truth flow through him, and submerged himself in the holy Scriptures. At those times he told himself that nothing had changed.

"My sons, the Lord forgives weaknesses of the flesh and understands temptation, but for you to receive salvation, you must fight the devil."

Pablo, apparently completely healed from his injuries, and Madariaga, handsome and strong beneath his unwashed garments, clasped their hands in prayer. They were both children and men, lambs to be led who, as soldiers, were part of the secular world—one not always in accordance with God's rule.

"Lord, look down upon these sinners and see that they are truly repentant. See also that temptation exists all around us and that we are in a heathen land, without the comfort and sanctuary of a church.

"By one man sin entered into the world, and by sin death, and so death passed upon all men. Behold thus the lamb of God. Behold him who taketh away the sins of the world. In those who are born again, there is nothing that God hates. There is no condemnation to those who are truly buried together with Christ, who are made innocent, immaculate, pure, harmless, and beloved of God. There is nothing whatever to retard their entrance into heaven."

Angelico opened his eyes, hoping to see the other soldiers coming to join them, but they were alone on the rock- and weed-strewn slope, alone except for the wind.

The wind that whispered of things he'd never heard before.

"We believe in one God, Father Almighty, maker of all things, both visible and invisible. And in one Lord, Jesus Christ, the Son of God, begotten—"

Something sang in the wind, the sound more essence than reality. Angelico shivered. Pablo shifted position as did Madariaga, who'd opened his eyes and was staring into the distance.

"Begotten from the Father, only-begotten, that is from the being of the Father, God from God, light from light."

Vibrations shimmered, unseen but felt, weighting down the air, adding to the heat, yet making Angelico shiver again.

"True God from True God, begotten not made, one in being with the Father, through—"

"Padre?"

"What?"

"Do you feel it?" Madariaga whispered.

"What you feel is the Lord's presence!" Angelico insisted.

Madariaga's lips tightened and his gaze turned inward. Angelico knew the soldier didn't believe him. He wasn't sure he did either.

After taking a deep but not calming breath, Morning Butterfly walked to the flap that served as the opening to Fray Angelico's dwelling place and called his name. She hoped he would order her to leave. Instead, she heard him shuffling about, and then he pulled back the flap and stuck out his head, looking first into her eyes, then behind her. The day was hot and nearly windless, making her wonder how he could stand to be inside such a close space. She'd worn a length of cotton tied at one shoulder and secured around her waist, leaving her arms and shoulders free; her dress ended modestly at her calves.

He now seemed fascinated by the way she presented herself, his gaze lingering on her arms before briefly touching her breasts. She knew to keep her distance from the soldiers, but to be looked at like this by the padre still confused her.

"Morning Butterfly. I am pleased to see you." He sounded unsure.

"You are?"

"Of course, my child, of course." His voice gained strength. "Pleased and yet surprised. I would ask you into my humble abode, but it would not be seemly. I am certain you understand."

She had no idea what he meant, but didn't say so as he stepped outside. "I must speak to you," she told him. "Of a thing that concerns all Hopi."

"The tribal leaders sent you?" He folded his arms across his narrow chest. "I will never understand you people, allowing women to conduct themselves with authority. Are you certain you have their permission?"

"I do not need anyone's permission—"

"Perhaps. Perhaps." For a moment, he looked as confused as she felt. Then his features brightened. "You are here to accept the Lord's words? That is why—my child, my child! I am delighted."

Unfolding his too-long arms, he reached to take her hand, and despite her determination not to show fear, she recoiled.

"What is it? Oh my child, you have no need to be afraid of me. A man of God is not like other men." His gaze again flicked over her breasts. "The devil has been testing me," he muttered. "Not in matters of faith, of course. My devotion to my Lord will never waver, has been my life so long that—" He glanced around.

"The devil seeks to distract me from my holy task by placing temptation in my path and weakening my resistance to that temptation."

"Fray Angelico," Morning Butterfly interrupted. "My people fear the soldiers' wrath and power. It is not the Hopi way to fight." *But maybe the Siliomono . . .* "We wish only peace, and yet—and yet things have happened which place that peace and our good hearts in jeopardy."

Although obviously disappointed that she hadn't come to

do what he called accepting the Lord's word, he nodded, and she took that to mean he wanted her to continue.

"You are part and yet not part of the soldiers," she said, Father Sun's heat on her back giving her courage. "You came with them, and yet you do not dress or act or speak as they do."

"No, I do not."

"It is our belief that your heart is different from theirs."

His features gentle, he indicated a nearby rock. She sat on it and waited as he selected another for himself, then he shifted position several times.

"Yes, my child," he said, "my heart is quite different from theirs because I am not conflicted by the opposing loyalties of Church and state; I suppose I should not be surprised that your people are aware of those differences. For one thing, I know that if one has given oneself to his Lord and master, then death is nothing to fear."

"The Spanish fear death?"

"Not death so much, but hell, certainly hell."

Hell was another of those words she could barely pronounce, let alone comprehend, but right now she was not interested in another long explanation of something that had nothing to do with her or her world. However, before she could think of a way to turn the conversation in another direction, he continued.

"Ah, Morning Butterfly." He sounded melancholy, yet determined. "I cannot yet expect you and your people to understand, but the time will come. I promise it will! It is not your cross to bear that you have no knowledge of the Christian God—Satan's hold on this land is that powerful—but the day will soon come when you no longer follow your heathen ways, when all of your people will commit themselves to walking on the righteous path that will assure you your place in heaven, not hell. If you do not take God into your life and heart and reject the beast, upon your death, your mortal soul will spend eternity burning in hell."

He tried to reach across the space separating them, but his arms weren't long enough. "You will understand. Once you have been baptized, the process of salvation will begin and you will turn your back on your heathen ways as you work for the glory of God and Spain. I promise you. I could have already baptized you as I did the Navajo and a fair number of your people, but it is my prayer that you, of all the Hopi, will seek salvation of your own free will."

Hopi ways weren't heathen—and why should they work for this god or for some place she'd never see and had no wish to? "This is not what I came to speak of today, but perhaps I must before we can talk of other things." She gathered her courage and began.

"For the Hopi, death is nothing to fear. When a heart ceases to beat, it means one cycle of life has ended and another is about to begin."

Fray Angelico clenched his jaw and his eyes narrowed.

"We leave one world and enter another; we embrace the journey. A man's body is wrapped in deerskin, a woman's in her marriage dress if she has one. A mask that symbolizes the rain cloud is placed over the face, and the body is arranged in a sitting position with the head bowed between the knees."

"No."

She ignored him. "Then the body is carried to where a grave has been dug. No one speaks as a bowl of food is placed on a nearby rock, and then everyone returns home, but for four days afterward, the women visit daily and place feathered prayer sticks and fresh food in the bowl. At the end of those four days, life goes back to what it was before the death and the soul of the one who no longer lives among us travels to the World Below to dwell among the kachinas." *And maybe the Siliomono.*

"This is what I want you to know," she finished. "That our ways are different from yours, different from the Navajo or other tribes, but right for the Hopi."

"No, no, no. Morning Butterfly, you are wrong!"

"Wrong? How?"

"The Scriptures leave no doubt that men such as myself must devote our lives to spreading the light."

"Why?"

"Because the Lord God so proclaimed. We are charged to go therefore and make disciples of all nations, baptizing them in the name of the Father and of the Son and of the Holy Spirit."

"The Hopi do not wish to become disciples."

He shook his head, spoke loudly and without looking at her. "It is written in Acts 8. Believe in the Lord Jesus, and you will be saved, you and your household!"

"There is no Lord Jesus in Hopi land."

"Silence! The Father Almighty, who made the heaven and the earth and the seas and all the things that are in them, is everywhere."

"Taiowa is the Creator. Taiowa—"

"You are a savage! A heathen! You cannot possibly understand the hold the devil has over you."

"Devil," like "hell," was another word she wanted to fling into the wind.

"I live the Hopi way. How can that be wrong?"

The padre's mouth opened and closed, opened and closed again. She had confounded him, that was clear. Maybe now—"Please, I do not wish to speak of these things. I came with a message."

Angelico collected himself, then asked, "Is this about the Navajo? You know who freed him?"

The sky had been an eye-pleasing blue this morning, but now it had taken on a hazy appearance. It might be a forerunner of rain, but there had been no Niman kachina ceremony yet to welcome the heaven's life-giving gift.

"It was I," she said.

"You? Why?"

"A Hopi does not willingly allow death to happen, not even to a Navajo."

"You feared the soldiers were going to kill him?"

"They were. We both know that."

Wincing, Fray Angelico repositioned his spare frame. "I still do not understand why that should concern you."

"Cougar did nothing wrong." *Except lie to the Spanish, but then so did I.* "Why should he die?"

"Cougar? That is his name?"

"Yes."

"How do you know? You've seen him before?"

"No, no."

"And yet you agreed to translate for him." The padre tipped his head to one side, his scrutiny so intense that she became even more uneasy. "He has a certain animal quality about him, a certain sensuality. Perhaps the two of you are lovers."

"He was a stranger."

"Maybe. Maybe not. I must never lose touch with the extent of Satan's influence here. So, Morning Butterfly, first you facilitated a conversation between the Navajo and the captain, then you freed him, and now you have come to me. What do *you*, if you are speaking of your own free will and not at Lucifer's command, want from me?"

What was he talking about, Lucifer's command? "I do not wish my people to be punished for my actions, but I do not dare take my plea to Captain Lopez."

He leaned forward, eyes narrowed. "So, you wish me to intercede on your behalf, do you? Ah." He pressed his hand against his forehead. "Tell me, do *you* want me to tell the captain about *your* personal involvement in his prisoner's escape?"

"I . . . no."

"Hm. No, I do not imagine you do. So, Morning Butterfly, *you* are confessing your sin to me, *correct?*"

"I . . . do not know."

"*You* do not know?"

"Was what I did something you consider a sin? I simply wished no blood to be shed. And today I came to you because I need to know whether my people will be made to suffer for my actions." Overwhelmed, she stared at the ground.

"Go on, my child," he whispered. "I do not want you, helpless child that you are, to ever fear me. Instead, I compel you to reach out for salvation."

His voice sounded so close. Looking up, she discovered that he'd risen to his feet and was standing over her, his outstretched and trembling fingers nearly touching her head. Men of God had been with the soldiers who'd all but destroyed Acoma and turned One Hand into a cripple. She cringed.

"I do not know what you will do with my words," she managed to say. "If you take them to the captain, maybe he will punish me. Still, that is better than having all my people punished."

The padre's hand descended, not on her head but her shoulder. She felt his fingers spasm.

"Yes," she whispered, tears in her eyes. "I confess my . . . sin."

"Child, child, praise be! Come into the fold and be saved. I will protect you and free you from the devil's clutches. I swear—"

Before she could ask him what he was talking about, he'd drawn her to her feet and wrapped his arms around her. He must be praying, but his words made no sense, prompting her to wonder if padres sometimes spoke to their god in another language. His arms felt like ropes, and she wished Cougar was here to free her.

"I will show you the path to walk, Morning Butterfly. Guide you out of hell's darkness and into the light of everlasting life. And when I am done—" his grip became even stronger, her breasts now flattened against his chest—"when I am done, you . . . you will be . . ."

Sobbing deep in his throat, he thrust his pelvis against her. She might be a virgin, but her people made no secret of what went on between a husband and wife, and she knew what he wanted, what her sister had been forced to endure. Still, if she repelled him, would her people pay the consequences?

"Fall on your knees with me, child! Together we will pray for protection and safekeeping, demand the devil cast himself out of you—out of me. Fall on your knees so your soul may receive salvation. Ask—ask for baptism and become a good Christian. If—if you do this thing, you will go to heaven—heaven. And—and . . . Eternal life of great bliss—in the presence of God."

Frightened by his tone, she struggled to free herself, but he continued to hold her with the kind of strength Cougar must have used to control the horses.

"If you do not become a Christian, you will be banished to hell where you will suffer . . . suffer cruel and everlasting torment."

"Padre, let me go!"

"I am your salvation, my child! Your salvation. I . . ."

He'd started to cry, his thinly muscled body shuddering as if in a storm-wind. His manhood, so hard that it made her think of a stick, ground into her belly.

"Kneel and kiss my hand. Render obedience. Render—obedience . . ."

He bent her back and off balance. She couldn't take her eyes off his blurry features. He reminded her of a stalking wolf. She wondered if he saw her as his prey.

But she wasn't a trapped and wounded deer, not with Siliomono at her side.

"No!" she screamed as she wrenched free. "No!"

Panting, his mind a dust storm of disjointed thoughts, Fray Angelico stared at his surroundings. Morning Butterfly was hurrying away from him, her thick hair no longer caught in coils on either side of her head but streaming out behind her.

His arms ached and his legs threatened to buckle; his manhood throbbed, but how could that be? He'd surrendered himself to the brotherhood and believed with all his heart and soul that he'd been chosen for life as a Franciscan monk. He was no longer a mortal man, was above such base desires and yet—

He'd wanted Morning Butterfly. Might have taken her if she hadn't yelled.

Mortification replaced confusion as he quickly remembered everything that had happened. His cheeks felt on fire, and he was drenched in a sweat that had only a little to do with the hot afternoon. It was incomprehensible that he'd lost control of himself and yet—

"Lord my God, please, please, I beg forgiveness. This country is indeed in the devil's clutches. What I experienced during my sermon at Oraibi was his doing, his attempts to turn me from You."

This was the first time he'd allowed his thoughts to return to that terrifying experience, but it was too soon. Later, when he felt stronger, he'd pray for understanding.

"And the people living here—the devil looks out through their eyes and has woven his evil way throughout their bodies, tempting . . ."

His throat was so dry that he was barely able to get the words out. Instead of forcing himself to say more, he took another, longer, look at his surroundings. To his everlasting relief, he saw no soldiers, and even the few Hopi he'd spotted in the distance appeared to be concentrating on their labors. But he could not assure himself that Morning Butterfly would keep what had transpired to herself.

"The creature you saw today was not me, Morning Butterfly. I was in Lucifer's clutches." He stumbled into his tent. There wasn't enough air inside, and he thought he might pass out. Bent over to avoid rubbing the top of his head on the low canvas roof, he reached for a long switch with a trembling hand. Then he stood in the center of the tent and closed his eyes and bowed his head.

"My Lord, I have brought shame upon both You and myself. My actions are reprehensible and if it pleases You to strike me dead, do so."

Barely able to breathe, he waited, but the thunder and lightning he half expected did not come.

"I will—I promise You, from this moment forth, I will walk the path You, in Your great wisdom, have set for me. I acknowledge the devil's temptation, fear it, understand that even the most innocent-appearing child . . ."

Was Morning Butterfly a child? Yes, she was a heathen, but a comely one nonetheless, ripe with untapped womanhood.

Groaning, he fell to his knees and gripped the switch so tightly that his knuckles turned white. "What have I done to deserve this torment? Please, Lord, what have I done?"

His plea echoed.

"I submit," he gasped. "And I seek atonement for my sins. Guidance and salvation."

Not sure where the strength came from, he nonetheless forced himself to stand. Then he pulled his robe over his head and stood naked in the dim light. Eyes clamped shut, he gripped the switch with both hands, lifted it over his head, and brought it down—hard—onto his back.

Pain flamed through him and forced out a cry, but he didn't stop. He lashed himself until blood ran down his back. At last, he collapsed onto the pitiful collection of leaves and rags that constituted his bed.

As darkness trapped him, he once again prayed for forgiveness and guidance, and to be free of Morning Butterfly's image.

It was still full light when Angelico regained the ability to think. The effort of sitting up caused him to gasp. Shaking, he reached for the faded leather satchel containing his worldly goods and drew out a pen and a precious piece of paper. After placing it on his Bible for stability, he began a letter to Governor Zotylo in Santa Fe.

"Much as I hoped to distance myself from civil matters, I find that is impossible, as I would be doing you a disservice if I did not apprise you of conditions here. Captain Lopez is an experienced military man, and I was initially much impressed with his leadership abilities, but I am deeply distressed by his disregard for the Church. He professes to be a servant of the Lord, but he is not. As a consequence, my holy task has become most difficult. Currently, Captain Lopez is little interested in anything except finding and punishing the nearby Navajo who have stolen a number of horses and ascertaining the existence of emeralds at or near the great canyon. Even more distressing is his and his men's treatment of the Hopi women, which is in direct opposition to the

Crown's orders. I have attempted to remind Lopez of his obligations to the Church and to me as the Lord's servant, but to no avail. Much as I hate writing these words, his morals and priorities are inexcusable. As a consequence, I must ask you to have him replaced with a man who fears the Lord and is faithful to the Crown."

Done, he carefully folded the letter and placed it inside a small deer-hide pouch. The next morning, as soon as early mass was over, he hurried—struggling to ignore his discomfort—to where the captain was instructing his men as to their duties for the day. Angelico presented him with the status reports he'd prepared—one for the missionary father Fray Bernardino de Luna, currently residing in Santa Fe, and an official one for Governor Zotylo. The private letter to the governor remained in his pocket.

"Captain," he said, "we are both eager, I'm sure, to let our superiors know of our accomplishments. My chronicles are now complete, as, I trust, are yours. My only concern is whether the documents will indeed reach the hands they are intended for."

"They will." Lopez's voice held only a touch of irritation. He nodded in the direction of the horse enclosure, indicating the two Indian servants who, although they'd been among the last to leave following the service, were already busy tending to his three personal animals.

"I chose those two with great care," he explained. "Not because they are blessed with any greater intellect than most of their kind—indeed, they do not appear capable of any independent thought and have learned only a few Spanish words. However, their families are working my father-in-law's land, and they are well aware that any disobedience on their parts will result in punishment to those they care about."

That announcement didn't surprise Angelico, who'd noticed that the two acted more like hostages than servants. Just the same, they faithfully attended all of his services and served as an example to the Hopi.

"Will you be sending both of them?" he asked.

"I considered it, since two would have a greater chance of reaching Santa Fe safely, but they are brothers. If one remains with me, the other no doubt knows his brother will suffer greatly should he not fulfill his mission.

"Yes, indeed. I see the wisdom of that. So, when will the journey begin?"

Lopez waved the two letters in the air. "You are eager for these to reach their destinations? I would think, given the little you have been able to accomplish toward establishing a church, that you would not have that much to report."

"Ah, but you are wrong—as I have no doubt you will realize when you read what I have written. You may see but small steps in my missionary work, but I have been laying vital groundwork, preparing the Hopi for acceptance of the true religion."

As he suspected, Lopez lifted his hand to stop him from continuing. Then he explained that he hadn't completed his own report but hoped to within the next day or two. As soon as that had been done, the messenger would be dispatched.

And when he was dispatched, Angelico thought, he would also be carrying the padre's personal letter to the governor.

11

From his perch on a rise a half day's walk from Oraibi, Cougar watched a number of Hopi men fan out over the land. They carried short, thick sticks that they used to turn over any large rocks they came across. Occasionally one or another would bend over, grab a wriggling snake, and shove it into a large deerskin pouch.

Cougar had never watched a Snake Ceremony but knew it was the most important of the Hopi traditions, part of Niman, which was essential if there was to be a bountiful crop. Until he'd spotted the men, he'd given little thought to the fact that their harvest season was approaching, but now he smiled, not because he concerned himself with whether the Hopi had abundant corn, but because the fact that they were preparing for the elaborate ceremony meant the Spanish hadn't changed them in this most fundamental of ways.

He was out today, not to spy on the Hopi but to learn how far a strong horse could travel. At the moment, his horse was eating on the far side of the rise, hobbled so it couldn't wander away. He'd chosen this particular one because it had the longest legs and didn't seem to have as many fears as some of its kin. If he was going to venture where soldiers might be, he must ride an animal who didn't easily panic and could be trusted, at least a little, not to betray its presence.

Walking back to the horse, Cougar allowed his thoughts to remain briefly with the Hopi—specifically Morning Butterfly who, he prayed daily, hadn't come to grief because of what she'd done for him.

His trip to Oraibi had accomplished nothing. The soldiers hadn't left for the great canyon after all, and he'd been left with the question of whether he'd been visited by a *chindi* and whether the *chindi* was Navajo or if the Spanish possessed such things.

The Snake ceremony had begun several days before Cougar spotted the Hopi men. The entire rite, designed to bring the rain that would insure a good harvest, lasted for nine days and was conducted by members of the Snake and Antelope religious societies. First, the societies' men had prepared themselves by praying, fashioning prayer sticks, and setting up altars inside their respective kivas. After that, every morning for four days, Snake and Antelope men would go in search of snakes. It didn't matter whether the reptiles were poisonous or not, just that a sufficient number were brought back.

On the eighth day, the marriage was held—not a marriage between two people who would spend their lives together, but one done in accordance with the Chu'tiva tiva ritual. As tradition dictated, it began before midnight when the Snake chief brought a virgin who'd been initiated into the Snake women's society inside the Antelope kiva. The upper half of her forehead, chin, and throat was painted with *tuma,* or white clay. The rest of her face had been painted black with *nananha* from a diseased ear of corn. She wore a woven black dress, a Snake dancer's kirtle, and a red-and-white cape. A small eagle-down feather had been tied to her loose hair, and a turquoise-and-shell necklace hung around her neck. She carried an earthen jar full of prayer sticks, corn, squash, melon, and bean vines.

She and the Snake chief were met by the Antelope chief

and a young man known as the Antelope Youth. His hair, too, was loose, with another feather tied in front. The youth carried a snake and also wore a ceremonial kirtle. In contrast to his "bride," his face was painted ash-gray except for his white chin. His body, arms, and legs had white zigzag lines on them.

The wedding ceremony consisted of a ceremonial washing of their hair in soapy water made from yucca roots, following which the girl was seated on a plaque of seeds brought in by the Antelope chief. The seeds symbolized food for birds, animals, and man. Once the boy and girl completed their part of the ceremony, the *pavasio* began, the singing of songs lasting until dawn.

Although Morning Butterfly was tired from last night's activities, which had brought together the Snake and Antelope societies, she eagerly awaited the dancers' arrival. Sitting in front of her family's pueblo, she divided her attention among the knot of soldiers standing to one side of the village plaza, her companions, including her silent sister, and the *kisi* where the washed and sand dried snakes had been placed.

She spotted Fray Angelico with the soldiers but did not acknowledge him. In truth, she reverently wished the Snake men hadn't allowed the outsiders to watch. There might be less conflict this way, and in the wake of no less than ten "baptisms" in the past two days, the padre needed to understand that his actions had had no impact on tradition; that Niman was for the Hopi.

"They come," her father whispered as the sun set.

"I pray the ceremony will strengthen you," she told him. "That you will become young again."

"Youth is a visitor, not something we can hold onto." His voice, although sober, wasn't filled with sorrow as it sometimes was when he contemplated his physical condition. "Perhaps youth can only touch so many people at once. If that is so, it is your turn, yours and Singer Of Songs. I gladly give you the gift."

She and Deer Ears seldom spoke of such intimate matters, in part because his responsibilities lay with his mother's clan, and now she cherished his every word.

"I accept the gift," she told him. "Still, I wish you could keep some of it for yourself so your legs could be strong and sure."

"Do not speak of that today, Morning Butterfly. Today we ask that our land be blessed with water."

Surrendering herself to the ceremony, she watched the Snake men dance into view, each with a snake in his mouth. Snakes were wise and sacred creatures capable of looking deep into a man and knowing whether he had a pure and fearless heart; no member of the Snake Clan who'd walked the way of his people all his life feared being bitten by one of the creatures, and all considered them their brothers.

Each Snake dancer was accompanied by a hugger who carried a whip which he occasionally used to keep the snake from biting. Once a dancer had made a circuit around the plaza, he removed the snake from his mouth and placed it on the ground, which was the signal for a third man, a gatherer, to pick up the snake and either drape it over his arm or hand it to one of the chanting Antelope men.

Although the ceremony was a lengthy one, Morning Butterfly was in no hurry for it to end. She still resented the newcomers' presence, but had been lulled by the deep chants meant to duplicate the sound of thunder, and focused on the *tipkayavi* or womb and the plaza in front of the Snake kiva with its sacred *sipapu*.

This was her motherland, the core of everything she was and would ever be. She would become whole with her people tonight. She glanced at the padre who stared open-mouthed at the *suta, yalaha,* and *tuma* painted dancers, each wearing a reddish-brown kirtle.

How strange this must be to him, how incomprehensible—just as the things he did during mass confused her. Maybe that explained the fear she saw in his eyes, his nervous, incessant movements. If she'd cared, she could have pointed out the dancers' dignity and explained that as each Snake dancer passed the snake-filled *kisi*, he stomped his foot against the *pochta*, or sounding board, so he could be heard by those living both below and above the ground.

Once again, she dismissed the man of God so she could give herself fully to what made her Hopi. Clouds had been building for several days and now hung low and heavy over Hopi land, but like the others, she was careful not to stare at them because one does not court the gifts of Taiowa the Creator, one simply accepts that if rituals and ceremonies are conducted with a pure heart, reward will follow.

Now, surrounded by her family, she pulled in the precious scent of water-laden air. The wind had picked up and was filled with an energy that came at her from everywhere. Her face uplifted and eyes closed, she began rocking to and fro in time with the chanting.

Tears of thanksgiving and acceptance filmed her eyes, but she didn't try to blink them away. One, two, and then more raindrops landed on her cheeks and forehead, and she drew in a shaky breath.

"Taiowa has heard us," One Hand whispered. Despite his hatred of the Spanish, he hadn't remained in hiding during Niman. "The Creator looks down on the People and knows our hearts are pure."

"Yes," Deer Ears answered while Morning Butterfly gave thanks, not just for the rain, but because Taiowa had seen fit to bless the Hopi even with strangers in their midst.

As the downpour began, she wondered if Cougar might be nearby and whether he understood what the padre never would. As for why those things mattered to her . . .

"This is appalling! Unacceptable! The heathens—how dare they defy me!"

"Are you saying they made it rain to spite you?"

Barely able to contain himself, Angelico waited for Captain Lopez to sit on the rock that would have to serve as a guest chair until he'd taught the savages how to fashion something decent.

The captain had finally dispatched one of the Mexican Indians to Santa Fe with the overdue military report, but the servant had days of travel ahead of him—if he could be trusted not to run away and hide among what remained of his tribe—and there was no knowing when the governor might read and respond to the letter Angelico had ordered the miserable creature to personally and privately deliver. In the meantime, he had no choice but to try to make the captain understand that the heathen ceremony they'd witnessed yesterday—had it been that long ago?—was the devil's work.

"I do not care about the rain," he said, although he couldn't help but question how a pagan ceremony could have been timed to culminate in a precious storm unless it was more of Satan's work. "I warn you, Captain. Do not mock me."

Captain Lopez, who, Angelico suspected, had once again spent the night with the female he'd taken a fancy to, shrugged but said nothing.

"I baptize the savages, but the moment I am done with them, they revert to their godless ways. I am at my wit's end trying to reach them."

"You are giving up?"

"Never! But I will need more of your help." Angelico made the admission very reluctantly. He did not miss the meaning in Lopez's sigh and the narrowing of the captain's eyes. When Lopez spoke, his voice was cold.

"I am aware of my responsibilities to you, Padre, rest assured. If I were not, I would be elsewhere."

"Elsewhere?"

"Searching for the emeralds." Leaning forward, he glared at Angelico. "However, if I made that my priority right now, you would waste no time informing the Crown of what you would surely call my desertion, would you?"

Did he know about the letter? Before Angelico could speak, Lopez continued.

"Tell me, why are we here?"

"Here" was in the valley, some distance from Oraibi. It might have made more of an impact if he'd insisted on meeting with Lopez on the mesa itself, but yesterday's ceremony had left him all too aware of the devil's grip on that accursed place.

"What was your reaction to what we witnessed last night?" Angelico asked.

"Reaction?" Lopez frowned and looked uneasy. "That was the most barbaric display I've ever had the misfortune of witnessing."

"You did not know the Hopi conducted such a ceremony?"

"How could I? My predecessors have hardly been thorough in detailing what to expect. Padre, I am in no mood to discuss this. If you wanted my men and me to put an end to it, you should have made your intentions clear then, not now."

True. However, he'd been rendered all but speechless by what he'd witnessed, the emotions and sensations he'd been forced to battle. "What I want is assurance we will never be subject to something like that again."

"And how do you propose to accomplish that?"

"Not me. You."

"Me?" Captain Lopez scoffed. "You are the one charged with their souls."

"I saw no souls last night," he countered. Then, determined not to give Lopez the opportunity to make fun of him, he hurried on. "I have spent hours praying on this. Unlike you, I did not—did not lose myself in matters of the flesh."

That earned him a glare. "A pity," Lopez said, "since all men, even you, would benefit from a release of tension. My men may come to you for forgiveness when they fornicate, but it will happen again—I dare say it already has, since they are only human, as are you."

How had the conversation taken this turn? "I prayed for guidance and it was given. God came to me in a dream which left no doubt of what must be done."

Captain Lopez started to get to his feet, then apparently thought better of it. "What must be done?"

"Captain, the military has been charged with facilitating Church representatives in their attempt to secure the colonies, so the various native populations can be put to service filling the Crown's larders, correct? That is why we brought so many horses with us, so they can take the goods back to New Spain, correct?"

"Correct."

"And our success in that regard has not been, shall we say, great, has it?"

"Go on."

"We both know that is because the devil is strong here. However, I know how to weaken his grip."

The padre was a fool, Lopez thought a few minutes later. It would take more than what Angelico suggested to break the heathens' resistance and bring them willingly into the Church's fold. Only might could accomplish that.

However, the Church and Crown in many respects were one and the same, and he'd spent years walking a line that accommodated both. Besides, although he had no intention of telling Fray Angelico so, the priest's plan was brilliant.

Lopez quickly gathered his men. Studying them, he was again struck by their youth and lack of preparation for venturing into hostile land. If only he'd been given seasoned troops . . . but there was a dearth of them in New Spain, and so he was forced to take these simple creatures. If not for the army, most of them would have been reduced to begging in order to stay alive. No matter. He would teach them how to be soldiers.

As concisely as possible, since he'd long held to the theory that underlings need only to obey—not fully comprehend and certainly not question—he outlined what was required of them. To a man, their reaction was disbelief, horror even, but, as he expected, most said nothing. Only Madariaga, who had yet to learn his place but would if it was the last thing Lopez did, had the audacity to ask why.

"So the heathens will have no doubt that the Crown and Church will not tolerate their barbaric ceremonies. Is that not clear? They are children, little more than animals in their ability to comprehend the world beyond this miserable land. The padre and I contemplated a less violent response, but my grandfather, Captain General Oñate—"

He leveled his gaze on Madariaga until the so-called soldier glanced away. "*My* grandfather succeeded in taming the

Keres because he taught them that resistance was intolerable."

"What resistance?" Madariaga ventured, still not looking at him. "The Hopi have responded to our requests for food and clothing by—"

"I am not talking about what we need to fill our bellies! The so-called ceremony we witnessed strikes at the very heart of our faith! Fray Angelico risked life and limb by coming here. So did all of us, but do the heathens comprehend that? Do they turn their backs on their godless ways and beg for forgiveness and redemption? No! There will be no more resistance, no more hesitancy on our part."

Making no attempt to temper his anger, Lopez stalked forward and shoved his nose in Madariaga's face. "If you do not understand that most basic of concepts, turn in your weapons and return to New Spain, now."

As he expected, Madariaga blanched.

"God will reward you for what we do today," Lopez exclaimed, although in truth he had limited interest in God's impact. "You men are the vanguard in taming this land and claiming it for the Crown, making it profitable. Your successes will be spoken of for generations to come. Do not ever lose sight of that."

The sun attacked with a furnace's strength as seven soldiers and their leader made the laborious climb up the ancient ladder. Yesterday's rain had made it necessary for the Hopi men to spend the day tending to their crops, with the result that only women, children, and a few elderly men were at Oraibi when the newcomers arrived.

One Hand, who'd wanted to go down to the farms to see how much the rain had benefitted the plants, had remained at home because he feared encountering a soldier; he was the first to spot them. Heart hammering, he ducked inside the safety of his pueblo, but a moment later, concern and curiosity prompted him to slip outside again and follow at what he hoped was a safe distance.

The newcomers walked slowly but unerringly toward the Snake kachina, their paces measured and, it seemed to him, reluctant.

"They do not belong there," Deer Ears whispered as he joined One Hand in the shadows. "Do they not understand?"

One Hand didn't waste time speculating, but set off at a run toward the opposite side of the village where Morning Butterfly had gone to visit. He spotted her outside a pueblo with Pumpkin Seed, whose youngest daughter had just given birth for the first time. Ignoring the talkative Pumpkin Seed, he grabbed Morning Butterfly's arm.

"The soldiers' faces are grim," he explained. "They speak only occasionally and look often at their leader. I am afraid to get close enough to make sense of their words, but you . . . they will not harm you. Please come."

Morning Butterfly stared at her trapped arm and struggled to gather her thoughts. It seemed as if her heart had forgotten how to beat in peace ever since the newcomers arrived; today was no different.

"Our men . . ." she began, stalling, "what do they—"

"They are not here. Surely you know that."

She did, unfortunately. "The soldiers have not tried to explain why they are here?"

"They ignore us. Perhaps—perhaps they only want to assure themselves that Niman is over."

After a glance at Pumpkin Seed, who obviously wanted to stay where she was, Morning Butterfly set off. One Hand hurried after her, his wheezing breath both adding to her concern and reinforcing her belief that she had no choice but to do this.

A growing number of women and children were climbing onto the roofs so they could watch the soldiers; the scene reminding her of how her people had gathered yesterday in celebration and ritual. She'd been certain the newcomers wouldn't approve of the Snake ceremony and Niman, but its time had come, and not holding Niman had been incomprehensible. If only she could make the newcomers understand—

"There you are! Come here, now!"

Fighting the pounding in her brain, she forced herself to face Captain Lopez, who stood a few feet from the Snake kiva with his men gathered around him. He hadn't spoken her name, and yet she knew he was talking to her. She glanced at One Hand for reassurance but saw only fear in his too-large eyes. Despite herself, her attention was drawn to the old man's scarred wrist.

"Morning Butterfly, forgive me," One Hand whispered. "I should not have asked you—"

"I do this because I am Hopi," she whispered, then stepped away from him, toward the Spanish.

Captain Lopez smiled, but there was no warmth in the expression. "You should have never revealed your knowledge of Spanish," he told her once she'd come close enough that he no longer had to raise his voice. "However, since you have, I intend to put you to use. I do not have to tell the Hopi of my intentions, but I will anyway. After all, a lesson fully comprehended has the greatest impact."

"What lesson?" she managed.

"You people have been coddled too long. The padre, for reasons better understood by him than me, initially attempted methods other than force to persuade you to reject your heathen religion, but he has not succeeded. Now, he has turned to me."

"What lesson?" she asked again.

His second smile held no more warmth than the first. "Yesterday's display will not be repeated."

"What—what are you going to do?"

"I do not need to spell it out for you, Morning Butterfly, do I? Nonetheless, it pleases me to do so. This hole in the ground obviously has religious significance—*had* significance. My men and I will do what we must. And if any of your people attempt to stop us, they will suffer the consequences." He held up his sword so the sun glinted off it. "Do you understand?"

An unwanted image of One Hand's wrist filled her vision, adding to her disbelief but at the same time reinforcing her determination to do what she had to. "Yes."

"Good. Good indeed that at least you are capable of comprehending certain realities and are, I trust, capable of sharing them with the rest of your people."

The sword still uplifted, he looked in all directions, taking in the rooftop watchers as well as those peeking around the corners of the closest pueblos.

"It pleases me to have so many here to watch. It would have pleased me more to have more men in attendance, but if they do not tend their crops, there will not be enough contributions to God, will there?"

"Contributions?"

"Your rewards will come once you are in heaven. For now, your people will be put to use harvesting what the Church requires, what is its due."

Barely comprehending, she couldn't think of a thing to say.

"The devil's handiwork will be destroyed today," Captain Lopez announced.

Still disturbed in his soul, Angelico hadn't wanted to be in attendance, but he had no choice. He'd heard everything Captain Lopez and Morning Butterfly had said to each other, but although the captain spoke more about the farms' produce than the need for absolute victory over the devil, he hadn't interrupted.

Let the captain and his forces be seen as instruments of destruction; that was why they were here, after all. His task was to gather the flock around him and guide them into the light. The Crown destroyed. He built.

Yes indeed, he would build and, through the process, atone for weaknesses of the flesh and thus face his maker with a clear heart and soul. Glory would be his!

Morning Butterfly had retreated back to her people, and if the padre hadn't been aware of her every movement, he might have lost sight of her. At first he paid little attention to the elderly man she occasionally spoke to, but as he fought to clean his mind of her unwanted physical impact on him—did the devil himself live in her?—he noticed that the old Hopi was missing his right hand.

For a moment, he thought the man had been born with the

deformity, but even at this distance, he could see the network of scars. There were, of course, any number of ways someone might have suffered such an accident. However, the brave was old enough that—

"Padre," Captain Lopez boomed, distracting him. "Today's action will have a lasting impact. Certainly you want to be part of it. I defer to you. If you wish to be the first to enter, do so."

"That—that is not necessary."

"Come, come, Padre. The men await your leadership, they are already convinced of mine."

With a growing sense of dread, Angelico looked into each pair of dark Spanish eyes. He'd been both pleased and relieved to learn that Captain Lopez was the exception and the men under him were as devout as any he'd ministered to over the years, but that, he now acknowledged, exacted a certain toll on him.

"All right." His throat caught. "All right. Let the Lord's work be done."

His pitiful footwear made a faint slapping sound as he approached the site that had garnered so much attention yesterday. Despite his effort to give himself up to God, he couldn't shake the impact of the watching, wary Hopi, and although he knew they'd be horrified by what was about to happen, he concentrated on the positive results that today would bring. Once their useless idols were no more, the process of making them understand why it had to be done would begin, but first—

First the tearing down.

After what seemed a long time, he stood less than a foot from the rounded pile of rocks that made up the walls of the so-called shrine. In order to get inside the cavity, he would have to climb the rough, uneven walls to the roof. A ladder stuck out of a small hole on the roof, leading into the strange creation's bowels. Like everything else, the rocks had absorbed the day's heat, but that didn't stop him from shivering. Stalling, he looked around for Morning Butterfly.

"What is it called?" he asked, once he'd located her in the crowd and gestured for her to come closer.

"Kiva."

"*Ki-va.* Tell me about it."

She squared her shoulders, looking older and more authoritative than he remembered—defiant even. "It is a Hopi place. For worship and beliefs that go back to the beginning of time."

"No one is inside?"

Her arms hung at her sides, but she didn't appear cowed. Surely she knew what was about to take place and should be begging—

"Hear me, Padre," she said. Her voice echoed off the pueblo walls. "You may destroy a kiva, but you cannot destroy what lives in our hearts."

"Enough!" Captain Lopez shouted before Angelico could think what, if anything, he should say. "She is threatening you, Padre. You *cannot* allow that to happen."

No, he couldn't. His head roared and his stomach knotted, but he'd forced this moment, and with his Lord and master looking down, he would accomplish what he'd come here for—what his entire life had been about.

He had to climb leaning forward in order to keep his balance on the sloping rocks. He wasn't sure the roof would hold his weight, and the ladder looked on the brink of collapse. Morning Butterfly hadn't answered his question about whether anyone was inside.

His hands shook as he gripped the ladder, but he refused to look around to see if anyone noticed. Eyes half closed in what he hoped would be interpreted as a prayerful attitude, he began his descent.

Sunlight filtered down from the hole in the roof, but that was the only illumination, leaving too much of the surprisingly large interior in shadow. There was precious little fresh air, the smell of earth and stone making him feel as if he'd entered a cave. He nearly ordered the captain to compel the soldiers to immediately follow, but instead he allowed himself to be absorbed by the alien place, to hear its silence, to feel its age.

To accept that he wasn't alone.

12

Every aspect of a Hopi kiva had meaning. The four levels represented the four stages of man's creation, beginning with Tokpela, Endless Space; Tokpa, Dark Midnight; Kuskurza, where the first People multiplied and spread out; and finally Tuwaqachi, which was World Complete.

As befitted their importance within Hopi society, the members of the Snake Clan had filled their kiva with a large number of kachina dolls. The largest, at nine feet in height, was Sio Calako, which symbolized the friendly relationship between Hopi and Zuni. Tawa, representing the relationship with the sun, was festooned with eagle feathers. Natashka, which resembled a buffalo head with sharp teeth, helped discipline children, while Ahote, with its protruding eyes and large horns, was a singer of sacred songs. There were literally hundreds of Hopi kachina dolls, but perhaps the most revered was Angwusnasomtaqa, the Crow Mother, with its oversized ears and white-and-black cape. Many considered it the mother of all kachinas.

All were supernatural beings with the power to bestow

abundant harvest and prosperity to those who revered them. Without kachinas, there would be no rain, food, or good health, and in recognition of their impact, ceremonies were conducted to honor them. Kachina impersonators, masked ceremonial dancers, took great care to prepare themselves emotionally. Children grew up with wooden dolls made in the likeness of kachinas, not as playthings but as objects to be studied and treasured.

None of the newcomers, however, knew about the integral role kachinas played in Hopi society. Instead, Lopez and then his men saw only grotesquely decorated doll-like objects—pagan idols.

His eyes showing too much white, Angelico stretched his arms toward the heavens, nearly touching the low ceiling as he invoked a prayer in Latin. Then, holding his breath, he grabbed the nearest idol and hurled it against the stone wall; the sound of its breaking filled the air. Above and unseen, a Hopi woman screamed.

"I destroy you in the name of the Lord!" Angelico shouted as the figure's dislodged eyes and nose rolled around on the packed-earth floor. "In the name of God and the Crown!"

Another scream, this one familiar, caught Lopez's attention. Singer Of Songs!

Shaking at the impact of his concubine's voice, Captain Lopez set himself to work, swinging his sword at a white, hairless thing with huge, shining, dark eyes, and decapitating it. Shouts and cries filled the air, but he ignored the unseen savages. His grandfather had chopped limbs off savages. He could do no less!

Pointing first at his men and then the shelves the dolls rested on, he encouraged the soldiers to do as he and the trembling padre had done. To his consternation, they were slow to respond, gazing first at Angelico and then at Madariaga, the most vocal of the lot.

"What is it?" Lopez demanded.

"Father?" Madariaga slid close to the little, brown man. "You are certain—"

"The devil *must* be vanquished!" Spittle formed at the corners of Angelico's mouth "God's might—God will prevail!"

Apparently that was what Madariaga needed to hear, because before Lopez could remind him of his loyalties, the soldier seized a small figure, held it a moment, then dropped it and smashed it under his boot.

The destruction was ridiculously easy, proof that the savages were incapable of creating lasting workmanship. Lopez delighted in the sight of feathers littering the stone floor or fluttering about in the stale air, and in the sounds of cracking wood, high-pitched wails, sobs, even what he took to be curses. As long as the creatures remained where they were, they represented no threat.

And if his men went about their work with grim faces and occasionally paused to study their surroundings, if they muttered prayers and frequently crossed themselves, that wasn't his concern.

Intent on what he was doing and aware of the strange sensation that he was being watched—but not by anything human—he paid no attention to his footing until his right boot stepped into nothing. He might have fallen if he hadn't grabbed the padre for support.

Looking down, he saw what appeared to be a small square cut into the floor. He thought it might be a fire pit, except there was no sign that anything had been burned there. He started to crouch down for a better look, but as he did, the strangest sensation—like cold fingers marching across his spine, heart, and lungs—stopped him. Straightening, he gripped his sword so tightly he might have snapped the hilt.

"What is it, Captain?" Angelico asked above the muted chorus of Hopi voices. "Did you hurt yourself?"

"Of course not." Lopez's jaw threatened to lock, making speech impossible, and he no longer cared what anyone else said or did. A moment ago he'd dripped sweat, but now he felt frozen. Despite that, a plan—perhaps both desperate and irrational—took life inside him.

"Look." He indicated the depression that was barely wide enough to hold two boots. "What do you make of that?"

The padre started to lean over, then froze. Lopez could see that the other man's thin shoulders were now as taut as his own felt. The soldiers had stopped what they were doing and watched from a distance.

"I . . . I do not know." Angelico's voice sounded strained. "Surely it is of little consequence."

"Surely," Lopez echoed, although he didn't agree.

Angelico took a queer stutter-step which effectively, if not gracefully, took him some distance from the pit. "There is so much I do not know about these people's beliefs," he muttered. "Morning Butterfly—she would tell me."

"Perhaps. Perhaps not." Now that Angelico was no longer between Lopez and the hole, he had no doubt that the cold emanated from it, but how could that be? It wasn't deep enough to have captured any of the earth's chill. His men, he noticed, had fallen silent. So too had the Hopi above them.

"You err in not having her see you as her master," he continued. "Treating her as if anything she says or does is worthy of merit or concern—you must consider the consequences of such behavior. If I once showed weakness—"

"Do not tell me how to conduct myself, Captain." The padre kept staring at the hole, now rubbing his hands together as if trying to warm them. "There is a clear distinction between our responsibilities. I . . ."

Lopez became aware of a sound he'd never heard before, like faint breathing. Thinking it came from his men, he studied them. They'd drawn close to one another, their eyes darting here and there, mouths agape, several crossing themselves over and over again.

"What is this?" he demanded of them. "You are the Crown's soldiers. Surely you have not become cowards."

"It is not right in here," Madariaga replied. "This place—it does not feel like anything I have ever felt before."

"Have you so recently left your mother's breast that the world frightens you?" Lopez's voice banged against the thick walls, bounced back at him. "Perhaps you wish you had her skirts to hide behind?"

The soldier's cheeks flamed, but he was wise enough not

to protest—either that, or he was unable to take his mind off his surroundings. Lopez would have given a great deal to say with confidence that he was immune to the misgivings that had overtaken his men, but he'd long prided himself on not lying, at least to himself. More than half of the bizarrely painted dolls remained untouched. He was determined to see them all destroyed, and yet . . .

"There is limited impact in what we are doing down here," he announced, startled because above the sound of his voice, he could still hear the breathing. "The savages must see the results of our work."

"Indeed they must," Angelico agreed, his words running together. Stumbling a bit, he hurried over to the ladder, obviously intending to reach the surface as quickly as possible. "Soldiers, gather up the devil's handiwork and bring everything out with you."

Angelico would have to be reminded of who was in charge, but not now and not with the men listening. Leaving the padre to the task of finding his footing, Lopez directed his troops to gather up the dolls. To his consternation, they were slow to obey, obviously hesitant to touch the crude objects they'd been so quick to destroy a few minutes ago; but they knew enough not to test his patience. Of course, it helped that he settled the largest figure on his own shoulder. The grotesque thing was every bit as heavy as he'd expected and then some, but he lost no time in climbing out of the kiva.

The moment he reached the surface, the day's heat attacked with such strength that surely he'd been mistaken about his earlier chill. Still, he saw no reason to look back into that gloomy place. Instead, he concentrated on his surroundings and was both surprised and discomfited to see that the number of Hopi had nearly doubled, some standing only a few feet away but most gazing down from the nearby rooftops. Disbelief and hatred had transformed their usually placid features.

"Morning Butterfly!" he yelled, looking around for her.

"I am here, Captain," she said from behind him.

"So you are," he retorted. "I trust I do not have to explain what I am up to, do I?"

Her gaze slid from his face to his burden; her flesh had been bleached of all color. "No. You do not."

"And you will make them understand?" He indicated the still tightly bunched, still silent Hopi. There, flanked by an older couple, the man looking on the verge of collapse, stood Singer Of Songs. She had hold of their hands; the love that existed among them struck Lopez like a blow. Had he ever touched his parents like that? Felt their love?

"Make them understand!" he demanded of Morning Butterfly.

Chest rising and falling, eyes heavy with hatred, she glared at him. "They already do," she said.

"Let me be the judge of that," he retorted, once again a soldier. "I could have set fire to that place the way my grandfather set fire to the Keres pueblo, but I am a benevolent man. Make them understand that."

She covered her throat with her hand, pressed hard enough to turn the flesh under her fingers white. "Your—your grandfather was the man called Oñate?"

He answered her question with no more than a brief nod. Then, taking advantage of her agitation, he described what had taken place in the kiva—not that the sounds could have left any doubt. Her features hardened, as did, he noted out of the corner of his eye, Singer Of Songs'.

I did what I had to, he silently told Singer Of Songs. Then, with an effort, he dismissed her.

"The death of the old comes before birth of the new," he said, pleased with his phraseology. "I do what I do today, not because I am a cruel man, but because your people *must* be brought into the light. Their salvation is assured once they have rejected their barbaric ways and embraced the Christian God. Only then."

For the second time, he hoisted the wooden statue to his shoulder, and if there was a moment, a second, when it felt like something alive, that was his secret.

Then, eager to have the task over with, he carried the

statue to the edge of the mesa and, screaming with the effort, heaved it into space. It tumbled down, hitting the mesa wall over and over again. Chunk after chunk broke off, the smaller pieces flying off in all directions, some of the larger ones finding perches. The hollow thud of shattering wood would stay with him for a long time.

Clouds—certainly left over from yesterday's storm—darkened and sagged toward him, weighed him down, threatened to surround him.

"Destroy everything!" he ordered his men.

He'd barely finished speaking when they hurried to obey, each holding their burdens as far from themselves as possible. Like him, they stopped so close to the edge that they were in danger of falling and, as one, threw.

Behind him, the Hopi began to wail.

Twisted together with the sobs and screams was another sound. Hollow. Deep. Dark. Not a cry of fear but a rage-filled bellow. There was nothing human about it. Rather, it seemed part of the earth itself.

Angelico had slept on the ground most of his adult life and had all but forgotten that his body had once known a less punishing rest. He'd spent so much time out of doors that he should have no qualms about falling asleep with the silent and uncaring stars looking down on him. Just the same, tonight he was acutely aware of his surroundings. In fact, he'd chosen to sleep out here because his tent's interior reminded him too much of the kiva. It wasn't that he wished the soldiers were closer, since he gained no sense of companionship from their presence and yet . . .

Fingering the cross around his neck, he began praying to give his mind something to focus on, but his concentration wasn't what it should be. Destroying the devil's handiwork should have brought him pleasure, and when he set about writing down his observations, he'd project confidence and thankfulness, but in the darkness, he had to be honest.

Certainly there'd been nothing sacred or holy about what the soldiers had destroyed. The kachinas—that's what Morning

Butterfly had called them, wasn't it?—were pagan idols and an abomination in the Lord's eyes. Why then was he haunted by the feeling, the conviction, that he'd done something wrong?

It was the setting. The tomb-like excavation he'd climbed into. The way the women, children, and old men had stared at him and the soldiers. The somber demeanor of the able-bodied Hopi men when they realized what was happening. Even the unseen wolves who'd set to howling at the end of the day were responsible for the way he felt.

All those things but most of all . . .

No.

His thoughts had skittered away from what had no explanation, but, despite his efforts, returned to it when he heard approaching footsteps. Startled, he sat up, then relaxed when light from a burning branch illuminated Madariaga's features.

"Come here, my son, come here," Angelico said in greeting.

"I am not disturbing—"

"No, never. You have been sent to look after my welfare?"

Madariaga shook his head. "I have not spoken to the captain, nor him to me. Given the mood he is in tonight, I have no wish to."

"Perhaps, if he has a woman with him, his mood will improve."

If Madariaga was surprised by Angelico's understanding of men's needs, he gave no indication.

"I—" Madariaga started. "I—today has unsettled me. I know that what we did was right and we were following God's dictates and yet . . ."

"Go on."

Grunting, Madariaga knelt. "Father, I believe in the Lord God. My faith is complete and if it had been possible, I would have embraced a religious life such as you have. If I had had any other option, I would not have become a soldier, but . . ."

"I understand. A man does what he must in order to feed himself."

"Yes, he does. When I heard that a mission was to be built in Hopi land and Christianity brought to the savages, I saw that as a sign that I could both fulfill my duties as a soldier and bring God to the godless."

"Have you told Captain Lopez that?"

"The captain has little use for me. I—in an effort to disguise the truth of my parentage, my . . . illegitimacy . . . I presented myself as someone other than who I am. Unfortunately, I made the mistake of choosing the name that belonged to his grandfather."

"This is a confession?" Angelico asked around a yawn.

"Not now, no." Madariaga sounded distracted. "I simply—Father, today tested my faith. I come to you asking for help in strengthening it. Some of the things that happened— what is God's explanation?"

Angelico didn't have an answer.

Captain Lopez had stuffed himself with mutton and drank more wine than usual. Following that, he'd sent his remaining servant for Singer Of Songs, and when she arrived, he'd buried himself in her. The last time he'd made use of her, he'd tried to teach her a few Spanish words. Tonight, however, he wanted only release—and to feel a woman's warm body against him. She'd remained with him until he fell asleep and then had crawled away, leaving him alone.

The dream was upon him before he'd a chance to ready himself. He saw the great, dark cape first, spreading over him like a massive rain cloud, but there was no welcome wetness in its depths, only cold.

Then the sound—like the distant screams of dying souls—began. Shuddering, he tried to recoil, no longer a seasoned soldier but a frightened child. Unmindful of what anyone might think, he struck out, his own scream much higher but no less sharp or penetrating than that which stalked him.

He was vaguely aware of trying to slither away, but even if he'd been capable of movement, he couldn't have escaped because the dying souls were everywhere.

Only, were they dying and defeated? Ruined enemies of the Crown, of his?

No, honesty said.

No, this was anger and warning.

Morning Butterfly had known she wouldn't be able to sleep. Praying, she'd waited for Singer Of Songs to come home. Even then, she'd remained awake, curled on her side, until she heard her sister's breathing lengthen out and finally, thankfully, become peaceful.

She was pleased her sister could rest and prayed she wouldn't be stalked by the nightmares that had begun after the first time Captain Lopez took her, but although she'd vowed always to be there for Singer Of Songs just as she had been for One Hand over the years, she needed activity.

After slipping out of bed, she went outside, hoping to find a measure of peace in the village's familiar shapes and shadows, but the mesa was too small to contain her tonight. Despite the soldiers below, Morning Butterfly climbed down to the desert floor, guided by memory and starlight. Although she felt capable of killing one of the Spanish after what they'd done, she had no intention of getting close enough to test her self-control.

Instead, drawn by forces she didn't understand or fight, she walked. The land's familiar sway helped calm her, and at length she was able to block out the horrible memories of destruction and focus on what else had happened while what was sacred to the Snake Clan was being turned into nothing.

Taiowa, Sotuknang, Kokyangwuti, and Paoqanghoya had cried along with the Hopi.

"Thank you, Taiowa," she said aloud in case the Creator couldn't hear around His grief unless she spoke. "Thank you for being there when we needed you. You and the others who were already here when the Hopi began. We sing the Song of Creation because it tells us of Taiowa's plans for life and makes us whole. Today we felt ourselves shattering and being torn apart, but the newcomers will not destroy us. Will not! As long as the earth remains, so will the Hopi. That cannot be taken from us."

Her prayer strengthened her, and when a distant wolf called, she nodded. The moon was newborn these nights, but from the beginning of time it had been growing strong and then fading before growing again, and she knew to be patient. If only she understood the ways of the newcomers as well as she did her people's past . . .

"Taiowa, I come to you tonight with my heart filled with questions. I do not want it that way. I want to bathe myself in the tears you shed today and let you carry my pain, my people's pain, but I do not know how. I need—please—I ask you to show my feet the way to walk."

She set off in the direction of the rising sun.

According to the ancient stories, the first Hopi migrated over the land while waiting for signs that they'd reached the place where they should settle. The Butterfly Clan wound up at Awatovi on Antelope Mesa, and although she'd never been there, she sometimes thought of the place that sheltered those who carried her name. The Bear Clan had been the first to settle at Oraibi, but they had only been there a short time when members of the Badger Clan asked to join them. To demonstrate the clan's worthiness, the Badger chief first moved to Third Mesa at Cha'aktuikaa, where they planted two fast-growing spruce trees, male and female.

"These two spruce trees are proof of our power and the gift we will make if you admit us to Oraibi," the Badger Clan had told the Bear Clan chief. "They are a sign that all the high places around the village will be covered with spruce trees whose power you may use in your ceremonies."

However, the Bear Clan chief had continued to refuse to allow the Badger Clan to join them, and the two spruce trees had died. Since then, the Hopi had to go all the way to Kisiwu for spruce for their ceremonies, and the Badger Clan settled at Tuwanasavi, the Center of the Universe, near Oraibi.

Tonight, Morning Butterfly wondered if her legs might take her to Tuwanasavi. If they would, perhaps there she'd find the sense of peace and acceptance she needed.

Perhaps.

"Taiowa, the Hopi have not strayed from the path taught us from the beginning. Our leaders are proud to lift their right hands as proof that they are responsible and religiously carry out their ceremonies to insure bountiful moisture. The Snake ceremony followed the path it always has. Everything about Niman was done as it should be; we did nothing wrong."

Shocked by the desperation in her voice, she again tried to settle her thoughts, but turmoil continued to hold her in its grip.

"Was it a sin that we allowed the Spanish to be there? Are we being punished? Is that why the kachinas were destroyed?

"What would you have us do different? Refuse to allow outsiders into Oraibi? But they have weapons and we do not. If we had opposed them as the Navajo do, they would have killed us."

She'd said too much. Spent, she leaned forward and rested her hands on her knees, sucking in as much of the night air as her lungs could hold. Fresh oxygen helped revive her and she felt less like crying than she had a moment ago. Still—

She wasn't alone.

A butterfly could fly, but she didn't have her namesake's wings. If she was being stalked by a restless or angry kachina or Siliomono, how could she possibly escape? Besides, if Siliomono wanted her, she should accept her fate, not fight. Still, she wasn't ready to die.

Maybe not Siliomono, the spirit people. Maybe a soldier.

That possibility turned her fingers into involuntary fists, and she berated herself for not having brought along a knife.

"Who is it?" she demanded. Her question swirled around her, then faded off into nothing. She swallowed and tried again. "Show yourself."

."Morning Butterfly, do not be afraid."

For one, maybe two heartbeats, all she knew was that the shadowy figure to her left spoke the language of her people and yet his command of it wasn't total. Then:

"Cougar?"

"Yes. I am sorry, I did not mean to frighten you."

As she waited for him to come close enough for the stars to expose his features, it seemed as if the night itself had both softened and become sharper. She wished she'd never spoken to Cougar, knew nothing of his existence, and yet she felt more alive in his presence. She told herself it was because she'd come to envy the Navajos' warlike ways and freedom, their courage in opposing the newcomers, and yet it was more than that.

"How long have you been here?" she asked.

"I saw you come down from Oraibi."

"It is not safe for you to be so close."

"I am careful."

No matter how cautious he might be, he couldn't be sure it would be enough. The thought of seeing him become the soldiers' captive again made her shiver.

"A Navajo brave is so full of himself that he has no fear?" she asked. "That is not a wise thing."

"Wisdom, and courage, are different now that the strangers are among us."

"Yes," she agreed. Her body felt different, warm and aware, almost as if it had been touched by lightning. Was Cougar responsible? "They are different. Are you the only Navajo here? Perhaps you and others are planning to attack the soldiers?"

"To do so would give me great pleasure, but no, we are not that foolish."

His voice had been touched with sorrow, not as deep as what she'd experienced while the Snake Clan kachinas were being destroyed, but impossible to ignore just the same. "Then why—"

"I wanted to see you."

If he touched her, she might shatter. Beyond caring

whether he sensed her emotional state, she took a couple of backward steps. It helped to have more distance between them, and yet his impact remained.

"Why?"

"To find out if you had been punished because you freed me."

"A Navajo cares what happens to a Hopi? The Navajo have never wanted anything from a Hopi except what they can steal."

"I cannot say you are wrong in that," he said after a short silence. "It has always been the way of the Navajo to take what they need."

"I know! I know."

He'd been standing with his arms at his side, perhaps to let her know he wished her no harm, but now he folded them over his chest, the gesture making him larger, maybe dangerous.

"The old ways are no more," he said, his voice filled with regret. "You are all right? They did not punish you?"

"The captain did not know I was responsible for your escape."

"Surely he suspected—"

"I am a Hopi woman, sister of the woman he has taken to his bed." She shuddered at the image of what Singer Of Songs was forced to endure. "A man who satisfies himself with a virgin who offers no resistance, a young woman who keeps her tears to herself—perhaps that man believes her sister is no different. A small mouse."

"Perhaps." He drew out the word. "And perhaps the padre protects you."

"That too," she agreed, surprised by his insight. When she laughed, the sound was without warmth. "I am valuable to the newcomers because through me they can make themselves understood."

He nodded, then turned as if to walk off into the night. She shocked herself by reaching out for him, though there was no contact. She snatched back her hand.

"I am glad," he said with his back to her. "My heart is no longer as heavy."

"The fate of a Hopi brings sorrow to a Navajo?"

"Yes." He whirled on her. "Is that so hard for you to understand?"

She didn't know anything tonight, certainly not why her heartbeat had become irregular simply because she was with a Navajo. "Maybe—maybe we should not speak of this. I—I accept your concern."

"Good."

She couldn't be sure, but it seemed as if he was studying her intently, taking in her hair, face, arms, body, legs.

"You do not carry a weapon, not even a knife?" he asked.

"No. I—"

"I know! You are Hopi and that is not the Hopi way!"

"Why do you care?"

"I do not know!" he retorted. "Perhaps I fear the Hopi will allow themselves to be taken down the way a newborn deer is overtaken by a wolf."

"All a wolf wants from a deer is what it needs to fill its belly. The Spanish have much more use for us."

"And the Hopi will stand there and allow the Spanish to rape them, take their food and belongings. I do not understand this, Morning Butterfly. I never will."

"Why do you try?"

"Tell me something," he said, sounding not angry any more but weary. "When the padre says the Hopi are wrong to believe the way they always have and orders them to walk the way he dictates, will you be like deer in this too? Will you expose your throats and hearts and allow them to be ripped out?"

"Stop it!" Her fingers became fists. "This is not your concern!"

"Yes, it is."

"Why?"

For a long time he said nothing, only stared up at the sky. "My people believe the First World was an island and the first beings not human beings as we are now but insects. If I was to say such a thing to the padre, would he accept my words?"

"I am sure he would not."

"How do you know? Because you have tried to tell him of Hopi beliefs and he has called them false?"

"No." Talking to Cougar both exhausted her and made her feel more alive than she ever had. "I would not waste my breath telling him something I know he would call a lie."

"But what the Hopi believe is their truth just as what the Navajo believe is their truth."

Some of her people called the Navajo savages, but Cougar was a wise man. "Yes," she agreed.

"And yet the newcomers cannot accept that there are ways other than theirs."

"No. They cannot."

"Since the first Navajo came to Hopi land, both our people acknowledged that we have different beliefs. We do not try to change each other, do not laugh at different beliefs. Why cannot the newcomers do the same?"

He sounded desperate, angry, his emotions all but tearing her apart. Unable to stop herself, she took his hand and covered it with both of hers.

"I have had the same thoughts," she admitted. "That—that is why I am out here tonight, because of what happened to our kachinas, to the Snake Clan kiva."

"Tell me."

She did, but not before dropping to her knees and closing her eyes. He sat nearby, breathing softly.

"Did they know what they were doing?" he finally asked.

"The padre said the Snake ceremony and Niman were the work of the devil and must not happen again." The words tasted bitter on her tongue.

"Will the Hopi conduct Niman again? Will men fill their hearts with pure thoughts so they do not have to fear poisonous snakes and will this please the spirits so the precious rains will come?"

"Do not ask me that!"

"Or will the Hopi walk a new way, Morning Butterfly? Will everything they have ever been be forgotten?"

"Stop it! I hate it when you do this to me!"

"I know you do," he whispered. "But I need to understand why the Hopi allow themselves to be treated like deer."

Sometimes the wind blew with such strength that the air filled with dust and other flying things, making it impossible to see. She felt as if she was in such a wind—blind. Afraid and angry.

"We are who we are, Cougar. Peaceful ones guided by spirits who teach great wisdom and patience, who . . ."

"What?" he prompted.

"The kachinas! The soldiers destroyed their likenesses, but their spirits remained. Siliomono was there as well."

"Tell me."

This man who should be a stranger was her courage, her test. Maybe her guide through her tangled thoughts.

"When—when the last kachina had been thrown off Oraibi, the spirits howled, their voices filling the air. Like crying night creatures, they wailed, and my people and I cried with them. Cried and were comforted."

"Did the soldiers hear?"

When the first notes reached her, nothing else had mattered, but once the initial shock had lifted and then realization set in, she'd turned her attention to her surroundings and had seen the look of awe on the faces of her people.

"Yes," she whispered, "I believe they did, but they said nothing."

"Morning Butterfly, listen to me," he said as he took her hands and placed them on his chest. She felt his heart beating through his cotton shirt. "Your people have been given strength by your spirits. This is my belief, your spirits want you to take hold of that truth and use it to repel the newcomers."

He was confusing her, taking her thoughts in a direction they'd never gone before.

"Do not let the spirits' cries be for nothing. Listen to their wisdom and guidance and fight for the land that has always been for the Hopi."

"Fight?"

"You are many, while they are few. Kill them."

"No!"

"Yes! Morning Butterfly, the Keres allowed themselves to be treated like deer, like mice. Their homes were destroyed and many, many Keres were killed and mutilated. You cannot want the same fate to befall your people. I risked a great deal taking the Spanish horses, not because I am a child who wishes to make everything mine, but because horses are strength."

She nodded.

"I am a Navajo man determined to make my people as strong as possible so they can drive back those who do not belong here. The day will come, I pray, when we will have their weapons, but already horses have made us swift. Powerful. It can be the same for the Hopi."

Despite herself, she'd watched and envied mounted soldiers, imagined herself sitting astride one of the fast-running animals. She'd also wondered what it would be like to hold a sword—for her sister to have one when the captain came for her.

"Defend what is precious to you. Fight! Fight!"

"My father's uncle cannot fight," she blurted as she scrambled to her feet. "The Spanish soldiers cut off his hand. I hear his nightmares. I see his helplessness, feel his fear! I share my home with an old man who will never be whole. I cannot forget that."

She'd backed away from him while she was speaking, but he came after her, stalking her as his namesake stalks its prey.

"My grandfather was at Acoma too," he said, his voice soft in contrast to his fierce posture. "He became Drums No More because of what was taken from him, but he is not afraid."

He couldn't move his arms. Panicked, he tried to strike out with his feet, but something heavy had been placed on them, holding him prisoner. In the dark recesses of his mind, Drums No More was aware that this had happened to him before, and that he must keep his fear to himself.

Fighting for control, he sucked what air he could into his lungs and held it, his chest swelling and burning with the effort.

Someone was coming, boots scraping on the earth, stiff uniform making its own angry sound. From where he lay, Drums No More tried to focus on his old, old foe, but he'd been doing this for nights without end and was weary of the battle.

When he felt himself becoming lightheaded, he expelled his breath in a harsh but hopefully silent breath and waited.

Waited for the Spanish soldier.

The walking, stalking sound began again, making him think of a great hoard of insects. Although it was useless, he again struggled and tried to kick. He screamed, but only deep in his throat, so no one would know his secret shame.

His night terrors.

As had happened, and happened, and happened, the darkness fell away and he saw the faceless man lean over him, grab his right arm.

'No! No! Please, no!

Pain beyond comprehension, old as life itself and yet always new and awful, seared its way into him. He saw his hand falling to the ground, blood pouring onto the earth, nerveless fingers turning white.

Again.

Again.

His silent scream went on and on.

Two days' foot journey away, One Hand writhed in the grip of his own nightmare.

13

By Angelico's reckoning, a full three weeks had passed from the time he had entrusted his letter to the Mexican Indian until the savage returned. Angelico gave little thought to the fact that the servant had driven himself to the limit of his endurance and caused the death of a horse during his journey. What mattered was that Governor Zotylo had responded to the padre's letter.

"Your accounting of conditions at Oraibi is indeed detailed," the governor wrote. "And, I must say, not consistent with your public document and Captain Lopez de Leiva's report received at the same time. Captain Lopez was chosen for the task of assuring your safety while you spread the Lord's word because he had proven himself a capable military leader. I have no doubt you are aware of his lineage, particularly the fact that his grandfather was among the vanguard in exploring this new land. I do not expect you to concern yourself with issues beyond your own calling, which is as it should be, but I wish to assure you, I have not taken your words lightly."

Angelico looked around to assure himself that he was alone, then continued reading.

"Padre, as governor, my responsibilities are vast. In addition to doing everything within my power to facilitate the Church's work, I am also charged with supplying the native labor force necessary to settle this wild land. Toward that end, I must insist the Indians be treated as humanely as possible and that nothing is done which might cause them to rebel. Rest assured, I have written Captain Lopez reminding him of that—just as I now remind you that the Church's concerns may, at times, not be in perfect accord with those of the State.

"In response to your suggestion that Captain Lopez be removed from his command, I am not in a position to entertain that possibility, the reasons being political in nature. Thus, I trust that you and Captain Lopez will work to forge a new and more positive relationship."

Confused, Angelico reread the letter, but it answered no more questions the second time. He would give a great deal to see what the governor had written to the captain. At the same time, he vowed to do everything within his power to keep the contents of what he held in his hands to himself. Thoughts of Captain Lopez's reaction to his complaint regarding his performance gave him an uneasy moment. However, he was doing the Lord's work; thus, his path and decisions were beyond question.

He'd just set his mind to what scriptures he wanted to focus on during Vespers when Pablo hurried up and informed him that Captain Lopez wanted to see him, immediately.

"Father, it was not a request but an order," the soldier said. "Please, you will come?"

"If I did not, it would place you in an awkward position, would it not?"

By way of answer, Pablo knelt before him, indicating he wanted his blessing. After giving it, Angelico tucked his letter into a pocket and started to trot toward the captain's tent. Before he could become winded, he forced himself to slow to what couldn't be taken for anything but a leisurely pace.

"Good afternoon, Captain," he said upon entering the

large tent that had been fashioned out of woven cotton cloth taken from the Hopi. "I am glad you have time for a conversation since there is something I wish to discuss with you."

Captain Lopez had been standing with his back to the door flap. Now he whirled and waved a piece of paper bearing the royal patent stamp at him. "How many Hopi have you baptized?" he demanded. "And their religious training? How is that coming?"

"I believe you know the answer to that. I pray. By all that is holy, I exhaust myself encouraging them to embrace Christianity, but they are slow to learn. Slow to—"

"Slow to do anything. Yes, I know. I swear, they are gifted with no more reasoning powers than sheep. That so few speak even a word of Spanish is of the utmost frustration."

"It is the same with Latin, which is why I use it only sparingly during services." He sighed. "How are they to accept the word of God if—"

"The word of God is not my concern." He waved the letter under Angelico's nose. "As if it were necessary, I have been reminded of the Crown's claim on what the heathens produce. According to the governor, I am remiss in providing the Crown with those essentials."

Governor Zotylo had assured Angelico that Captain Lopez would be reminded of his duties regarding the Church. Was it possible the captain had misinterpreted? Before he could think how to voice his question, Lopez signaled for the padre to sit on a wood-and-leather stool.

As farmers, the Hopi were expected to supply a given amount of corn, wheat, beans, squash, and other food stuffs for the State. In addition, they and other Pueblo Indians were expected to oversee the State's livestock herds both in New Spain and throughout the territory. Lopez stated that the governor had written that he had received, from good authority, word that the Hopi's willingness to work for the Crown was in jeopardy because of the way they were being treated.

"Was it you, Padre?" Lopez demanded. "According to this—" he again indicated the letter, "my men and I have been accused of availing ourselves of the local women, a situation which, officially at least, will not be tolerated by the Church. Does this sound like you? Does it?"

"Do not threaten me, Captain."

"By all that is holy, I—if you were a man, a real man, you would understand!"

Angelico's back burned and itched, reminding him of the devil's hold. "You are right," he said nonetheless. "A mortal man's weakness is beyond my comprehension, but not my concern. If you came to me, we could pray together for you to receive forgiveness, but you do not—"

"No, I do not." Lopez pressed his hand to his forehead and squeezed his eyes shut. "We are worlds apart, you and I."

"Yes, we are," he said, although the truth was, the only true conversations he had were with the captain. Until now, he'd given scant thought to Lopez's responsibilities where the State was concerned. Was being charged with filling a produce quota or supplying a workforce more important than guiding savages out of darkness? No.

Never.

"You do your work. I do mine," Angelico said.

"My task would be much easier if you did not interfere in it."

"I only did what, in good conscience, I knew I must."

"Damnation!" For the second time, Lopez pressed his palm to his forehead. "Do what you are determined to, Padre. All I ask is that I be allowed to do the same."

"Granted."

"Granted? Just like that?"

"Yes." Angelico stood and drew back his shoulders in what he believed was a show of strength. "Take what Hopi workers you need. I will do the same."

"What? I do not understand."

"Then I will educate you," he said, measuring each word. "The Lord was testing me when He had me consider building my church at Oraibi. Now I know what He wants. Now I can truly begin."

"*Consider* building your church at Oraibi? I understood the matter was decided."

"Not at all. Not at all, which is why construction has not gone forth. Captain, you know as well as I do that the Hopi consider the mesa sacred. Oraibi is an ancient village, and as such it has become the center of their heathen traditions." Why couldn't he come out and admit he never again wanted to set foot on that accursed place?

"It was enough that we made a statement of force by destroying their idols. I do not wish my church to be seen as competing with their primitive beliefs."

"*Your* church?"

Ignoring the interruption, he hurried on. "The Lord's word will spread its own light and live in its own holy structure. It will not stand in the shadow of heathen kivas."

"Padre, I have tried to exhibit patience in your presence, but by all that is holy, will you please come to the heart of the matter?"

How wrong he'd been to think he could continue to work with this man! The next time he wrote the governor, and that would happen before the day was over, he would state his position in the strongest way possible.

"The church—this celebration to our Lord—will be erected on virgin land so its glorious message can sing out loud and clear. So there will be no confusion as to the direction the Hopi are to bend their hearts from this day forth."

"In other words . . ." Captain Lopez's smile was a fearful thing, half predator, half snake, "you do not want to risk provoking their wrath, or the wrath of their supreme beings."

"*Their* supreme beings? They have no such thing!"

Long after the padre left, Lopez made no attempt to turn his attention to what else he needed to accomplish today. Fury at the governor's condescending tone continued to rankle him, but he would deal with that later. First, he needed to absorb what Angelico had said.

"You were afraid," he said softly, secure in the belief that no one could hear him. "When that . . . sound began, you thought you had been thrown into hell, didn't you? You

think I do not notice how seldom you have gone near the kivas since then, but I am not stupid, Padre. Not stupid at all."

Sagging forward, he stared at the ground beneath his
boots. Little sound reached him in here, a condition that
sometimes disquieted him, since he wasn't a man comfortable with his own thoughts. At times like this when there
was no distraction, no activity to expend energy on, he was
forced to come face to face with himself.

And what confronted him now was the fact that his senses
still vibrated with the awful echo of those accursed wails.

Even with Singer Of Songs lying beside him, he hadn't
had a decent night's sleep since then.

The weight of his thoughts closed in around him and
forced him outside. He set off toward the Hopi gardens.

Not that he felt a need to express it to anyone, he admired
the Indians' ability to coax life from worthless land. The various plants were spaced far apart, obviously in deference to the
limited moisture, usually on a slope in order to take advantage
of any water runoff. He'd noted how quickly everything ma-
tured and that the hardy varieties were all but impervious to
desert temperatures, but real success was due to how deeply
everything was planted. The seeds had been dropped into
holes some twelve to sixteen inches deep where, despite the
scant rainfall, the subsoil remained damp because it was protected by surface sand. The plants had strong root systems
which allowed them to withstand the constant wind.

The savages were simple creatures; he'd spent his entire
military life believing that and having that reinforced by
how easily the Indians in New Spain had given way before
the expanding Spanish presence, but here the indigenous
population remained essentially as it had been for centuries,
independent and resourceful, in harmony with the land.

Much later that day, Angelico opened the second letter he'd
received, this one written by a fellow Franciscan stationed
among the Zuni. According to the letter, Fray Francisco
Letrado and another padre had made great strides in the year
they'd been at Halona.

"It is so seldom that I have opportunity to communicate with my brethren that I trust you will be patient with my ramblings," Fray Francisco began. "I also realize this might not reach you for many months and that conditions here may have changed by then, but my blessings have been great; I feel compelled to share them."

He went on to describe the initial hostile reception the group had received from the Zuni, a hostility that proved to be short-lived.

"I give credit for much of our good fortune to the governor who, along with a large contingent of cavalry men, visited our humble mission shortly after I arrived. He personally and quite emphatically informed the soldiers of what their behavior toward the natives should be. He ordered that, 'no soldier should enter a house of the pueblos, nor transgress in aggrieving the Indians under penalty of his life.' But, for me at least, most powerful were his edicts concerning how I was to be treated. He was convinced the Zuni would approach me with reverence and awe if they saw that self-same behavior from the soldiers. In the presence of the savages, he and the soldiers fell to their knees before me and kissed my feet. That display has made all the difference."

With a growing sense of frustration, Angelico read that Fray Francisco had succeeded in building a church in no more than three months, had baptized the vast majority of Zuni in Halona, and had made great strides in teaching them Spanish.

"Once the church was to my liking, I turned my attention to the rest of my duties," Fray Francisco continued. "As dictated by the Crown, of primary concern was making the mission self-sufficient. With the willing assistance of both soldiers and natives, our crops flourish, a good two-score foals were born this spring, and the sheep herd has grown beyond my counting. Truly the Lord's blessings shine upon me, as I am certain they do on you."

The Lord's blessings! Barely able to contain himself, Angelico took stock of his "accomplishments." He had a small tent for shelter, barely enough food to fill his belly, not so much as a stick or rock yet set in place for a church, and less than half of the Hopi had submitted to baptism.

Even more disturbing, he couldn't sleep because he was haunted by what he'd heard and felt after ordering the Hopi's barbaric effigies destroyed.

"Lord," he prayed, "I seek Your guidance. I am a humble man and Your most devout servant, but I also wish all who are touched by my commitment to my Lord to see You in Your full glory and power. The Hopi *must* be shown the light and guided to salvation. What better way to force them to give up their barbaric beliefs than in service to You—in celebrating Your greatness?"

And if I do not succeed, my life is failure.

"You cannot be serious!" Captain Lopez exclaimed when the padre faced him for the second time that day.

"Completely. Captain, surely you agree that we have not accomplished nearly enough. Is that not what your missive from the governor was about?"

"The letter was addressed to me. Let me be the one to interpret it."

Angelico shrugged. "As you wish, it is not my concern. This is: Hundreds of Hopi live at Oraibi. It is only fitting that the church be large enough to accommodate all of them."

He would never understand the padre's thinking. Wasn't it just a short while ago that Fray Angelico had agreed with the State's claim on the savages' possessions? Now he was proposing a structure whose building would necessitate putting all able-bodied Hopi to work just as their crops were reaching the point of harvest.

Speaking as a father might to a young child, Lopez pointed that out. "All I am saying is that wisdom dictates you put off your plans until fall is full upon us," he suggested. "By then, the crops will have been collected and shipped off."

"Celebrating the Lord's glory has been delayed long enough, Captain. The holy objects I brought with me and have placed in view of the infidels is only the beginning. From the moment we reached here, from the moment fate cast us together, I begged you to lend me your assistance, but that has not happened. Instead, you and your men allowed yourselves to be distracted by a few inconsequential Navajo raids. When you are not engaged in an ill-conceived and so-far futile search for that wild tribe, you send out scouts to look for the area's mineral wealth—wealth that may not exist and means nothing to our Lord God. And then, do I need to mention this, there is the amount of time you devote to pleasures of the flesh."

"At least I am accomplishing something," Lopez countered. "Unlike you, you have wasted so much time trying to decide where this precious church of yours should be built. Any other padre would have made that decision long ago."

As he'd expected, Fray Angelico's face reddened. "A simple decision, you think!" he blurted. "The placement—by all that is holy, I do not know why I persist in trying to educate you!"

"Believe me, it would please me no end if you would stop. So." He sighed. "Since there will be no peace until you have had your way, show me this latest drawing of yours."

With trembling hands, Fray Angelico spread out a detailed rendering of a structure some forty feet long and nearly thirty wide. It was to be topped, not with the cross he'd brought with him, but with one even larger and constructed of wood available only in San Francisco. At least the padre had the good sense to use stone for the majority of the structure. Still, this was a far more ambitious undertaking than any frontier church he'd ever seen or heard of. He opened his mouth to point that out, then thought better of it.

"I am not a builder," he said. "How long do you anticipate this will take?"

Angelico blinked. "I am not certain. Much depends on how well the labor force understands what we require of them."

"Yes, that is a problem."

"But it will happen! The Lord has spoken."

"The Lord?" Lopez asked archly.

"I am but God's servant. My words are His."

For a day marred by the critical letter from the governor, Lopez had to admit it had turned out quite well. Fray

Angelico's determination to throw the village into turmoil over a structure still puzzled him. He would probably never understand the Catholic religion's insistence on pomp and show, but now that he'd given it serious thought, he realized how well this would work to his favor.

"Come here," he said to Singer Of Songs, who'd just entered his tent.

Her eyes were unreadable, her newly ripened body nearly hidden under her shapeless dress. As he reached for her, a wave of loneliness washed over him. He certainly didn't miss his wife and seldom thought of her, but there was no one here he could truly talk to, no one to share his small triumphs and all too oppressive frustrations.

The land was to a large part responsible. It was so damnably inhospitable, without so much as a spot of greenery to ease the unrelenting gray. Why anyone had made this their homeland was beyond his comprehension. If the Hopi or Navajo had had an interest in gold or the other precious stones he never doubted were here, he might understand, but why the miserable savages struggled to support themselves on barren rock—

"No, no," he chided as she tensed under his touch. "How many times do I have to tell you, if you do as I say, no harm will come to you."

She gave no indication she understood. In truth, the words were for him alone since he had no wish for anyone to know about this softness in him. "You are spring. A blooming flower and a gentle breeze. A pocket of serenity in a hard world."

The act of lifting her sleeveless dress over her head distracted him. Ignoring the look of resignation in her beautiful eyes, he covered her breasts with his hands and began kneading them. He'd started to turn her around so she couldn't watch while he divested himself of his uniform when he heard a horse approach, followed by someone calling his name. Angry at being interrupted, he clenched his teeth. Then he recognized the voice.

"Come in, come in," he announced, then pushed Singer Of Songs to one side and threw her dress at her. She hadn't had time to put it on before Pablo entered. The young soldier, who'd nearly lost his life at the hands of the horse-stealing Navajo, reeked of sweat. He'd removed his helmet, revealing filthy, wet hair. His eyes strayed to the Hopi, then fixed on his superior officer.

"I did not expect you back yet," Lopez told Pablo.

"I did not think I would succeed in my task as soon as I did. However, the moment I was certain, I pushed myself to the limit in order to report to you." He inclined his head at Singer Of Songs.

"She speaks not a word of Spanish," Lopez assured him.

"I understand, Captain. If I could—if I could trouble you for a drink of water . . ."

Although impatient, Lopez indicated where Pablo could find a water bladder and waited while he satisfied his thirst. At least the young man knew enough to remain standing.

"I found the Navajo village."

Lopez's heart began to race. "Tell me," he ordered.

Pablo did just that, and if his tone and demeanor gave away some of the tension—no, fear—he'd felt while in enemy land, at least he had the presence of mind not to dwell on it. As directed, Pablo and another soldier had headed north. They'd spent the first night hiding in the shadow of a barren, steep-sided mesa and in the morning had discovered that they'd lain their heads mere inches from a hideous looking lizard, one Pablo had no doubt was capable of inflicting a painful if not fatal bite. Feeling almost fatherly toward Pablo, Lopez suggested it must have been a highly poisonous Gila monster. For a moment, Pablo concentrated on swallowing, then went on.

"That morning we came across horse tracks. It was an easy matter to follow them."

"They must have been fresh. Otherwise, the wind would have blown them away."

"We came to the same conclusion, sir, and doubled our efforts to remain as inconspicuous as possible, but there was no way we could be sure of our safety."

Lopez nodded. "Go on."

Looking disappointed at his commanding officer's apparent lack of concern for his life, Pablo forged ahead. As he detailed the rugged terrain, Lopez gave silent thanks to the God he all too often discounted for looking after his men. Life was cheap in this land, and yet each was precious; if his troops were depleted, he would be at the savages' mercy.

"It was nearly dark on the second day when we first heard the horses," Pablo explained. "We waited until the moon was up, then left our own mounts behind and continued on foot. The eight Navajo hovels are grouped so most are within sight of each other. They have not built a corral but hobble the horses. In addition, guards are stationed among the animals."

"How many guards?"

"I saw two, but there might have been more."

"Hm. What did you see in the way of weapons?"

Pablo shook his head. He hadn't taken a chance on getting closer to the settlement. A few Navajo men had been sitting in front of one of their houses, but it had been impossible to determine how many savages called the village home.

"The element of surprise," Lopez said, returning to the matter at hand. "That is what will conquer the Navajo. The Indians who make this godless land their home are little more than animals, untrained in modern fighting techniques. Once we begin firing, they will surrender."

Pablo fingered his side, where he'd been wounded, but said nothing.

"Do not concern yourself with strategy, Pablo," Lopez snapped. "That is my responsibility. Yours is simply to obey my commands." He licked his lips. "And now that we know where the Navajo are, I can put my plan into action."

14

_____

While she waited for her sister to return from the captain's tent, Morning Butterfly busied herself by repairing One Hand's moccasin, and remembering the time she'd spent with Cougar.

He wasn't the first man she'd been alone with, but tonight she couldn't remember the others. She wanted to believe that was because his words challenged everything she'd ever believed about being a Hopi, but she knew it was more than that. He was handsome and tall, strong and reckless—as witnessed by the way he'd stood up to the captain. A man like that would be a good hunter, capable of providing everything she needed. Only . . .

Only he was Navajo and she'd told him she hated him.

A faint scraping outside the pueblo provided her with the distraction she badly needed, and she scrambled to her feet to welcome her sister. So far the captain had left no marks on Singer Of Songs. Just the same, by coal light, she studied her sister's every movement.

"You are late." Not wanting to risk waking the other family members, she kept her voice at a whisper. "He has never kept you this long."

"No." Singer Of Songs glanced at her parents' sleeping mats before indicating she wanted Morning Butterfly to go outside with her.

"I will tell everyone what I heard," Singer Of Songs said once they stood under the stars. "But I want to discuss it with you first. To see if you find the same meaning in the soldiers' words that I did."

Morning Butterfly wrapped her arm around her sister's shoulder.

"They think so little of us," Singer Of Songs said. "It does not occur to them that you are not the only one who has learned at least a little Spanish."

"It is best that way."

Singer Of Songs studied the stars and the nearly full moon for several moments before going on. "I wish I was a child again," she said softly. "A girl learning to dry corn and gather what our mother needs to make baskets. To be curious about deer and wolves, insects and snakes. To not—to not be a woman."

"In your heart, you—"

"No, not in my heart. And not my body either. I fear . . ."

"What do you fear?" she prompted.

"Nothing. The missing soldiers returned today," Singer Of Songs said, and then proceeded to describe the conversation between Captain Lopez and the one known as Pablo.

Morning Butterfly had guessed the soldiers were either looking for the Navajo or had gone in search of the stones the captain set so much store by. Learning that finding the Navajo village had been their goal, and that they'd succeeded, chilled her.

"What will happen now?" she asked. "Will they attack the Navajo?"

"I do not know. The captain spoke of his desire to find emeralds. That is what he is determined to have the Navajo tell him."

"There can only be one way. He and his soldiers will attack the Navajo, kill those he has no need for, capture Cougar."

"Surely that is not your concern."

"But it is," she whispered. "Sister, if a Navajo knew the newcomers planned to attack us, you would want his warning, would you not?"

"A Navajo does not care what happens to the Hopi." Singer Of Songs gripped her sister's arm and pulled her close. "Your thoughts frighten me. Please tell me you will not leave Oraibi. Promise me."

"Do not ask for what I cannot give."

Sometimes the Snake ceremony caused it to rain for several days afterward, but this year there'd only been one brief storm. As Morning Butterfly hurried toward the Navajo settlement after gathering up what she would need for a journey of several days and asking Singer Of Songs to do what she could to calm their family, she took note of how dry everything looked, the air brittle and spent.

She'd heard enough from the Spaniards to know that other parts of the world were blessed with abundant rainfall, but she couldn't imagine what it was like. Nor would she ever want to be anywhere else. Every morning, Sun emerged from his house in the east, traveled in a circular path above the earth, and, at sunset, descended into his house in the west. During the night, Sun completed his journey by traveling west to east through the underworld. In the same way, every year at the time of the Winter Solstice, Sun left his winter house and traveled to his summer place, a journey that lasted until the Summer Solstice.

In gratitude for the everlasting cycle, the Hopi held ceremonies to assure that the rhythm would continue for all time. The Home Dance would be held, the women of the Lakon, Marawu, and Owaqlt societies would perform their fall ceremonies as they always had.

Without those things, here, there would be no Hopi.

Lost in those thoughts, she barely noticed the red and white cliffs in the distance, now highlighted by the rising sun. She made no attempt to hide herself and had no doubt the Navajo would spot her once she neared their village. She wanted to be found. Wanted to be taken to Cougar.

No, not just Cougar, although his presence was essential since he might be the only one she could communicate with.

A gray-brown rabbit broke from beneath a bush to her right, causing her first to start and then laugh at the way its overlarge hind legs slapped the ground. Suddenly she realized that something, or someone, was in the small depression to her left, something large that sent fingers of alarm through her. Acting instinctively, she changed directions, but although she'd already started to run, she'd only gone a few steps when something slammed into her and she was sent sprawling to the ground.

A man's voice, the words harsh and incomprehensible, helped calm her. Although she didn't understand Navajo, the language itself told her she hadn't been captured by a soldier.

"Please," she gasped. "I . . . I mean no harm."

Her captor said something else, his tone less angry. Then, to her gratitude, he lifted himself off her. Before she could think what to do, he yanked her to her feet and turned her so her face was in full sunlight.

"Cougar," she said, carefully pronouncing the one Navajo word she knew. "I must see Cougar."

The sun had completed its journey and she was both thirsty and hungry by the time she and the brave reached the Navajo village. For the first time in her life, she'd sat astride a horse, and although at first she'd been terrified, she'd soon been in awe of the amount of ground a running horse could cover. She hadn't liked having the Navajo's arm around her waist, but she'd also felt safe with him behind her; most of all she'd been grateful that he hadn't seen her as an enemy and understood what she wanted.

Because Sun's light hadn't fully faded, she was able to make out several separate, rounded Navajo hogans. Although she'd heard them described, she'd never seen one, and despite her unease at being here, she took a moment to study them.

From where she sat on horseback, she spotted as many structures as she had fingers on one hand, but because the land here buckled and swayed, she suspected there were more.

Like her people's homes, the hogans blended with their surroundings, but where a pueblo took its strength from stone, the hogans were held together with dirt and bark. What made the most impact was how far apart from each other they were, like lonely creatures isolated in the wilderness instead of interwoven the way Hopi houses were. Perhaps the Navajo valued privacy; perhaps each family had its own separate piece of land. Just the same, she found it strange that they didn't need to take strength from each other's nearness.

A couple of young boys came out of the closest hogan and stood staring at her with their mouths open. When she smiled at them, they didn't smile back, but the older one came a few steps closer. Learning Spanish had been an unwanted necessity, but she looked forward to learning enough Navajo to at least communicate a little with the children.

The man who'd brought her here pointed toward a flat area, and after dismounting, she walked over to it, hobbling a little from being on horseback so long. A number of other children had already joined the boys, and several women now stood near them. They wore cotton dresses covered with complex designs.

She'd just settled herself and begun to look around when one of the women approached, shook out a sheepskin, and placed it on the ground. Using a combination of grunts and hand signals, she commanded Morning Butterfly to sit on it. She did so, wondering as she inhaled the scent of wool how many sheep the Navajo had killed, and how much longer the Spanish would tolerate the loss of their livestock.

How long she sat there, with at least twenty women and children studying her, she couldn't say, just that the day had ended and night begun when she felt a faint thudding that seemed to vibrate through the ground. As it came closer, she prayed to Taiowa to protect her. If the sound and vibration was caused by a Navajo spirit, would the Hopi creator be powerful enough to keep her safe? She couldn't imagine any being greater than Taiowa, but she was on Navajo land.

Seven or eight men started walking toward her. In the rapidly dying light, she couldn't tell whether they were armed.

"Humbly I ask my Father, the perfect one, Taiowa, our Father, the perfect one creating the beautiful life, shown to us by the yellow light. To give us perfect light at the time of the red light. The perfect one laid out the perfect plan and gave to us a long span of life, creating song to implant joy in life. On this path of happiness, we the Butterfly Maidens carry out his wishes by greeting our Father Sun. The song resounds back from our Creator with joy, and we of the earth repeat it to our Creator. At the appearing of the yellow light, repeats and repeats again the joyful echo, sounds and resounds for times to come."

Strengthened and steadied by her people's Song Of Creation, she folded her hands in her lap and waited. The men formed a circle around her, their bodies so warm that she guessed they must have just come from their sweat lodge. One sat on the sheepskin with her, his knees touching hers.

"Do not be afraid, Morning Butterfly," Cougar said in Hopi. "No harm will come to you."

He was voice and warmth, a shadowy outline so close she could easily trace his features and form with her fingers if she reached out. So he wasn't a dream after all, not a kachina born of her young heart. And he was alive.

"It is good to see you," she said as yet more Navajo appeared. The number eventually swelled to nearly a hundred.

"It is good to see you. When Laughs At Thunder offered to watch for any sign of the newcomers, I said it would be a good thing, even though I knew what he really wanted was to spend the day with one of the horses. Now I see the spirits' hands in what happened."

"The spirits?"

"They brought you and Laughs At Thunder together and eased your journey. Your people are well?"

"Yes."

"And are they happy?"

"Happy? No, they are not. We fear we will not be able to harvest this year's crops," she began, then told how she'd been forced to pass on the padre's orders that everyone capable of working spend their days building something he called a church. She'd explained to Lopez and the padre that the Hopi would starve if they neglected their corn, beans, and squash, but her pleas had fallen on deaf ears.

"The captain pointed to our store of dried corn and piki and said that would be enough to feed us through the winter. Winter, maybe, but what about spring and summer? They must believe we can survive on grass and weeds the way their horses and sheep do."

"You said those things to him?"

She nodded, then said yes in case he couldn't see her gesture in the dark. "The lives of the Hopi means little to the captain and his men. Only one thing does—emeralds."

He expelled his breath with enough force that it reached her cheeks. She wished it was daylight so she could study his expressions, look into his eyes and find the truth of him.

"Cougar, he knows how to find you," she said when he'd finished what she assumed was a translation of what she'd just told him.

Numerous shadowy bodies crowded even closer, but she concentrated only on Cougar, spoke to him alone. "I fear—I fear he will force you to take him to where he believes the emeralds are."

"He knows where I am?"

She hadn't said that well, but with apprehension crawling through her, choosing her words was difficult. After gathering the Song Of Creation around her for courage, she told him what she'd learned from her sister.

"Soldiers gazed upon us and we did not know," he whispered after he'd passed on the latest. "This is not good."

"They followed the tracks of horses," she explained. "But they were fearful, and so took care to hide themselves."

"Witchcraft," Cougar said, shaking his head.

"What?"

"Witchcraft may be responsible for what the soldiers were able to do. I feared—I knew I had seen a witch-wolf, a *chindi.*"

"A *chindi?*"

"Darkness and evil, sometimes the hate-filled ghost of a dead Earth Surface People."

"And your people fear them?"

"Yes," he said after a brief silence. "No good Navajo becomes a *chindi,* because in order for the change into evil to take place, a relative must be sacrificed. Ours is a peaceful village because we have no such cursed one among us, but what I saw when I was returning from my first visit to Oraibi may not have been a true wolf. I sought out our elders and shamans and asked for their wisdom, but all they could do was tell me they did not believe the evil came from the Navajo."

"Then where?"

"The Spanish. I was foolish to think I could get rid of the newcomers by sending them off in search of green stones," he continued. "They are still here, still dangerous."

"Cougar, you told me that the Navajo are different from my people, that yours would never allow their enemies to take their food, their women, their freedom. I do not want to say this, but is it possible the Navajo could become sheep because the Spanish have *chindi* among them?"

"No! Never!"

"Then you will leave? Go where you and your people will be safe?"

A man who'd been standing behind Cougar started to speak. Cougar responded, and then several others joined in. Morning Butterfly listened closely and tried to duplicate some of the sounds of their words in her mind, but the sounds lacked meaning and she didn't know what—if anything—she was saying. She felt exhaustion creeping through her.

"They wanted to know what we were talking about," Cougar finally explained. "Everyone is troubled because the Spanish came so close. You are certain you were not followed?"

She explained that she'd been careful to sneak away at night when neither the soldiers or padre were nearby, but added that they might be looking for her now.

"They will not know where to search, but I cannot stay long," she told him. "Cougar, please, go where you will be safe. Hide from our shared enemy."

"Me? What about the rest of my people?"

"I cannot tell you what to do. But if you were captured again, the soldiers would force you—they are not gentle men. I fear . . ."

"You are afraid for a Navajo?"

"Yes."

"Why?"

The question left her momentarily speechless, but after looking up at the newborn stars for guidance, she spoke.

"This land nourishes those who understand and honor it. We accept its richness, but we, Hopi and Navajo alike, also know we are blessed to be allowed to live here. The Spanish do not. Instead, they take from the land but do not replenish it, do not give thanks. That places your people and mine on one side of life, the outsiders on the other."

He gave her knee a brief squeeze, then said something to the others which she took to be an explanation of what they'd been talking about. Several responded, and she waited through the discussion, absorbing the night, her surroundings, and what Cougar had shared with her earlier—the gifts and cautions of his belief. Her people had no *chindi,* but that didn't mean they didn't exist for the Navajo. She could only pray that he—they—would heed the warning she had brought before it was too late.

"When will you leave?" she asked when the conversation fell away.

"Nothing has been decided."

"What? Cougar, my people want only peace and the Spanish know it. That is why they have no need to smash us, but the Navajo stole Spanish horses and sheep, angered them."

"Morning Butterfly, do not make our burdens yours."

She wouldn't have risked coming here if she hadn't already done that, didn't he understand? Still, telling him that would make her even more vulnerable to him.

"Morning Butterfly, listen to me," he went on. "What you brought to us must be discussed and prayed over. In the morning, after everyone has had time alone with their thoughts, the tribe will meet."

"That is wise." Morning Butterfly yawned, sagging in her place.

Cougar nodded, then said, "Tonight, after you have had something to eat, you will sleep in my hogan."

Morning Butterfly was relieved to see that Cougar didn't live alone, but with his parents, his grandfather Drums No More, two younger brothers, and a sister.

A small fire burned in the middle of the hogan, the coals supplying enough light that she could see the dirt floor, the short tunnel from the door to the main room, the beds radiating out from the fire, a large loom almost identical to her family's, and several storage containers. The room smelled of dirt and wood, cooking meat and corn, those scents reminding her of home.

Without saying a word, Cougar's mother spread a deerskin blanket on the ground next to her own bed and pointed to Morning Butterfly, indicating that this was where she should sleep. Then, still silent, the older woman handed her a bowl filled with venison stew. Morning Butterfly gave her what she hoped would be interpreted as a grateful smile, then quickly filled her belly. Cougar's little sister returned her smile with a shy one before scurrying outside, followed by her brothers.

Cougar was outside, and Morning Butterfly's inability to communicate with his family weighed on her. Once she'd finished eating, his parents left and only Drums No More remained, a silent, staring presence that in many respects reminded her of One Hand. He made no attempt to hide his disfigurement; in fact, he seemed to go to some length to make sure she saw it. She was fighting sleep and thinking about the similarities between Navajo and Hopi housekeeping when Cougar finally entered. His first words were to his grandfather, but before long, he squatted near her, and when he did, she thought of nothing or no one else.

"This is my mother's home," he told her, his deep voice like a low rumble of thunder.

He didn't take his eyes off her, made her feel as if they were the only people on earth. "Once my grandfather decided that my father should marry my mother, her family built their first hogan for them. Although we have moved many times, each hogan is hers." He drew in a long breath. "When I married, I entered my wife's hogan, but then she died and I came back here because my parents and grandfather needed me. I tell you this so you will understand that everything here belongs to my mother; her words carry great weight."

"You have been married?"

"Yes."

"I—" Was she so tired she was in risk of saying too much? No matter, her need to learn more about him was too great to be swept aside by caution. "I did not realize I knew so little about you," she admitted.

"It is the same for me," he said after another of his silences, "except that when I saw how you wear your hair, I knew you did not have a husband."

Flustered, she fingered the squash-blossoms her mother had taken such pains to create. "I am sorry your wife died. Do—do you have children?"

"No." He breathed the word. "I wanted them, we both did, but then Sweet Water sickened and I stopped living with her as a man does. Stopped dreaming . . . Morning Butterfly—" He reached out as if to touch her, then pulled back. "My grandfather wishes to speak with you, not now, but before you leave. He wants to learn what is in your heart and for you to know certain things about him."

"Like what happened when he lost his hand?"

"Yes. His heart does not beat a single time without that being part of him."

Nodding, she looked over at the old man, but he appeared to be ignoring her.

"Whatever he wishes to tell me, I want to hear it. Cougar, I am glad for tonight, to learn things about your people and hold those things to me so I can take the truth back to my people."

15

Although sunlight had yet to touch the hogan's entranceway when Cougar woke, he quickly turned his mind from thoughts of getting any more rest. Determined not to unleash bad luck on those he loved, he took care not to step over the sleeping bodies as he made his way outside. Once there, he picked up a handful of sacred corn pollen from a nearby bowl and sprinkled it on the hogan's poles so the Holy People would know his first waking thoughts were of them.

That done, he prayed to Changing Woman, the Earth Mother, who was always benevolent, asking for her guidance in living in harmony with nature.

"My gratitude to you knows no bounds," he whispered. "It is you who built the first hogan out of turquoise and shell, you who gave us the gift of corn. I have asked myself if you are responsible for allowing horses into our lives, but it is not for me to know those things."

His mind still on his place in the universe, he sat on a rock and stared at the ground, the newborn sun warming his back.

The sun, life itself. A gift which could be taken away if

the Navajo strayed from the Beautiful Rainbow Way Of Life.

"Spider Man," he called out, "you are he who warns of coming danger. I come to you today in my mind, asking you to show me what the future brings. If we have done wrong, if we have incurred the wrath of Corn Beetle, Gila Monster, Big Snake Man, Big Fly, or Crooked Snake People, and they have decided to punish us, so be it. I bow before the power and anger of Wind People, Cloud People, Thunder People, and Coyote the trickster. If they wish me dead, I will not fight. I took horses because I believed my people would be made rich and powerful and could better withstand the new-comers. If that is wrong—"

"Cougar?"

When Morning Butterfly spoke his name, her tongue took it in a slightly different direction from what he was accustomed to. He would have laughed if he hadn't been concerned she would think he was making fun of her. After a short, silent prayer to Spider Man, he turned and acknowledged the young Hopi woman. Her hair had come undone in the night and flowed around her face, protecting and defining it. She was rubbing her arms—at night warmth left the land and even in the heavy months of summer, dawn brought a chill—yet she seemed unaware of any physical discomfort. He was struck once again by her graceful walk, her lively eyes, her gentle features.

"I am sorry," she said, her soft tone one he'd never forget. "I did not mean to interrupt your prayers, but I wanted to talk to you before the others woke."

"What we said to each other last night was not enough?"

"Perhaps it should have been," she told him as she found a nearby rock to settle herself on, "but it is not."

"Do not tell me that the Navajo must flee. You have spoken your mind on that, and the decision is not yours."

"I know." She sighed and briefly studied her surroundings. He hoped the sight pleased her. "This morning I speak of another thing. Sleep was a long time coming to me. I heard someone cry out."

Tensing, he looked around. "A *chindi?*"

"I think, if a *chindi* is about, that a Hopi would not know; but no, this sound was made by a human. By your grandfather."

"Sometimes his night thoughts are too much for him to keep to himself."

"That is so for all of us, but Cougar, his cries were the same as One Hand's."

"What are you saying?"

"Not what you want to hear." She briefly studied her hands, then lifted her head to meet his eyes. "You told me that Drums No More had not been made fearful by what happened to him, and if that is what he wishes everyone to believe, so be it. But I think, deep inside, he relives that horrible day. That it is a burning, bleeding knot in his heart."

She was Hopi, an outsider. How dare she think she understood his grandfather better than he did.

"I do not want to take his secrets and hold them up to the light," she continued. "That is not my intention."

"Then what is?"

A horse squealed, momentarily distracting her. "Simply to say that what happened to two men at Acoma touched them in the same way."

"That is for Drums No More and One Hand to decide."

"Perhaps the time will come when they can do that, together."

"I would like that," he admitted, surprising himself.

Cougar and Morning Butterfly were still sitting together when one by one, and then in groups, the other Navajo emerged from their hogans. Little was said as they ate breakfasts of fry bread, squash, and corn. Then Drums No More stepped to the middle of the village and began to chant. The men settled themselves on one side of him, the women and children on the other. Under Cougar's guidance, Morning Butterfly took her place near his mother. He would not be able to sit beside her and tell her what was being said. He would try to whisper to her from his place, but it would not be easy.

"The First World was an island," Drums No More said,

"surrounded by oceans. There lived the first beings, the Insect People. They were twelve in number and lived on the borders of three streams in the middle of the First World, all of which emerged from a central place. Two streams flowed to the south and one to the north.

"I say this because before anything is discussed, I want us to think of our beginning and how the Insect People had to leave their home when the wall of white that was water arrived. The Insect People flew high and looked down to see that water covered the First World. I am only a man without the wisdom of the Holy People, but it has come to me that the strangers' arrival may be like when the ancient water came."

"That cannot be!" Blue Swallow exclaimed. As the murdered Blue Corn Eater's older brother, he had every right to speak, and for his words to be taken to heart. "The newcomers are also known as Mexicans, and Mexicans came to be when Klehanoai, the god who carries the Moon, created them, as well as sheep, asses, horses, swine, goats, and birds for Nohoilpi after the gambler lost everything to the Navajo. Mexicans are nothing but servants."

"Perhaps they were when they were first created," Cougar pointed out, "but legend says they left Mexico and moved north where they built towns along the Rio Grande and in time enslaved the Pueblos who lived there. From servant to servant owner is the lesson we must heed."

"What are you saying?" Blue Swallow challenged. "That we should run from them?"

"No," he said somberly. Morning Butterfly was giving him a puzzled look, but he didn't dare take the time to translate for her. "What I say is that we must weigh everything before deciding what direction to walk."

"There is no time!" Blue Swallow insisted. "Listen to me! Last night I met with the others who went from boys to manhood in the same season I did, and we spoke at length about what the Spanish did to my brother. We are young, yes, but we are the future of the Navajo. Our bodies are strong. We may not have the wisdom of our elders, but our courage is great."

What a brave needed was wisdom as well as courage,

Cougar believed, but his grandfather, not he, had called this meeting and it was for him to speak.

"So you and others talked last night, did you?" Drums No More said. "Did your words go in a straight line or were they like wind-circles?"

"A straight line." Blue Swallow glanced at the knot of young men around him. "My brother's death was a warning so we would know what the Spanish are capable of. I hate what was done to him, but that does not make me afraid." Again he looked at his companions. "We say it is a good thing that the soldiers have found us. They will come, and when they do, we will kill them."

"No!" Drums No More gasped.

"Yes!" Blue Swallow insisted. "In your youth-time, when the newcomers first reached Acoma, they were met by Keres armed with stones, arrows, and clubs. A large number of the Spanish were killed. That was the Keres's victory, one never to be forgotten."

"One which angered the remaining Spanish and caused this to be done to me." Drums No More held up his stump. "Do not forget that."

Blue Swallow met the old man's eyes. "Your sacrifice was great and the lesson will live with us always, but we will not make the same mistake the Keres did. We say we must destroy the Spanish at Oraibi and then hide, taking the horses with us. By the time more soldiers come, we will have found a new home far from here."

The braves near Blue Swallow nodded agreement, and even Drums No More pursed his lips in concentration. For a moment no one spoke. Then an elderly woman pushed herself to her feet.

"This is Dinehtah, home of the Navajo!" she fairly shouted. "Does that mean nothing to you?"

Looking offended, Blue Swallow placed his hand over his heart. "Of course it does. Leaving here would cause me great pain, but perhaps we must if our children are to be safe."

"Cougar, what are they saying?" Morning Butterfly demanded. "Please, tell me."

Several Navajo glanced at her but most kept their attention fixed on Blue Swallow and Drums No More. She'd risked a great deal by coming here and deserved to know what was being discussed. Although tradition said she should remain with the women, Cougar signaled for her to join him. Once she'd sat beside him, he outlined Blue Swallow's plan.

"You cannot think such a thing!" she gasped. "To murder—to cause Spanish blood to flow—No!"

"You love them so much you wish no harm to come to them?"

"I wish I could die without having seen one of them," she said through clenched teeth, "but it is too late for that."

"Yes, it is. And you are one of the Peaceful Ones who would give up her own life before taking another."

"Do not throw those words at me! You and I have been down this path before and know each will continue on our way."

"I am glad to hear you say that. Do not forget, this is . Dinehtah and a Navajo decision, not Hopi."

"You are wrong. Wrong!" Her eyes blazed. "When you cause the soldiers' hearts to stop beating, you think you have won, but you have not. This is what the Keres believed and their village was nearly destroyed."

"Blue Swallow spoke of that, which is why we will be gone by the time more soldiers arrive."

Leaning closer, she glared at him, her eyes hot with emotion. "The Navajo, yes, but what about the Hopi? What about us, Cougar?"

"The Hopi are not at war with the Spanish."

"Do you think that matters to them?" she demanded. "They call us all Indians. If the Navajo kill, the Spanish will insist on revenge, and my people—*mine,* not yours—will feel the burden of that revenge. Tell your people that, Cougar. Tell them!"

"Morning Butterfly—"

"Do my people mean so little to you?"

"No, I care, but my family comes first in my heart."

She sagged, but not before he had glimpsed her tears. Neither he nor any other Navajo would willingly hurt another person's feelings, but he meant what he'd told her about his family with every fiber in his being, and prayed she understood.

"If the Navajo are willing to leave this village," she whispered, "why do they not do so today? Not to bring harm to the soldiers but to flee, now."

"Leaving them free to make slaves of your people? Forcing the Hopi to turn their backs on everything they have ever been and embrace a Christian god? Is that what you want?"

She didn't answer, but pulled her knees tight against her belly, rocking slightly. He needed to concentrate on what his people were saying, to weigh those words and add his own to them, but unable to walk away from the pain, he tried to put his arm around her. For a moment he thought she'd allow him to comfort her, but then she jerked away.

"Be Navajo," she hissed. "Just as I am Hopi."

The pros and cons of embracing the plan Blue Swallow and his companions wanted to follow was debated until the children grew restless and wandered away. Cougar asked several boys to tend to the horses so he could remain where he was. Morning Butterfly stayed at his side, even though she didn't understand what was being said.

At length, Drums No More announced that nothing new was left to be said. It was time to take guidance from the Beautiful Rainbow of Life. In ageless lessons, he explained, answers would come.

"I wish there was time for the Blessing Way Ceremony," he said, "because the story of our Emergence, told in its entirety over nine days, is at the heart of what we are. There is much wisdom in the story of Changing Woman and her sister White Shell Woman, who created the first Navajo and started them on their journey to Dinehtah. For it to be right, for our children to attain the wisdom of the old people, each word should be right."

"Grandfather, we hear your wisdom," Cougar deliberately softened his voice so the love he felt for the old man came through, "but I say there is not even time to discuss this. I ask you, will we not find peace in a Rainbow song?"

Drums No More called several of the elders to him, and they spoke quietly among themselves. Cougar stretched his legs and back and tried not to think about the thirst he felt.

"What did you say to them?" Morning Butterfly asked.

"That this is not the time for old men to wear out their voices telling us things we already know."

She turned toward him, revealing the slightest smile. "What things?"

"The paths the Holy People compel us to walk. In the stories of our beginning, what we call our Emergence, are the lessons for how we should live our lives. Those things are important, and no Navajo child can become an adult before learning the Rainbow Way, but sometimes old people lose themselves in the past."

Her smile broadened and for the first time since reaching the village, she didn't look burdened.

"It is the same with our old ones," she admitted. "They love to talk about the different kachinas, how they came into being, and what befalls those who displease them. When I was a child, the stories fascinated me, but now . . ."

"You want to tell the old people you have taken those things into your heart and do not need the lesson again."

"Yes." Her laughter was a beautiful thing, a warm spring breeze. Then she indicated the conferring men. "This will take a long time?"

"I am afraid it will."

"Then—Cougar, I spent last night in a Navajo village surrounded by Navajo. I did not think that would matter, but I have become a child who wishes to learn everything about your people."

The urge to embrace her washed over him, but even if they had been alone, he wasn't sure she would want his touch.

"There is not time," he pointed out.

"I know. But, please, tell me about the Way Of The Rainbow. Why is walking its path so important?"

Wondering if she had any idea how complicated her question was, he nevertheless went deep inside himself for an explanation she could take home with her.

"The right way is narrow," he began, "and it is all too easy to stray from it. But no one wishes it was different."

"Why not?"

"The path is there," he said, not sure that meant anything to her. "If you walk where you have never gone before, if the day is new and there has never been one like it, you feel safer if others have been on that journey before, do you not?"

"Yes."

"And if you know how to stay on that path and not stumble off into the darkness, you feel safe, do you not?"

"Yes."

"That is how it is for us. *Chindi* are fearsome things, the ghosts of Earth Surface dead. Even if the person was good and gentle, his *chindi* can be evil. That's why we want nothing to do with someone who has just died, and why, if he dies inside a hogan, the body must be removed through a hole broken in the north wall, which is the direction of evil, and the hogan burned. But we know how to protect ourselves from *chindi*. We may not always do it the right way, but we know and that brings us comfort."

"What can you do?"

He patted the small medicine bag he carried around his neck and explained that it contained a mix made from the gall bladders of mountain lions, bears, eagles, and skunks, which protected him from *chindi* poison.

"That is only a small part of the path we walk," he explained. "Our ceremonies are times of complex rituals and chants. We have ceremonies before a child is born, then take care to place a newborn at its mother's left side and anoint its head with corn pollen. A father sings a special chant as he makes the cradle board, and when the child has reached his seventh year, he becomes an adult through the Yeibichai ceremony. If such things are done as they should be, there is little to fear."

"But if your *chindi* are angered—"

"Then the person who has earned their wrath will go to a singer, who will perform rites to protect him; most powerful is a dry painting that takes a long time to make and may cost a great deal. Each painting is destroyed as soon as it has been created." He frowned, then said, "I am sorry I cannot show you the symbols used to banish *chindi*."

"Why not?"

"Because I was stalked by a wolf-*chindi* and still may be a target. I do not want to anger him or make him stronger."

"You were stalked . . ."

"Yes," he said simply. "Today I will not speak more of it with you."

She nodded. Then, as the old men's conversation increased in intensity, she stared intently into Cougar's eyes. "The padre will never understand what you and I have shared."

"I know."

"I will never understand why he and those of his religion believe there is only one way."

He wanted to tell her how much it meant to have her care about his people's beliefs, but his concentration was fading, floating . . .

From where he sat, he could see as far as he could run in a long day. The land included depressions deep enough to shelter any number of creatures, twists and turns in the earth, but the horizon, although hazy, was well known to him. A few clouds rode in the sky; not strong enough to support rain, they were whimsical things that gathered and then fell apart. The elders' voices were like distant drumbeats, part of his being, and yet they did not command his attention.

When he'd first known he'd marry Sweet Water, the same thing had happened. He'd mentioned the experience to his uncle, who was of his mother's clan and thus bore much of the responsibility of guiding him to adulthood, and his uncle had nodded and smiled.

"A man's heart is not his to control," he'd told him. "Once

a woman touches it, it becomes like a bird, flying this way and that in the wind."

It couldn't be happening again. It couldn't!

"It is my turn, Grandfather."

Drums No More folded his arms across his chest, his stump tucked under a bony elbow. The meeting among the elders had finally come to an end, and in his long-winded way, Drums No More had been explaining their decisions to the others. Much as the elders wanted the wisdom of the Blessing Way ceremony, he'd told them, the soldiers might come while they were in the middle of it, forever marring what was sacred. When he announced it was time to discuss Blue Swallow's suggestion, Cougar rose.

"You have already spoken, Grandson," Drums No More pointed out. "We gave your words weight and will continue to do so."

"I am grateful for that, but the words I need to say are new ones. I will speak in both Navajo and Hopi so Morning Butterfly can understand."

At length, Drums No More nodded.

"I have been here since early morning," Cougar began. "I have listened and spoken, and told Morning Butterfly what was happening." He pointed toward the distant clouds. "They called to me, commanded me to look deep into them. I saw countless horses. They gave my heart strength and I knew I had done right by bringing them here. But then the spirit-horses faded and were replaced by . . ."

Speaking first in Navajo and then Hopi wasn't easy, but one look at the expression in Morning Butterfly's eyes told him he was doing the right thing.

"The cloud-horses became a wolf."

Gasps followed that; even Morning Butterfly looked alarmed.

"It was not an earth-wolf but born of the *chindi.*"

"You are sure?" Drums No More asked.

"Yes." He forced the word through his tight throat. "Some

of you know that when I returned from Oraibi after Blue Corn Eater's death, I was followed by a *chindi*-wolf."

More gasps accompanied by low muttering briefly distracted him from the haunting image.

"I do not fear the *chindi*-wolf; if it wishes me harm, so be it, but I do not believe that is why the ghost showed itself in the clouds."

He waited, wanted someone to question him, but no one did.

"My vision is a message from the gods. The *chindi*-wolf was not alone. The Hero Twins were also there, speaking to me with their presence. Making me remember that it was they who saved our ancestors from the Naye'i."

His fellow villagers silently accepted the explanation, but Morning Butterfly asked to be told about both the Hero Twins and Naye'i who were alien to her.

Long before his people came to Dinehtah, they'd scattered over the land in an attempt to escape the Naye'i monsters. They carried with them a small turquoise image of a woman which became Estanatlehi, Changing Woman, and a white shell that became Yolkai Estan, White Shell Woman. The two bore twin boys who in four days grew to the size of twelve-year-olds. Compelled to travel, the boys passed through the country of the cactus and into the land of rising sands. There they encountered a number of monsters, which they appeased by chanting sacred formulas. Finally they reached Tsohanoai, who held the sun.

Tsohanoai put the twins through a series of tests, which they passed. Then Tsohanoai showed them how to defeat the remaining Naye'i by using lightning bolts as weapons. Each fierce battle caused a great deal of blood to flow, but finally Bear that Pursues, Traveling Stone, White Under the Rock, Black Under the Rock, and even Sa, which was Old Age, were destroyed.

"This is what I say." Cougar now addressed everyone. "I do not have the strength of the Twins but neither are the Spanish as powerful as the Naye'i. A *chindi*-wolf appeared before me and yet did not kill me. I now believe that is because my reason for being born is not over. The first time I spoke to the captain, I believed in what I was doing. I was wrong to have run away. I must return, must make them so greedy for what they call riches that they will leave on their own and leave all Indians safe."

"I ask for strength in this," he said, addressing Storm Wind, who was the most respected shaman and whose beautiful Enemyway dry paintings had cured uncounted sicknesses. "I ask you to create a Slayer of Enemy Gods painting for me so that when I look into the eyes of the captain, I will not falter and he will believe my lies."

"That was my thought even before you asked," Storm Wind. "This I will willingly do, but first I want you to look deep into your heart."

"I already have."

"But is your heart clear?"

"Clear?"

"Unencumbered by a man's thought." Storm Wind indicated Morning Butterfly. "My son, it is good that a woman has touched your life, but she is not Navajo. A woman can make a man's thoughts turn to other things. If that has happened to you, you may be in danger."

What Cougar felt for Morning Butterfly was new and untested, like a morning mist that might not survive the day. Surely he could walk through the mist and into the sunlight. That's what he told Storm Wind and the others.

"A wise answer," Storm Wind said. "One which makes me proud. Yes, Cougar, it would please me to create a Slayer of Enemy Gods painting for you so the soldiers will see you as we want them to."

As Storm Wind, Drums No More, and other elders retired to begin their preparations, Blue Swallow walked over and sat beside Cougar. When his cousin thrust out his hand, Cougar grasped it.

"I did not say what I did because I wanted you to be the only one to take up a weapon," Blue Swallow said. "What I wish is the soldiers' deaths, all of them."

"So do I, but Morning Butterfly is right. If we kill these,

then others, filled with the need for vengeance, will come. The first path I walked around them must be walked again."

Although he still clasped Blue Swallow's hand, he remained aware of the warmth at his side and admitted that Storm Wind was right; Morning Butterfly had touched his heart.

16

Cougar sat cross legged in Storm Wind's crowded, sage-scented hogan along with the tribe's elders—and Morning Butterfly. Cougar had been relieved when the old shaman had guided her inside so she could witness the sacred ceremony. Her eyes had filled with fear when she'd realized he intended to again try to convince Captain Lopez and the soldiers to leave Oraibi in search of emeralds, but she hadn't argued with him. He was grateful, because he couldn't do it without her.

Creating the dry painting took the better part of the day. Although Storm Wind asked another man to help him lay out the bed of clean sand that formed the painting's base, from then on, he worked alone. The white, red, yellow, black, and blue powders were made from ground sandstone, charcoal, gypsum, and ocher, and Storm Wind shaped them into the familiar Slayer of Enemy Gods, a war deity with lightning bolt weapons. Once the painting was completed, Cougar sat on it while the shaman shook his sacred rattle, prayed, and chanted at length. Following that, Storm Wind destroyed his creation.

Seated on the painting, embraced by his people's prayers for his success, Cougar let go of his physical body and went back through the ages to when the Hero Twin known as Monster Slayer confronted Tsetahotsiltali, He Who Kicks People Down the Cliff. The Hero Twin killed the Naye'i by repeatedly striking him over the eyes with his great stone knife. Nothing in life happened without meaning; no dream was simply a collection of random thoughts. If the Hero Twin had destroyed his enemy with a knife, Cougar would carry a knife when he confronted the captain.

He had been blessed and made strong by cloud-visions, the shaman's ceremony, and his own belief in his courage. He would not, could not fail, because the alternative might be that the soldiers would attack his people's village and do to them what had been done to the Keres at Acoma. With Morning Butterfly there to supply the words he lacked—

"Wait. I have something to say before my grandson leaves," Drums No More announced, his firm tone pulling Cougar into the present. "I tried to push my concerns aside and tell my heart that what just took place will be enough and no harm can come to someone I love, but our enemies are strong, maybe as powerful as those the Hero Twins confronted. And Cougar was not born of Changing Woman or White Shell Woman. He is a man, not a god."

Cougar whispered a translation for Morning Butterfly.

"My words are not meant to make less of Cougar's courage," the lean, sun-dried Navajo continued. "I have always been proud of him, no more than I am at this moment, but—but that does not silence an old man's fear that he may never see his grandson again, because our enemies have killed a warrior."

"You say my ceremony was not enough?" Storm Wind challenged.

"I say your skills were learned during a time which no longer exists. We are not just Navajo here; there is a Hopi among us, one with a pure heart, yes, but still her presence changes things . . . just as this new enemy does."

Once again, Cougar helped Morning Butterfly understand. When he mentioned her possible impact on the ceremony, she responded with a somber nod.

"These are my thoughts," Drums No More continued. "My beliefs. I spread them before you so each can take them and look at them.

"Once before, my grandson went to the soldiers and they made him their prisoner. Instead of heeding his words and going to the great canyon, our enemy is still here. What I ask myself is what must be different this time so we will be rid of them."

Cougar had asked himself the same question, then turned from it as he buried himself in ceremony and prayer.

Drums No More lifted his mutilated hand over his head. "Look at this, not as something you have seen all your lives but as a Spanish soldier would. What does it say to you?"

At first no one answered. Then, as what his grandfather was getting at made itself clear to him, Cougar spoke. With all his heart he wished he didn't have to.

"A soldier would see a man who cannot fight."

"Yes." Drums No More's voice was filled with resignation.

"A Navajo who has reason to fear the Spanish."

"Yes."

"Perhaps even a man too afraid for anything except the truth."

"Yes."

"Do you think I want him to travel with us?" Cougar asked Morning Butterfly when, finally, they stood in sunlight. "He has lived all his life hating the Spanish and should not have to look into the eyes of men like those who hacked off his hand. That is why I want the Spanish gone, so his memories can go back to their sleeping place."

"I understand." She stood across from him, her arms

hanging at her sides, her hair still flowing over her shoulders as it had when the day began.

"You understand?" he repeated in surprise.

"Drums No More's fears are the same as One Hand's."

"No! My grandfather walks with courage. However, his words have merit because the Spanish do not know the truth of him."

Morning Butterfly continued to look doubtful, but she didn't argue with him. Instead, she questioned his decision to return on horseback.

"I know the journey will take much less time that way, and I do not want to see your grandfather walk that far, but the soldiers will be angry when you approach riding what was theirs."

"Listen to me and tell me if you believe my thoughts have wisdom," he said. The soon-to-be-sleeping sun had spread red lights over her hair, making him wish he could touch it. "When we reach Oraibi, you will tell the captain I took you captive, but you convinced me to free you and try to win favor by returning three of their horses and promising to tell them where the emeralds came from."

"I was not your captive."

"You and I know that, but the captain does not. He will trust you."

Running her fingers through her hair, she frowned. "I should have given my actions more thought before I came looking for you," she admitted. "Only once I was underway did I ask myself how I was going to explain my long absence."

"I know you do not want to lie, and if I could think of another way, I would not ask it of you. I would not—" giving into impulse, he brushed a strand off her neck—"would not have you standing at my side when I tell my own lies to the captain."

"I am not afraid."

"No?"

She shook her head, hesitantly it seemed, then began to

nod. "You say lies are not the Hopi way and you are right, so I will tell you the truth. What I want is to spread corn on the roof of my family's pueblo so it will dry, nothing else, but I fear there will not be enough corn to see us through the winter. More than that, the padre says our beliefs are the work of the Catholic devil and we will spend eternity burning in his hell. If the Hopi are ever going to go back to the life they once knew, the newcomers must go away."

So she'd been forced into her role just as he had. That bound them together in a way that would last as long as they lived and surely was why he ran his fingers over her throat.

"I stand in awe of your courage, Morning Butterfly."

"Will he follow you?" she asked Cougar, who'd helped her onto the mare he'd chosen for her to ride before mounting himself, his easy leap filled with confidence. "My horse, I mean. When yours walks, mine will do the same?"

"If you tell him to."

She looked at the twitching ears ahead of her, then started when the creature shook its head to dislodge a fly.

"How do I do that?"

"You did not watch the way the soldiers controlled their horses? I cannot believe you were not curious."

"I was, but I tried to stay as far from the soldiers as possible."

His features became grim at that, but he didn't say anything, only waited as Drums No More walked his horse over to a rock and used that to help him climb onto the animal's back.

Cougar could have boosted his grandfather up, but Morning Butterfly guessed he hadn't wanted to draw attention to Drums No More's deformity. She and the other members of her family did the same around One Hand, quietly assisting with what he couldn't accomplish on his own but leaving him with as much of his dignity as possible.

"I wish Drums No More and I could share our thoughts,"

she told Cougar. "I would like to learn from his wisdom, to know what his life is like."

"He is not a man who easily opens himself to others." Cougar said something to his grandfather, then nodded at the response. "He is ready."

"Not afraid?" she asked.

Cougar started to shake his head, then paused. "If he is, he keeps his fear to himself. Let him walk his way, Morning Butterfly. It has gotten him through his life."

Her people called the Navajo simple, but there was nothing simple about either Drums No More or Cougar, especially Cougar. As they set off, accompanied by waves from what looked like the entire tribe, she fixed her gaze on the broad, naked back ahead of her, remembered the feel of Cougar's hand on her throat as he brushed back her hair. By imitating what Cougar and Drums No More did, she managed to get her horse to start walking, and although she didn't think she'd ever get used to the uneven rocking motion, remaining on horseback wouldn't take all of her concentration. The rest went to Cougar—Cougar, who had tucked a knife under his kilt and, like his grandfather, carried a pouch filled with green stones.

Maybe he'd taken the burden of keeping the soldiers away from his village onto his shoulders because risking his life was easier than facing a conflict between the young and old that might tear his tribe apart. If that was so, he was truly a brave man.

Maybe more.

Maybe he was a man she could love.

On horseback, with Cougar setting a hard pace, the distance from the Navajo village to Oraibi was traveled in less time than it took the sun to complete a single journey. They'd spoken little during the trip, each lost in his or her own thoughts. When Oraibi came into view, they stopped for a bite of food and a drink of water for themselves and their horses. Then, still silent, they plunged ahead.

Pablo announced their arrival to Captain Lopez. The captain had been watching the padre attempt to show a group of children the proper demeanor for prayer. The soldier told his superior that two Navajo men and a Hopi woman were riding toward Oraibi, and Lopez grunted in surprise. Angelico, on his knees, still forcing a Hopi child to kneel, looked up and insisted, "In the name of God Almighty, there will be no killing today!" He asked Pablo, "They are not armed, are they?"

"I saw no weapons, Padre," the soldier answered.

"See! They come in peace and to ask the Lord's forgiveness."

There were times when the padre's thinking left Lopez shaking his head in disbelief. Biting back a criticism, he asked Pablo how he could be sure the woman was Hopi.

"Because it is the one who cared for me when the Navajo tried to kill me."

"Morning Butterfly?" the padre and Lopez exclaimed in unison.

Angelico was the first to regain his composure. He explained that because he hadn't seen her for several days, he'd been afraid she was sick. Lopez didn't buy it for an instant. Why Angelico hadn't gone up to Oraibi to search for her, he didn't know, but he had his suspicions.

Lopez studied the newcomers as he neared them, Angelico at his heels. He couldn't be sure, of course, since all savages looked the same, but he suspected that the warrior riding beside Morning Butterfly was the self-same one who'd earlier tried to buy his favor with emeralds. Morning Butterfly herself looked about to jump out of her skin, her eyes flashing from him to Angelico, then back to him again. As for the old man . . .

"I beg you," Morning Butterfly said once they were close enough that a decent conversation was possible, "do not kill us before you have heard us out."

Lopez laughed. "If I order my men to kill you now, I can devote myself to more important matters."

She blinked rapidly several times, but to her credit, she

didn't try to run—not that he had any intention of shooting her until he had learned all she knew of the Navajo village.

"Where have you been?" he demanded.

She told him, her words rushed and awkward. Although he had to struggle to concentrate on what she was saying instead of the way her skirt slid up her thigh when she dismounted, he realized that she wanted him to believe she'd been a captive of the Navajo.

He might have swallowed her story—except she and Cougar occasionally spoke to each other in Hopi and she even seemed to want to argue with him—hardly something a terrified captive would do. He wondered if the padre had caught on or was so besotted with her that he'd believe anything she said.

"Enough!" he exclaimed when, for the second time, she insisted that Navajo hadn't wanted to incur his wrath by stealing horses. "If the Navajo were truly quaking in fear, they would have already brought the animals back. Ask them, where are the Crown's horses?"

He assumed that was what she was doing during the long conversation she carried on with the two men. He'd be a fool to trust Cougar, who didn't seem to give a damn whether he lived or died and undoubtedly had a weapon hidden on him, but what was the old man doing here? Maybe he was some kind of spiritual leader. If that was the case, Lopez thought with a rueful smile, it was a shame he and the padre couldn't communicate, because they might kill each other during the attempt at conversion.

"Navajo legends foretold of the time when horses would come to them," Morning Butterfly finally told him. "They believe the animals are gifts from their gods."

"You cannot be serious! All right, all right," he said, calming himself. "So—so why are they apologizing?"

"Because the legends did not foretell the coming of the Spanish. They do not know which way to walk."

The whole thing was nonsense! "I will tell them which way to walk; straight into hell."

"Captain," Angelico interjected, nodding at Pablo for reinforcement, "that is for the Lord to decide, not man. Only He determines whether a person has lived a godless life."

"Will you be still! I swear, I cannot say a word without you spouting scripture."

Pablo positioned himself between the two men. Not for the first time, Lopez acknowledged the padre's hold over his deeply religious troops. "Look, Morning Butterfly," the captain said. "I want you to ask these braves one question and one question only. Are they going to return the Crown's horses, or am I going to have to go after them?"

If she had any reaction, she kept it to herself—hardly for the first time since the conversation began. He assumed she was posing the question to the two, because the old man took an abrupt backward step, then looked around as if seeking an escape route. Cougar, however, remained impassive, and his response was short and clipped.

"He says the horses must remain with his people as the gods ordained," she said.

"There!" Angelico exclaimed. "That is what my work is all about. You see how misguided they are, how ignorant? The church cannot be built soon enough."

"This is not about that damnable church of yours. It is about horses. Horses!" *That and the fact that I'll have the devil's own time accounting to the Crown and my father-in-law if I don't get the nags back.*

He supposed he could have given Cougar one last chance to change his mind, a generous offer that would have sat well with the padre, but it was getting dark and he was hungry—and for more than just food.

"Pablo," he said, "I place these three under arrest."

Pablo aimed his musket at Cougar's chest. The Navajo stepped back, his hand sliding to his waist. In response, Lopez lifted his own weapon, but instead of drilling a hole through the savage the way he wanted, he aimed at Morning Butterfly. Cougar stared defiantly at him, then, slowly, let his hand drop.

"So, you are not as ignorant as certain people would have me believe. Pablo, throw a rope over him."

"But—"

"Now! Believe me, he will not do anything that might endanger her life."

Despite his confident words, Lopez breathed a sigh of relief once Pablo had lashed Cougar's hands behind him and taken away his crude knife. The savage continued to glare at Lopez and although helpless, he looked dangerous, wild.

"Now the old man," Lopez ordered.

"Captain Lopez, I must protest. These people came in peace."

"Go build your church, Padre. Or if you are so inclined, baptize more of the savages. I am certain they will see the light once they feel the weight of your hand on their heads."

"You will regret this!'

"Padre, what we have to say to each other is not fit for a public airing."

"No," Angelico agreed. "It is not."

Pablo had been shuffling from one foot to the other during the exchange, but when Lopez jerked his head at him, the young man hurried over to the old Navajo and grabbed the arm that had been angled behind his back. As the end of that arm came into view, Lopez and Fray Angelico sucked in their breaths.

"By all that is holy," Angelico began, "what—"

"He was at Acoma," Lopez interrupted. Striding forward, he jerked the ruined arm of Pablo's grip and held what was left up to the dying light. "Tell me, old man, when you heard the others scream, did you scream too?"

Although he trembled slightly, the old man gave no other indication he'd heard a word, and Lopez belatedly remembered the language barrier. Still gripping the disgusting stump, he hauled the Navajo over to Morning Butterfly. Out of the corner of his eye, he saw Cougar's chest expand, his leg muscles contract. By his grandfather's memory, if Pablo hadn't done an inadequate job of securing him—

"You heard me." He addressed Morning Butterfly. "You know what I asked him. I do not care what you have to do, but I demand an answer."

Morning Butterfly had heard Fray Angelico speak of how he couldn't tolerate her people's slow understanding of the word of God. When he did, his voice rang with an emotion hot as the hottest summer sun. This, she believed, was hatred, and she'd never wanted to feel anything like that herself. Now, as she looked up at Captain Lopez, she wondered if she might catch fire from the heat of her own emotion.

"Do not do this," she warned, defiance boiling out of her. "Do not take him back to that time and place."

"I warn you, do not test my patience. Ask him!"

"Morning Butterfly," Cougar hissed in Hopi.

She told him what Lopez had said.

Cougar nearly growled. "Say my grandfather prayed to die and has lived in that place they call hell from that day on."

"What?"

"Do it! Trust me."

Trust me. Despite everything that was happening, his words burrowed deep inside her. Before Lopez could demand to be told what they'd been talking about, she said Cougar had insisted on an explanation. That seemed to please the captain, who repeated his demand that she probe into Drums No More's past.

"His name is Drums No More because he was once a Navajo singer but is no longer able to make a drum sing in time with his words," she said after Cougar fed her the words. "He was a young man, not much more than a youth, who had gone to Acoma to trade when the Spanish arrived."

"Not just any Spanish, Morning Butterfly," the captain corrected. "My grandfather."

"Yes, I know. Soldiers threw him to the ground and placed his hand on a rock," she continued. A wave of nausea momentarily rendered her speechless. "He tried to tell the soldiers he was not their enemy, but they did not listen. When the axe came down, he prayed to die and then he fainted."

Glancing at Drums No More, she saw that his remaining fingers had turned white around the knuckles. Maybe he didn't understand her words, but he had to know what she was talking about, had to be reliving the nightmare. Fighting the horror emanating from him, she took a calming breath. "When he woke up, he prayed it had been a nightmare because he could not bear the truth."

Captain Lopez's lips twitched. "What has it been like since then for him?" he prompted as he fingered Cougar's knife.

"Why are you asking this?"

"You are not a military man, Morning Butterfly, so you cannot understand how fear weakens the enemy. Ask him, damn it!"

Hatred nearly clamping her throat shut, she told Cougar and Drums No More what she had to. Speaking in short, harsh bursts, Drums No More said something in Navajo. Although she couldn't understand the words, she felt his tension.

"Listen to me," Cougar said with his eyes fixed on Drums No More, his words slapping at her raw emotions. "If I live, I will avenge my grandfather."

"Cougar, please, your fury imperils us all."

"And you feel no hate?" he asked as Drums No More's jaw clenched and his nostrils flared. "Can you tell me that and still speak the truth?"

She couldn't and he knew it, she realized, feeling more vulnerable than she had in her entire life.

"What do I say to the captain's question?" she forced herself to ask.

Cougar expelled a harsh breath that reminded her of the sound his namesake made after a kill. If he felt the loss of his weapon, he gave no indication. "Tell him—tell him Drums No More often consults the shamans and has them perform peace-thought ceremonies for him, but they do no good."

"Cougar!" Drums No More hissed. Then he said something that Cougar didn't translate.

"Is that true?" Morning Butterfly asked. "The shamans are of no help to him?"

"No. But it would please the captain and padre to hear that—and today I will please them. Tomorrow . . ." His chest expanded as he tested his bonds. "Tomorrow I will have my revenge."

I pray for that.

As she relayed Cougar's words to the captain, she felt herself draw into a tight, small ball. If only she could run from here! Instead, she was forced to remain where she was as Lopez told the padre to direct some of his workers to build a fire. Once the flames reached for the emerging stars, he would have her, Cougar, and Drums No More brought to it.

Cougar remained impassive, but Drums No More tried to shrink away from their captor. When Captain Lopez pointed his sword at Drums No More's throat, the old man reached inside his shirt and withdrew the emerald-filled bag. After a short hesitation, Lopez accepted the gift and opened it. His eyes narrowed, and he ordered Pablo to search Cougar.

"What is this?" he demanded after Pablo handed him the second bag. "Morning Butterfly, they will tell you everything, understand?"

The hate-heat that had threatened to consume her earlier had begun to fade. Now it returned, but she fought it just as she fought the need to look at Cougar.

"And when you have your answer, what will happen to them?"

He chuckled, then glanced at the padre as if expecting him to see the same humor in the situation. When he received no response, he shook his head.

"Good."

"Cougar, how can you say that?" Morning Butterfly demanded. No matter how much she tried to banish the image, she saw the three of them as hunted deer. Maybe the arrows had already been launched.

"In his eyes, I was dead the moment I rode into sight of him."

Her head screamed in pain that became nearly unbearable when she looked at the old man sitting on the ground, his ruined arm cradled in his lap. She'd freed Cougar once and given him back his life, but tonight she had no knife.

Captain Lopez stood behind her with his hands on her shoulders. His breath smelled of the roasted sheep he'd just eaten. She desperately needed to say more to Cougar, but Captain Lopez was an impatient man and she'd do whatever she needed to keep him from killing Cougar and Drums No More.

"Tell the captain that the great canyon where the emeralds came from is sacred to the Navajo and to speak of it in certain ways may bring danger," Cougar said, "but I will do so if he promises to set my grandfather free."

"When he knows where to look, he will kill you."

"Maybe."

17

After what seemed a lifetime, Captain Lopez told Morning Butterfly that he had no further use for her. Although Cougar felt a wrenching loss as she slowly walked away, looking over her shoulder at him, he also breathed a sigh of relief.

Once she was out of earshot, Captain Lopez spat a few words at Pablo, glared a death-making stare at Cougar, and hurried away. Cougar's stomach growled and his shoulders ached from the unnatural position they'd been forced into, but his concern for his grandfather made it possible for him to ignore his discomfort.

Fray Angelico and Pablo were speaking, or rather the padre's voice droned on and on in what Cougar took to be a prayer as the soldier knelt before him with his face uplifted. Cougar remembered when the padre had placed his hand on his head and said the words that meant he'd been baptized. What was taking place between these two was no more important to him.

"They are done with us," Drums No More whispered.

"Maybe."

"Through the Hopi woman, you told them where to find emeralds, and they have no more use for us."

"You are wrong. Until we have guided them—"

"Do not say that again. It does not make a lie of the possibility that they will kill us now."

The soldier had driven a stake into the ground and tied Cougar to it, but he'd left Drums No More free. Hopefully, as intended, the Spanish thought he was too undone by fear to raise his single hand against them, but although his grandfather gave the appearance of someone on the verge of tears, Cougar knew better. Still, if Morning Butterfly was right and Drums No More had hidden his true emotions all these years, having to see, hear, and smell the Spanish might have brought back the nightmare.

"You are all right?" Cougar whispered.

"All right? They are poisonous lizards and bear dung, something to be avoided."

"Grandfather, I love your words. They speak the truth."

"More truth than you did."

"Do you think I should have done otherwise? Did you want me to tell them there are no emeralds at the great canyon? That they risk their lives by looking for them? That it is both sacred and dangerous and that once there, you and I can escape and hide?"

"No." Drums No More sighed. "You did what you had to. As for whether your plan will work . . ."

"I know." How long would the padre continue to pray? And when he'd finished and gone away, would the soldier then run his sword through him and his grandfather? Was that what the captain had ordered him to do? "They believe we are helpless. Defeated."

"Yes, they do."

"Is that your belief as well?"

Drums No More didn't immediately answer. Then: "I have lived a long life, watched my children grow up and become mothers and fathers. A man could not ask for more."

"You could have had both hands."

"A wise man does not pray for what will never be. Our

fate is in the hands of a man we both hate." Then, to Cougar's surprise, his grandfather chuckled. "I was going to prepare myself for death with prayer. Instead, I will think of when the Hero Twins took the multi-colored hoops their father Sun God had given them back to their mother Changing Woman. She blessed them and sent them in the earth's directions. After that, thunder was heard, the sky grew dark, and a great white cloud descended. That was followed by whirlwinds that uprooted trees and tossed great rocks around. The storm killed many Naye'i and created the great canyon. Perhaps when the soldiers go to it, Sun God and Changing Woman will see them as Naye'i and destroy them."

The dream had always been the same. His first child had just come into the world and he was reaching for it when, to his horror, he discovered he had no hand with which to cradle the infant. As the newborn fell to the earth, blood spurted from his ruined wrist and his mouth filled with the need to scream. Something, however, stopped him from giving the cry freedom—he'd always silenced it, the effort exhausting him.

The soldier who'd tied his grandson to the stake stood before Drums No More, the man's stench pulling Drums No More out of the nightmare.

The soldier, who had left and then returned, walking alone and like one who does not wish to be seen, now held his sword awkwardly in both hands, firelight glinting off the shining surface. He kept glancing in the direction the captain had gone, and he muttered to himself, the unintelligible words reminding Drums No More of the padre's earlier prayer. Drums No More didn't know or care what the soldier was thinking; nothing mattered except the deadly weapon and the one that had come before it so many years before.

Cougar's large black eyes burned into his grandfather, searching for the truth of his heart, but Drums No More didn't return his grandson's gaze because he was afraid the courageous young man would see his fear.

He forced himself to concentrate on his enemy. The man's

awful smell became even stronger, pungent and hot like a horse after a long run.

Up, up went the sword, its strength all-consuming, and Drums No More knew—as he'd known on the day they hacked off his hand—that he was about to die. He didn't fear death, sometimes cried out for it. Would welcome it.

But it wasn't his grandson's time.

The soldier's eyes were an agony of determination, his prayer going on and on.

"No!"

The earth was strength and life, Mother and Father. Everything. It flowed through Drums No More and became him. Young again, he gathered his legs and charged. His head slammed into his enemy's belly and the man flew back, a surprised grunt his only sound.

Drums No More followed him to the ground, landing on him. The sword flew off into the night and the soldier was scrabbling, reaching. . . .

"No!"

It didn't matter whether the cry came from Drums No More or Cougar. His hand, his one hand, locked around the soldier's hair, yanked his head up and then slammed it down onto the summer-hardened earth. Again and again he pounded until the soldier stopped struggling and blood spurted from his mouth and nose. The blood-smell became Drums No More's thoughts, his reality. He had been made to bleed and now he had returned the deed.

"Grandfather! Free me."

"Madariaga de Oñate" stopped in mid stride, but although he held his breath in an attempt to hear better, he couldn't say what had caught his attention. A quick prayer wouldn't hurt—not that he hadn't already asked God on numerous occasions to see him safely through the night, or day.

He'd barely begun to cross himself when he heard what sounded like a sigh. Quite possibly one of his companions had chosen a nearby spot to take one of the native women . . . and yet—

The sigh—or whatever it was—was repeated. Drawing his sword, Oñate inched his way forward. Although he still strained to hear, now there was nothing except the usual night sounds—sounds he'd become accustomed to while working on the farms of wealthy New Spain landowners. Unfortunately, familiarity with what crawled, walked, or flew at night wasn't enough to make him comfortable, not with so many savages about.

Cursing the sound his well-used boots made, he slipped closer until firelight told him what he didn't want to know. The Navajo was no longer tethered to the stake. Beyond, a dark shape lay unmoving on the ground.

Instead of hurrying toward what he feared was Pablo's lifeless body, Oñate spun and raced for Fray Angelico's tent. It wasn't until he'd burst into it that he asked himself why he hadn't gone looking for his captain. The answer was simple. He'd do everything he could to avoid his superior officer.

"He is dead!" he blurted. "Pablo. The Navajo killed him."

Angelico, who'd already gotten to his feet, froze. "What?"

Please, Padre, I beg of you, come with me." Madariaga dropped to his knees and clutched the hem of Angelico's robe. "Wrap me in God's goodness. Ask Him to take pity on me so that my—my captain . . ."

His words fell away, but not before they'd echoed back at him and revealed him as the coward he was.

"I am ashamed," he managed. "Pablo may yet be alive, but did I go to comfort and protect him?"

To his everlasting relief, he felt the padre's warm hand on his head. "Listen to me, my son," Fray Angelico said softly. "Do not chastise yourself for your actions. The devil's influence here is great; no mortal can attempt to vanquish him."

"My friend—"

"Is in the Lord's hands. My son, we will pray for his soul and then do what we must."

Banished to Oraibi, Morning Butterfly eagerly returned her family's welcoming hugs, but even as she told them about her trip to the Navajo village and why she'd returned with two Navajo, her thoughts and heart remained far below, with Cougar.

Was he dead?

Singer Of Songs had once again gone to spend the night with the captain. Since Morning Butterfly had left, her younger sister hadn't once returned to her pueblo until nearly morning, and when she did, all she wanted to do was sleep. Her chores had gone undone, not that anyone blamed her. Instead, they'd prayed for her, just as they'd prayed for Morning Butterfly.

Her mother begged her to never again go to the Navajo village, but her father, brothers, and sisters, and even One Hand wanted to know what she'd seen and learned. She tried to satisfy their curiosity, taking time to share what Cougar had told her about Navajo beliefs and ceremonies, but the whole time she heard his voice inside her, and she prayed for him.

Her youngest brother fell asleep first. Then her mother started to snore and even her father, who had turned more and more to talking as his physical ability lessened, stumbled off to his sleeping mat. Finally it was just her and One Hand in the faint glow of what remained of the cooking fire.

"If you do not want this question, tell me and I will be silent," she said. "But when I was with the Navajo, I met a man like you."

"Like me?"

"His hand had been hacked off."

"Atch!"

She reached out to wrap her arms around him, but he pulled into himself and the shadows, distancing himself from her. Still, she continued. "Do you remember a Navajo—"

"I do not think of that time. You know that."

Maybe not during your waking moments, but at night . . .
"He is now Drums No More, and I do not remember what he was called before that. His grandson is the one who took the horses, the one I freed earlier."

If anything, One Hand seemed even further away than he'd been a moment before. "The grandson is a brave man."

"Yes, he is." *Please live, Cougar. Please! I should not have left*—"One Hand, I thought—I thought that if you met someone who had survived what you did, that you two could learn from each other."

He expelled his breath in a harsh gasp. "I do not live in the past! And if he does, he is a fool!"

"I meant no harm. I only—"

"Morning Butterfly, my heart continues to beat because I turned that time into darkness. It has died inside me."

"Has it?"

Again she heard his breathing, only he didn't seem so angry any more. Rather, he sounded like a very old man whose lungs have grown weary.

"I will not speak of where my thoughts go when I am asleep," he told her, "because if I do, they may follow me into morning."

"I understand," she whispered, loving him, "but I cannot forget the words you sometimes utter when you dream, or your need to be held."

She'd never thought they'd speak about that and was afraid he'd throw her words back at her or deny the truth of what she'd just said, but he only pulled his stump against his chest and gently massaged it.

"I can walk just one way, Morning Butterfly." His words sounded hollow and lifeless. "The way that keeps me from drowning in darkness, from screaming to the sun. Do not ask me to speak to the Navajo Drums No More. Do not."

One Hand's plea still echoed inside Morning Butterfly when the endless, sleepless night came to an end. Her sister hadn't returned, and between worrying about her and the awful question of whether Cougar and Drums No More were alive or if Cougar had wanted her near him as he died, she'd been unable to quiet her mind enough for sleep to invade it.

She'd gone outside and was watching dawn touch the

horizon when she spotted someone walking slowly toward her. Jumping to her feet, she started forward, then, alarmed by her sister's haggard appearance, she stopped.

"Morning Butterfly?" Singer Of Songs said once she was close enough that the sisters could look into each other's eyes. "The captain said you were back. I prayed he spoke the truth."

"He knows you understand Spanish?"

"No. That is the one thing I can keep from him."

Singer Of Songs looked so small. When Morning Butterfly held out her hands, and her sister snuggled against her, she wished with all her heart that she could wrap her in a blanket and carry her into the wilderness.

"You are all right?" she managed around her tears. "He still treats you well?"

"He has not injured me."

Not your body, but what about the rest of you? "I give thanks to Taiowa for that. Sister, I must ask you something. The captain, did he say what happened to the two Navajo?"

Singer Of Songs leaned back slightly in Morning Butterfly's arms. "No. He had fallen alseep when one of his men woke him. They spoke so rapidly that I could not understand. The captain started to leave, then with gestures ordered me to stay. I thought he would return, but he did not."

The knot in the pit of her stomach Morning Butterfly had lived with all night returned, forced her to struggle to speak. "I am afraid he killed them," she admitted. "I tell myself he still has need of them, but . . ."

"They are Navajo, sister. They angered the captain and he hates them."

"I know," she admitted, "but . . ."

"Do not burden your heart with thoughts of the Navajo. The Spanish have changed our lives; the weight of that is enough."

As if to add emphasis to what she'd just said, Singer Of Songs rested her head on Morning Butterfly's shoulder and a shuddering sigh rocked her slight frame.

"What is it?" Morning Butterfly demanded. "You heard something that fills you with fear? Something you are afraid to tell me?"

"Yes, yes." Singer Of Songs began to weep, soundlessly tears dripping down her face.

"What?" *Please, do not let it be about Cougar!*

"I will say this to you first because I pray you will give me the courage I need to share it with the rest of our family." She took a deep breath and the tears stopped. "I . . . I am with child."

"Spider Woman, no!"

"Yes."

Taiowa the Creator had ordered Spider Woman to create trees, bushes, plants, flowers, and other growing things out of the earth. When she'd finished, Spider Woman used more earth to fashion birds and animals, and told them to travel to the four corners of the land to live. Finally, she'd gathered yellow, red, white, and black earth and mixed that with *tuchvala*, the liquid from her mouth, before covering everything with her white-substance cape that was creative wisdom. Then she sang over her creations until the forms became human beings. Spider Woman gave life; she didn't take it away.

"I wish it was otherwise," Morning Butterfly managed. "I prayed your body would not accept a Spanish seed."

"So did I." After another shaky breath, Singer Of Songs pulled free so she could study the rapidly emerging horizon.

"Maybe you are mistaken."

As she feared she would, Singer Of Songs shook her head. "My breasts feel different, heavier. And my stomach does not want to keep food in it."

"No one else knows?"

"No. I tried to tell our mother, but she is so seldom alone. She looks at the Spanish and our father with fear and sorrow in her eyes, but when she speaks, it is about things that do not matter—things that make her laugh. It is easier to tell you first."

Morning Butterfly had been learning how to talk and run when her mother had called her own mother and the other women to their clan together and retired to a small room. Morning Butterfly had heard the women's encouraging voices and her mother's occasional groan, and when, finally, they'd emerged, her mother carried a small bundle which she placed in Morning Butterfly's arms. From that day on, she'd loved her younger sister and taken care of her as best she could. Today, however, there was little she could do.

Maybe one thing.

"This child will be Hopi, not Spanish," she said. "It was conceived on Hopi land and will grow up as a member of our clan. Its father is nothing to it."

"You—you think so?"

"Yes. Listen to me. From the time of the first Hopi, children have always belonged to their mother's clan. When we need guidance, we call on our mother's brother. Our father is but a visitor in his wife's house and his responsibilities are to his sister's children. You will never welcome the captain into where you live, will you?"

"No. Never."

"There." She spoke with confidence, reassuring both herself and her sister. "It is done then. This little one will be yours, mine, our mother's. Hopi."

Singer Of Songs started to cry again, and this time Morning Butterfly cried with her. Then she began to undo her sister's hair. A pregnant Hopi woman had to be careful not to have knots in her hair, so the baby wouldn't be "tied-up."

"After the others awake, we will stand before them and ask them to celebrate the coming of another Hopi child," she said.

"You will stand beside me?"

"I will not have it any other way."

Morning Butterfly and Singer of Songs faced their family as they gathered for breakfast. Although Roadrunner was concerned about how long her daughter could keep her condition from the captain and what he would do when he found out, everyone agreed the child would grow up learning what it meant to be Hopi.

"I am a fortunate man," Deer Ears said. "My sisters' children and my sons have blessed me with grandchildren, and when I die, they will remember me. Now—" he squeezed his youngest child's hand. "Now I wish to live even longer so this one will carry memories of me in his or her heart."

Her eyes damp with fresh tears, Singer Of Songs embraced her father. "Do not speak of your death," she begged. "I want to wrap my child in a blanket you have created just for him or her." She nodded at the small, now seldom-used loom set up in a corner of the room. "Your skill with cotton . . ."

Deer Ears swallowed. "I could make one from wool, warm and soft."

"No. I want nothing from the newcomers covering my child."

Finally, her head pounding from exhaustion and the breath-stealing fears she hadn't been able to share with anyone, Morning Butterfly excused herself. Singer Of Songs asked where she was going, but all she said was that the captain or padre might have need of her and she didn't want to run the risk of a soldier being sent up here.

The day had the calm, dead feeling of late summer. It was as if the land had spent itself weathering endless heat and barely lived while it waited for the relief of winter. She sensed promise in the wonderful scent of ripening corn and the fact that the days weren't quite as long as they'd been before Niman. Yet the time of resting and cold was still a long way off.

Morning Butterfly turned slowly and saw the newborn church. Now that he'd received the signs he'd been waiting for, Fray Angelico hadn't wasted any time starting work. Already a large, square rock wall nearly hip high existed where days before there'd been nothing. The necessary flat rocks hadn't been that hard to gather from the surrounding desert, but before long the Hopi would be forced to travel long distances in order to continue the work.

The newcomers had brought wagons with them, but one was in need of repair and the other was not sturdy enough to bear the weight of more than a single layer of rocks. As a result, the Hopi men were forced to hand-carry many of the stones. In the meantime, their crops were being neglected.

Seeing the emerging church filled Morning Butterfly with the anger Cougar had forced her to acknowledge, and for some time she couldn't make herself look to where Captain Lopez had interrogated her and the two Navajo last night.

The stake Cougar had been tied to was still there—but unused. Her heart thudding, she stumbled closer, then stopped. Strands of rope hung from the stake, the ends ragged, as if they'd been cut. Had Cougar's life ended here? Had the soldiers dragged his body away where wolves and buzzards would find it?

Sick, Morning Butterfly stared at the ground, but she couldn't see any drag marks. Perhaps the earth was too hard to give away its secrets. If there was blood—

Something had stained the ground nearby, something that had given up its moisture to the sun but left behind shadows of what it had once been.

"Cougar," she moaned. "I grieve for you. A Navajo's body may mean nothing to those of his people who continue to live; but—but I cry for you with a Hopi heart."

Shocked at the sound of her voice, she quickly studied her surroundings, but she had the area to herself. As she continued to stare at the dried bloodstain, she felt her heart, her soul close in around itself. Cougar's death was more than she could bear. Still, she vowed to try to find Cougar's body, and his grandfather's, and wrap them in deerskin so the kachinas might understand that these Navajo, who'd died on Hopi land, weren't their enemy.

Her vision blurred and a wave of nausea nearly bent her double.

Captain Lopez's favorite horse stood outside his tent. Saddled and bridled, the gelding had fallen asleep and didn't stir as Morning Butterfly walked toward it. Her fingers clenched and unclenched; if she'd had a knife, she would have ended the captain's life today—or died in the effort. Then, despite her resolve, strength flowed from her legs and left her incapable of movement. How could she possibly look into the eyes of a man capable of murdering a helpless prisoner?

She was still praying for guidance when the tent flap lifted and Captain Lopez and Fray Angelico stepped outside. They were arguing, their hostility so intense that they didn't notice her, and she quickly moved so the horse was between her and them.

"I will not be silent!" Fray Angelico was saying. "By all that is holy, what you are doing is the devil's work. If you believe you can get me to bless—"

"That is the problem, Padre," the captain retorted. "You believe having taken vows puts you above the Crown's influence, but you are wrong. I am the emissary of the State here, not you."

"The king would never condone what—"

"You have sat at a dinner table with the viceroy who is, after all, the king's emissary? Shared wine with him and discussed whether the Crown's current policy regarding the conquered Indians of New Spain is prudent? Until you have, do not pretend you know what is important to His Majesty."

"We—you and I—were sent here to bring God's word to the savages. That and nothing else."

"How wrong you are. Just because that is all you care to concern yourself with . . ."

The thud-thud of approaching horses caused Morning Butterfly to whirl in that direction. Captain Lopez's mount, awake now, walked toward the other animals, revealing her to the captain. She didn't know which she feared more, being seen by Lopez or the sight of six mounted soldiers in full uniform, each leading another animal weighed down with provisions.

"Morning Butterfly, what are you doing here?" the captain demanded.

"I . . ."

"How quickly word travels," he continued, his long, heavily muscled legs erasing the distance between them. "I would be well advised to never forget that. What do you think? Are my men well equipped for a lengthy journey?"

"You . . ." She swallowed and tried again. "You are leaving? All of you?"

His laugh sent shards of pain through her. "Excellent deduction, excellent. And I dare say you and the rest of your people will greet my decision much more positively than the padre does."

Fray Angelico hurried over to the soldiers, but when he tried to take hold of the nearest horse's reins, the animal reared and he scrambled back.

"God will punish you for this!" he bellowed. "Cast off your allegiance to Captain Lopez and surrender yourselves to your Lord. That is the only way you can avoid hell."

"Padre," one of the men said, "we *have* to obey him. He will see us dead if we do not." Eyes wide as if just realizing what he'd said, he now addressed his superior officer. "I meant no disrespect, Captain. We would never—"

"I know, I know," Captain Lopez interrupted. "You are loyal to me, all of you." Sarcasm tinged every word. "Besides, after last night's events, I trust there is nothing any of you want more than to put Oraibi behind you."

He turned from the soldiers. "I am sorry things came to this end, Padre. Truly I am. When I accepted this assignment, I did so believing I would be overseeing the establishment of a mission, but I have no intention of letting the opportunity of a lifetime slip through my fingers. I would think you would understand. My servants are yours to do with as you wish."

With that, he grabbed his horse's reins, pulled the animal around, and mounted. On horseback now, he stared first at Fray Angelico and then at Morning Butterfly.

"For your sake, I hope you told me the truth last night," he practically spat the words at her. "Because if you did not, it will be the end of you. And if you did—" He yanked on the reins, causing the horse to rear.

"And if you did, my men and I are all going to be wealthy!"

* * *

For as long as it took for the hoofbeats to fade into nothing, Morning Butterfly stood motionless. Only when she again heard the wind's whisper did she think to look at Fray Angelico. To her surprise, he didn't appear devastated.

"Where . . ." she began, then faltered.

"To the great canyon to search for emeralds, of course. He insisted he would take you with him, but I reminded him, in his men's presence, that you serve the Lord, that taking you from your duties would earn him God's everlasting wrath, and that only the cruelest of men would leave me without the means to communicate with the neophytes. He is not a particularly religious man, but his men are, and he will only test their loyalty so far."

"Then—then he believed . . ."

"Did he believe the Navajo? It appears he did, although I will go to my death proclaiming him a fool. Wealth or the possibility of wealth does strange things to men, Morning Butterfly. Makes them take leave of their senses. You would have thought he had learned from his grandfather's experiences. However . . ."

A gust of wind sent the tent walls to flapping, the sound both hollow and lonely. "Will he return?" she asked.

"He does not know. I swear, there is nothing he knows any more."

"He believed Cougar—before he killed him."

"Killed—no."

Afraid she hadn't heard right, she begged the padre to explain.

"The savage means that much to you?"

Silent, she returned his gaze.

"My God, the devil is everywhere! His terrible influence—"

"Is Cougar alive?"

"My child, what does it—all right, all right," he said when she lifted her hand as if to silence him. "From what I understand, the Navajo somehow overpowered Pablo and killed him. Although the unfortunate young man was beyond help,

I administered last rites, thus assuring his entrance into the kingdom of God and giving peace to those he served with. The soldiers spent most of the night digging a grave." The padre sighed.

"Where are Cougar and—"

"What do you care? Pablo's head was caved in; he had been beaten to death. The Navajo are gone."

Gone. Alive.

"The way he ranted, I initially believed the captain would head for the Navajo village and burn it to the ground, not that I would have stood in his way. The killing of a soldier of the Crown is an act of war, and war against God and State cannot be tolerated, but—"

She didn't care about that. Nothing mattered except that Cougar was alive.

18

"It was indeed my intention to make the most of the situation which has presented itself," Fray Angelico wrote. "Following your communique, I redoubled my vow to devote myself fully to the natives' spiritual needs and bring them into the Lord's graces. My heart filled with joy at the prospect of being able to save so many souls, and after much thought, I made the decision to build my—" He stopped. He'd had no intention of claiming ownership of the church. After marking out the final word, he continued his letter to the governor.

". . . build the church on virgin land so the savages will understand that their pagan ways must be put behind them. Impressive progress has been made on the structure, in large part because the Hopi, like the children they are, are most eager to begin worshiping the Lord in His house."

It was once again night, the darkness barely kept at bay by the precious candle. Although he was grateful for the illumination, the tallow stench had prompted him to sit outside, and shadows caused by the flickering candle made him wonder what existed beyond the light. All he heard were the ever-present wolves, but did their howls have to echo endlessly?

Did he have to feel so alone?

"However," he continued, "I fear work will not be completed because Captain Lopez has deserted his post, taking with him those under his command and one of the wagons. His leaving was so sudden and unexpected—prompted, I hesitate to say, by greed."

He spent close to a page detailing the latest confrontation with the Navajo, the murder of a soldier by the Navajo prisoners before they fled, and Captain Lopez's subsequent determination to ascertain the truthfulness of what he'd been told about emeralds at the great canyon.

"I do not fully lay blame at the captain's feet," he continued—he wasn't foolish enough to alienate any military men who might read his letter. "It is my unpleasant but holy responsibility to report that this area is rife with the devil's might. Satan is indeed most powerful here, no doubt strengthened and encouraged by the ignorant natives in his grip. There is not space within this letter to detail all proof of the devil's presence, but I trust you are aware of how committed I am to eradicating the dark forces."

He was in danger of allowing the letter to veer off in the direction that caused him untold sleepless nights but was beyond the governor's sphere of influence. He had to control himself.

"Your excellency, I am forced to repeat my insistence that another post be found for Captain Lopez." Yes, that was good; he wasn't suggesting Lopez be stripped of his rank. "Although a man of proven military intelligence, I believe he is, nevertheless, not suited for this particular enterprise. I most humbly request that a replacement be sent posthaste."

His fingers cramped, he set down the pen and shook his hand until circulation was restored. Holding the paper up to the yellow light, he reread what he'd written. He wasn't particularly satisfied with it and wished he could modestly remind the governor of his own commitment and sacrifices. He also worried that Captain Lopez's influence might be far ranging and thus that by writing, Angelico had alienated powerful men, but the fact remained that he *had* been deserted.

After going back over a number of the words to make them easier to read, he carefully folded the paper and got to his feet. Despite his resolve not to, he acknowledged his surroundings. Didn't the wolves ever stop howling? From dusk to dawn, it seemed, they cried. No other sound could rival it. No wonder he had had trouble falling asleep ever since coming here and had such unsettling dreams. It would be even worse tonight in the face of the soldier's desertion—and the reality of the pile of rocks that marked where Pablo had been buried.

A chill ran from the back of his head down his spine, weakening his legs and causing him to stumble. Righting himself, he grabbed the candle and held it out in a less than successful attempt to illuminate his surroundings. A man whose heart is at peace with the Lord has nothing to fear; he knew that, believed that with everything in him, and yet—

Just last year, three of his fellow Franciscans, Fray Francisco de Porras among them, had set out to minister to far-flung Hopi villages, accompanied by eighteen soldiers who had subsequently returned to Santa Fe. At Awatobi, the Hopi medicine men had called Fray Francisco a liar and ordered the tribe not to attend his sermons. Francisco had fallen to his knees in the pueblo plaza, crossed himself, and begun praying. Then he'd spat on his hands and made a mud ball, which he'd placed on the eyes of a blind Hopi boy, immediately restoring his sight. Although the padre had written humbly of the miracle, he'd incurred the wrath of the medicine man, who'd soon after fed him poisoned food. He'd died as another Franciscan was administering last rites.

Appalled at the memory of the worst the savages were capable of, Angelico dropped to his knees and prayed, loud and long, for protection and guidance, for unwavering faith and the courage to face Satan in all his guises.

When there was nothing left to say, he forced his weary legs to once again accept his weight, but before he could pull back his tent flap, a whisper of sound reached him, this one different from what the wolves were capable of, hollow and deep at the same time, haunting and haunted.

Had it come from Oraibi itself?

Old Willow, a member of the Water Clan, was telling the story of how Palatkwapi, the ancient Red City of the South, had become a great village that had subsequently been destroyed when the Hopi living there ignored the warnings of the kachinas Eototo and Aholi to continue their migrations.

Because she'd heard the legend more times than she could count, Morning Butterfly paid little attention to Old Willow's words but lost herself in the sounds his fellow clan members made with their soft drumming. As a young girl, she'd been frightened by the details of how Palatkwapi had been destroyed by a serpent that rose from a new grave and shook his coils, thus shaking the earth and toppling buildings. By noon, the great city had fallen and hundreds had been killed, the survivors fleeing the smoking ruins.

One house had remained untouched. In it lived a couple with twins, a boy and a girl. As all twins did, these two had special powers and were called *choviohoya,* or young deer. Deserted by their parents, who'd believed them dead, the twins had followed the survivors' tracks. When their food ran out, the boy had shot a magical deer who instructed them how to use its body so they would have new clothes to keep them warm. Eventually the twins reached another village and shared what they'd learned about utilizing all of a deer's gifts.

Cougar had told Morning Butterfly about Navajo twins. They were different from those of the Hopi, and yet she couldn't dismiss the similarities: Each pair, in their own way, had improved the lives of their people. If she ever saw Cougar again, she would tell him that.

During their desperate run for freedom, Cougar had given no thought to reclaiming the horses they'd ridden to Oraibi, and although he didn't doubt his ability to return to his village, he'd been concerned about his grandfather. From the moment the old man had sawed through Cougar's bonds, Drums No More had been a man possessed, excited because he'd saved his grandson's life and determined to avoid recapture. Still, the long hours had exacted their toll on him and he'd started to stumble.

Pretending a weariness he didn't feel, Cougar had convinced his grandfather that it was wise—and safe—to spend the day resting.

"We each have our own mission, Grandfather," he'd told Drums No More when night arrived. "Our people must be warned. We could do this together, but my thoughts are not yet ready to leave Oraibi."

"Oraibi, or Morning Butterfly?"

He'd ignored his grandfather's question, instead pointing out that they needed to know what the soldiers were doing—why one had tried to kill him, whether they were getting ready to attack the Navajo, or, as he'd hoped, were riding toward the great canyon.

"I will return there," he'd said, "and use my eyes and ears to learn all I can. I have no wisdom about the soldiers' ways. I thought I could turn them in the direction I want, but I was wrong. If their anger is such that they punish the Hopi—" He'd faltered over that. "If that has happened, their actions will tell me much about what exists in their hearts."

Drums No More insisted that the soldiers didn't have hearts, but although he was afraid for Cougar, he'd seen the wisdom in his grandson's plan. As a result, the old man, rested and determined, was now on his way home while Cougar was nearly back at Oraibi. All day, he'd kept his senses turned for any sign of the soldiers, but there had been none. It was inconceivable that the Spanish wouldn't be determined to avenge the death of one of their own . . .

From where he stood in the sheltering and welcome dark, he could just make out a faint glow near where the padre had set up his tent. Uninterested in what the man was doing, he made his way toward where the soldiers slept. As he did, his ears absorbed wolf howls and drum sounds from the top of the Hopi mesa. The message wasn't that of the Navajo, and yet the deep notes made him think of home and belonging. He prayed Morning Butterfly was up there, safe, surrounded by her family. He also prayed she knew he was alive, and that the knowledge had given her joy.

The soldiers weren't there. He couldn't hear them and their smell had faded so much that the land had nearly absorbed it. The corral didn't contain as many horses as it had yesterday.

Patient in the way of one who has learned that patience means life, he waited for the moon to spread its silver light before taking the final steps that brought him to Captain Lopez's tent. Then he nodded in understanding. The ground had recently been trampled by numerous hooves.

Bending low, he followed the trail of disturbed pebbles. At first he had difficulty determining which marks were new and which had been placed there earlier, but it soon became clear that many horses had gone in one direction at the same time. He was loping now, bending low, running like a wolf on a scent. The thought that he resembled a wolf gave him pause, but he couldn't stop, couldn't turn from his task. If he ceased to be a Navajo warrior and became a *chindi*-wolf, so be it.

His breath came faster and his back had started to ache but at last he knew—*knew*—that the soldiers had left Oraibi. They weren't on their way to his village; instead, their tracks headed toward the great canyon.

Stopping, he lifted his head to the night, opened his mouth, and howled like the wolf he'd become.

From inside his tent, Fray Angelico heard the howl and shivered.

And, high on the mesa, Morning Butterfly thought she caught the note of something both animal and human.

The next morning, Fray Angelico instructed both Mexican Indian servants to once again set off for Santa Fe. His orders were simple: They were to safeguard this latest letter to the governor and return as soon as they'd received a response.

Once the frightened but obedient Indians were gone, the padre drove himself nearly to distraction trying to get the Hopi he'd managed to gather around him to understand what he wanted them to do. They couldn't already have forgotten what size and shape stones he needed, or where to search for them, but even when they fell to their knees and bowed their heads as he prayed over them, he doubted their sincerity.

Struggling between his impatience to get the job done and his fear that the Hopis might rebel, or worse, if he pushed too hard, he ordered each and every one of them to relay to Morning Butterfly the message that he had urgent need of her. Although they nodded their heads like weeds bobbing in the wind, as soon as he'd finished, they wandered off instead of going in search of her. If this was deliberate disobedience on their part, the day would come when they would regret their actions. And if they were simply too limited in intelligence to grasp the simplest command, he prayed for patience.

Most of all he prayed for an end to his isolation.

Morning Butterfly had spent the three days at Oraibi since the Navajos' escape and the soldiers' subsequent departure. Like Singer Of Songs, she gave thanks that the captain and his demands no longer impacted on their lives, but while Singer Of Songs was content to learn from the women about what to expect as her pregnancy progressed, Morning Butterfly paid close attention to what others told her about the padre's state of mind.

He was, they all agreed, an impatient man who was also as nervous as a young deer stalked by a wolf pack. He prayed more than before, his prayers louder and longer as well. He sometimes lost his temper and yelled at those he'd commandeered to build his church, then his tone turned into that a parent uses when trying to get a small child to stop playing and help with chores.

The padre's behavior was a source of great amusement, and despite her unease, Morning Butterfly laughed at some of what she was told. She knew that she would have to present herself to the man before his threats of punishment became reality, but she put it off as long as possible.

The end of her reprieve came on the afternoon of the fourth day, when she heard a child crying as she clambered up the ladder to Oraibi. She looked around for the little girl's mother, but Slow Walker was nowhere in sight.

"Why are you alone?" she asked the little girl.

Between hiccups, the girl explained that she and her mother had been collecting water from one of the few springs that had survived summer when the padre approached. Although Slow Walker had attempted to avoid him, he'd ordered her to give him a drink. After that, he'd made it clear that Slow Walker would supply water for his workers as well. He'd grabbed Slow Walker's hair and started to drag her with him. Afraid, Slow Walker had ordered her daughter to run home.

It was her fault, Morning Butterfly knew. By avoiding the padre, she'd put her people at risk. After entrusting the girl to an aunt's care, she gave her pueblo a last look and did what she had to do.

She had no trouble finding the padre, since she heard him before she could single him out from the men working in the afternoon sun. Two had lifted a boulder onto the church wall, but the boulder had no level side and kept threatening to fall off. Fray Angelico, his face streaming sweat and his hood thrown back to reveal his tangled hair, was berating the men over their choice of a stone.

"Please," she said, "let them stop before they hurt themselves."

Fray Angelico whirled on her. Then he composed his features, but not before she saw an expression that made her think a *chindi* might look like him.

"Where have you been?" he demanded. "I have been asking for you for days. Surely—"

"You could have come to Oraibi yourself."

Something flickered in his eyes but was gone before she could make sense of it. He still put her in mind of a *chindi*, and she took the warning to heart.

"My sister needed me," she said, her half-lie coming almost without thought. Then, studying his reaction, she explained that Singer Of Songs carried Captain Lopez's child.

"By all that is holy! The man's debauchery knows no bounds."

Although she'd never heard the word debauchery before, she had no doubt of its meaning. Hoping to keep him from asking too many questions about her sister, she repeated her concern for the Hopi men's safety.

"You tell them," he insisted, "that they are doing this all wrong. I am *so* glad you are here." As if emphasizing his point, he flattened a hand against his chest. "My patience has never been tested like this and without God on my side, I would have given up. I cannot understand how people who can build an extensive village have no comprehension of what I require."

Because they choose not. "Their minds are elsewhere," she said, "on their need to harvest their crops."

"Morning Butterfly, I am not going to debate this with you any more than I was willing to debate it with the captain. The Lord's work has priority. Until *His* majesty has manifested into something tangible, until this Church is completed, the converting of souls cannot truly begin."

His hand had dropped to his side, but now he placed it over his heart again. "If only I could make your people understand that this is my life's work . . . If only they could comprehend the extent of their reward for having bent their backs so God's glory can be fully realized . . . Why do I bother?" he asked with a groan.

For a heartbeat she felt sorry for this man who was so alone. In truth, the ways and whys of his religion interested her just as she'd been fascinated by everything Cougar had told her, but if she told the padre that, he would force his beliefs on her until their weight crushed her. If only he would open himself to Hopi wisdom, maybe the two of them could sit down together and hand each other their gifts.

Sighing, she acknowledged that that could never be and

turned the conversation to the subject of Captain Lopez. As she suspected, Angelico didn't know when, or if, to expect his return.

"If he does come back," he said, "it will not be for long."

The two men charged with trying to lift the too-awkward boulder had set it down and now each propped a leg on it. Others had also ceased working. If they started to walk away, if they refused to obey the padre, he couldn't stop them. It was as Cougar had said; the Hopi did not have to see themselves as animals. They could fight.

With a start, she realized the padre was speaking. Still trapped by the enormity of her revelation, she struggled to keep up.

". . . not as all-powerful as he believes himself to be," Fray Angelico was saying. "He believes I will blindly accept his every decision, but he is wrong."

"How is he wrong?"

"I have influence. He chooses to discount that influence, but he will live to regret his decision because I have set certain things in motion."

She'd never heard of this thing called a letter, and wasn't sure what it had to do with what he called "bringing pressures to bear," but that didn't matter as much as his final comment.

"It is my fervent prayer, my hope that, within the month, Captain Lopez and his troops will be replaced by others who put God's work before all else."

Her dream of seeing her people walk away from Fray Angelico and again take up the pattern and tempo of their lives spluttered, threatened to die.

"Within the month?" she repeated although she had no idea what that meant.

"Perhaps sooner, but these things take time. It is not as if this new colony is overrun with soldiers awaiting assignments, but the Crown is committed to working with the Church to civilize the natives and make the land ready for Christianity, so yes, I do not anticipate having to wait overly long."

Dizzy from the effort of trying to make sense of everything he'd told her, she nodded.

"In the meantime, God's work will continue. I vow this! With you passing along the necessary elements of what is required . . ."

Tell him you will not do this.

But if you anger him and he passes his rage onto new soldiers, what price will your people pay?

"Cannot the work wait until—" she began, but instantly his features became shadowed as if a great bird had flown between him and the sun. Stunned by this evidence of his mood, she fell silent.

"It should be enough that I am the emissary of God's word and was chosen for this great work," he muttered. "And yet . . ."

He lifted his hand to his forehead and pinched the sides with his long, bony fingers, his expression pained, and she reminded herself that he'd never physically harmed one of her people. She remembered his gentle, loving eyes when he'd just baptized someone, particularly a child.

"God came to you, told you what he wanted you to do?" she asked.

"How little you understand of the Lord's work." He sighed, but no longer looked anguished. "God's ways are mysterious indeed. I was brought into my calling when I was but a child and have wanted no other life, cannot remember anything else, but even I do not pretend to have God's ear."

Once again confused, she tried to nod.

"The work to which I devote my life is easily stated. I am here to free the natives from the miserable slavery of the demon and from the obscure darkness of their idolatry."

His words had a rote-like quality, as if he'd heard them countless times and was simply repeating what he'd memorized.

"Who is this demon?" she asked, even though she wasn't sure she wanted to know.

"The devil, of course! Surely you have grasped that simple fact. My child, your people are of vicious and ferocious habits; they know no law but force and must be rescued from their barbarism. It is my burden, my duty to punish those who worship the devil so they will not infect others with their wicked ways."

She felt as if she was sinking into his words, surrounded by swirling dust, bombarded by nonsense that, nevertheless, carried the core of his belief.

"Before I came here," he continued, "I committed the theology of this mission to heart. What I know, what I embrace with all my heart, is the truth—the absolute truth."

"The truth?"

"That those who could prevent a given sin and fail to do so cooperate in the offense committed against God and therefore share in the guilt."

"Guilt?"

"Not embracing the Lord God. Child, child, you are a Hopi of rare intellect. Nothing would gladden my heart more than having you as my most devout convert, your praise of the Lord Jesus Christ ringing from the mountaintops."

Spittle had formed at the corners of his mouth, and his eyes didn't seem to focus on anything. His sparse body trembled and, alarmed, she reached to steady him, but his eyes suddenly became intense, and once again she wondered if a bird's shadow had passed over his features.

"The promise of showing the Hopi of Oraibi the road to eternal life fills me with the greatest joy, but joy unshared is lonely. So lonely." Without warning, he grabbed for her, raking her forearm with his nails. Somehow, she yanked free.

"Padre," she warned. "I am not my sister and you are not Captain Lopez."

Would weaknesses of the flesh never be done with him? Anguished, Fray Angelico ripped off his robe, leaving himself naked in the wilderness with God knew how many savages watching. His mind screaming denial, and praying for forgiveness, he yanked a needle-encrusted bush out of the ground and slapped his back with it over and over again until his world turned red with pain and his flesh bled. Only then did he pick up his robe and stumble away.

He'd been walking for what seemed forever when self-hatred and doubt faded, to be replaced by cold realization. It wasn't his flesh that was weak, not at all. Rather, being surrounded by savages had brought him too close to the devil's clutches.

The devil would not win! No matter what the effort, a lifetime of devotion to God would sustain him and he would come through the test all the stronger for the effort!

Stopping, he looked around, more than a little disconcerted to realize he could barely see Oraibi in the distance. As for the remaining horses and his barely-begun church, there was no sign they'd ever existed.

Only—

Only faint hoofbeats coming closer.

19

Panicked and nearly breathless, Fray Angelico raced for the dubious safety of a large, seemingly dead bush. As he crouched behind it, he yanked his robe on, gasping in pain as the rough fabric caught on his flayed back. Prayers multiplied inside him, but the threat of death left him unable to decide which of them was most likely to convince his maker.

Something seemed wrong about the sound, or rather the direction it was coming from, but his mind refused to take hold of these pieces of knowledge. Impelled by an instinct for self-preservation he hadn't known he possessed, he made himself as small as possible. The bush's upper branches reached out in all directions and would have afforded him adequate protection if the base hadn't been so spindly.

Through an act of will that gave him a small measure of pride, he forced himself to focus on the approaching dust. Whoever was out there moved slowly, saddle creaking and—

A saddle? The Navajo hadn't stolen any, had they?

Just as panic had, relief now nearly robbed him of the

ability to breathe. At the same time, it would take more than this to put an end to his fear.

Was that a glint of metal? Leaning to one side of the bush, he struggled to make sense of what he'd spotted. When the glint reappeared, for a moment he was convinced his prayers had been answered and that these were new troops. Then reality once again intruded; he'd heard the sound of a single horse.

Madariaga de Oñate took an impossibly long time to reach him, time Angelico used to mull over the reason for the young soldier's return. If something had happened to the rest of the troop . . .

Angelico stood and positioned himself so Madariaga couldn't see his back and the blood soaking through his garment. The soldier immediately slid off his horse, dropped to his knees and touched his forehead to the ground. Pleased, Angelico placed his hand on his shoulder.

"Welcome, my son, welcome," he said. "I will pray for you."

"I . . . I need prayers."

"There has been an . . . accident? You and the others were attacked by hostile Indians?"

"No," Madariaga reassured him. He remained bent so low that Angelico had to strain to hear him. "The captain ordered me to return."

"Because he believed I needed protection?"

With a low groan, Madariaga straightened. He looked older, drawn and tired. "No," he whispered. "Because I have displeased him. He—he no longer assumes responsibility for me, does not want me in his sight."

"Why not?"

Madariaga blushed. "I asked that we have prayers before going to bed the other night. I also questioned why no services had been held on the Sabbath. The others had the same concerns, but it fell to me to ask. My captain vented his displeasure at me and dismissed me. Padre, I do not know if I have met a less religious man than Captain Lopez. He is—was—my commander and I respect his military expertise, but not to put the Lord foremost in his life . . ." The young man looked about to cry. "The Lord moves in mysterious ways. The more I see of this world the more convinced I am of that, but the devil's influence—Padre, is it possible that the devil's hold on a human heart and soul can be greater than God's power?"

Angelico might have taken offense, since his ministrations to the soldiers always centered on God's supreme force, but the young man was genuinely confused by his commander's behavior and was only searching for an explanation.

"The battle between our supreme savior and the powers of darkness has raged since Adam and Eve," he said as he helped Madariaga to stand. "Those who truly seek salvation and guidance find the strength to cast off the devil, but not everyone is capable of hearing His word."

Madariaga frowned. "The captain is an intelligent man, educated far beyond what I will ever be. His collection of novels, such as Cervantes's *Don Quixote*, fills me with envy, and yet I cannot help but wonder if an excess of secular reading might draw a man far from the Bible's truth."

"I am certain such material has influenced his thinking, but I cannot pretend to fully understand why Captain Lopez has chosen the direction he has. My son, understanding of God's great plan for us can only come about if we immerse ourselves in His truth and wisdom, which, I fear, the captain has not done. You say you wish you had access to his book collection." He deliberately kept the conversation off what had happened between Madariaga and Lopez. "I must be wrong. I was under the impression you had not been afforded a formal education."

Madariaga had started to relax while they were talking, but now he became agitated again. "Padre, my blood is impure. I am—my mother is—Indian."

"And because of that, school was denied you," Angelico finished for him.

Madariaga nodded, then brightened slightly. "Unlike most of my kind, my father acknowledged me and taught me to read. I have read the entire Bible several times. Not only that, I put it upon myself to learn from my surroundings; there is an education there for anyone with a willingness to listen."

"I am certain there is."

"Not all of it is truthful. That is the thing, the hard part—separating falsehood from truth." Sighing, he scratched under his chin. "Padre, if I may, a confession?"

"Of course. Of course."

"I did not become a soldier simply because I wished to be free of the constraints placed upon me because of my heritage, but because I became convinced that this new land presented opportunities I would never have elsewhere."

"Opportunities? To help spread the word of the true and only faith?"

Looking somewhat abashed, Madariaga shook his head. Then he glanced over at his horse who'd wandered a few feet away in search of food. "Padre, so many spoke of this land's mineral wealth, gold and silver. The explorers who first came here, like the great and courageous Estevanico, who led Fray Marcos de Niza up the Rio San Pedro, left such details that I am surprised so few have ventured here."

Estevanico the Black had been a slave, a Moor and not a Christian; he'd been killed and torn apart by Zuni savages. It had been Fray Marcos, not the slave, who had garnered support from Bishop Zumarraga of Mexico City because of his fine religious zeal and approved virtue. With an effort, Angelico restrained himself from pointing out the falsehoods in Madariaga's story.

"I have committed what they found to memory." The youth closed his eyes and sighed. "How much I would sacrifice if only I could have been with them when they came across the great city of Cibola! Estevanico's words stick to my mind like clay: 'The houses are as they have been described to me by the Indians, all of stone, with terraces and flat roofs, fine in appearance, the best I have seen in these regions.'"

That accounting had come from Fray Marcos, not Estevanico and, unfortunately, time had determined it to be the product of Fray Marcos's overactive imagination and enthusiasm. Equally unfortunately, "news" of Cibola had spread and taken on a life of its own since that early expedition, giving rise to persistent stories about the Seven Cities of Cibola which many—perhaps Captain Lopez among them—persisted in believing were rich in gold and jewels, well stocked with rare foods and fine wines. The search for the—to Angelico's mind—nonexistent cities had resulted in the death of many explorers.

"I have studied maps," Madariaga continued, no longer looking at all crestfallen. "Pored over all I could get my hands on until I became convinced that finding a heretofore undiscovered river would lead me to the riches."

A boy could hardly get his hands on what few maps of the territory existed. Beyond that, Madariaga's blind belief in what educated men had determined to be a falsehood made Angelico want to weep. Not only had Madariaga staked his future and maybe his life on accomplishing what no one had done, but his obsession kept him from seeing what was truly important—devotion and sacrifice to the Lord. Only through those things could he hope to separate himself from the limitations wrought by his birth.

"My child, while I applaud your courage and determination, in good conscience, I cannot encourage you to continue on this course."

Instead of arguing, Madariaga responded with a shuddering sigh. "My childhood, although simple, did not lack for physical comforts. It was only while making my way here that I learned the meaning of fear. Attempting to establish a military presence here has exacted its own toll, I must confess; it is so strange and different, dangerous. Ever since the Navajo killed Pablo, I have been unable to sleep."

"It is a loneliness of the spirit, my son, one which can only be banished with the grace of God. It was He who led you back here, He who placed you in my care."

Madariaga didn't respond, only continued to survey his surroundings. His stomach rumbled and he pressed his hand against it.

"You and I will pray together and through prayer, you will find salvation and peace," Angelico protested.

"The nights are the worst," Madariaga said, seemingly unaware that he'd interrupted. "By day the land seems so vast and unpopulated by anything except vile creatures, snakes and lizards, birds that feed off rotting flesh. There is so little sign of moisture, and I cannot see how even the most desperate savages would make this godforsaken place their home. At night . . ."

"What about the nights?"

"The darkness is so complete. It—it is as if I have fallen into a cave and a demon, maybe the devil himself, has placed a stone over the opening." He wrapped his hands around his stomach. "I hold my hand up to my face but cannot see it. My fellow soldiers and I—sometimes we talk through the night because we hate the silence so—we hear each other but we are voices without bodies. Padre, Father, does it ever feel the same to you?"

"Does what?"

"As if you will never be free of the nothingness? This desert—it seems to go on forever, to be everything. To be waiting for me to die so it can pick over my bones."

"I have seen the vultures," Angelico said, his heart suddenly cold. "They are indeed vile creatures, but they perform a necessary task and are not something to fear."

"I know. Father, there is something I think about a lot." Madariaga swallowed. "Something that allows me no peace."

Madariaga was a lost soul, lost but not beyond the Lord's reach. Thinking to comfort him, Angelico reached out to touch him, but the youth jerked away and let out a frightened squeak.

"I—I am sorry," he muttered. "It is just that I have spent so much time looking over my shoulder."

"That is all right. Please, my son, unburden your heart," he said.

Except for the ever-present wind and Madariaga's ragged breathing, for a long time nothing broke the silence. Then: "The Indians are savages. That is why you came here, to make them stop their evil ways—"

"My mission is to guide the Indians into the light."

"I know. But they were not without beliefs before we arrived. I did as you and the captain commanded, destroyed their false idols, but before that, when we were new to Oraibi and just exploring their village, I walked near the underground rooms where their men go."

"Yes, yes."

"The sounds that emanated from those places—they were like prayers."

Angelico's throat constricted and he swallowed loudly. "I have heard the same thing," he admitted.

"You have?" Madariaga visibly set aside his surprise. "That is what I keep thinking about—if they are praying, who do they pray to? Do they worship the devil? Maybe—maybe they have made gods of vultures and snakes, lizards."

The mind of a simple people was beyond Angelico's comprehension, and yet he half believed Madariaga was right.

"They knew nothing of the Lord Jesus Christ, did they?"

"I have made great strides in leading them to God's grace." Angelico prayed that was true.

Madariaga breathed in and out. "If I had known nothing except this barren place, if that was all my ancestors had known, maybe I would worship snakes."

The devil had this man in his clutches! There could be no other explanation for what he was saying. But even as Angelico wrapped his belief around him, he remembered the hellish sound he'd heard after the kachinas had been destroyed.

Although she didn't want to, as soon as she'd heard that one of the soldiers had returned, Morning Butterfly forced herself to seek out Fray Angelico. She found him standing with his hands behind his back while he stared at what existed of his church. Thinking he was engaged in prayer, she waited.

On the day the first stone had been set in place, he'd gathered around him as many children as the soldiers could find and baptized them. The next day he'd done the same with an almost equal number of women. Perhaps half of the Hopi men had been compelled to kneel before him while he muttered words they didn't understand. Even as he welcomed them into what he called the light and protection of his lord, she'd filled her mind with her people's Song of Creation. Today, as she waited to speak to the padre, she again took comfort in those words.

"The perfect one laid out the perfect plan and gave us a long span of life, creating song to implant joy in life. On his path of happiness, we the Butterfly Maidens carry out his wishes by greeting our Father Sun."

She and other Hopi had listened to the padre's sermons. Would the time ever come when he would do the same?

"Morning Butterfly, I did not see you coming."

She indicated the sleeping soldier. "He returned alone. Why?"

Angelico blinked several times before speaking. "Because Captain Lopez wants to provide me with protection. If my prayers are answered, he will shortly be joined by others sent here by the governor."

Her stomach clenched, and she struggled to keep her reaction to herself. "But Captain Lopez and his men took much food with them and we have little left. If more soldiers come—"

"The Lord provides, my child. The Lord provides."

Did this lord of his help harvest crops? Knowing the folly of asking him that, she turned her attention to the church, posing to him the question of whether he intended to use the services of the anticipated newcomers in continuing work on it.

"Undoubtedly. My first concern will be, of course, with the state of their souls." He glanced upward. "God will show me the way to minister to my entire flock, but I already feel the weight of those added responsibilities. What sustains me is the prospect of having the church completed by fall."

"Fall?"

"Before winter. You know what that is, do you not?"

Although the Spanish looked at the seasons in ways different from the Hopi, she nodded. "And then?" she asked. "Once there is a church at Oraibi, will you go elsewhere?"

The question seemed to surprise him. "Oh no. At least I do not anticipate being given another post in the foreseeable future. A religious structure is simply my first responsibility.

After that, I plan on making a true contribution to God."

"A true contribution?"

"Yes." He smiled, obviously warming to the conversation. At the same time, she noticed that he kept his distance from her. She was careful to do the same.

"I wish you could see what has been accomplished in Santa Fe," he said. "There is a plaza and the Palace of the Governors which is both a chapel and, of necessity, a prison. Within its walls is a garden and beyond that stables and quarters for the guard. East of the plaza is a fine church, and south of that, the chapel of Saint Michael. An acequia madre has been constructed to carry water from the river throughout the settlement, and the resultant pastures and cultivated land are most extraordinary. The days of Captain General Oñate are no more. Great strides have been made in bringing civilization to the wilderness. The same will happen here, my child. Much of it within your lifetime."

In the days that followed, it seemed as if Fray Angelico's promise would become reality, not as she walked toward old age, but even before Singer Of Songs' child was born. The lone soldier remained by the padre's side at all times and they appeared to take pleasure from each other's company, although the younger man obviously saw Angelico as his superior. He was always armed. Fray Angelico continually exhorted the natives to follow his directives. If they did not, he said, commanding Morning Butterfly to translate, God's wrath would fall upon them. She did as he ordered because she feared that either Captain Lopez and his men or others from Santa Fe would soon arrive and punish any disobedience.

He had, Angelico told Morning Butterfly, devised a plan by which church construction could continue while the Hopi tended to their farms. He'd noted a glaring lack of efficiency in the way a single man took responsibility for a plot of land, working it by day and returning to Oraibi at night. Instead, he instructed—commanded—able-bodied Hopi of both sexes to remain near the crops at all times, a necessity with the sheep running loose. The majority, however, worked on the church.

Nights had always been for meetings in the various kivas, for prayer and ceremony, but that was no longer possible. Instead of the various clan members gathering strength from their brothers, a Snake Clan member might find himself working alongside a Badger, two Eagles, and three Hawks. Yes, they were all Hopi, but they hadn't grown into manhood knowing each other's hearts. There was a desperate need for a Council of Chiefs, but how could the heads of the various clans gather when they were kept separated for days at a time?

What distressed her the most was what might happen to her sister and the other women once soldiers were once again in their midst. As it was, Madariaga had already had his way with one woman when she'd tried to hand him a bowl of water. Afterward, he'd prostrated himself before the padre, but she had no doubt that he would "sin" again.

"The newcomers are deer in rut," her mother insisted one afternoon as she and Morning Butterfly ground corn on their metates. "They were like that at Acoma and nothing has changed. At least the captain was gentle with Singer Of Songs and he was the only one to touch her. I fear what will happen if many newcomers are here. Atch, I do not have the words for it."

Neither did Morning Butterfly. She'd grown up knowing it was right for young Hopi to have *dumaiyas* with a number of partners, because how else could they decide who they wanted to spend the rest of their lives with? Once a marriage partner had been selected, however, neither boy nor girl looked at anyone else. Intercourse was for the purpose of creating children, and because it was enjoyable, because people cared for each other.

Among the Hopi, a man never forced himself upon a woman.

It wasn't the same for the Spanish.

"It is not right," Morning Butterfly finally told Fray Angelico. As usual, their meeting took place in the middle of the day, near the church. "When the soldiers left, my people were happy because they believed there would be no more rape, but now everyone fears what the future will bring."

The padre, his wind-torn hair reminding her of a discarded mouse nest, blinked rapidly. "Madariaga confessed his sin and was forgiven."

"Can you tell me he will not sin again?" she demanded.

"He is a mortal man," he said.

"Does that excuse him? Padre, the night before the captain and his troops left, a woman I call my sister because she is of my clan was forced to submit to three men. It is not right!"

His mouth sagged open, then closed. "No," he muttered, "it is not. However . . ."

"When they come, cannot you talk to them? Tell them we hate them for what they are doing."

"It does not matter to them." He sounded both frustrated and angry. His fists clenched at his side; he looked around at the church, which was now higher than a tall man's chest, but seemed to take no pleasure from it. "You have no comprehension—your world is so small, so isolated. The world beyond your vision means nothing to you. It is easier that way, but it is not the way I have to live."

He looked small with the newly built rock walls behind him, and there was a desperate note to his voice. Those things made her feel almost sorry for him, might have made more of an impact if she wasn't still filled with the sound of Little Bird's sobs.

"It was you who came to our world." Morning Butterfly turned her attention to the horizon where, maybe, Cougar and other Navajo rode free. "We did not ask you here."

"Without me, your souls will never be saved."

"Without you and other newcomers, our women and girls would not be full of fear and sometimes cry themselves to sleep. Our men would work and pray and hold ceremonies as they have since our Emergence."

"Stop it!" He clamped his hands over his ears. "Have you not heard a word of my sermons? You, more than anyone else, should know what I am saying! Believe in God and vow obedience to Him, disavow your pagan—"

"What is pagan? Because our beliefs are not yours, they are wrong?"

"Stop it. Stop it!" He pressed against his temple so hard that the skin there turned white. "Oh Lord, why must I suffer so? I gave my life over to You, gladly devote myself to Your teachings, and yet these children are blind to Your wisdom."

She'd heard him speak like that before and knew his words would blind him to anything else. Still, she couldn't walk away yet.

"Padre, you are a gentle man, unlike other Spanish. Hopi women too are gentle. When they are forced to submit, their hearts tear and bleed. Cannot you tell the newcomers that, order them to—"

"You want me to command young men to live lives of abstinence?"

"Yes."

"You do not understand. You never will."

After Morning Butterfly left, Angelico struggled to turn his attention and energies back to the question of how to construct an adequate roof given the few suitable materials at his disposal, but his mind refused to dismiss the just-finished conversation.

In the past, Morning Butterfly had been unassuming, keeping her eyes respectfully downcast and attending most of his sermons. It had pleased him—no, it had pleased the Lord—to watch her, and he'd allowed himself to believe the rest of her people would follow in her footsteps.

But it had all been deception. She understood nothing. Worse, she did not seem to want to understand.

20

On their bellies, Cougar and Blue Swallow worked their way closer to Oraibi. The two had left their horses at Little Wind Canyon, which was halfway between the Navajo village and the Hopi pueblo. Cougar would have preferred to come alone, but Blue Swallow had insisted on accompanying him, pointing out that if something happened to one of them, the other might live to warn their people. Although Cougar acknowledged the brave's courage, Blue Swallow reminded him of a young elk determined to challenge an old bull's dominance.

At the moment, Blue Swallow was slightly ahead of him, frequently rising to peer over brush and boulders. Perhaps the time would come when Blue Swallow would learn the wisdom of caution, but if he didn't and his recklessness cost him his life—

"The padre's house grows taller and taller," Blue Swallow pointed out unnecessarily. "There must be many in his family. Otherwise, what need does he have for something that big?"

"Perhaps the Spanish believe they need to build walls

around everything," Cougar offered. "Maybe they think they can keep the Hopi from escaping that way."

"The Hopi will never run. Look!"

Blue Swallow pointed at a distant shadow east of the unfinished church. Shading his eyes, Cougar recognized a gray wolf, its nose pointed into the wind.

"Perhaps your *chindi*-wolf . . ."

"Perhaps," Cougar said when his companion's voice trailed off.

"Has it approached you again? Have you dreamed of it?"

"Dreams, yes, but although I sat alone for a better part of a day and a night, what I saw once has not returned."

"Maybe it was not a *chindi* then?"

Instead of replying, Cougar continued to study the creature as he asked himself if Blue Corn Eater had turned into a *chindi* after the soldiers burned his body and either blamed Cougar for his death or wanted revenge. Although the motionless wolf made him uneasy, he knew to wait for the answer.

"Perhaps," Blue Swallow continued after a short silence, "the wolf has never seen a church and seeks to make sense of it."

"If that is so, he will starve before the truth comes to him."

Blue Swallow chuckled, then turned serious. "I did not say this before because . . . maybe because I wanted my words to be heard only by you—but you were right. You saw into the soldiers' hearts and knew what was most important to them: emeralds. I am glad they are gone."

Cougar tried not to think about what Captain Lopez and his men were doing, where they were, and what they might do after they'd searched the great canyon, but trying and accomplishing weren't the same thing. If his prayers were answered, a *chindi* would send the soldiers to the edge of the canyon—and then over it to their deaths.

And if no spirit heard his prayers—

Forcing his thoughts off what he wasn't ready to face, he concentrated on Blue Swallow. Silent as a snake, the brave had started crawling forward again. A spider the size of his thumbnail clung to Blue Swallow's shirt, reminding him that Spider Woman had taught the Dineh how to weave. Perhaps this tiny creature was one of Spider Woman's children.

They were getting close enough to Oraibi that speaking was unwise, and he was grateful for the silence—or he would have been if he wasn't consumed by thoughts of Captain Lopez.

Blue Swallow seemed to have forgotten the wolf; either that or his attention was now fully on remaining hidden. A wise man puts safety before anything else when he is among his enemies, and Cougar struggled to take his cue from Blue Swallow's wisdom. He'd taken note of the increased activity in the various Hopi farm plots and was glad the crops hadn't been left to die. He'd heard that other priests at other villages claimed most of every harvest and sent it far away. If Fray Angelico attempted to do the same thing, would the Hopi rise up against him?

Blue Swallow stopped so suddenly that Cougar nearly ran into him. Chiding himself for once again allowing his thoughts to distract him from what he was doing, he peered in the direction his companion was staring. So close that he could reach him in no more than two bounds stood a soldier. The young man was unclothed from the waist up, revealing a broad chest and surprisingly slender arms. His legs were long, his boots large. His shoulders had been burned by the sun and the skin was flaking off in places. He held nothing in his hands but had strapped a short knife to his waist.

Shocked to see a soldier when he'd thought they had all gone with Captain Lopez, Cougar signaled to Blue Swallow that they should move around the man. Blue Swallow nodded agreement, but instead of crawling away, he continued to study the stranger while Cougar, who had felt cruel Spanish hands on him, only wanted to leave. He was still trying to get Blue Swallow's attention when the sound of approaching voices froze him. By blocking out the wind's soft laughter as it played with the grass, he managed to identify several Hopi women's voices; not only that, he could understand their conversation.

One was convinced that the padre was little better than a

coyote because he let the Hopi do the work and then claimed what food he wanted. Another pointed out that at least a coyote had a sharp nose and long legs with which to protect itself, while the padre would be easy prey for any scavenger if he ventured too far into the desert.

The last to speak had little to say beyond warning her companions that no one except a fool would dismiss a coyote's teeth; despite her near whisper, Cougar recognized Morning Butterfly's voice. It swirled around him like fog, light as a hummingbird.

Even in his dreams, he hadn't allowed himself to believe he'd see her again, and as she came into view, his surroundings faded. He was barely aware of Blue Swallow, and the soldier no longer mattered.

She was alive, healthy if he could believe what her voice told him. No harm had come to her, and most important, she hadn't been forced to accompany Captain Lopez.

With his body pressed to Mother Earth, he caught only glimpses of her. She walked in the middle, the other two shielding her from his view, insulating her and—

Alarm slammed into him at the realization that they were approaching the soldier, who'd turned toward them. If he hadn't spent his life in tune with his world, Cougar might have dismissed the man's hungry look. As it was, he sent out a silent warning to Morning Butterfly.

In the middle of taking a step, she halted, placed a restraining hand on the other women's arms, then squared her shoulders. Fear shared space with respect in Cougar, for truly this was a woman who faced life and all its dangers.

He couldn't understand what she said to the soldier, just that whatever it was made him say something that caused her to draw away from him. With his hand pressed low on his belly, the Spaniard stepped toward Morning Butterfly and the other women. Gasping, first one and then the other turned and fled, but Cougar paid them no attention because Morning Butterfly hadn't moved.

Barely aware of what he was doing, he inched forward. Blue Swallow gripped his ankle, but he didn't take his eyes off the scene in front of him. Morning Butterfly hadn't looked around for help, which told him a great deal, not just about her but about her people as well.

The Spaniard, silent now, reached for the knife at his side. Drawing it free, he held it up for her to see.

"Cougar, no." Blue Swallow hissed as Cougar's muscles tensed.

Morning Butterfly said something to the knife-wielding man, then stepped toward him. When she spoke again, she'd dropped her voice so low that Cougar couldn't catch it. Like his namesake Cougar knew he was ready to attack—he would do anything to protect her.

A ray of sunlight touched the knife blade Madariaga held, then danced away, uninterested in human concerns. Morning Butterfly took note of its deadly message, but it didn't distract her from the Spaniard's face. His eyes, so dark they might have belonged to one of her people, said he wanted her, and yet he wasn't a stupid man.

"You will not touch me," she ordered. "If you try, my clansmen will call on our kachinas and your blood will flow."

"Kachinas?"

Cougar knew kachinas were peaceful spirits, and a Hopi would never ask one to harm someone.

"You know who I am," Morning Butterfly continued. "The padre—"

"He understands my weakness. And he needs me."

"Put away your knife," she ordered. "Why do you draw a weapon against me? I have done you no harm, I am no threat."

"Hardly. Every other female runs away the moment she sees me. Only you look me in the eye and can talk to me. Do you have any idea how long it has been since I've talked to a woman? I have been so lonely," he continued. "Fray Angelico, all he talks about is fulfilling his vows. He does not understand what it is to be a man alone; he cannot possibly."

Wondering if she'd made a mistake by talking to Madariaga, Morning Butterfly glanced around, but if the padre was nearby, she couldn't see him. The sense that she and the soldier were being watched tugged at the corners of her consciousness, yet she didn't dare let herself be distracted.

"I will not give myself to you," she told him. "If you touch me, you will feel my body's hate."

To her surprise, he sighed, and his face took on a wistful look. "Coming here was the biggest mistake I ever made. Only one thing makes it bearable."

Whatever sympathy she might have felt for him died with his first step toward her.

"No." She swallowed and spoke again, forcing courage into the word. "No."

She was certain he was going to say something, felt the words gather inside him, but he remained silent. His forward progress and the steady knife spoke for him. Something, tears perhaps, glinted in his eyes; despite herself, she backed away. After a lifetime of going barefoot, her feet were hardened yet sensitive to the land she walked; they told her she was balancing on a downward slope and if she weren't careful, she risked falling.

"I will not kill you, Morning Butterfly. I would never— you are so beautiful. I never thought I would say that about one of your kind, but you cared for Pablo and you and I have talked and . . . a man—a man can only take so much. This godforsaken place is driving me insane."

Madariaga launched himself at her, but she was ready for him, whirling to her left and propelling herself forward. Balanced on her toes, she fled up the incline, but the slope slowed her enough that he slammed into her and knocked her off balance.

Recovering before she hit the ground, she shoved the soldier away and started to run. He moved quickly, locking his arms around her, clamping his free hand around her waist. The knife was so close to her side that she felt the whisper of contact.

She spotted movement out of the corner of her eye even as Madariaga's breath washed over her neck and sent fingers of heat into her hair. Repulsed, she jerked away, but the knife touched her side again, this time slicing through her dress.

Movement again, closer, large and dark.

Then she was free. Her attacker was locked in an embrace with a nearly naked man, and the one who'd come to her aid was the larger and stronger. Madariaga twisted his wrist so the knife was aimed at her rescuer's naked flesh, coming closer, closer.

"Look out!" Morning Butterfly screamed.

Her protector reacted by shoving the Spaniard away. As he did, the knife sliced through air—then briefly found a home.

Blood streamed from the warrior's side. Ignoring his wound, he kicked out, his foot connecting with the soldier's chin and propelling him backward. Madariaga threw his hands behind him in a desperate attempt to cushion his fall, and as he went down, his hands slammed against the ground and the knife flew out of his grip.

Without thinking, Morning Butterfly dove for the weapon. Its weight was unfamiliar, but she felt stronger and more powerful with it in her grip.

"Morning Butterfly, run!"

Cougar!

"What are you doing here?" His side streamed blood as he advanced on his fallen foe.

Certain he meant to kill the momentarily helpless Madariaga, she grabbed Cougar's arm, made his wild strength hers. "Please, if you harm him, his captain will kill you."

"You wish him to live?"

No! Holding the word inside, she took in their surroundings, noting several Hopi who stared at them from a distance. She still couldn't see the padre, but that didn't mean he wasn't nearby.

"Cougar, I beg you, leave!"

He continued to strain toward the man he'd bested, but the fact that she could hold him back told her that her plea had reached him—or his wound had weakened him.

There was so much she wanted to say to Cougar. He'd saved her from attack; maybe she would have died today if it wasn't for him. And because of her, he'd been wounded.

Those things needed words known only to the two of them, but there wasn't time.

"You are not safe here," she said. "Our enemies will kill you if you stay."

"You want me gone?"

"I—I want you alive."

He nodded at that, his sleek hair lifting and falling, chest and shoulders moving in unison. Then he turned toward her and looked into her eyes, and his smile heated her as the sun never had.

"It is the Holy People's will that I am here today," he told her. "They guided me to you."

Maybe they did. "Cougar, my heart—my heart thanks you."

Someone shouted and, together, they turned to face the sound. A Hopi woman with a baby strapped to her back pointed in the direction of the church. Fray Angelico was running toward them.

"Go! Now!"

"This is unforgivable. You were commanded to sin no more, were you not?"

Madariaga's gaze remained on the ground.

"I will pray for your soul, my son; none is so deep into the devil's clutches that he is beyond redemption, but I require some assurance from you that you are truly repentant this time and will not allow yourself to again be swayed by weaknesses of the flesh."

"Father?"

"What?" Angelico didn't attempt to disguise his irritation.

"It is not as if I did anything wrong."

Nothing wrong! If it hadn't been for the Navajo's intervention, the man he'd befriended would have ravished not just any Hopi, but Morning Butterfly.

"Pray!" he ordered. "Pray for your mortal soul. We will discuss the manner of your penitence once I have decided upon its proper course. Mark my words, if you so much as look at Morning Butterfly again—"

"What about the Navajo?"

"What?" Angelico demanded, his anger at being interrupted barely in check.

"The savage who tried to kill me, the one I wounded." Madariaga continued his study of the ground. "Who knows what he might have done to her if I had not stopped him."

"He stopped you."

"No."

"Silence!" A modest, calm manner was a virtue, but there was only so much any man, even one who has devoted his life to God, can abide. "You think I did not see? Believe me, my son, there is little that takes place here that I am not aware of. Little that is not my responsibility. Just this morning, I offered you prayers, but obviously you are not capable of receiving them. Perhaps you believe you can stand up to the devil on your own."

"No, no," Madariaga whispered, as the padre knew he would. One thing about simple souls, their fear of the devil's influence was limitless. They might sin—they did sin—but then they were overcome by the need for repentance.

Without prompting, Madariaga knelt and kissed Angelico's feet and remained bent forward. Although Angelico believed himself to be without selfish pride, he nevertheless gained satisfaction from Madariaga's attitude. In a world with few tangible rewards and endless trials, was a moment of victory a transgression?

They were inside the roofless church, and although perhaps he should have dealt with the young man's transgressions in a more public place, he'd labored too hard on the structure not to put it to use. He'd allowed—encouraged—the Hopi to follow them in here, but only a handful had.

It didn't matter. Morning Butterfly was here. She would tell her people what had happened.

Morning Butterfly.

"Go my son," he told Madariaga, and if his tongue hesitated over calling him his son, he would face that later. "Go, and this time truly sin no more."

Madariaga hurried away and finally, finally, Angelico turned his attention to Morning Butterfly. It was late enough in the day that the sun had begun its downward march, and as a consequence, the church was in shadows, as was she. Although he was grateful that she couldn't easily see his expression, he wanted to look into her eyes.

"Come here, Morning Butterfly." As always, he took pleasure in speaking her name. "You and I need to speak of what happened."

"He tried to rape me."

The Hopi's openness about sexual matters would never cease to astonish him and would be the basis for many of the sermons he was planning.

"And I trust he has finally seen the error of his way and will pray for restraint. It will not happen again."

She said nothing to indicate she believed him.

"The Indian who interceded in your behalf? The one who fled."

"Cougar."

The Navajo! He'd known it! "What was he doing here?"

"I do not know."

She shifted her weight from one foot to another, reminding him of both her femininity and the fact that she hadn't shown him the respect that was his due and was unawed by their holy surroundings.

"Perhaps it was as he said." She folded her arms under her breasts. "He was guided to my side by the Holy People."

"The Holy People? You mean the disciples?"

"No."

"He said? My child, I saw the way the two of you acted around each other. I insist on being told; did you object to Madariaga's advances because you and Cougar—because you have been with him?"

"No."

There was no emotion in her voice.

"I ask so little of you," he heard himself say. "Your assistance in communicating with your people, yes, but that is something any Christian would do willingly."

She drew away when he called her a Christian, and he didn't push the issue. He had no way of knowing that his next words echoed what Madariaga had said just before the soldier had attacked the maiden.

"When I began this journey, I never thought I would meet someone like you. Intelligent, compassionate." A *woman*. "You cannot possibly comprehend how desolate my surroundings have become."

He was shocked to hear his feelings expressed in his own voice. "I find joy in doing the Lord's work," he told her. "Joy beyond measure. I trust you will never doubt that."

She nodded but didn't say anything. There was a shadow in her eyes.

"But God does not concern Himself with my every waking moment. Nor does He seek to control my every thought. As a consequence, I seek intellectual stimulation, of which there is precious little here."

"I understand."

"Do you?" He hated himself for sounding like a small, hurt child.

Sighing, she went on. "Perhaps you believe I concern myself little with what you do, but you are wrong," she said.

He opened his mouth, but she stopped him. "We always believed the old ways would walk us into tomorrow. We were content with that and yet . . ."

"And yet what?"

"Perhaps the wind will change the way it blows and the moon and sun cease or alter their journeys. Much changed as the Hopi were on their migrations, so who are we to believe that would not happen again. You—sometimes I wonder if you are the first of new winds."

For a moment so brief he wasn't sure he'd seen it, her features aged. Then she drew in a deep breath.

"Is that what you are?" she asked. "The beginning of a new way of life for the Hopi?"

21

"This was no random dream, of that I am certain. Dreams without meaning are like rabbits, jumping here and there, coming from nowhere and going noplace. But this one, I say we must look deep into it for its wisdom."

"That is why we are here, Drums No More."

"As it should be," Drums No More agreed. "I am uncertain of my dream's beginning. When I woke this morning, I looked deep into myself and prayed for wisdom, but—" He sighed. "Perhaps that remains lost in mist because I do not want to look at the truth of it."

Cougar shifted position, careful not to jar his still sore side. Although the wound the Spaniard had inflicted on him had bled freely, Blue Swallow had packed healing herbs around it, and by the time they'd reached home, Cougar had regained most of his strength. He'd told his story during several sweats attended by members of his clan, but this was the first time since his return that a formal meeting had been held.

"I was sleeping beside you when you first sat up," he reminded his grandfather. "You reached for me and called my name. Do you remember that?"

Drums No More looked around at the other men who'd crowded into the sweat lodge. He stared for a long time at the shaman Storm Wind, who'd encouraged him to speak, then at his sons, but not, Cougar noticed, at him.

"Spider Man was there," he finally said.

"Spider Man," Storm Wind echoed. "He who warns of coming danger."

Drums No More sighed. "I did not want him there, told him he was wrong to seek me out."

"Who then?" Cougar asked.

"No one! That is what I said to Spider Man. In my harshest voice, I ordered him to go away because the Navajo had no need of him. I reminded him that we faithfully follow the Holy People's way to assure no harm will come to us. When he did not leave, I—I picked up a rock and threw it at him."

Several men gasped, and even Cougar, who'd vowed to listen to everything his grandfather had to say with an open mind, struggled to imagine this gentle old man lifting an arm in anger against anyone.

"The rock bounced off him, but Spider Man gave no sign he had felt it," Drums No More said. "He—when he spoke, I heard no anger in his voice, so perhaps I only imagined what I had done."

"That can be," Storm Wind agreed. "Spider Man spoke to you. What did he say?"

Drums No More leaned forward and rested his elbows on his crossed legs. For a while the only sound was that of the men's breathing.

"His words remained in the mist. I do not know how it happened, but soon Spider Man was no longer there. In his place stood the Hero Twins."

Despite the heat from the nearby fire-heated rocks, Cougar felt a chill.

"They spoke to me," Drums No More continued, his voice stronger. "Of many things. They reminded me of the powerful spirit-beings who travel on the wind and sunbeams, on lightning flashes, rainbows, and thunderbolts. They told me to take into myself the truth that only Changing Woman, the Earth Mother, is always benevolent. Then they reminded me that Changing Woman was their mother and Sun their father."

"No one has ever questioned that." Storm Wind pointed out. "Did the Hero Twins say someone had?"

"They spoke no such words. They took me back with them to when they walked the earth and killed the monsters."

"Ah, yes! They were indeed powerful!" Storm Wind exclaimed.

Drums No More nodded agreement, but Cougar wondered if he was irritated by the shaman's continued interruptions.

"Before the Hero Twins took me with them, they reminded me of the monsters they did not destroy."

"Poverty. Hunger."

This time Drums No More glared at Storm Wind. "Shaman," he said, "I am a patient man who understands everyone needs a time to talk. It is right that you lift your voice at a time like this, but if I am not allowed to give my thoughts freedom now, I fear I will lose them. When I am done, I will listen to what you have to say, but now—now I ask you to be silent."

No one ever confronted the shaman like that since shamans were responsible for keeping everyone on the path laid out by the Holy People. Drums No More's request was proof of how serious he was. Teeth clenched, Storm Wind nodded.

"When the Twins completed their tasks," Drums No More continued, "the Holy People came together and created us, the Earth Surface People, and taught us how to find food, face life, build our homes, marry, and protect ourselves against disease. They told us what we must do in order to walk a righteous path. Those things the Twins spoke to me about.

"Then they were no longer the Hero Twins but came together in a single form—a man who sits among us today."

The chill he'd experienced earlier returned, forcing Cougar to suppress a shiver.

"My grandson," Drums No More said, speaking to him, "in my dream I saw, not the sons of Changing Woman and Sun, but you."

Storm Wind gasped, then clamped his leathery hand over his mouth.

"I saw you as a youth, traveling east although Changing Woman had told you not to. You saw an animal with brown hair and a sharp nose and pointed your arrows at it, but it jumped into a canyon."

That creature had been Coyote, a spy for the alien god Teelget.

"It was you who saw the great black bird seated on a tree, you who aimed your arrows at it but could not hit it because it spread its wings and flew away."

That had been Raven, spy of Tsenahale, the great winged creature that devours men.

"You spotted the dark bird with a skinny red head and no feathers. This one too flew away before you could pierce it."

Buzzard, spy for Tsetahotsiltali, He Who Kicks Men Down the Cliffs.

"You," Drums No More continued, "who tried to shoot Magpie, spy for the Binaye Ahani who slay people with their eyes. After that, Changing Woman spoke to you, begged you."

Begged him to comprehend the awful consequences of his disobedience, since those spies of the alien gods would tell their masters, who would come to devour him as they had devoured so many before. But that was only part of the legend, the rest of it having been played out as the Twins faced their enemies in battle and finally destroyed them.

"I did not want to see you in my dream," Drums No More continued. "I am proud of you, eldest of my grandchildren. My heart swells in memory of your courage in taking the horses and confronting the captain, but you are not Changing Woman's son."

"No, I am mortal." *A man who does not want to carry the weight of change.*

"And that is why I fought to end my dream, but instead, everything happened as it had in ancient times. The monsters appeared and you, the Hero Twins, fought them. Only—only the monsters were not Tsetahotsiltali, Teelget, Binaye Ahani and the others. They were, all of them, Captain Lopez and his men."

"I was alone?" Cougar made himself ask.

"No. Other Navajo men were with you and you were their leader."

"And when you dream was over, were all the monsters dead, or—or had they killed us?"

"I do not know."

The next morning, Cougar slung his bow and arrows over his shoulder, thanked his mother for the leather bag she'd filled with food, and turned to face the ten braves who would accompany him. Storm Wind had created a dry painting during the night, and at dawn Cougar and the others had knelt around it while they prayed and chanted the Door Path Song.

He had no doubts about the message in his grandfather's dream or the way the painting had been created or whether they'd chosen the correct song to start them on their way, but he'd never imagined himself following in the Hero Twins' footsteps. His birth and childhood hadn't been different from any other boys', so why had he been singled out this way?

During the sleepless night, he'd asked himself this so many times that his head had pounded with it. His wound ached because he'd tossed about so much; he continued to hear Morning Butterfly's words, to acknowledge that he was embarking on a path of war while she spoke only of peace.

What would she think of what he was doing now? Would she hate him—refuse to ever speak to him again?

Did she even know he was alive?

"Cougar?" Blue Swallow prompted from where he stood

beside him. "What will we do when we overtake the soldiers?"

"What?" Shaking his head, he fought to dismiss Morning Butterfly from his mind. "I do not know."

"Not know?" The other brave indicated his arrows. "Surely our weapons speak for themselves. There can be no peace with the newcomers, none."

Drums No More was standing beside the shaman. Instead of puffing out his chest because his grandson would be leading the group, the old man looked shrunken and sad.

"Cougar?" Blue Swallow pressed.

"You are right." He touched his side. "The Navajo and newcomers will never walk together as one. This is Dinehtah, our land, and the Spanish do not belong here."

"Then they must die."

Them, or us?

Because he'd never made the journey on horseback, Cougar was unsure how long it would have taken the soldiers to reach the great canyon. The captain might have forced some Hopi to guide him and his men across the desert, through the forest and to the canyon. They might already have discovered that the canyon wasn't a place that easily gave up its wealth. They might already be on their way back to Oraibi.

With that possibility foremost on his mind, Cougar directed his companions to accompany him, not along the well-worn trails used by generations of Indians, but through the wilderness, where they could more easily hide. Although that slowed them, no one argued with him. Instead, they readily agreed with his every suggestion, and he accepted the sense of power even as he fought a thousand uncertainties. Did Captain Lopez ever feel this way, or had the man readily embraced his many responsibilities? Was he so convinced he was right that no doubt ever entered his mind?

After five days and an equal number of nights, they reached the canyon's edge. Although he'd been here twice before, Cougar felt awed by it, made small, insignificant, humble. Nothing touched the massive cut in size or depth;

nothing else could possibly so dominate the land. No matter what Captain Lopez had been told about it, he couldn't have prepared himself for its vastness. The canyon was everything, this world and beyond.

Had Morning Butterfly ever stood here and taken proof of the gods' power into her soul?

Almost as one, each man took a pinch of corn pollen from his medicine pouch and cast it into the air, watching the golden flakes fall and fall until they disappeared far below.

The wind blew as it so often did here, and in the breeze lived the memories of all those who'd come before. Listening intently, Cougar "heard" of when the first Spaniards reached the vast earth-wound created by ancient gods and spirits. The Hopi had agreed to lead a man called Garcia Lopez de Cardenas and some twenty followers along one of the twisting trails leading here. Upon seeing the immense gorge, one of them, Padrode Castaneda, had made many marks on his talking leaves so that those who lived after his death would know what he had witnessed. The Hopi hadn't understood why he hadn't simply ordered his experience passed from mouth to mouth into forever, but such was the ways of the newcomers.

Three of the early explorers had wanted to climb down to the river, but they hadn't asked a Hopi to accompany them, so no one could say for certain how far they'd gone. They'd left at dawn and returned before night, their eyes speaking of awe, disbelief, exhaustion, and fear.

The Hopi still laughed at the foolish newcomers who hadn't thought to take along enough water and whose eyes hadn't told them the truth about the steep descent or climb. If they'd let go of their prideful ways, the Hopi would have told the Spanish that no one made such a journey without filling gourds with water and burying the gourds on the way down so they'd have something to drink on the way back.

What had caused the most laughter was that the three foolish explorers had tried to make the descent on horseback. Cougar hoped Captain Lopez hadn't done the same, not because he cared what happened to the soldiers, but because it would be a shame to risk a horse's life in such a way.

He'd dismounted and, along with the others, was staring at the ground where the soldiers' horses had left marks when he became aware of movement so far to his left that he couldn't be sure what was responsible for it. He pointed, to call the others' attention to possible danger.

"Soldiers?" Blue Swallow whispered.

"Perhaps."

Blue Swallow nodded and offered to accompany him. After vaulting back onto their horses, they started forward. The closer he came, the more convinced Cougar grew that they were indeed looking at human beings, but because those figures were on foot, he didn't believe they were soldiers. Blue Swallow rode as if he and his horse shared the same heart, as if he'd been born sitting there.

"I look at you," Cougar told him, "and I know it is right for the Navajo to have horses. Whether the gift came from Changing Woman or a Spanish god does not matter."

"Perhaps the Spanish gods looked at Changing Woman and the Hero Twins and saw that what is Navajo is greater than anything they call theirs."

"Perhaps." It felt good to laugh, even if only briefly.

"Cougar? I want to ask you something. I thought to wait until I was certain my question would not anger you, but if you and I do not live past today—"

"We are not going to die!"

"You have looked into the future and know what it brings?"

"No, of course not, but this is a peaceful day, full of what has been from the beginning of time. The wind carries no warning in it."

"And the wind speaks to you?" Blue Swallow's reprimand had much humor in it.

Cougar had been wrong to try to voice his sense of peace, and much as he resented being corrected, Blue Swallow was right to remind him how little it took to stray off the

Way Of Life. "No," he admitted, then asked Blue Swallow to continue.

"When your grandfather told us of his dream, did you believe he brought a message from the gods or—or did part of you wonder if it was simply a dream, like countless others?"

"A man should want to be touched by Changing Woman," he said. "What greater glory is there than to be told he is more than mortal?"

"None."

"But I am a man. A man."

Blue Swallow grunted but didn't say anything.

"No," Cougar admitted, "I did not want to hear my grandfather's dream."

"But you did not turn from it."

"No."

"I think . . . that is why I am with you, not because of a dream but because you accepted the weight of Drums No More's words. Why did you?"

He was older than Blue Swallow, experienced in ways the other man wasn't, and yet today he considered him his brother. "Because I looked at what the Spanish did to my grandfather; they turned him into an old man who cannot fight." *Who, maybe, was scarred in ways he has kept from everyone except Morning Butterfly.* "Maybe the time for war with the Spanish is here. If so, I will fight for my grandfather."

"And die for him?"

What Cougar had spotted turned out to be three Zuni hunters who'd been as leery of the Navajo as they'd been of them. Using trade language, the Zuni explained that they'd come to the canyon after deer, but although the signs had been plentiful, they hadn't followed them because they wouldn't risk exposing themselves to mounted Spanish soldiers. The Spanish had been here when the Zuni arrived, and the Zuni watched them entering and leaving the canyon over and over again the way ants wander in and out of their underground homes. Several times the soldiers had tried to ride their horses into the canyon, but after one animal broke its leg and another had to be abandoned, screaming in pain after it fell a great distance, they'd made their trips on foot.

The Zuni hadn't been able to make sense of what the soldiers were doing. They'd speculated that the foolish newcomers were trying to get to the river, but surely any observant man who would have used one of the several trails that showed the way down. Instead, the soldiers had taken a different route each morning and returned either late in the day or, occasionally, not until the next day, obviously having spent the night clinging to the steep sides. They were looking for something, the Zuni had concluded.

Cougar asked if the soldiers were still here. Yes, he was told, the crazy newcomers were a morning's ride to the south.

"So we go there?" Blue Swallow asked.

Caught in the memory of the look in his grandfather's eyes, Cougar nodded.

"And then we rid Dinehtah of those who do not belong?"

"Yes." *If Changing Woman so wills it.*

Perhaps his heart wouldn't beat like that of a captured bird, Cougar thought, if his companions had filled the air with boasting, but Blue Swallow and the others had been silent. They'd camped for the night so they could rest their horses and prepare themselves with stories of how the Navajo had come to Dinehtah.

To his surprise, he'd slept soundly and had no disturbing dreams, perhaps because he'd taken strength from the legend of how Changing Woman's younger sister, White Shell Woman, had been visited by Hastseyalti, Talking God, and Hastsehogan, the House God who'd created the people who became the House of Dark Cliffs Clan. That clan, along with others, had moved from where White Shell Woman had been living and traveled west until they finally reached the land the gods had given the Navajo.

Now, touched by the reality of daylight, he remembered the rest of the story—that the clans had left the East because they'd been few in number and their enemies many. If the past ever repeated itself, maybe there were as many Spanish as rocks littered the ground and his people would be forced to leave the land where their hearts belonged.

If that time came, would he be among those who gathered up their belongings to flee, or would his blood already have been shed?

He didn't want these thoughts! Didn't want to be doing what he was! If he could follow his heart's desires today, he would be with Morning Butterfly while she told him of ways other than war.

The day was hot and without a breeze to keep a man from sweating. Their precious water supply was running low and although there was a spring nearby, if they stopped there, it would be dark before they reached the soldiers. Cougar didn't mind traveling at night, but forcing the horses across ground they couldn't see would increase the risk of injury. Besides, the soldiers might hear them coming and hide in wait.

Again and again his gaze turned to the sky as he looked for clouds with messages in them, but nothing disturbed the endless blue. The clip-clip of the horses' hooves calmed him a little, but he still wished he had something to think of other than what might happen once they overtook the Spanish.

Finally the sun had passed the midpoint in its daily journey and was on its way to where it spent its nights; it was time to send a brave out alone. Cougar studied his companions. Over half were married, and even those who hadn't yet moved into a woman's hogan and fathered children were responsible for their sisters' children. They were warriors, yes, but they were also hunters, and if they died, their families would go hungry.

"Wait here," he told them. "I will go on alone, on foot. When I have found our enemy, I will return and we will discuss what must be done."

"Alone?" Blue Swallow questioned. "What if something happens to you?"

"Then you will know my grandfather was wrong to place his trust in me."

Sweat and dirt clung to every inch of Captain Lopez's body. The skin under his beard itched unrelentingly, and whenever he scratched, he dug into the scabs there and they started bleeding again. Under his arms and between his legs his flesh burned and throbbed, red and irritated. He'd been sunburned enough times that he knew new skin would eventually replace what he'd lost, but not until he got out of the sun for several days at least. Tired, hungry, thirsty, filthy, disappointed, and furious, he barely cared whether he lived or died.

He forced his eyes to focus and stared at his surroundings. He and the others, miserable excuses for men that they were, clung to the canyon's wall. They were so deep into that gash in the ground that from where he was, he couldn't see the sun. In and of itself, that was a relief, because at least he was spared its relentless rays.

For the life of him, he couldn't remember how many times they'd ventured into this hell-hole. In the beginning, each expedition had filled him with great enthusiasm. Surely this time the canyon would give up its secrets; surely this time what from a distance glittered like jewels would turn out to be emeralds—or gold.

But one failed attempt had turned into two and then three and then—then what?

Had the Navajo lied? Half sick and exhausted both in body and spirit, he still ordered his men to follow him into this godforsaken entrance into hell.

Because he'd never failed before.

"Failure."

Shocked by the raspy sound of his voice, he forced himself to set down his pick and stare at the cuts he'd made in the stone, dully accepting that a half-day's effort hadn't accomplished much. Due to the rough terrain, he and his men were all at considerable distance from each other, not that he had any desire for companionship. Still, being able to talk to someone—

There wasn't a soul! Never had been and never would.

His wife wanted only one thing from him, a husband capable of satisfying her demanding father, though Lopez still wasn't sure he ever would. What he did know was that he hadn't been the first to bed Bonita Marie. He'd expected to find her an inexperienced virgin and had put his mind to what he should do to ease their wedding night for her. In a rare moment of fantasy, he'd seen himself guiding her from innocence and fear into womanhood. He'd never confess this to a living soul of course, because a military man wasn't expected to have tender thoughts. Compassion and kindness only weakened a soldier's ability to do what he must on the battlefield. He never was certain who had deflowered Bonita Marie, though he suspected it had been her confessor, from the looks they exchanged. Yet another reason he did not trust religious men.

All his wife wanted from him was a home worthy of her station in life—and service in her bed. If he couldn't do that, he knew, she would find another man, just as he replaced one horse with another when the first broke down.

Singer Of Songs was a spring flower, simple and innocent, gentle. True, the language barrier made honest communication impossible, but perhaps that was better. This way he could imagine Singer Of Songs was everything he needed in a woman.

Fighting what couldn't possibly be tears, he suddenly knew with absolute certainty that his entire life to this point had been a failure. In a dim way he recognized that exhaustion was partly responsible for his dark mood, but there was only so much a man could endure, so much pain, so much disappointment . . .

Crying, he gripped his pick with both hands and swung it against the rock with every ounce of strength left in him. In his mind he saw not stone, but the face of the heathen known as Cougar.

* * *

With their front legs tethered, the soldiers' horses couldn't travel far; still, Cougar was surprised to find them unguarded. It was also unlike Captain Lopez to leave them in plain sight like this. After assuring himself that he was truly alone, Cougar studied the animals. They'd all lost weight and two were lame; none more than glanced at him before going back to the task of trying to find something to eat. He considered freeing and stampeding them so the soldiers would be reduced to walking, but with no way of finding water on their own, he'd be condemning the valuable animals to a miserable death. He could rope them together and lead them to his companions. And then—

Absently rubbing the chest of the nearest horse, he turned his plan around in his mind. He'd never heard it said that the soldiers were skilled trackers, but even they should be able to follow the missing horses' tracks. They wouldn't know a Navajo had taken them; maybe they'd believe the animals had managed to shake off their tethers on their own.

No, they wouldn't, he admitted. One horse might pull free, but not all of them. Still, the soldiers would have no choice but to try to find their missing animals. No matter how tired they were, the men would head after them, even walking through the night.

Dying, lost, alone and on foot.

But Drums No More's dream had been of a Hero grandson, not one who abandons his enemies to the elements.

"Is that what you want?" he asked, not sure whether he was speaking to his grandfather or Changing Woman—or himself. "For me to face the soldiers? To go to war with them? To die, maybe, at their hands?"

22

Last harvest season, Morning Butterfly's mother had been so proud of the piles of dried corn which took up one wall of the house that she'd daily pointed out the heaps of the brilliant white, red, yellow, and purple-black ears. Now much of that was gone—confiscated by the padre and added to the pile he intended to send far away.

This morning, although her mother had wanted, once again, to discuss her concerns about the dwindling supply, Morning Butterfly had left Oraibi and was busying her hands, if not her head and heart, by collecting rabbit brush. She intended to add it to the basket she'd been working on at night—the only time Fray Angelico didn't need her. Wondering how long it would take him to find her today, she kept looking over her shoulder.

As she wandered here and there, she tried not to think about the march of time, but this year's corn stalks had already bent low under the weight of ripe ears. From the beginning, corn had sustained her people and been part of their religion, but if what Fray Angelico had told her came true, that would end. He called the taking of Hopi crops and other belongings and sending them far away "contributions to God." When she'd questioned why her people should contribute to a deity unknown to them before the coming of the first Spanish, he'd launched into an explanation that had made no more sense. The Spanish leaders, governors, and viceroys, even the king, had proclaimed that not only the Church but the State as well should profit from what was in the land discovered by Spanish explorers. The Crown had proclaimed that all land north of New Spain belonged to Spain, not to the Hopi, Zuni, or Navajo.

Shifting her small load from her right arm to her left, she shaded her eyes and stared at the horizon. Sound carried great distances on the wind, and she could hear a stone-laden wagon approaching. Unwilling to acknowledge the seemingly endless parade of building materials, she turned her back on it. As she did, her attention was drawn to movement in the direction of the setting sun—the way the soldiers had gone. If they were returning . . .

Teeth clenched, she set down her bundle and half walked, half ran to a rise. At the top, she again shielded her eyes. To her relief, the approaching figures were on foot, which meant they were probably traveling Indians. Still, if they'd been near the great canyon, they might have news.

Not wanting to appear overanxious, she waited for the travelers to approach. She wasn't the only one eager for news, and by the time the few Zuni were close enough to yell out a greeting, she was surrounded by other Hopi. Because Broken Toe Mends often traded with the Zuni, he easily communicated with them. After a long conversation, Broken Toe Mends passed on what he'd learned. And with each word, her despair grew.

The Zuni had camped near the soldiers for several days, hoping the newcomers would grow careless so they could steal some horses. Unfortunately, the soldiers had remained vigilant even as they drove themselves to the brink of exhaustion while exploring the great canyon. The Zuni had been about to leave when a number of Navajo braves appeared.

"The Navajo were looking for the soldiers," Broken Toe Mends explained. "They were all on horseback, well-armed, with enough food and water for a long journey. Their leader told the Zuni they had come to kill the soldiers because Changing Woman had ordered it."

"What was their leader's name?" Morning Butterfly forced herself to ask.

"They do not know. What he did say was that his grandfather, a man who was mutilated at Acoma, had dreamed what he must do."

Cougar!

She was still trying to absorb this when Broken Toe Mends continued. One Navajo had gone alone to study the soldiers. After his return, there'd been much discussion about what to do, but in the end they'd declared they would continue on the path laid out by the dream's prophecy. The Zuni, who wanted to see what would happen, followed them.

"The Navajo waited for the soldiers to come out of the canyon," Broken Toe Mends explained. "Then, although they could have lain in wait and attacked the soldiers while they were unaware, the Navajo showed themselves. There was much yelling on both sides, and when the soldiers began firing their weapons, the Zuni fled."

"They do not know if any Navajo were killed?"

"No. The Zuni say the soldiers' weapons surely pierced flesh because the fire sticks screamed so many times."

Someone asked if the Zuni knew whether any soldiers had died, but Morning Butterfly didn't care. In her mind she all too clearly saw the uneven battle—simple bows and arrows against powerful, far-reaching powder and balls.

"Did the Zuni go back after the battle was over?" she asked. "Perhaps then they counted the dead?"

"No."

* * *

"You cannot breathe life back into him if he is no more," Singer Of Songs said.

"I know."

"Then do not think of him. What happens to a Navajo is not the concern of a Hopi, is it?

"No."

"Then—"

"I cannot stop what I feel inside!" Morning Butterfly blurted. Before she could stop herself, she'd jumped to her feet and stalked from one end of her family's pueblo to the other in a futile attempt to escape her sister's words.

"The last time I saw him, blood flowed from a wound in his side, and although he seemed strong, I feared he'd died," she said. "To learn he survived that injury but may have been killed at the canyon—I do not know if I can bear it."

"This is not right," Singer Of Songs said, her tone a mix of concern and irritation. "Sister, you must put your thoughts on what it is to be a Hopi woman. I see the way the unmarried men look at you. They want you to choose one of them."

It didn't matter. Ever since yesterday, when she'd learned of the battle between Navajo and soldiers, nothing else had mattered. She hadn't slept at all last night, couldn't remember where she'd set down her rabbit brush, and had deliberately avoided Fray Angelico although he'd sent a messenger after her.

"How can I think of marriage when so much has changed for our people?" she asked distractedly.

Singer Of Songs got to her feet. Although her body hadn't yet been changed by her pregnancy, her movements were slow. "Sister, listen to me. When I knew what the captain had done to me, that I was carrying his child, I was in despair. It was you who reminded me that I was Hopi and the baby would be as well. I smile again because my heart is Hopi. That is what you are."

"I know."

"Singer Of Songs looked at her closely, then said, "You love him, do you not?"

On the tail of a sigh, Morning Butterfly turned back around and faced her sister. At the moment, they were alone in the pueblo and whatever she said in confidence to Singer Of Songs would remain that way.

"I feel different when I think about him," she admitted. "I remember what his voice sounds like. When I close my eyes, I can see him looking at me. The things we said to each other remain inside me and . . ."

"And what?"

"I do not know! His beliefs were—are—not the same as mine and he would go to war when that will never be the Hopi way."

"But those things do not mean your heart cannot be touched by his."

"How do you know? You are wise in the ways of love?" Regretting the words the moment they were out of her mouth, she reached for her sister. "I am sorry. I attack you when it is I who should feel my anger."

"Why? Because to love a Navajo is wrong?"

"No. Yes. I do not know."

Chuckling, Singer Of Songs hugged her. "Our legends tell us what our rhythm for life should be, but they do not say enough about matters of the heart."

"No," Morning Butterfly agreed. "They do not."

"Perhaps that is because there is no wisdom where the heart is concerned. I hope—I pray—the day will come when a Hopi man comes to me and asks me to become his wife and my heart answers yes."

"I want that for you," Morning Butterfly admitted around the lump in her throat.

"As I want the same for you."

Nothing had changed about the damnable place. Oraibi still stood sentinel over the inhospitable land and the wind continued its hellish sound as it ripped its way over the worthless earth. A man with more in his belly and less weight in his heart might feel pride at seeing the work that had been done on the church, but Captain Lopez was hard put to find anything positive about the day. His back throbbed and his left knee was swollen to twice its normal size. His lips were split in numerous places.

As he expected, his appearance caused the miserable Hopi to stop what they were doing and stare at what remained of his troops. Only the fact that they had no way of communicating what they were witnessing to his fellow Spaniards kept him from utter despair. Let the creatures point and laugh; at least his superiors and father-in-law would never know. Maybe.

Whether he was glad to see the padre or not was hard to say. Still, Fray Angelico took his responsibilities seriously and was a compassionate man. Without comment or question, the little brown man hurried over to him, then waited patiently as he dismounted.

"Food and water," Captain Lopez said, his tone as unhurried as he could make it. "Care for our horses. And medical attention."

"I will see to those things," the padre assured him. "And prayer? Surely you wish—"

"Later. Later." In truth, his need for prayer was stronger than it had ever been, and if his knee's throbbing hadn't been so persistent, he would have bent before the padre. "Some of my men were wounded and their injuries have become infected. Whatever Morning Butterfly used on Pablo, that is what they need."

"Of course, of course. Captain, you left with six men. One is missing."

"Dead." He forced the word. "Killed by murdering Navajo."

"I will pray for his soul."

A harsh laugh worked its way up from somewhere deep inside him. "If you are determined to pray for the dead, you have your work cut out for you."

"What do you mean?"

Eyes half closed, he went back to the hot, exhausted afternoon four days ago when he and his men had been attacked. The hatred he'd felt then surged back, shoved aside everything else. "The miserable savages paid for what they did. By all that's holy, they paid!"

His outburst must have exhausted him, because he didn't remember saying or doing anything for a long time afterward. He had a dim memory of someone, probably the padre, taking his arm . . . and somehow he found himself inside the half-finished church. His men were there as well, stretched out on the ground, one or two moaning.

There was another dim memory—of "Madariaga de Oñate" first warily studying him and then assisting in making the others as comfortable as possible. Later he'd demand that Madariaga give an accounting of himself, but for now only one thing mattered—drinking until his sunken belly threatened to burst.

The blessed water revived him. He realized that he was sitting in a surprisingly comfortable wood-and-leather chair. When he commented on it, Fray Angelico explained that he'd spent considerable time overseeing the work the Hopi women did on it. He wanted more, but getting the women to work with any degree of enthusiasm was proving difficult.

"At first I told myself they were so lacking in intellect that I should not berate them for their inability to comprehend the most basic of instructions," Fray Angelico said. "But I know different now."

"I could have told you that a long time ago. Still," he said as he looked around, "I compliment you for what you have accomplished. I did not expect to find the work here so far advanced."

Looking pleased, Angelico said, "God's hand is truly here. My prayers are indeed being answered."

"Perhaps prayers," Lopez muttered. "And perhaps it is simply in the Hopi's nature to bend their backs to any task."

Ignoring his comment, the padre explained that he'd sent for Morning Butterfly. "I must confess that having to rely on her has proven burdensome."

"Oh?"

"No matter how strongly I word my desire to have her at my side at all times, she professes not to understand. Also, I cannot trust she is faithful in her translation of what I need to impart."

"She defies you?"

A look of pain touched Angelico's features, but instead of explaining, he got to his feet and started toward the church entrance, but before he reached it, a small figure passed through the opening. For a moment Lopez thought it might be Singer Of Songs, but of course she wouldn't care about his welfare.

"You took your own sweet time getting here," he told Morning Butterfly. "Could it be you do not care whether a soldier lives or dies?"

She met his gaze. "I came as soon as I heard."

"Hm. I want you to immediately treat my men's wounds. And you had better pray no one's condition worsens. If it does—"

Although she nodded to indicate she understood, she didn't look at all intimidated. In fact, if he was as shrewd a judge of human nature as he prided himself on being, she had her own reasons for being here. If nothing else, her attitude pulled him back to reality. After telling him she'd brought along a supply of healing herbs and would apply them as soon as she'd assessed the soldiers' wounds, she asked if it was true that they'd been attacked by Navajo.

"I do not believe I said. In fact, I am certain this is the first time the miserable tribe has been mentioned today. Tell me, why did you say that?"

Confusion briefly clouded her dark eyes, and she held herself so taut that he half expected her to snap in two. Her fingers were fisted, the flesh around her knuckles white. Hoping his injured knee wouldn't give way, he stood, stepped toward her, and took hold of her wrist.

"You do not care whether I live or die," he told her. "In fact, it would bring you great pleasure to be looking at my lifeless body right now, wouldn't it?"

As before, she boldly returned his gaze.

"I thought so. Ah, Morning Butterfly, you remind me so much of my own 'dear' wife. She too does not show respect to a man who is in every way her better. But where she is well schooled in what emotions she should reveal and those she should keep to herself—at least in public—you are all too easy to read."

A slow blink was her only reaction.

"You are here, not just to nurse the injured, but because you want to know what happened. I am right, am I not?"

"Yes."

"And why does it matter to you?"

"One of your men is missing," she said after a brief silence. "He is dead?"

"I think you know the answer to that."

"Was his the only death?"

"The only— Wait. I understand. You want to know how many of the savages we killed."

Yes, she answered without saying a word.

"Oh yes, my dear Morning Butterfly, my men and I won that battle. Overwhelmed by our superior weaponry, the creatures fled."

"Fled?"

"Tried to run away like the cowards they are. But they had nowhere to run except toward the canyon's edge. The sounds of their screams as they fell to their deaths was music to my ears."

"They are all dead?"

"It gives me great pleasure to report to you that, yes, they are."

Morning Butterfly's hands belonged to someone who knew what had to be done and went about the necessary tasks. She knelt over one soldier after another, washed dirt and dried blood off scratches, blisters, and wounds, covered them with healing poultices, sometimes spoke a few words, but heard nothing of what they said to her.

These men had forced the Navajo over the canyon's edge that had no gentle slope, nothing for a desperate warrior to cling to. Death might not come until a man reached the river at the bottom, but there could be only one end.

And as that man fell, he'd know what that end would be.

She prayed that Cougar—and the others—hadn't suffered, that their fear had soon been extinguished and their souls were at rest. When she wasn't praying for that, she prayed for forgetfulness for herself.

And, although maybe she was deluding herself, she prayed that Captain Lopez had lied to her.

Lopez slept without moving until nearly noon the day after their return, then ate until his stomach refused to take in any more. He'd tried to get Morning Butterfly to send Singer Of Songs to him, but she'd pretended not to understand. He and the padre would have to decide how to deal with her defiance, but the truth was, he still wasn't up to sex, or even facing the young woman who'd become more than a way of releasing physical tension. Calling Madariaga to him was easier.

"What were my final words to you?" he demanded of the dark, handsome young man.

"That you never wanted to see me again." Madariaga didn't meet his gaze.

"Then why have you defied me?"

"You know," Madariaga whispered, "I have just a single horse. If it did not survive the journey back to Santa Fe . . ."

"Go on."

"It is not just that," he went on after a minute. "A man out alone in that wilderness—he might not survive."

"You should have thought of that before questioning my leadership."

"Not your leadership, sir. Never that. I simply . . ."

"Go on."

"We—we were sent here to assist in the spreading of God's word. It concerned me that He was not being given His due at a time when His guidance and protection were needed."

They—at least he—were here for reasons beyond religious ones, but instead of telling Madariaga that, Lopez pondered whether the expedition to the great canyon and the confrontation with the Navajo might have turned out differently if he'd done more to assure that God rode at his shoulder. Never mind; he hadn't.

"I am not going to discuss that with you," he said, eager to finish the conversation. "For once disobedience has turned into a benefit. Until my men have recovered, you must assume their duties."

"I have been assisting Fray Angelico. The supplies are nearly ready to be sent to Santa Fe, and the church—you see how much has been accomplished."

"Hm. Be that as it may, from now on, you will again report only to me. Do you understand?"

Although he nodded, Madariaga hesitated just long enough to let Lopez know where his loyalties lay; it didn't surprise him. After all, the Church's hold on its subjects was a powerful one. Only a few, like him, ever questioned that control.

Captain Lopez had turned back into a strutting stallion. When he'd first dragged himself back to Oraibi, he'd been a cowed, even frightened man, but that hadn't lasted. Why had he expected it to? Angelico asked himself as he watched the captain take inventory of the garrison's weapons. A man's basic nature doesn't change, at least not that of a worldly man incapable of surrendering himself to the Lord.

"Lord," Angelico prayed aloud, "whatever path You choose for me, I gladly walk it, but I believe You have sent me a message. If I am to do Your work here, I must be free of certain oppressive presences. The Hopi need not a heavy military hand, but my gentle guidance—only that."

He cast about for something to fix his attention on but found only a small, dark cloud. Perhaps he was that cloud, alone and yet secure. Free to roam the heavens—free to spread the Lord's Word.

That, he prayed, would happen once his latest letter of complaint reached the governor.

23

────────────

"He may be dead." Morning Butterfly threw back her head and stared up at the sky. Her eyes burned from her sleepless night, but she didn't dare close them for fear an image of Cougar's lifeless body would appear.

"Listen to me, my child," One Hand said. "It is not for us to know what happens beyond where our eyes take us. What I say to you is, live with what is around you; that is your truth."

"The truth is not always what we want," she said, her gaze going to his stump.

"Hating reality does not turn it away."

Most of the conversations she and One Hand had had over the years had been about practical matters, the day-to-day concerns of life. By unspoken agreement, they'd never brought up his nightmares or her efforts to ease his mind. His insight this afternoon touched her deeply.

"I need to take your words into me," she admitted. "I must learn from your wisdom so I no longer resist the changes to our way of life. So—so Cougar's death becomes part of reality."

"You ask much of yourself, more than I have been capable of."

"No. You are teacher. I—"

"Do not look at my footprints and plan your journey from them, Morning Butterfly." His words were as soft as hers had been. "I am not one man, but two. The one you see now is as you say, accepting of reality. But there is another—fearful."

"I know." She dropped to her knees before where he was sitting and covered his stump with her hand.

He stared at what she'd done. "Yes, you do, because you have seen and heard and held that fearful man. Because you do not turn your back on my weakness."

"Never! One Hand, I love you."

"As I love you, granddaughter of my heart." Leaning forward, he kissed her forehead. "Your eyes speak of great weariness. Caring for the soldiers took much from you."

"Not so much," she admitted. "Their injuries were not mine, and what I saw and did today did not touch my soul. When they cried out, the sounds were nothing like what escapes you at night." There. She'd said it.

Nodding, he met her gaze with eyes as weary as hers felt. She started to stand, but he rested his hand on her shoulder, stopping her. "It is right that you and I are together today, and that I see your fears for Cougar. Morning Butterfly, you have given me gifts without end. I want it to be my turn to give to you."

How could anyone have thought this gentle man was their enemy!

"You are not at peace," he went on. "Your heart struggles for answers, as does your soul. You must walk with a man who believes everything about the Hopi is wrong and should be changed, a man who wants us to renounce all we have ever been and follow only his teachings. Maybe that is what has torn your heart."

"No," she told him without the slightest hesitancy. "I—I

feel sorry for the padre even as I acknowledge that his belief is as much a part of him as his need for air. I listen to his prayers, but they will never become mine."

"Have you told him that?"

"I tried once. I no longer do." A memory washed over her and took her from thoughts of Fray Angelico. Not fighting, she buried herself in it.

"Morning Butterfly, what are you thinking?"

"Of—when I was with Cougar, he and I spoke of what is different about our people, but there was no anger between us, only understanding."

"He did not tell you to cease being Hopi and become Navajo?"

"He would never do that."

"And you did not ask him to leave his beliefs and embrace yours?"

"No. I would never—"

"I know," One Hand assured her. "What I say to you today is that that, in part, is why Cougar touched your heart."

Unable to speak, she could only nod in mute agreement.

"Morning Butterfly, you are more than heart and soul." He touched the top of her head. "Remember the lessons from the First People. As long as we listen to the earth, wisdom and peace are ours."

"I know." Had she ever known peace? Lost in turmoil, she couldn't remember.

"When a child is born, certain ceremonies are held that make that child one with not just his family, but also the earth. As a child grows, he learns that his real parents are not those who live with him but Mother Earth, from whose flesh all are born, and Father Sun, who gives life to the universe."

"Why are you saying this?"

"Because Mother Earth and Father Sun will give you the answers that Hopi people cannot." He increased the pressure on her head. "When you were born, this place was not hard as it is now but soft, your *kopavi*."

Kopavi, the open door through which Hopi received life

and communicated with their Creator. With every breath an infant took, the soft spot moved up and down with a vibration that communicated to the Creator. At the time of red light or Talawva, the soft spot hardened and the door closed, remaining that way until a person's death when the door reopened so his life could depart as it had come. Below the *kopavi* was the second center, the brain, which carried out the plan of all Creation. Third was the throat which, along with the mouth and nose, accepted the breath of life and had the ability to speak and sing praises to the Creator. The heart came next, where man felt the good of life and its true purpose. The navel was the Creator's throne; from there he directed all of man's functions.

"Be one with the Creator, Morning Butterfly. One with the earth so it can speak to you."

When the Creator gave life to the First People, they'd known only peace and happiness and had multiplied and spread over the land, but eventually they forgot Sotuknang and Spider Woman's commands to respect their Creator. When they did, animals drew away and people became estranged from one another. According to legend, Sotuknang told the few believers that the world as they knew it would be destroyed and another created so harmony could return. They were directed to listen to their *kopavi*'s wisdom, which allowed them to see a certain cloud they should follow by day and a star to lead them at night, taking them far from the destruction.

"I am confused," Morning Butterfly admitted. "My thoughts are full of the Creator and what he did to make us one with the earth, but I am only an earth woman, not Sotuknang or Spider Woman."

"But you believe."

"Yes."

"Because of that, if the time has come again when the Creator is no longer respected, you will not be destroyed, will you?"

She couldn't answer, could only head into the future

guided by the past. She stood and began to walk. The sky was blue and pure, contrasting sharply with Oraibi's gray walls. As summer gave way to fall, the blue would fade, and by winter, sky and Hopi home would be nearly the same.

A single cloud hung in the distance. White as a newborn sheep's coat, it looked forsaken, silent, and untouchable. Cloud-shapes were like the wind, always changing, and yet this one held a warrior's features. No matter how long she looked at it, the features remained.

Sotuknang had directed the ancient believers to follow a magical cloud.

Feeling suddenly weightless, she looked around for One Hand, but he had not accompanied her.

The cloud was west of her. If she stood directly under it, she would be—at the great canyon.

"Sotuknang, is this cloud for me?"

After filling a bladder with water, selecting several pieces of piki so she'd have the finely ground and baked cornmeal to eat, and picking up a length of rope, Morning Butterfly scrambled down off the mesa. She'd debated telling her sister and parents what she was doing, but her father had fallen twice recently and her mother's eyes turned dark with concern whenever she looked at him. Singer Of Songs had been spending much of her time with their aunt's newborn—and waiting for Captain Lopez to again demand her presence. Hopefully Morning Butterfly's family would think she was with the padre or tending to the soldiers.

Although she avoided the areas where the soldiers and other Spanish were, she gave them little mind. Her heartbeat seemed so loud that she wondered if her heart had been touched by thunder, and her head throbbed. When she covered her throat with her hand, she felt the rise and fall of each breath, and when her hand moved to her navel, she thought of the woman-part of her, the Creator-given gift that made it possible for her to create life. Her feet—Hopi feet—stood on Mother Earth.

With each step, she became more and more one with the earth. She was surrounded by kachinas, guided and protected by them, a Hopi woman seeking the truth.

Seeking a Navajo man.

Her hands belonged to someone else as they untied the cord holding the corral gate in place. Moving among the horses, she breathed in their scent and remembered the first time she'd seen Cougar as he galloped away on one of them. When a long-legged mare stepped toward her, she secured the rope around its lower jaw as she'd see Cougar do. Then she gathered her muscles and sprang onto the animal's back. She was closer to the cloud now and although night would swallow it before she stood under it, she prayed a star would emerge to show her the way.

And if it took her to where Cougar's body lay . . .

With her eyes on the sky, she cantered away from Oraibi.

Only one person saw her leave. Captain Lopez.

The cloud had given way to a blue-silver star that cast a steady light through the night while Morning Butterfly slept. Her horse remained nearby, perhaps comforted by her steady breathing. At dawn, the cloud reappeared and held steady throughout the day. On the second night, the star returned; the same thing happened the third night. By then she'd reached the forest, and the trees often hid the star's light from her, but she knew it was still there. She ate a little yarrow and needle grass to supplement the piki, not enough to completely silence her hunger but enough to keep her strong.

A child of open spaces, she wasn't sure what to make of the close-growing trees. She was grateful for the cool shade they provided, and their crisp scent fascinated her, but the trunks and branches hemmed her in, stole her view of her world. Accustomed to the wind's constant presence, she missed it. She heard it pressing against the treetops, the branches' random movements a kind of dance, but her flesh needed to be touched by moving air.

When the shadows threatened to take over everything, she told herself that the forest wasn't that different from the walls of Oraibi, but although remembering her home and family comforted her a little, she couldn't stop thinking about how strange and new everything felt.

The first time she caught a glimpse of movement in the shadows, it was all she could do not to turn and run. Quickly dismounting and sliding behind a tree, she peered around it, didn't think to breathe until she realized she was looking at a doe—by far the largest she'd ever seen. Relief flooded through her, causing her to sigh so loudly that the doe bounded away. After that, she trained herself to let curiosity take precedence over fear so that when she spotted a creature nearly the size of a newborn sheep but covered with what looked like a blanket of pine needles, she guessed it was a porcupine. Her people had long traded with other tribes for porcupine needles, but she'd never imagined the animal itself looked like that.

Easier to accept were the different kinds of birds, such as the large but skittish turkeys and loud jays, dark red squirrels, tiny, shy mice, and once—fleetingly—a short-eared bobcat that melted into its surroundings with a single, graceful leap. She'd heard of great bears who lived in the woods and knew no fear, but surely, she told herself, if one of the fierce creatures was about, the other animals would warn her. At least she prayed they would.

She'd always thought of the earth as something hard and dry, soil robbed of richness because of the lack of moisture, but here everything felt faintly damp as if earth and trees had wept cool tears. It seemed impossible that every drop wasn't precious, that in fact there was more than enough, and she vowed to tell her family of her discovery.

The days and nights she'd spent alone had made it possible for her to dismiss the Spanish presence from her mind. Although she occasionally tried, she couldn't recall a word of what Fray Angelico had told her about his God.

The cloud was nearly overhead now. In the past, the canyon hadn't been any more interesting to her than any other place she hadn't seen. She'd been told that looking over its edge was like staring into the center of the earth where Sotuknang had once taken First People so they could live with Ant People. She wanted to pull the vision into herself and make it a part of her so she could eventually describe it to her children.

That was what she would concentrate on, not what might wait for her once she was within the cloud's shadow.

She'd been following the child of the river that ran through the canyon's belly, sometimes riding along its banks, occasionally veering aside when it twisted and turned upon itself. No matter how many times she gazed at it, her wonder at this much water never ceased. If she could pick it up and carry it back with her, there would no longer be a need for Niman and corn would grow so thick and rich that it might become like the forest. She chuckled at the image of herself dragging a river behind her. Her horse started to lower its head to eat, then stopped, its muscles quivering.

Morning Butterfly heard the sound then, not part of the forest's song, but set apart and existing on its own. Sotuknang and Spider Woman might have shown her the way, but she wasn't so foolish as to believe they would guide her every step, be her eyes and ears, her wisdom.

After a quick prayer asking the horse to forgive her for leaving it exposed, she dismounted and slipped into the low-growing vegetation. Sharp branches scratched her calves and thighs, but she was barely aware of the discomfort. The sound grew stronger and closer, taking shape inside her mind, becoming horse and human.

Like a teasing child, the forest gave up its secret by slow degrees, but at length she knew the truth—a truth that filled her with tears, laughter, and prayers of thankfulness.

Cougar rode at the front of a line of men and horses. They were all Navajo, none wary of their surroundings but easy and relaxed. Occasionally, Cougar turned to speak to those behind him, and Morning Butterfly warned herself to take measure of them, but her eyes saw only Cougar, her ears strained only for his voice.

Alive. He was alive.

She was still taking him into her when he spotted her

horse and instantly became like his namesake, cautious and aware but not afraid, passing on his knowledge with a minimum of words. In her mind she saw herself walking toward him, lifting her hand in greeting, telling him how relieved she was to find him alive, but she felt suddenly naked and vulnerable. For now she would remain hidden.

Through a blur of tears, she saw the others gather around Cougar, their eyes scraping over their surroundings as they reached for their bows and arrows. Cougar took hold of her mare's rope, and it occurred to her that he would know it hadn't been ridden by a soldier. Would he think—

She placed her hands, fingers splayed, on the ground. This was Mother Earth, and she owed her existence to it and Father Sun. Belief had brought her here and belief would see her through what came next.

The song resounds back from our Creator with joy, and we of the earth repeat it to our Creator. At the appearing of the yellow light, repeats and repeats again the joyful echo, sounds and resounds for times to come.

Surrounded by the Song of Creation, she stood and walked toward the Navajo. The first man to spot her cried out a warning and aimed an arrow at her, but instead of shrinking away, she continued forward.

"Cougar," she said in Hopi, "I have been sent to you."

Morning Butterfly hadn't said anything about being hungry, but Cougar had seen it in her eyes and gladly shared some of his venison with her. He still didn't understand how she'd found him or what she'd meant by her greeting.

That could come later. It was vital for him to learn everything he could about what Captain Lopez had been doing and what he might do next, but although she willingly answered his questions as everyone sat in a circle in a small clearing, her explanations were like pollen on the wind— gone before he could capture them.

Morning Butterfly had come here alone, the journey taking three days and nights, riding fearlessly through land unknown to her, unarmed.

"No one knows you are here?" he asked, although she might have already told him.

"One Hand, maybe. I should have said something to my parents and sister, but . . ." She pressed her hand to her forehead. "Changing Woman came to me and told me what to do."

"She told you to come to the canyon to look for Navajo?"

"No." She didn't meet his eyes. "Captain Lopez boasted he had killed you, but my heart would not hear those words."

Something hummed between them, but how could he concentrate on it while surrounded by those who were family to him? "The captain lied," he said.

"I know that. Now."

But you did not for a long, hard time. "I am sorry for his lies."

"I thought—it came to me that he might be like a stag, full of himself."

"The Navajo were the stags, not soldiers," he said, laughing a little. "We came at them like grizzlies, killed one and forced them to flee."

"Not grizzlies," she whispered. "Your name led you into battle."

"Not just my name. Captain Lopez's grandfather sought to destroy mine. The time for that to be made right had come."

"I know."

"Do you? Can a Peaceful One understand—"

"Cougar, you and I have said these words to each other before; I do not want to do so again. Besides . . ."

"Besides what?"

Closing her eyes, she lingered behind her lids for a long time. "It is not so easy to be Hopi these days. When I see what is happening to my people . . ."

With a little prompting, she told him and the others about the recent changes at Oraibi. Although he tried to imagine what the church looked like, that didn't concern him as much as the hardships being forced upon the Hopi and what might happen now that the soldiers had returned.

Although the others occasionally asked questions of her

through him, she seemed barely aware of their presence. Instead, her eyes remained on him, her words were for him, her body leaned toward his. She'd started to ask about Drums No More when her eyes filled with tears. He took her hands in his and then flattened them on his chest.

"I am sorry," he whispered.

"Sorry?"

"When I took my grandfather's dreams of the Hero Twins into my heart and said I would act on them, I should have thought about what my decision would do to you."

"Me?"

"My actions touched you, became part of your life," he started, then fell silent because there were no words for what he now felt. Seeking wisdom, he looked around at his fellow braves, but of course they didn't understand what she and he were saying to each other.

"What are you going to do now?" he made himself ask.

"I must—must return to my people."

Singer Of Songs was rubbing her father's legs when she heard the first warning cry. Jumping to her feet, she hurried outside in time to see Captain Lopez and the other soldiers walking toward the center of the town. They were all heavily armed, but with helmets shading their features, she couldn't see what was in their eyes.

"What are they doing here?" her mother hissed from behind her. "They cannot—they have already taken so much."

"A little food remains, but if they know . . ."

Singer Of Songs glanced behind her long enough to spot her father silhouetted in the doorway and leaning against it for support. If Morning Butterfly was here, she would walk up to the soldiers and with her presence ask for an explanation, but her sister was gone—looking for Cougar, she had no doubt.

"He will not hurt me." Singer Of Songs indicated the captain.

"You cannot be certain of that."

The pueblo rooftops were already dotted with Hopi and

even more were climbing onto them for a better view. All she wanted to do was run, but she couldn't. Her heart hammered so she could barely breathe, and yet she forced her legs to move. She stopped a few feet in front of the soldiers, the sun beating down on her.

Recognizing her, Captain Lopez stopped in mid-stride, and despite the helmet-shade, she thought she saw hesitancy in his features, but it didn't last long.

"We are here for everything which belongs to us," he announced. He turned toward the soldier who'd returned before the others. "Get it. Get it all."

Food was a wonderful thing. Once eaten, it turned into strength, flowed into the muscles and brought the mind back to life. Morning Butterfly had always known that, but she couldn't remember ever having been as hungry as she'd been before Cougar fed her.

And yet food wasn't responsible for the way she felt now, she acknowledged, still drinking in Cougar's reality. She'd been starved for him without knowing it. He'd told her that he and the others hadn't attempted to follow the soldiers but had gone into the canyon, where memories and wisdom of the Before Ones waited. She understood why standing where the Before Ones had once lived had been important, even wished she could walk into the rock homes of the Anasazi so she could study the artwork and carvings they'd left on the canyon's sides and look for discarded pottery, jewelry, cooking utensils, or weapons. There was indeed wisdom and continuity to be learned from the Before Ones, and these days she ached for that.

Still, if Cougar hadn't spent days and nights within the canyon's great walls and in its shadows, her fear for him wouldn't have stripped her of every other emotion.

Looking around, she took note of the rapidly dying daylight. Cougar's companions had remounted and were getting ready to ride away. Only half aware of what she was doing, she started toward her mare, but Cougar stopped her.

"This is our time," he said simply. "Nothing else."

"But . . ."

"You do not want to be alone with me?"

"No, that is not it. My family."

"Send them a prayer. Maybe their hearts are open and they will hear it."

Closing her eyes, she concentrated on her parents, Singer Of Songs, and One Hand. In her mind, she saw herself touch each of them on the shoulder and whisper that she was all right and would soon return. That done, she looked up at Cougar.

She thought night must love him because although it was still coming to life, its shadows embraced him and painted him in dark, bold colors. He'd soon have to put on a shirt or blanket but the mountain chill hadn't yet touched him. Instead, he remained nearly naked, part of his world.

"This is as it should be," he said as they listened to the retreating hoofbeats. "Spider Woman and the Cloud People guided you to me because it is right for us to be together."

"You believe in her and the Cloud People?"

"They are not Navajo, but they exist for the Hopi."

"Just as *chindi* are part of the Navajo world?"

He nodded. "Kachinas live in the Hopi world; Navajo have Changing Woman, White Shell Woman, the Hero Twins. Those are separate, not right or wrong, simply part of one tribe or another."

"That is what I tried to tell the padre, but he would not listen."

Night was bringing the forest closer and closer. She could no longer distinguish between the different trees. Cougar was saying something, and she struggled to concentrate on his words, but with his body calling to hers it wasn't easy.

"I do not want to talk about Fray Angelico or the others who do not belong here," he said. "We have done that before and will do so again, but not now."

He was right. Still . . .

"What is it?" he asked.

"I—I am afraid."

"Of me?"

"No." Giving weight to her words, she wrapped her arms around him and rested her head against his chest. "Of what I feel for you," she whispered from the cocoon and challenge of his embrace. "Of the ways you have touched me."

"You touch me too."

"How?"

"In every way. I hear your words and although I make them Navajo in my mind, they remain Hopi. I take what it means to be Hopi into my heart and am made wiser because of that, but then I ask myself if I am becoming less Navajo."

"Is that wrong?"

"I do not know. What it means to be Hopi is the ability to look at the world as it is and as it is becoming and walk in peace with those things."

"Yes."

"It is not the same for my people."

"I know."

"We are not afraid to go to war, to die." He glanced at his surroundings. "But if we continue on this path, will the time come when the newcomers are so many that even if we prepare our hearts, minds, and bodies as the spirits guide us, will we all be killed?"

"Do not say that! The Navajo have always been. Surely—"

"I know," he softly interrupted. "These are things I do not want to speak about, to think of. I am with you." He'd bent his head toward her; his breath whispered over her forehead. "That is where I want my heart to be tonight, with you. For nothing else to exist.

"Can that be?"

"Yes," she whispered.

24

The moon was a thin, silvery arch that only occasionally peeked out around the canopy of trees. Although there were no clouds, the stars too seemed subdued. Maybe, Cougar told Morning Butterfly after they'd made love, summer's heat had exhausted the stars along with everything else and they were resting until cooler temperatures coaxed them back to life.

That was possible, but she had little interest in stars tonight; nothing mattered except Cougar and the easy way her body had welcomed his into it. Yes, there'd been initial pain, but she'd known to expect that and had waited without breathing until it passed. Then she'd learned what it is to be a woman.

Snuggled against his side with her hand over his chest and her head resting on his arm, she asked what he and Sweet Water had talked about when they were together like this.

"My wife belongs in yesterday," he whispered. "She will always live in a place in my heart, but she is not with us tonight."

"I am glad, but . . ."

"But what?"

"My parents have slept together for many years and what they say to each other is familiar and easy . . . but I do not know what you want to hear from me."

He chuckled, then admitted that words weren't coming easily to him either. "Perhaps we should try to sleep," he suggested. "In the morning—"

"I do not want to talk about tomorrow, to think about it even."

"Neither do I. Morning Butterfly, this was your first time with a man, was it not?"

"Yes. I—I wish I was wiser in such things and knew what I was supposed to do."

"Your body sang to mine. That is all that matters. Did I hurt you?"

"Only a little."

"I tried to be gentle." Then, although his body was beginning to respond to her again, he continued speaking. "This thing we have done may bring new life. If a child begins to grow inside you, I want to know as soon as you do."

"A baby? I should have thought—" Morning Butterfly felt a flicker of fear—if Singer of Songs could become pregnant, did Morning Butterfly think she could not? Yet she had not thought of it at all.

"It is all right," he reassured her. "Listen to me. The Hopi and Navajo are the same in that a child belongs to its mother's clan, and if there is a baby, it will be raised Hopi—unless we are together."

"Together? How can that be?" She started to sit up, then collapsed, trembling a little, against him. "Is it possible? Can a child be raised both Hopi and Navajo?"

His fingers were a current flowing over her shoulders and back. "I do not know. It has never happened before."

"If the Spanish were not here, you and I could move freely among each other's people, and Hopi and Navajo would soon think nothing of it, but that is not reality."

"Maybe after what happened to the soldiers at the canyon, they will leave."

"There is nothing I want more. It is not right for them to stand on Hopi land, to try to make Oraibi theirs!"

Cougar pulled her closer. What he was about to say might anger her, and he wanted her body to know the truth of what he felt about her. "If they insist on making Oraibi their home, the Hopi must leave."

"Leave? Cougar, I will *not* speak about this with you again."

"Morning Butterfly, for many generations the Navajo traveled from one place to another and called nothing home. Until they came to Dinehtah, it did not matter where they slept. Now our feet draw strength from Dinehtah, but we have not built immovable houses. Cannot it be like that for your people? If moving means freedom, then—"

"Oraibi is everything to us. Listen to me, listen so maybe you will understand. Like the Navajo, in ancient times the different Hopi clans migrated, but it was not because they did not care where they lived. The clans were guided by sacred tablets and sent on their journeys by the Creator. When our ancestors came to two sacred and mighty rivers and saw the three high mesas between them, they knew this was the place to build our fourth world, the one the Creator said we must call home for all time."

"Even if staying means death?"

"Stop it!" She tried to free herself, but he refused to let go, and after a moment, she relaxed against him. "Why are you doing this to me?"

"Because I want you alive."

"It is the same with me," she whispered. "I would do anything to protect you."

"You cannot walk my walk for me."

A hot tear trickled off her cheek and ran over his arm. "Cougar," she whispered, "you have changed me, showed me another way."

"The Spanish have done the same."

"They force their ways upon us. You let me see what it is to be Navajo. That is very different." She took a deep breath. "I smell you," she told him. "I think I will never forget what the

Navajo called Cougar smells like. I also now know the scents of this forest. My nose is like a child exploring its world for the first time, and my head says it is good to smell something other than Oraibi, but Rock Place On High is my home."

"Rock Place On High? Has it been called that from the beginning?"

Her words vibrated against his chest as she said yes and then explained that the Bear Clan was the first Hopi clan to complete its migration. Machito of that clan had been given the task of determining whether the other clans were worthy of settling at Oraibi as well. If they'd used their powers wrongly or for evil purposes, they were refused entrance, but if they'd come out of trouble the humble way, Machito then asked what special power their deity had given them and what ritual or ceremony they used to evoke it. Finally they were required to demonstrate how their power would benefit everyone. Only those whose ceremonies were proven to bring rain or snow, control underground streams, prevent cutting wind, or help crops grow were given farming land.

In his mind, Cougar saw the various clans build permanent homes, prepare the ground, and, most important, establish the shrines and altars that marked Oraibi's boundaries. The kachinas brought blessings from other stars and planets. Grass grew on the vast, dry plains and herds of antelope grazed within sight of the village. Bighorn sheep were nearby, as was other game of all kinds. The Hopi depended on their ceremonies, prayers, and the universal plan of life and lived a religious life, and in return, the land gave them what they needed to survive.

All that was as it should be, part of the spirits' plan, a path to be walked forever.

Captain Lopez ran an appraising hand over his hair. He'd had Singer Of Songs trim it after his return from the hellish canyon.

This day, the eighth since he'd seen Morning Butterfly leave, had started out well enough. His favorite horse had stopped limping and no longer picked at its food. He'd intended to let it rest a little longer, but now he was looking forward to a long ride, during which he would clear his mind and make plans for the future.

That pleasant thought, however, had been shoved aside when an Indian from New Spain had unexpectedly shown up a little after the midday meal. The Indian, a personal servant of his father-in-law, had been sent ahead of the wealthy landowner's party. Gregorio de Barreto and the rest of his entourage expected to arrive at Oraibi before nightfall.

With as much detachment as he'd been able to summon, Lopez had passed that piece of unwanted information on to Fray Angelico, who'd looked as displeased as the captain felt. Following that, he'd conducted a hurried inspection of his troops, during which he'd berated them for inattention to their uniforms, weapons, horses, and personal belongings and insisted they send away any Hopi women they might have with them. As for him, he'd satisfied himself with Singer Of Songs last night and would survive at least one night without her.

Now, as shadows lengthened, he sought to calm himself by reminding himself of how much he'd accomplished since coming here. Yes, there were problems with the Navajo, but the bulk of the compliant Hopi's possessions and food supply would be making its way south within the week, satisfying the demands of both State and Church and improving his standing.

In addition, work on the church had stepped up even more now that he and his men were here to oversee its progress, facts his father-in-law would undoubtedly take note of. Still, the last thing he'd expected was to have Gregorio come here. Only one explanation made sense: The man was checking up on him.

Lopez hadn't seen his own father since he'd left home and didn't know whether his parents or siblings were still alive; he only rarely thought of them. If he'd known his father-in-law would have this much impact on his life, would he have jumped at this marriage for the chance of bettering himself that it presented? No matter; the deed had been done.

With deliberate slowness, Lopez drew back his shoulders, stepped forward, and waited for Gregorio, an imposing man with keen dark eyes and a gray-flecked mustache. Although Fray Angelico stood only a few feet away from his father-in-law, Lopez didn't bother introducing him. Let the padre satisfy his own curiosity.

"Welcome," he said as his father-in-law dismounted, looking a little heavier and older but no less authoritative than the last time he'd seen him. "Welcome indeed. I trust you had a safe journey?"

"Quite."

Gregorio turned his horse over to one of his servants, then knelt before the padre, who blessed him but, uncharacteristically, didn't ask any questions. After Gregorio had inquired about Angelico's health, he clasped Lopez by the shoulder.

"I swear you have become as dark as the Indians themselves," he said. "And you are leaner than when you left. You have been well?"

"Yes, yes," Lopez answered. "Food is plain but serviceable, and fortunately we brought along adequate salt and other seasonings."

He explained that living where there was precious little shelter exposed a man to the sun's unrelenting rays. If he had lost weight, it was because his duties and responsibilities came before personal concerns. He pointed toward the partly completed church for emphasis.

Gregorio was a large man with arms and legs like tree trunks and a voice that had always reminded Lopez of thunder. He was every bit as hard and durable as his many leagues of land and mines. Unless some accident befell him, he would probably live to see the century mark.

"So," Lopez said, "to what do we owe the pleasure of your presence? I would think your responsibilities would have kept you in New Spain."

That made Gregorio chuckle, the sound more growl than laugh. "A piece of advice. As you go about making your mark in this world, spend as much time in pursuit of tomorrow as you do attending to today."

"That is why I am here," he reminded Gregorio unnecessarily. Then, assuming the role of host, he asked Gregorio if he wanted an immediate tour of Oraibi or was in need of rest first. As he expected, Gregorio shrugged off the suggestion that the journey might have tired him. However, he wasn't at all opposed to something stout to drink.

"Do not worry," Gregorio boomed. "I do not expect you to provide either wine or whiskey, since I dare say whatever supply you brought with you no longer exists."

"A little remains, but you are correct, I was unable to bring an amount adequate for a lengthy post."

Gregorio chuckled again, then looked around. "This place is even more desolate than I expected. Does it ever rain?"

"Once since I arrived. It still amazes me that the natives are able to grow crops. Their farming methods are quite ingenious and will, I am certain, fascinate you." No way was he going to tell Gregorio that the rain had come on the heels of a Hopi ceremony designed to accomplish precisely that. "If you have wondered whether my letter to you adequately described its worthlessness, I trust you now have your answer."

"I do indeed. Even if there were no savages to contend with, I cannot see how I could possibly make this place profitable."

"It is profitable," Angelico cut in, "in the souls that have been saved."

"Indeed. Indeed. And I wish to hear about that, but first, it would greatly please me if you would join us in a little taking of spirits."

To Lopez's consternation, but not surprise, Angelico agreed, and for the next hour the padre sipped blood-red wine and answered Gregorio's questions about his progress in the saving of souls.

Lopez was more than a little relieved to hear Angelico praise him for providing the necessary military presence and then sat back and listened as Angelico gushed that there would be no missions in this colony if it were not for the generosity of God-fearing men like Gregorio de Barreto. Nodding to himself, Lopez came to the not too complex conclusion that Fray Angelico would do whatever he felt was necessary in order to court favor with Gregorio. No matter what Angelico privately thought of Lopez, he wouldn't say anything negative around the soldier's wealthy and influential father-in-law. When Lopez had noticed that his former servants were gone, he'd concluded that Angelico had sent them to Santa Fe with another letter of complaint, but he'd concern himself with that when the time came.

As the sun was setting, Angelico asked if Gregorio wanted to tour the church, but Gregorio said that could wait until morning. In the meantime, if the padre didn't mind, he had need of a private conversation with his son-in-law.

"Fray Angelico is a most devout man," Gregorio observed once he and Lopez were alone. "I have occasionally wondered if I might be more successful if I could summon a Franciscan's zeal."

"I cannot see you taking a vow of poverty," Lopez pointed out. Night, as it always did here, was rushing in to take over everything. He took a moment to light a couple of candles and place them on the small table holding their drinks, then settled back in one of the chairs the Hopi had built. Orange and red lights flickered over Gregorio's features, making him look suddenly old.

"Why are you here?" Lopez asked bluntly.

Gregorio let loose with a booming chuckle. "That is one of the things I admire about you. Your directness. Why am I here? To offer you two things. First, congratulations, and then a business proposition. Maybe."

"Congratulations?"

"My daughter, your wife, has given birth. You have a son."

Bonita Marie, despite her church-sponsored and -dictated education, barely knew how to write, and communication from New Spain was all but nonexistent, which meant Lopez had had to content himself with speculation in that regard. In his mind, he now saw his wife with a baby clutched to her breast, a gentle smile replacing her usually somber expression. The infant's tiny fingers would open and close, its bright eyes fixing on whatever came close. It would laugh and cry, see the world as something wondrous, and one day the word "daddy" would flow from his lips.

"I have an heir. The baby and my wife are healthy?"

"Quite. He is robust, with a set of lungs that do his grandfather proud." Gregorio, to his everlasting chagrin, had fathered four daughters—and until now, his only grandchildren had been girls.

Gregorio cleared his throat. "Lopez, there is nothing I want more than to have my estate settled within the next few years, but it is much too soon to decide how much of it will go to Salvador."

Salvador? Was that what his son had been named? Feeling oddly bereaved because he hadn't been part of that decision, Lopez waited.

'Before I can come to any conclusions about what kind of man my first grandson will turn out to be," Gregorio continued, "I must see what kind of man his father is."

I am a captain in His Majesty's service. Grandson of a great explorer. "I see."

"No, I do not believe you do."

Lopez leaned forward. He hadn't had enough to drink that his reasoning power was impaired, just enough that any false modesty had been put to rest. He was ready to point out his accomplishments at Oraibi, the hardships he'd endured, even his determination to find the precious stones that so far had eluded him, but before he could open his mouth to begin, he was struck with the knowledge that whatever he said would be a mix of truth, lies, evasions, and pontification.

Somewhere out there in the dark were Cougar and the other Navajo, alive and boastful, maybe laughing at him this very moment. Morning Butterfly, too, was somewhere beyond his reach.

"What do you believe I do not understand?" he finally asked.

Gregorio leaned forward, so their foreheads were mere inches apart. "When I told Bonita that I had decided to come to Oraibi, she demanded to be told why; she is direct in that way, is she not? I explained the obvious: that I wanted you to know you have a son and so we could talk about that son's future as my potential heir."

I see, he almost said, then stopped himself. "The obvious? Then you have other reasons? Reasons that also concern me."

"Yes, they do, but probably not in ways you suspect."

This sparring had gone on long enough. If it had been anyone else, he would have ordered him to speak his mind. However, no one, not even a viceroy or governor, ordered Gregorio de Barreto to do anything.

"Good," Gregorio said, breaking the silence. "You have patience."

"This land has taught me that."

"The land?"

"It has secrets buried deep within it. Great mineral wealth. But I have learned that that wealth will reveal itself in its own time, its own way."

"Hm. Fascinating. I am tired of sitting. Come, walk with me."

Aided by the candles they each held, they made their way from the military camp to the nearest farming plots. As they walked, Lopez explained how the crops were planted and grown and how they managed to survive despite limited rainfall. He even touched on the Hopi's dependence on ceremonies, but made it clear that he considered them primitive and barbaric. Gregorio asked enough questions to let Lopez know he was more than casually interested in the natives' thinking processes.

"They are indeed a simple people," Gregorio said as they looked at the impressive pile of blankets, baskets, animal hides, dried corn, and other foodstuffs that would soon be on its way to New Spain. "When I first began to educate myself about this territory, I assumed all Indians were alike, but they are not, are they?"

"No. The Hopi are quite manageable while the Navajo are a savage lot."

"A savage lot with no earthly use."

They were getting somewhere with this conversation, finally. Lopez waited.

"I am pleased with what I see here." Gregorio indicated

the impounded possessions. "It appears we did not underestimate the number of horses that would be needed to carry what you have found here."

"No, we did not. As soon as I feel secure in assigning at least three men to travel with the pack animals, I will have them loaded and on their way. Unfortunately, they have already eaten much of the grass here." He said nothing about the horses the Navajo had stolen.

Gregorio walked in silence for several seconds. "There are other crops," he said. "Other produce, if you may. A commodity much more valuable than squash and beans."

Had Gregorio heard about the emeralds? "Oh?"

"Indeed. I am speaking of a useful workforce. Slaves."

From his perch on the church wall, Angelico studied the two flickering lights. That Captain Lopez and Gregorio de Barreto had excluded him from their conversation shouldn't have caused him consternation, but it had, not because he cared what they said privately to each other, but because if Gregorio had caught wind of the complaints he'd registered against Lopez, the powerful man might at this very moment be discussing his letters to the governor with the captain.

Too upset to fall asleep, he slid off the wall and began an aimless pilgrimage. When he'd first realized who their guest was, he'd engaged in several fantasies about conversations with Gregorio de Barreto. He would modestly show him around Oraibi, not so much as hinting that more supplies such as a reinforced wagon or adequate tools would make the process of building a mission much easier, because surely Gregorio would see that on his own. He might admit that, yes, conversion of the heathens would go smoother if they had a greater understanding of Spanish power, but he wouldn't have to do more than that because Gregorio would assure him he had every intention of bolstering the military presence.

But if Gregorio knew he didn't believe Lopez fit for command—

With a start, he realized how close he'd walked to the two

men. His first reaction was to slip off into the night, but that would only postpone the inevitable.

"Padre," Gregorio boomed when he stepped forward, "we did not interrupt your evening prayers, did we?"

"Not at all. Not at all. I confess, I have so little knowledge of the outside world these days that I hoped you would have a few minutes in which to educate me."

"Of course. I should have done so already. It is just that I first wanted to tell my son-in-law that he is a father. My daughter has given birth to a son."

Angelico congratulated both men, and if his gaze lingered on Lopez, so be it. Lopez knew he didn't approve of his liaison with Morning Butterfly's sister. The captain probably was concerned he might say something to Gregorio.

Lord, please forgive me. Humility is a virtue while to engage in manipulative concerns is not. I beg You, keep my heart clear and clean.

"I imagine you are anxious to see the infant," he said to Lopez. "Do you think you may return home any time soon?"

Lopez shrugged and if Angelico thought he saw a wistfulness in the captain's eyes, it was probably due to the inadequate light.

"I do not see how that is possible." Lopez glanced at Gregorio, who nodded. "Not with the proposal we have been discussing."

When Gregorio looked at him, Angelico drew himself as tall as possible. Just the same, he remained nearly a foot shorter than the landowner. Gregorio said, "I believe it would be counterproductive to be anything but totally honest with Fray Angelico. Padre, my son-in-law and I are of one mind about this land's greatest resource."

"Souls?"

"Souls? Indeed no. Slaves."

25

Morning Butterfly had been wrong to fear returning to Oraibi because when she reached it, her senses told her that what was going on made her absence unimportant by comparison. Yet more newcomers had arrived, four of them waiting patiently in a small group while the fifth, a large man dressed in rich, deep blue clothing and black boots that looked as if they'd never been touched by dust, walked with Captain Lopez.

Although she wanted to see her family, she decided to first present herself to Fray Angelico. She found him just outside his tent, his well-worn Bible open on his lap. He glanced up when she approached, surprising her with his haggard if determined look.

"Where have you been?" he demanded.

She'd already decided to tell him the truth and did so as concisely as possible, leaving out only what had taken place between her and Cougar.

"You believe the Navajo?" he asked when she told him that no Indians had been killed or even injured during their confrontation with the soldiers. "Their natural boastfulness and need to save face might have caused them to lie."

"I believe. If you do not, so be it."

Angelico started to say something, then shrugged dismissively. "I cannot think about that now. I take it you saw Gregorio de Barreto?"

Guessing that was the big man, she nodded. "Is he looking for gold and emeralds?"

"It would be easier if he was, but no, he is after what he considers far more valuable."

Feeling lightheaded, she settled herself on the ground. "Not more of our food stores? Surely he can see how little is left."

"No. Not that."

Even more alarmed, she asked him to explain, but long before he'd finished, she wished he'd never said a word. Gregorio de Barreto, Captain Lopez's father-in-law, owned so much land that Angelico could only speculate at the extent of his holdings. Gregorio believed all his leagues capable of growing fine crops, but in order to make full use of it, he needed a large number of hands to work the land. He'd commandeered much of the local labor force, but the Mexican Indians were a poor lot, highly susceptible to disease, and far from willing workers.

Angelico sighed. "He is after slaves. Not just for his own use, either. He intends to sell the surplus to other landowners."

"Slaves?" The word wasn't new to her, but the thought that armed men would kidnap and exploit others was almost more than she could comprehend. "Hopi slaves?"

When Angelico shrugged, she shivered. "No! He cannot—"

"Not him alone, no, but with Lopez working at his side . . . When they first told me of their plans, I warned them they would incur the Lord's wrath, but greed—greed is indeed the devil's work."

"You cannot stop them?"

Angelico gave her a look she couldn't comprehend, and

she was again struck by how weary he looked. "The matter is much more complex than I could possibly expect you to understand."

"Then you will do nothing?"

Anger briefly contorted his features, but although she wondered if he might try to strike her, he only gripped his Bible tighter. "If I turned my back on this vile practice, I would be failing my duties as a member of the clergy. And more than that, I would be failing myself."

The time she'd spent with Cougar had been like a spring morning. She would give anything to be back with him as they watched a hawk play with the air currents and their bodies whispered to each other, but he had returned to his people and she to hers.

"You are but one," she said. "How can you stand in the way of two?"

"Two? There are many, many more involved in the slavery trade, and much as it appalls me, I can understand de Barreto's position."

She didn't care what the oversized man did or thought. She simply wanted him gone.

"He will remain wealthy only if he is able to exploit his land, and what more productive way to accomplish that than by making use of free labor?" the padre went on.

"And you embrace his words?"

"No, of course not." Although quiet, his words held determination. "What I am saying is that I understand why he and others like him are so committed to this course of action. My vows call for me to forsake all personal property, but a life embracing poverty places me and my fellow priests in the minority. Wealth, Morning Butterfly, is power and position."

Once a Hopi had grown enough to feed his family, he joined the other men in the kivas and participated in religious ceremonies. A Hopi woman was known for her basket-weaving skills and her children's health; nothing else mattered.

"I would not be here if it was not for the generosity of men like de Barreto. It is not an easy position to be in, and determining what I must do now has caused me a sleepless night." He rubbed his eyes. "However—" He lifted his gaze to the sky—"I have only one true loyalty and that is to the Lord. He is my master."

Trying not to call attention to herself, Morning Butterfly shifted position and rubbed an aching instep.

"No matter what the personal consequences," he went on, "there is only one course of action for me."

"What is that?"

"I must remain true to my calling."

"How?"

"I had already set my course by penning a most strongly worded letter to the governor."

A letter, Morning Butterfly knew, was words placed on paper, but how could that stop Lopez and his father-in-law from doing what they wanted?

After she'd asked him that, Angelico looked at her in astonishment. "Morning Butterfly, surely you know you and your people are under the Church's protection."

"That is what you have told me."

"Yes, I am sure I have. My child, the soldiers have no jurisdiction over the Oraibi Hopi. If Lopez and de Barreto attempt to place your people in slavery, they will be in direct conflict with Catholic mandates. In a struggle between Church and State, there can be only one victor. The Lord God would not allow it to be any other way."

But what about my people and the Navajo? Are they the losers?

Lopez wasn't surprised when Fray Angelico handed him a copy of the letter he'd sent to the governor. What caused him the most consternation was that his father-in-law obviously believed he had little influence with the padre.

"I am disappointed," Gregorio told him, his lips barely moving. "I had hoped you had been more successful in your dealings with that man. His opposition to my endeavor, although not unanticipated, cannot be tolerated. But to have to personally set myself to the task instead of trusting you to take charge—perhaps I was wrong in assuming you would be instrumental in supplying the necessary workforce."

Lopez hadn't asked Gregorio how he intended to deal with Fray Angelico, not because he didn't care, but because he had seen Morning Butterfly. Thoughts that might, with nurturing, become the solution to a great deal flooded him.

Despite the cost to his nervous system, Lopez forced himself to bide his time until evening. Then he took leave of Gregorio by informing him that he needed to tend to the stationing of guards. The assignments took only a few minutes; after that, he hurried to the plot owned by Morning Butterfly's family and, using now familiar signals, made it clear he wanted Singer Of Songs brought to him.

Waiting was hard, not just because he'd have to explain to Gregorio why he was gone so long, but because he still hadn't fully formulated his plan of action. Not one but two women arrived, Singer Of Songs walking behind her older sister.

"She does not want to be with you," Morning Butterfly announced. "She knows you wish to make slaves of our people."

"How quickly news spreads. Has Angelico not already enslaved you?" he scoffed.

"You think we are sheep," she countered, her body so taut he half expected it to shatter. "We are not. Our hearts—" she pressed her palm against her breast—"our hearts are not those of animals."

No, they aren't, he thought, his attention torn between her and Singer Of Songs. He suspected Singer Of Songs was pregnant because her breasts felt swollen to his touch and she'd twice thrown up around him. So he was going to have not one child but two, was he—not that this bastard counted.

"I do not recall asking for you," he told Morning Butterfly. "Suppose you tell me why you are here."

"Gregorio de Barreto is a powerful man, is he not?" she asked without emotion.

"Yes, not that it is any concern of yours."

"The padre says that what he wants to do—making slaves of my people—is wrong, but it is not easy to oppose him."

The relationship between Morning Butterfly and Fray Angelico had been complex from the beginning and was becoming even more layered; he would be wise not to forget that.

"I repeat my question," he prompted. "What concern is it of yours?"

"A powerful man, more so than you."

"What are you getting at?"

She stepped closer, a silent shadow. He thought he detected a certain nervousness in her demeanor but couldn't be sure. Singer Of Songs' attention went from him to her and back to him.

"If you rape my sister again," Morning Butterfly said, "I will go to your father-in-law."

"The hell."

"And tell him what you have been doing to her, satisfying yourself with her instead of as a man should with his wife."

"Do you think he has not done the same himself?"

She blinked, then nodded. "But you are married to his daughter. Besides, what you do with my sister, what you allow your men to do as well, is against the Church's teachings. I see how de Barreto conducts himself around the padre. When your father-in-law hears how you have fallen in the priest's eye, he will turn against you. Cast you out."

Despite everything, he had to admire her. She was in over her head and couldn't possibly understand the complex relationship between Church and State or the unique position someone like Gregorio de Barreto held within that society, but she was willing to risk a great deal—her life—defending not just her sister but the rest of her people as well.

"You came here so you could threaten me, did you?" he said, sliding closer to Singer Of Songs.

"Not threaten. It is a promise. Leave my sister alone and have nothing to do with the taking of slaves or I will go to him."

On the tail of an oath, he lunged, wrapped one arm around Singer Of Songs' neck, and hauled her against him. "You aren't the only one with an agenda," he informed Morning Butterfly. "I have my own. And ways of tipping the scales to my advantage."

She started toward him with her hands uplifted and already fisted, but although he had no doubt she'd like nothing better than to attack, she didn't.

"Stay right where you are," he warned her. "And if you have a knife on you, I'd better not see it, because if I do, your sister is going to have a broken neck."

"No!"

"Yes." For the first time since his father-in-law's arrival—before that even—he felt in control. "I have a damn good idea where you have been," he continued. "With the Navajo." He kept his choke hold on Singer Of Songs, studying Morning Butterfly as she stared at him with eyes of cold fire. "You were wrong in thinking I wanted your sister tonight. Actually, it was you I was after."

"Why?"

"We will get to that in a minute." Singer Of Songs put up no resistance; it might be because she was half unconscious, but maybe she was too afraid. "First, it is time you learned something about me. All my life I was groomed for one thing, a career in the military. As a soldier of the Crown I have rights and responsibilities you cannot possibly comprehend, and I am not going to waste my breath explaining them to you. What I will say is that those rights and responsibilities have become valuable assets."

Why was he pouring himself out to a savage? What she thought of him didn't matter, only getting what he needed from her did.

"You found the Navajo, right?" he demanded. When she didn't immediately answer, he tightened his grip on Singer Of Songs so her breathing became even more tortured. "Answer me! You were with them—him."

"Yes!" She tried to pull his arm off her sister, but he

kicked at her, his boot connecting with her knee. Gasping, she stumbled back.

"That is what I thought." He tried to keep his voice down, but the need to get everything he could out of her drove him. "Where are they?"

"What?"

"Where *are* they? When you found them, what were they doing?"

"Let my sister go."

"No! You want her to live . . ." He yanked Singer Of Songs off her feet. She clawed at him with sharp but weakened fingers. Despite himself, he wondered if the baby inside her felt the lack of oxygen, whether he was killing it. "You will tell me what I want to know."

"What do you want? Please, let her go!"

"Did you see emeralds?" he demanded. "You went to the canyon and the Navajo were still there because they were mining emeralds."

"No!"

"You lie!" The jewels were his bargaining chips. If he had the stones, Gregorio de Barrato would see him for what he was, a man he couldn't demean or desert.

"There are no emeralds."

"No!" He was shouting, unable to control himself. "I do not believe you, no!"

Fray Angelico had been praying when he first heard the distant sounds of argument. He'd told himself it was none of his concern and that his relationship with God was more important, but then he realized that at least one of the voices belonged to a woman. He scrambled to his feet, then nearly collapsed because the circulation in his legs had been cut off for so long. Wincing, he stumbled in the direction the sound had come from.

As he drew near, he saw that Captain Lopez had hold of someone and was being confronted by Morning Butterfly. Gregorio de Barreto, whose demands for an explanation now overrode every other voice, stood nearby.

"What are you doing?" Angelico interrupted. "How can you—"

"Padre!" Morning Butterfly gasped. She briefly turned toward him, then went back to trying to pull Lopez's arm off his captive. "He is killing her!"

"Stop it!" he ordered Lopez.

"Stay out of this, Padre," Lopez warned. "Tend to religious concerns all you want, but leave me alone."

Lopez's captive tried to suck in air, but the sound was a harsh rasp. Sobbing, Morning Butterfly doubled her efforts to free the other woman.

"If you want her dead, be done with it!" de Barreto shouted.

"No!" Angelico gasped.

"My sister," Morning Butterfly interrupted. "He is killing my sister!"

He should have remained where he was, safe within the cloak of prayer. Now he had to act. Propelling himself forward, Angelico took hold of Morning Butterfly's flailing arms and tried to pull her off Lopez. His effort earned him an elbow in the throat, but though he could barely breathe, he refused to let go. Instead, he locked his arms around her and knocked both of them to the ground.

Despite his efforts to contain her, she wriggled out from under him and surged to her feet. Before she could resume her attack upon Lopez, de Barreto himself interceded with a violent shove which sent her to the earth. He cocked his leg and would have kicked her if Lopez hadn't yelled at him to stop.

"Why?" de Barreto demanded, his attention still fixed on Morning Butterfly. "The animal was attacking you. She must be punished!"

"No," Lopez said again.

Angelico scrambled to his feet and quickly straightened his robe. He wanted to help Morning Butterfly stand, but after the way she'd fought him, he thought better of it. Besides, graceful as a deer, she proved she didn't need any assistance.

"All right," she said, ignoring everyone except Lopez, addressing only him. "I will tell you what you want to know, but only after you have let my sister go."

"She speaks the king's Spanish," de Barreto gasped. "This savage—how is that?"

It seemed to Angelico as if the night had begun to breathe. Everything was chaos and tension, anger and desperation, and still the darkness, or maybe something within it, called to him. By the time he'd gathered his senses again, de Barreto had repeated his question, but no one had answered. Morning Butterfly and Lopez stood like statues, each taking the measure of the other.

At last Lopez slowly released Singer Of Songs. The girl slumped forward and would have fallen if Morning Butterfly hadn't caught her.

"That is my good faith gesture, Morning Butterfly," the captain said, his tone thick with hatred. "Her life in exchange for certain information."

"You cannot bargain with a savage," de Barreto insisted. "If one stands in your way, you bury your sword in the creature."

"Not her."

"Why not?"

For a moment, Angelico was certain Lopez was going to strike his father-in-law, but although fury vibrated throughout him, his fists remained clenched by his side. He strode toward Morning Butterfly. She stood proud and desperate and determined. The captain grabbed hold of her hair and drew her, almost gently, toward him. Morning Butterfly released her sister and then, after briefly stroking Singer Of Songs' cheek, went with her captor.

"I do not fight with women," Lopez said, although Angelico wasn't sure who he was speaking to, maybe himself. "Not—" his mouth twitched,—"when there is a better way."

"Women?" de Barreto scoffed. "These two are animals."

"No," Angelico insisted, although by all that was prudent he should remain silent. "They have souls and are human beings. This one—" he pointed at Morning Butterfly—"has assisted me in untold ways, and if anything happens to her, I will not rest until the wrong is righted."

"Are you threatening me?" Lopez asked through clenched teeth.

Once again the night seemed to reach out and touch his nerve endings, but this time, strangely, Angelico felt stronger for the contact. "I vow, before God and this assembly, that you will be held accountable for each and every action you take against her."

"Damnation," de Barreto blurted. "Padre, I warn you, do not interfere in matters which do not concern you. Your role is religious, not secular."

"Stay out of this, Gregorio!" Lopez interrupted. "You have no idea what has been happening here."

"How dare you speak to me like that. Surely I do not have to remind you of who I am."

"As if you would allow me to."

"Silence! I can make or break you."

"Is that a warning?"

"No. It is a promise. Damnation, Lopez, you are pushing me too far."

When de Barreto stepped toward Lopez, Angelico was struck by the older man's bulk and had to accord Lopez grudging admiration for not cowering. In truth, Lopez seemed barely aware of his father-in-law's presence.

Instead, the captain split his attention between Morning Butterfly and Singer Of Songs, who was massaging her throat and still breathing raggedly. Although it certainly, couldn't be, Angelico half believed Lopez was concerned about Singer Of Songs.

"This has gone on long enough," Lopez said, his voice thick with what might be both resignation and determination. Barely acknowledging the others, he jerked Morning Butterfly's hair, pulling her with him.

Despite the way he'd confronted his father-in-law, it was clear to Morning Butterfly that Lopez knew enough not to incur his wrath any more than he already had. Instead, he'd invited de Barreto into his tent, along with the padre who'd insisted he had no intention of leaving.

As the night drew on, she prayed Singer Of Songs had heard her desperate warning to flee and was no longer at Oraibi but somewhere in the wilderness's sheltering vastness; nevertheless, she didn't dare let her attention stray from what was being said around and about and to her.

For the most part, Fray Angelico remained silent except to make it clear that nothing short of his death would deter him from assuring she remained under his protection. As for de Barreto, except to occasionally remind Lopez that his standing in the family was in jeopardy, he too had little to say.

"This is the crux of it, Morning Butterfly," Lopez said. In the uneven candlelight, his eyes had taken on a yellow, wolflike cast. "You took off after the Navajo so you could spread your legs for Cougar. You have your hooks in him all right. And you are willing to risk your life—and your sister's—to be around him."

It wasn't like that at all! Morning Butterfly wanted to shout.

"What are you going to do?" de Barreto asked.

Lopez leaned forward, which allowed the candlelight to reach deep into him and pull out something dark and deadly. It was all she could do not to recoil.

"Use her."

26

When the Hero Twins went in search of the alien gods, they traveled east and entered the house of the Sun. As soon as they'd sat on the floor, lightning shot into the lodge, and they were alarmed, until Wind whispered that they had no reason to be concerned. Then Sun entered and offered the Twins a seat made of shell and another of turquoise, but Wind advised them not to take the gifts because they were seats of peace and they should choose the ones made of red stone, which were warrior seats. Pleased with their choice, Sun, who was their father, complimented them on the number of monsters they'd already killed. As a gift to their mother Changing Woman, Sun gave the Twins five hoops of different colors.

On their way home, they beheld a beautiful vision; the gods spread out before them the country of the Navajos as it was to be in the future, after the Navajo had multiplied and grown happy and rich. When they saw Changing Woman, the Twins gave her the hoops, and she rolled them to the ends of the earth.

Four days later, the Twins heard thunder and the sky grew dark and a great white cloud descended. The cloud was followed by huge whirlwinds that uprooted trees and tossed boulders about. The storm lasted four days and nights before quieting to a gentle rain. Changing Woman believed the storm had killed all remaining monsters, but Wind whispered in the Twins' ears to let them know that Old Age, Cold Woman, Poverty, and Hunger remained. The Twins confronted each monster in turn, and in exchange for sparing the monsters' lives, the Twins learned that the monsters were not enemies, but part of their family.

Eyes closed, Cougar lifted his hands to the stars and gave thanks to Wind for warning and advising the Twins. He couldn't say why the legend had been with him all night and why, instead of returning to his people, he remained near Oraibi, but he didn't question either his instinct or the directions his thoughts took him.

When Sun courted Changing Woman, he'd done so with respect for her flowing through him, and although she'd been content to live alone for many years, she'd finally accepted him. Whether it would ever be like that for him and Morning Butterfly, Cougar couldn't say, but he had no hesitancy about listening to the legends' wisdom

Maybe that was why he was here tonight, because Morning Butterfly, who might have been touched by Changing Woman, had sent her thoughts to him.

The nights were now cool enough that they carried hints of winter, and before long he'd dream of warm nights, but now it was enough that the breeze invigorated him. Sleep? He had no need for it and even if he did doze, his dreams would be full of Morning Butterfly and the gift she'd given him—her body.

A wolf turns in ever shrinking circles before settling itself on the ground, and as he turned first one way and then the other, always aimless, he wondered if he might be turning into a wolf. That his mind accepted thoughts of wolves made him a little uneasy, and yet maybe he was wrong to have feared his earlier vision of the *chindi*-creature. Only the wisest of old men and women knew everything there was to know about wolves, or *chindi*. He—

Like a strong hand propelling him forward, the wind pushed against his upper back. Instantly alert, he turned to face the wind, but it had already become the slightest of breezes again. Confused, he pulled the land's scent deep into his lungs but learned nothing new. What he'd felt might have been the beginning of a storm or, if One Hand's dream had indeed been a telling one, maybe he'd become one of the Twins, and the wind warned him of monsters.

"What is your message, Sun?" he whispered. "Changing Woman, is it you who speaks to me?"

Neither entity responded, but then why should they? He was a Navajo warrior, nothing else. Wasn't he?

"Nich'i, Wind? Are you laughing at my foolishness? If you are, speak to me so I will learn."

Understanding came in the form of the sound of running feet. Instantly alert, he dropped to the ground and hugged it until he realized that only one person was on the move, his or her progress uncertain. The Hopi didn't fear moving about at night, but they didn't run unless they were in trouble. He couldn't say if it was the same for the newcomers.

His nostrils flared, and the flesh across his shoulders came alive, sensitive to any disturbance. Although being on foot made him vulnerable, it also increased his ability to move silently over the land, and he did that now, bent low, senses as finally tuned as those of any predator. Imagining himself as a wolf brought a smile to his lips.

Closer and closer he came to his prey, muscles ready, one hand on his knife, the other clutching his arrows. Still, if the truth was in the soft thud-thud of feet against earth, he wouldn't need either. The slender moon had ducked behind a wispy cloud, and the stars were like fox kits reluctant to leave their warm den.

The first time he heard the word, all he felt was surprise at the realization that the other night traveler had spoken. Then the sound was repeated and he understood, or at least thought he did.

"Cougar," the wind itself seemed to say. "Cougar."

His heart jumped and skittered; his ears let him know it wasn't Morning Butterfly's voice, still, there was something—

A woman walking alone where maybe it wasn't safe for anyone to be about. Armed with that knowledge, he eased closer to what moved in the middle of the slumbering desert. She called his name again in heavily accented Navajo, the sound wavering at the end, letting him know that whoever she was, she didn't want to be here.

"Do not be afraid," he said in Hopi. "I mean you no harm."

She gave a little squeak, and he imagined her shrinking back.

"Who are you?" he asked. "Who has come looking for me, Cougar?"

"You?" she managed. "It is you?"

"Yes."

"Spider Woman, thank you for guiding me to him. Where—where are you?"

"Here." He stepped closer, slowly enough, he hoped, that he wouldn't frighten her. "Who are you?"

"Singer Of Songs, Morning Butterfly's sister."

"Where is she? What are you doing here?"

"I would ask you the same question."

He searched within himself for the answer, but all he could tell her was that Navajo spirits controlled his legs and thoughts these days and he didn't fight their wisdom. She grunted, the short answer making him believe she didn't fully understand but accepted.

Forces he didn't yet and might never comprehend were at work here tonight, but because his soul was Navajo, he accepted them.

Singer of Songs was wary of him, and Cougar had no doubt that she carried a weapon somewhere within the folds of her skirt. Even now, standing so close that he occasionally felt the warm puff of her breath, he couldn't make out more than the faintest outline.

"My sister feared I would not be safe at Oraibi," she told him, "that the captain would come after me again, but that was not the only reason I fled. Morning Butterfly risked so much for me. I listened to my heart and soul and they told me of what exists between her and you—that I should try to find you."

"You knew I was here?"

"I knew you had come to Oraibi with my sister; my heart said you might not have left. And that you should know what has happened."

"I thank you."

"I wish I could tell you more, but Morning Butterfly and I had little chance to speak because as soon as the captain released me, he made her his captive. I have become important to the captain, but he is two men, one capable of gentleness and the other a stalking wolf."

"What about Morning Butterfly?"

"He ordered her into his tent; his father-in-law went with him, as did the padre. The Spanish men do not trust each other and perhaps there is hatred between them, but their greed is even stronger."

"Greed? For emeralds?"

"I do not know. An old man from our family, One Hand, had been hiding nearby as the Spanish threw words at each other. As soon as I was free, he called me to him."

"I know who he is. What did he say to you?"

The sound she made was half sigh, half sob. "One Hand has lived many years and has seen many things—learned truths he does not want."

"He is not the only one."

"I know. Cougar, my sister fears for both of our people. When I spoke to One Hand, his words were the same, that the man called Gregorio de Barreto is dangerous and may bring grief to both Hopi and Navajo."

"In what ways?"

"He is a slaver."

Briefly robbed of the ability to breathe, Cougar neverthe-less faced what he had to. He'd first heard the word slave from his grandfather when Drums No More explained that many of the Acoma captives had been sent far away. Most, including an uncounted number of children, had never been seen again, but a few had escaped and returned to tell of being forced to work for Spaniards who taught them, with whips and chains, to care for their livestock and till the ground. They'd had barely enough to eat as they sweated and bled and cried far from the land that had sheltered their ancestors.

"How many men did Gregorio bring with him?" he made himself ask. "Enough to force many of our people to go with him?"

"Only four, but Cougar, there are other soldiers already here. All of those—how can our people fight them?"

She wanted an answer he couldn't give her. "First I must speak to Morning Butterfly, try to free her and make her safe."

"No, do not take that risk," she whispered. "My sister has reached the padre's heart, and he will not let anything bad happen to her. I believe he will fight to have my people remain here so he can continue to save our souls and because—" she gave a short, mirthless laugh—"so we can build his church."

"Perhaps there will be a battle between the padre and the others."

"There is only one of him, yes, but he carries his god with him and the Spanish fear that god. Maybe . . . maybe he will win and the others will leave."

If there'd been time for ceremony and dry paintings, that might come to pass, but he was alone tonight—alone and afraid for the woman who'd touched his heart and soul.

"If the slaver wins, my people will not resist," Singer Of Songs whispered. "We will be like sheep, hiding from the memory of what happened at Acoma. I would rather be dead than live anywhere except here, but I do not know how to fight."

True, but the Navajo did.

* * *

"I have never doubted your military expertise," Gregorio said, "but by all that is holy, I do not understand your present course of action."

"It is not necessary for you to comprehend everything I do," the captain returned. "Just that you trust me to turn the current situation to both our advantages."

Gregorio snorted. "I would like to, but how can I?" He rubbed his eyes with his large fingers and yawned. "Perhaps I did not adequately explain myself, but it was certainly never my intention to rob the Church of souls, even heathen souls. I intend to reassure Fray Angelico of that since the last thing either you or I need is to incur any more of his wrath. After all, the Franciscans, despite their pious appearance, are a powerful force and the Church's influence extends—"

"You do not have to remind me of that."

"Hm. It is indeed a delicate balance we must walk." Gregorio leaned forward and although they were alone in the tent except for a bound and silent Morning Butterfly, he lowered his voice. "I am going to ask you a question, and I expect an honest answer. The only way for you and me to profit by our relationship is by being totally open with each other."

As if I'm enough of a fool to do that. "Certainly."

"I—no, I think I will begin with a bit of a background, a reminder if you will. Your family's fortunes never fully recovered from the disastrous consequences of what happened to your grandfather, true?"

"You already know the answer to that."

"Indeed I do, indeed I do. I have no doubt you sought my daughter's hand as part of a plan to improve your position. You saw marriage to her, not as a love match, but as a financial one, did you not?"

Lopez shrugged and allowed himself a small smile. Why shouldn't he? After all, he and Gregorio had already had this conversation.

"As for myself, I had four daughters to settle in advantageous marriages. Bonita is not, how shall I put it, gentlenatured or over-blessed in intellect. The best I hoped for was to give her a prestigious name, which you supplied. And now I have a grandson, an heir, which, you trust, makes me even more favorably disposed toward you. You are right, but what I feel when I contemplate the infant's future only goes so far."

"I would do the same if I was in your position."

Lopez glanced over at Morning Butterfly, but she gave no indication she understood what they were talking about. How could she when she had no comprehension of the world beyond this miserable place?

"I hope to live many more years," Gregorio said, "but who knows what God has decided in that regard. I need to have my estate settled. I will need a competent overseer, a master capable of taking charge of my holdings—who is as ambitious and determined as I have been."

"Yes, you will."

It was Gregorio's turn to smile. "You know what I am driving at, do you not?" He'd settled back in his chair but now leaned forward again, causing the wood and leather to protest. "The position can be yours, if . . ."

If what, old man?

"If I turned my land over to you at this moment, what would be your priority?"

He didn't have to think about the answer. "Increasing the workforce so the land would be even more profitable than it already is."

"And how do you propose to acquire this workforce?"

"Through slaves of course." Out of the corner of his eyes, he noted Morning Butterfly's sudden alarm.

"Hopi slaves? How do you propose to wrench them free from the Church?"

"Not Hopi. Navajo."

Gregorio nodded but said nothing.

"The Church has little use for them," Lopez continued. "In fact, I have no doubt that Fray Angelico and his fellow priests would like nothing more than to be rid of the entire tribe."

"And how to you propose to round them up? They are wild animals."

Turning from his father-in-law, Lopez directed his response at Morning Butterfly. "By baiting the trap," he said.

His grandfather, Don Juan de Oñate of Zacatecas, had worn the title Governor and Captain General, which had once made him the new colony's highest judicial officer. The drive to accomplish at least a small amount of what his grandfather had managed consumed Lopez. The time when a man could become lord and master of everything his eye beheld was past, but with luck he would one day step into Gregorio de Barreto's shoes. However, he wanted something to call his own.

No, not just something. The legend of the Seven Cities of Gold, which had prompted the initial expeditions north from New Spain was just that, a legend. However, this country was wealthy—but not just in slaves.

Emeralds were everything, his salvation and pride—once their location was finally revealed by the miserable Navajo when they'd become his captives!

And then, finally, he would no longer question what his life was about.

"First People lived with wisdom flowing through them. They understood that the earth, like them, was alive. The earth was their mother. First People were made from her flesh and suckled at her breast. Her milk was the grass upon which all animals grazed, and corn had been created specially to supply food for mankind."

One Hand straightened and looked around the kiva at the assembled men. They were all looking at him, their expressions both grave and·expectant.

"The corn plant was also a living thing with a body much like man's," he continued. "And the people brought its flesh into their own, making corn, too, their mother. Thus First People had two mothers, Earth and Corn."

"Yes, yes," the men muttered in unison.

"It was the same with their father. He was Sun, the solar god of the universe, and it wasn't until he appeared before First People at the time of the red light, Talawva, that they became fully formed. Yet Sun's face was but the face through which Taiowa, the creator, looked. These things, thus, were First People's true parents. Their human parents were but the instruments through which their power manifested itself."

"Yes, yes."

Outside, the sun had already risen, but although his bones needed its warmth, One Hand's need for the kiva was stronger. "I speak of these things because in this time of change, it is important that we remember our beginning."

"We are like a newborn," Sun In The Sky said, his voice equally low and somber. "An infant spends its first twenty days with a perfect ear of corn beside it because that is Corn Mother. The infant sleeps in darkness because although its body is of this world, he is still under the protection of his universal parents. In darkness, with Corn Mother beside us, we are at peace. Safe."

"Sun In The Sky, I do not find fault with your words, but it comes to me that we cannot think of ourselves as infants. We have not been washed with water in which cedar has been brewed, and fine white cornmeal has not been rubbed over our bodies since we became men. I wish," he told the Bear Clan elder, "that all of us could nurse from Earth Mother's breast, but our feet do not walk that way."

Sun In The Sky frowned but didn't say anything. One Hand would have liked nothing better than to speak of the rituals and ceremonies that guided all Hopi throughout their lives, but the men who shared the kiva with him knew those things, and if he was going to help his people, he had to do more.

"My dreams have long been of things I could not bring myself to speak of and they were born of memories of this." He indicated his stump. "I buried my nightmares within me, at least I told myself I did, but one among us knew the truth."

Morning Butterfly's father and another man nodded, making him wonder how many had been aware of what he'd thought had been his secret. It didn't matter.

"The time has come for me to live beyond those nightmares. I looked at Morning Butterfly's courage and gave silent thanks to her for showing me the way, but I cannot lean on her. Instead, I have to find my own truth. My own wisdom."

"That is good."

"My journey is not complete and it may never be, but ever since the newcomers arrived, I have opened my heart to Hopi wisdom as never before. That is what I wish to speak about today."

He waited for encouragement, but all he saw were expectant faces, faces as familiar as his own.

"My thoughts are of Tokpa, the Second World."

"Where First People were sent when they forgot how to be pure and happy."

He nodded agreement with Sun In The Sky. "Tokpela, Endless Space, is where we would still be if the First People had not lost their way, but they did, and that, I believe, is what has happened again."

"How can that be?" Wanderer demanded. "We conduct our ceremonies as we always have. During Niman it rained, did it not? What more proof do we need—"

"It rained only a little," he interrupted the senior chief. "Because our hearts were not pure."

Several clan heads disagreed, but he waited them out. As he did, he placed both his whole hand and the stump on the ground and imagined earth's life force flowing into him.

"Our hearts are not pure," he repeated. "Not because we have forgotten ancient truths, but because strangers, who do not understand that these rocks and dirt are part of us, walk on our land. The padre speaks of a god unfamiliar to us, a god Hopi land has no need of."

"That is true, but we do not dare tell the padre that."

"Morning Butterfly has tried. Perhaps her words have reached his heart; perhaps, because he is not Hopi, he cannot hear them."

One Hand explained Morning Butterfly's conversations with Cougar, his voice thick with emotion.

"Why a Navajo accepts Hopi wisdom while the Spanish

cannot is not for me to say," he concluded. "We cannot turn the newcomers from what they are; we can only be Hopi—more Hopi than we have been since their arrival."

He expected more disagreement from the clan leaders, but all they did was study him.

"Go with me back to when First People lived in Tokpela, when they stopped being pure and happy and were banished to Tokpa. How did that happen?"

"Before that, they multiplied and spread over the face of the land as the Creator told them to do," Wanderer supplied. "Although they were of different colors and spoke different languages, they breathed as one and understood one another without talking."

"Yes," One Hand agreed. "It was the same with the birds and animals. They all suckled at the breast of Mother Earth who gave them her milk of grass, seeds, fruit, and corn. People and animals, they all felt as one. But then—"

He took a long, calming breath before continuing. "Then came some who forgot the commands of Sotuknang and Spider Woman to respect their Creator. They used their vibratory centers for earthly purposes instead of carrying out the plan of Creation, and were punished. This is where my thoughts have been, on how Sotuknang treated those whose hearts still had a song in them.

"Sotuknang caused the world to teeter off balance, spin around, and roll over. Mountains plunged into seas, seas and lakes splashed over the land, and the world spun through cold and lifeless space, freezing into solid ice. But those with songs in their hearts were spared and placed in the underground world where they lived happy and warm until the world once again began to rotate on its axis. The ground—" again he pressed his flesh against the earth—"the ground became their home and they were safe because they believed.

"The world is teetering off balance again," he finished. "And if we are to survive, we must trust, body and soul, in Mother Earth."

27

After feeding and watering his exhausted horse, Cougar announced he had something of great importance to discuss inside the sweat lodge.

Now, surrounded by relatives, clan members, and fellow warriors, he passed on what he'd learned from Singer Of Songs. He'd told the young woman she would be safe with his people and asked her to come with him, but she'd explained that even if she could leave her sister, her parents needed her. In the end, he'd clasped her hand and vowed to do whatever he had to in order to free Morning Butterfly.

"My sister says courage runs through you," said Singer Of Songs. "I believe her, and know that what lives in a man's heart is more important than the tribe he belongs to."

He couldn't look into the hearts of the newcomers, but the fact that the captain had imprisoned Morning Butterfly deeply disturbed him. Before anyone could ask why it mattered so much to him, he explained that not just the padre, but the soldiers, too, depended on her to communicate with the Hopi.

"She sacrificed a great deal and spent much time away from her people because she sought peace between Hopi and Spanish," he said. "Despite her own beliefs, she walked beside the padre and gave his words to her people. For that she was rewarded by being made a prisoner."

"If the padre sets great store by her, he should free her."

"He is but one man."

"What concern is it of ours, Cougar?" Drums No More asked. "We share the same land with the Hopi, but that does not mean their problems are ours."

"She ate with us and listened to Navajo words and prayers," he reminded him. "She did not step on our beliefs."

"No, she did not. But those things do not make her, or her people, Navajo. Cougar, I watched when the two of you were together and know your heart walks with hers. Perhaps that thing has made you forget that your first heartbeat was Navajo—and can be nothing else."

"I have not forgotten."

"Have you not? Cougar, I am an old man, and yet I remember what it is to be in love. It is a wonderful time, new and exciting, but I caution you—that emotion is not everything."

He hadn't called this gathering to talk about what he felt for Morning Butterfly, and he certainly didn't want to be told she might have turned him from the path he'd always followed.

"Her people will not free her, so I will make the attempt, but I do not want to do so alone," he said as evenly as possible. "I also wish for the Hopi to look at the Navajo and learn to be cougars, not deer. Otherwise, they will become slaves."

In response to their puzzled expressions, he explained that the captain's father-in-law, a landowner, was searching for a way to make his property even more productive. Everyone had heard about the taking of slaves, and a number of Navajo from other villages had been kidnapped and never seen again. Still, as long as the Spanish were interested only in Hopi laborers, his fellow tribesmen believed they were safe. He disagreed.

"Morning Butterfly is the voice of her people," he continued. "Through her, the Spanish have learned what little they know about the Hopi, but now they have silenced her and with that act, thrown her people into darkness. I cannot, will not allow that!"

"If it was anyone except Morning Butterfly," Drums No More asked, "would you still say that?"

"To be Hopi or Navajo is not so different," he said. "And it has come to me that if the padre says they cannot take a single Hopi, they may come after us."

Several of the men nodded uneasily, but although his brow furrowed, Drums No More simply pointed out they had no way of knowing that.

"No," he agreed. "But Morning Butterfly can tell us those things."

"Maybe. Maybe not. My grandson, I do not wish to bring you grief. It would please me to give your heart peace, but what if you free her? Perhaps she will be safe here, but I fear her presence would place us in danger."

"We are already in danger!" Shocked by his sharp tone, he tried to gather his thoughts but only partially succeeded. "Grandfather, Morning Butterfly and I are wiser together than we are apart. We each bring wisdom to the other. If the Navajo reach out to the Hopi, if we say something about who we are and our courage by freeing her, then the Hopi will no longer see us as their enemies. United, Hopi and Navajo can repel the newcomers."

Although the various tribes traded with one another, no one had ever suggested they take up arms together against a common enemy. Still, he could tell his people were carefully weighing his words. Several agreed with him, and Blue Swallow pointed out that Hopi knowledge of the soldiers' strengths and weaknesses was greater than theirs. However, Drums No More continued to scowl, as did most of those his age, which concerned Cougar, not just because this was his grandfather, but because the words of the elders carried the most weight when decisions were made.

After Blue Swallow had finished, Drums No More said, "Once I was a young man who thought nothing of traveling wherever I wanted, and we all know the hard lesson I learned. Now I see only Navajo faces and walk on Navajo land and my heart is full. Navajo wisdom and belief is enough for me. We are Dineh, the People. Sun, Moon, and First Man brought the Dineh into this, our final world. Us, no one else."

"But we share the earth with other tribes, the Hopi among them."

Although he shook his head, Drums No More looked troubled. "Do our dry paintings heal or guide others than the Navajo? No. Did the Hero Twins appear to other tribes? No. Only *we* ascended to the surface world through the Hole of Emergence. Only *we* are guided by the Rainbow Way."

"Yes," Cougar agreed, "and only we are plagued by *chindi* and ghosts. Perhaps in that, we should share with other tribes."

His attempt at humor failed. Scowling, Drums No More pointed out that someone who walks the Beautiful Way Of The Rainbow knows he's on the right path. Cougar, he suggested, questioned the Way because he'd absented himself from too many songs and ceremonies recently, and because he'd allowed himself to get close to a Hopi.

"They are not us," Drums No More said solemnly. "Only the Navajo were created by Changing Woman. All others walk their walk just as the Dineh walk theirs."

In an effort to calm himself, Cougar ran his fingers over the ground, reminding himself that the first Navajo had dwelled beneath the surface and their memories were still there for him to take strength from.

"You say Changing Woman fashioned us and no one else." Looking up, he fixed his gaze on his grandfather's ruined arm. "That is so, but the path of the Navajo and Hopi walk have become the same."

"Our feet are not imprisoned like the Hopi. We can—"

"Yes, we can run and perhaps that is what we will do, but Grandfather, there is one among the Hopi who has long walked in your footprints as you have in his."

Drums No More started to shake his head, but Cougar stopped him.

"He is like a grandfather to Morning Butterfly. When she was here, she knew the truth of your nights because the nights of someone she loves are the same."

The old man's lips thinned, but his eyes told him to continue.

"I wish you no disrespect. I would never do that, but things are happening which never have before. You say we should not reach out to the Hopi because we are different, but the Spanish made you and One Hand the same. Your pain was the same, your nightmares are twins of each other's, your views of the future—"

"One Hand?" Drums No More interrupted.

His eyes never leaving his grandfather's, Cougar nodded. "He, too, was at Acoma. I say that made him your brother, but only you can decide if he truly is."

"I still do not understand how you propose to get the Navajo to come here," Gregorio said. "Why they should risk their freedom for one Hopi woman—"

Anger burned a hole in the pit of Lopez's stomach, but he forced himself to speak in a measured tone. "I already told you, one of their leaders fancies himself in love with her. When I parade her about in chains, he will no doubt hear of it—if he does not already know. He will try to rescue her—and he will not be alone."

"I am not a military man, but I am a student of battle and I know how often deaths are a consequence of such actions. I need live bodies, not dead ones."

"I have no intention of sacrificing my men," Lopez pointed out. "Besides, Cougar and his warriors are not my primary target. Let them 'rescue' her. In the meantime—" he allowed himself a smile, which was doubly gratifying because Morning Butterfly could see it—"in the meantime, my men and I will be surrounding the Navajo village."

Gregorio, who'd appeared more interested in the state of his nails than what his son-in-law had been saying, stopped his perusal of his thumb. "You know where it is?"

"Of course. When the warriors arrive here, they will find only Hopi and a frightened padre all too willing to release her. By the time the Navajo realize what has happened, it will be too late and you will have the slaves you require. The savages will need to be taught what is expected of them, but you have experience in that regard."

"Indeed I do," Gregorio said with a small, satisfied smile.

Morning Butterfly was so still and silent that she reminded Lopez of a statue, or she would have if life hadn't taught him to take nothing and no one for granted. In the two days since he'd initially sketched his plan to Gregorio, she hadn't said more than a half dozen words. Although she often looked longingly at the tent flap, he'd kept her inside except when he took her out so she could relieve herself, not because he was afraid she'd try to run away, but because there was considerable advantage in keeping her isolated from her people—and to hell with what the padre thought.

What frustrated him was that he'd wanted to implement his strategy from the moment it occurred to him, but he'd been unable to fully garner Gregorio's attention until now because the pompous, self-assured man had made surveying the countryside and scratching certain itches a priority. In the meantime, he'd refined his plan.

"So," he said, "you agree that my course is the prudent one. I may not be able to hand you male Navajo in their prime, but they prove to be the most troublesome anyway. Females and youth, and the horses the savages stole from us are another matter."

"Females can have more than one use. All right," Gregorio said with finality. "You are right that we would alienate the Church by taking Hopi. As a result of the time I have spent with the padre . . ."

Although his father-in-law continued to talk, Lopez didn't listen. His skin crawled; no matter how many times he'd checked to see if insects were on it, he saw nothing. Still, he couldn't shake the feeling that his flesh had been invaded by something alien. He hated inactivity, no more than he did right now, and that might be responsible. Still . . .

Did he really give a damn whether his father-in-law had the slaves he insisted he needed? Bringing the Navajo to their knees would give him great satisfaction, but beyond that—

Why had he believed Cougar when the miserable savage told him there were emeralds at the great canyon? As far as he'd been able to ascertain, there weren't. . . .

And yet the canyon's rock walls had looked *so* promising. If only he could return—

"Are you listening to me?"

"What?" Lopez asked, startled.

"I said—never mind. What is more important is whether you will be able to lead your men in a successful raid on the Navajo village."

"You doubt my leadership?"

Gregorio stood. "Lopez, I would not have accomplished what I have in life if I took anything at face value, and since you asked, I am not fully convinced of your ability to succeed."

"My men and I would already be attacking the Navajo village if I had been able to garner your attention," he said.

He got to his feet and stalked over to Morning Butterfly.

"I hate you," she hissed. "I wish you dead."

"Wish all you want; it is not going to happen," he retorted.

"You took my sister's virginity from her, raped her again and again. That is not the Hopi way."

"I am not a Hopi! Never was and never will be."

He yanked her after him, and if his grip on her wrist was so tight that it caused her to gasp, so much the better. He'd already decided to secure her to the stake he'd used to imprison Cougar, and with his mind on how long it would take his men to reach the Navajo village while staying concealed, he paid little attention to his surroundings. However, when Morning Butterfly said something in Hopi, he looked around to see who she was talking to.

More than a hundred Hopi stood within easy speaking distance. A number were women, but the majority were men, some gripping the crude tools they used to work the land, others holding knives. How they'd gotten so close without him knowing gave him a moment of disquiet, but there wasn't time to think about that.

"What is this about?" he demanded of Morning Butterfly as Gregorio joined him.

"Ask them," Morning Butterfly said, and there was no mistaking the challenge in her voice.

"You know I cannot—what is this about?" he repeated, belatedly remembering he had a hold on her and there was no better bargaining chip. "If you want to go on living, you will tell me."

Instead of immediately supplying the answer, she spoke to several Hopi men, and he noted that most of her comments were directed toward the elderly man missing his right hand. He'd initially been of the opinion that the Hopi were little more than sheep because they were so easily dominated, but only a fool would think that now. There was something dangerous in the way they looked at him, and they held themselves, not like sheep, but more like wolves.

He'd just noted that Fray Angelico was standing off to himself but within earshot when Morning Butterfly switched to Spanish.

"They will not allow me to remain your prisoner," she told him. "And they have come to tell you and de Barreto that they would rather be killed, here, than be made slaves."

Their edict, given the inequality between muskets and arrows, would have been laughable if there hadn't been so many Hopi here and even more doing God knows what where he couldn't see them.

"They want my soldiers to shoot?" he demanded. "Believe me, if I feel it is necessary, it would give me great pleasure to—"

"No! You cannot—I beg you, you cannot!" the padre shouted.

"This is *not* your concern, Padre," he retorted as the little man hurried up. "I would think you would know better than to risk escalating an already explosive situation."

"You cannot allow anything to happen to the Hopi," Angelico sputtered. "They are my responsibility."

"They are threatening us."

Lopez signaled to let his soldiers know he wanted them to come closer. Because he'd trained them well, they did so with a show of force, their still-unprimed weapons making more of an impact than knives and hoes ever could. Just the same, he felt the weight and impact of the Hopi presence.

"Morning Butterfly." Despite the energy dancing inside him, he kept his voice even. "Tell your people to look at my men. Soldiers will draw first blood."

Because he'd had the presence of mind to keep his hand on her, he felt her tremble. Good. Her fear would surely be transmitted in everything she said.

"Do it," he insisted. "Tell them, now."

She did so without looking at him—at least, he assumed she was passing on his ultimatum. As he waited, it occurred to him that for once Gregorio had nothing to say, perhaps because his father-in-law was receiving an unforgettable lesson in his competence in military matters.

When this confrontation began, he'd estimated the enemy force at no more than a hundred, but that number was growing as more and more grim-faced Hopi joined those already present. According to Angelico, more than a thousand souls lived at Oraibi. If all of them showed up—Seeking to reassure himself of his men's superior force, he glanced at them, but instead of being comforted, he noticed that they were looking at Angelico. If they believed they owed more allegiance to the Church than to him—

"Navajo!" a man suddenly screamed in Spanish. "Navajo!"

28

As armed warriors galloped into view, Morning Butterfly strained for a glimpse of Cougar, but the sight of so many grim-faced Navajo was nearly more than she could comprehend. Even Captain Lopez, who surely had faced attack before, stepped back, nearly releasing her, but before she could put her mind to fleeing, his grip intensified.

"Where is he?" he demanded of her. "Cougar. Where the hell—"

"What is this?" Gregorio interrupted.

"They are here because you would not let me implement my plan in time," Lopez countered. "This is on your head, all of it! Damnation, Morning Butterfly, where is he?"

How he thought she knew was beyond her, not that it mattered, because somehow she'd found Cougar in the midst of the horsemen, and as their eyes locked, she knew she wouldn't be the one to point him out to the captain.

"Have they come to kill us?" Gregorio asked; if he was afraid, his voice didn't give him away.

"How the hell should I—"

Before Lopez could finish, an arrow arched through the air and landed at his feet. A heartbeat later, Fray Angelico cried out. Looking at him, Morning Butterfly saw he was trying to shake an arrow out of his robe's hemline. For an arrow to come that close and not wound must have been deliberate.

"They are going to kill us!" The padre's voice rose, more sob than warning.

"Damnation, Morning Butterfly!" Lopez jerked her against him, using her as a shield between him and the Navajo. "Where is he? You have to talk to him—"

She heard the hard twang of a bowstring, and once again the padre cried out. As before, only his robe had been struck.

"The church!" he wailed. "We will be safe there!"

He began running toward the hated structure. Several soldiers made as if to follow him but stopped at an order from their captain. Why the padre thought he would be safe in a building without doors or roof mystified Morning Butterfly, not that she had time to ponder that, because Cougar was urging his horse forward.

At the moment he was indeed a predator, proud and unafraid, and although she should have told him to flee, she didn't. Instead, with a nod, she acknowledged Drums No More, who rode at his grandson's side.

Lopez bellowed something, but she couldn't concentrate; then she felt herself being transferred from him to Gregorio and larger, equally hard hands held her in place. Lopez grabbed a musket from one of his men and started priming it.

"Tell him," Cougar said, his tone confident, "that he is to release you or we will kill him and his men."

"What is it?" Lopez insisted. He held up his weapon, the barrel pointed at Cougar's chest. "What did he say?"

She could tell him anything and Cougar wouldn't know, but the Navajo had risked so much that she couldn't be anything except truthful. Her eyes never left Cougar's as she repeated his order.

"Cut off a snake's head and the body dies." Lopez sounded as self-assured as Cougar had, as if he'd been waiting a long, long time for this moment. "Tell him that my first ball is for him and once he is dead, the rest of his people will scatter, at least those we do not kill."

She relayed Lopez's message.

"My life does not matter," Cougar told her. He had to speak loudly to be heard over the sound of restless horses and muttering Hopi. "Tell him that."

"I do not want to see you die."

"I would spare you that, but he needs to understand I am not the head of a snake. The Navajo are warriors."

"I know. But why? What happens here should not matter to your people."

"What are you talking about?" Lopez demanded, shattering the connection between her and Cougar. "If you are plotting—"

"He says—" Cougar was an eagle; without freedom, he was the same as dead. "He says there are no snakes here, only warriors."

Gregorio snorted. She was still trying to decide how much of a danger the man represented when Lopez's body turned into stone, all except for his arms. A silent scream propelled her forward, but even as she fought Gregorio's grip, she knew she couldn't stop Lopez from firing.

The snap of hammer against flint barely registered before the accompanying sparks ignited the powder. A boom, so close it filled her head, spread and echoed, became everything.

After a long, frozen moment, Drums No More pitched forward; if he had cried out, the musket blast had buried the human sound under it. Cougar grabbed him, his eyes never leaving Lopez, and she felt his hot hatred for the captain.

Cougar was still trying to hold up his limp grandfather when the other Navajo began to spread out. For a moment, she didn't understand, but then she saw that at least two and sometimes more Navajo were riding toward each soldier. Another hell-explosion from a musket forced a gasp from her, and yet she heard a gurgled sob. Turning in that direction, she saw an arrow protruding from a young soldier's neck.

"Lord help us!"

"Jesus Christ!"

Spanish oaths swirled around her and clashed with whatever the Navajo yelled to each other. Overwhelmed by the unfamiliar sounds, she concentrated on Hopi words. Instead of backing away from the confrontation between Spanish and Navajo, her people remained part of it.

A Hopi woman screamed. Madariaga, his eyes wide and white, had grabbed hold of New Corn, a girl no older than Cougar's sister, and was forcing her in front of him.

"They're going to kill us!" Madariaga whimpered, his words all running together. "Dear God, they're going to murder—"

"Oraibi! You will be safe there!" cried Angelico. What was he doing back here instead of huddling in his church? For a moment it seemed as if no one had heard him, and then, like rabbits fleeing an eagle, the soldiers raced for the mesa. Madariaga and his youthful prisoner brought up the rear, and to Morning Butterfly's great relief, no one endangered the child's life by releasing an arrow.

When Gregorio jerked her arm, she slashed at his face with her nails. His pain-filled cry gave her a heartbeat of satisfaction; then she felt rough fingers around her free hand and turned to face Lopez.

"The padre is right," Lopez said to his father-in-law. "Oraibi is sacred to the Hopi. They will not allow any killing up there."

"What are you, a coward?"

"We are out-manned! Can you not see—"

"I see a coward."

On the tail of a curse, Lopez wrenched Morning Butterfly free of Gregorio, causing flames of pain to sear her shoulders.

"Stand there and die if that is what you want," Lopez told his father-in-law. "Me, I am going to live."

Angelico had prided himself on being in decent physical shape for a man his age, thanks to his rugged lifestyle, but by the time he and the other Spaniards had reached the top of the mesa, breathing had become such torture that he couldn't speak. He was soaked in sweat and had lost both sandals, and if there'd been any other way, he wouldn't have come up here. But he'd had no choice because—

Because a full half dozen of the heathen Navajo had ridden their horses into his church and forced him back until he'd stood under the cross he'd sacrificed and sweated to bring here. They'd thrown ropes around the cross and pulled it down. Destroyed what was sacred.

Unable to bear the memory of the splintered wood, still shocked and horrified by the sacrilege, he forced himself to take in his surroundings. He hadn't been up here in weeks, and even when he had, his visits had been infrequent and far from relaxing. As a consequence, he had only a rudimentary understanding of the placement of the various structures, though he had no trouble recognizing the kivas.

"What are we going to do?" he asked Lopez with what breath he could summon, each word a heartbeat behind Gregorio's as the landowner asked the same question.

Instead of answering, Lopez turned in a slow, hesitant circle. He still had hold of Morning Butterfly, but she no longer fought him. Instead, except for keeping a wary eye on Madariaga and the frightened soldier's young captive, she seemed a disinterested observer.

Angelico had been wrong to think the majority of the Hopi had been below because he now saw just how many women and children were watching them from a distance. At least he didn't see any men, a thought that should have relieved him, but didn't.

"This is insane!" Standing toe to toe with Lopez, Gregorio shook his fist at his son-in-law. "A proven fighter would have known not to let himself be trapped this way. How are we ever going to get back down?"

Gregorio had been all too eager to join the others in taking refuge on Oraibi, not that Angelico felt compelled to tell the man that. At the moment, all that mattered was that he was alive—alive to ask both himself and his God how the Navajo could have desecrated his church.

"You know these savages, at least I should hope you do," Gregorio said when Lopez didn't respond to his question. "Is it likely the two tribes will join forces against us?"

That was a question Angelico wouldn't even have had to ask a short while ago. Ignoring the men, he limped over to Morning Butterfly.

"By all that is holy—" he began. Then he caught the look in her eyes and a chill spread through him. "That does not matter to you, does it?" He couldn't raise his voice above a whisper. "Everything I have tried to tell you—"

"They are your words, Padre, not mine."

His legs threatened to collapse, and for a moment he couldn't swallow around the knot in his throat.

"Your god is not mine, Padre." She sounded like a mother comforting a heartbroken child. "And I do not want him to be part of what you and I say to each other."

Lopez breathed in loud, noisy snorts, his mouth open in an effort to draw enough air into his lungs. Gregorio stared at him as if he was some loathsome insect he'd uncovered; the hostility between the two was unnerving.

"We will prove—we will prove our forces are superior," Lopez gasped. Blinking as if he just now realized where he was, he briefly studied his surroundings.

"The Hopi have always repelled their enemies from up here," he said, his voice again rich with authority. "That is what we will do—when our enemy attempts to overwhelm us, we will be ready for them." He pointed at the top of the ladder. "The moment they show their filthy heads, we will shoot."

"With what?" Gregorio insisted. "In case you have forgotten," he punctuated each word, "most of the ammunition is below. By all that is holy, Lopez, this is the most ill-conceived—"

"Ill-conceived?" Lopez interrupted. "If you thought that, what are you doing here? When we run out of powder and balls, we will use the savages' weapons—rocks."

The thought of the Crown's soldiers being reduced to throwing rocks was ludicrous, yet Lopez was right—they had no other options.

Rage no longer transformed Gregorio's features but neither did he look convinced of his son-in-law's plan. Turning toward the soldiers, he asked if they agreed with their captain.

"Our lives are in God's hands," Madariaga said while the others stared at him. "There are so many places here the savages can hide. And the way they look at us . . . they are waiting for us to turn our backs on them. Padre, I beg you, pray for our souls."

The mesa wasn't flat but sloped away and had several minor depressions in it. The uneven terrain, along with the randomly spaced houses, made it impossible for anyone to see everything. A number of Hopi were bold enough to now be standing in full view and there might be God knows how many others waiting their opportunity to attack from the shadows. Lopez might have a plan for repelling the enemy below, but what about those who already surrounded them?

Perhaps Gregorio had come to the same conclusion, because he stepped in front of his son-in-law and addressed the soldiers.

"You know who I am." His voice, although not overly loud, rang with authority. "And that I am a wealthy man. Before God and man—" he inclined his head toward Angelico—"I vow I will most handsomely reward whoever comes up with and implements a plan which gets us safely out of our predicament."

"The kivas." Lopez spoke so softly that for a moment what he'd said didn't register with Angelico. "We will seize control of them."

"What are you talking about?" Gregorio demanded. "What does—"

"I have already demonstrated to the Hopi what we are capable of," Lopez interrupted. "With her help," he indicated Morning Butterfly, "they will be made to understand that either peace will be restored and the Navajo made to leave or we will destroy them all—each and every one of their idols."

Morning Butterfly whimpered, low in her throat, but said nothing. With his head clamoring and his nerve endings screaming, Angelico struggled to assess the wisdom of what Lopez had just proposed.

"Father, I beg of you." Madariaga pulled his captive even closer. "Pray for us. I do not want to end up like Pablo."

Instead of acknowledging the soldier's request, Angelico turned his attention to the nearest kiva. A solitary old man stood in front of it. Holding a small, finely decorated basket in his hands, he appeared harmless, and yet—

The mesa known as Oraibi was far from impenetrable. Over the generations its residents had chosen a primary route from their gardens to its top, but there were other, less well-trod ones, and Cougar had chosen one on the opposite side of the mesa. Both his fellow Navajo and a large number of Hopi had wanted to accompany him, but he'd pointed out that they'd risk exposure by going up en masse. If and when he wanted them to join him, he would scream like a cougar and trust the wind to carry his message.

The various buildings were all made of stone, hard and lifeless and yet he felt something—not simply the essence of those who lived and even now stood here but something else. A *chindi* could have followed him and his awareness might be the only warning he'd receive that he was going to die today.

A cougar is a solitary hunter. Although one might occasionally charge a deer herd, it would have already picked out its prey and would follow that particular creature to the ground. No matter what the danger to Morning Butterfly and her people, Cougar wouldn't attack his gathered enemy, but if one stood apart from the others, he wanted nothing more than to sink his claws—his knife—into that vulnerable flesh.

But would killing one Spaniard alter Morning Butterfly's fate? Or his own?

The sound was heartbeat and rhythm, older than the oldest Hopi and part of everything she'd ever been and would ever be. As the chanting from the nearby Bear Clan kiva grew louder, Morning Butterfly pulled the murmur deep into herself. The Spanish had drawn closer together and stared nervously at the sound's source, but she and New Corn didn't share their fear because they understood that a number of Bear Clan members were singing the Road Of Life Song.

"What is that?" Gregorio demanded. "What are those devils doing?"

Fray Angelico and Captain Lopez looked at each other as if waiting for the other to supply the answer; the soldiers began praying. The padre had cleared his throat and opened his mouth when another sound began.

This one didn't come from human lips, Morning Butterfly was certain of that, but seemed to belong to the wind. It was as if earth and sky had reached out to each other in exploration and this soft, low whisper was what they'd created. If she'd had time and freedom, she would have run to the Bear kiva and asked the clan members to be silent so everyone could hear what remained.

"What is that?" Gregorio repeated. "What are they doing?"

"Singing. Praying. Nothing for us to concern ourselves with." Angelico tried to sound secure in his opinion, but it amused Morning Butterfly to see him slide closer to Captain Lopez. The military man continued to search his surroundings, his eyes narrowed.

"Make them stop," Gregorio ordered over the soldiers' rote-like prayers. "Damnation, force them to—"

"Listen to the sound," she interrupted. Ignoring everyone except the powerful older man, she addressed him. "Listen and learn the truth."

"What truth? Damnation . . ."

The wind-music had already grown stronger and held the potential for even more strength. Caught by the wonder of what was happening, for a moment she couldn't do anything except listen. Then:

"It is the song of who and what the Hopi are," she told him. "A song as old as the ground we stand on, ancient and wise."

"Shut her up," Gregorio barked.

A single knife-stroke would silence her forever but it didn't matter. Nothing did, except what she was hearing.

"End me if you must," she told Lopez, who gripped his sword with white-knuckled fingers. "But if you do, you will never understand."

"Make them stop," Angelico pleaded. "By all that is holy, make them stop."

"I cannot," she said, "because what we hear are more than human voices."

"The hell they are!" The oath burst from Lopez's throat, a man shocked back to life. "Damn you, I will not—"

"Listen!" she ordered. Although the captain's weight was nearly twice hers, she didn't shrink from him. "The kachinas are singing. If you tell yourself that you hear only the voices of those of the Bear Clan, it is a lie. Today is not for lies, only the truth."

"What truth?"

So Gregorio was capable of doing more than ordering people about. "The kachinas belong to the Hopi and we to them," she told him. Because the soldiers had fallen silent, she addressed them as well. "Today they sing of Tokpela, which is Endless Space."

"Blasphemy," exclaimed Angelico.

Turning her attention back to the padre, she shook her head at his ignorance. "The Niman ceremony, the one you said was the devil's work because it involved snakes, is our way of telling the kachinas that the harvest season is coming and they can leave the earth and return to their below-ground home until winter is over. But that did not happen this time, not because the Hopi did anything different or wrong, but because of what was done to the Snake Clan kiva."

For a moment the memory overwhelmed her, then, after giving White Corn an encouraging nod, she continued. "You destroyed what is sacred to our people and angered the kachinas. They are still here, among us, singing today."

"No!"

"Listen! Listen and tell me different."

The sun had darkened and dried Angelico's face, but today his flesh appeared stripped of color. Instead of doing as she'd ordered, however, he clamped his hands over his ears.

"Only God exists!" he shouted. "Everything else—all this is the devil's work."

"Not the devil," she replied, noting that for the first time the soldiers weren't looking at him as if expecting all answers and truth to come from his lips. "Taiowa, who is the Hopi creator. He cries with the kachinas."

The padre must still have been able to hear because he shook his head violently. "No, no, no," he muttered over and over.

Music danced on the air and echoed off ancient stone buildings. The sound reminded her of a bear's low growl, a distant wolf howl, restless wind pushing past grass and brush. She heard something a great deal like this every time her people drummed and sang during their ceremonies, and yet this was different—inhuman. If she had been surrounded by Hopi, Morning Butterfly would have dropped to her knees, closed her eyes, and become one with the vibrations.

"Taiowa is the beginning," she said, timing her words with the chant's rhythm. "And yet there was no beginning and no end, no time or shape, just the great void that was life in the mind of Taiowa the Creator. Taiowa is infinite and yet the Creator fashioned us. That is what we now hear, Taiowa saying that you had no right to destroy what he created."

"No. No. No."

"Why cannot you believe?" she asked, her voice laced with sadness. "You ask us to accept your belief but you cannot do the same?"

"No. No!"

Before she could begin to react, Angelico sprang forward, but instead of attacking her, he snatched New Corn from Madariaga. At the same time, the padre pulled a knife from somewhere deep in his robe and pressed it against the girl's throat.

"Tell them to be silent!" Spittle dribbled from the corner

of his mouth, and his eyes darted about. "Make them stop or I will kill her."

Morning Butterfly started forward, then forced herself to stop when she saw how the padre's hand trembled. "Even if I ask the Bear Clan to be silent, what you hear will not end. I am only a Hopi woman and cannot control the kachinas or Tokpela."

His mouth flapped open, but instead of speaking, he stared down at New Corn as if he'd never seen her before.

Someone was emerging from the Bear Clan kiva. Whoever it was wore a kachina mask designed to represent a bear. Although there was nothing to fear from an old Hopi man in a wood-and-fur mask, several of the soldiers gasped and Madariaga dropped to his knees and extended his clasped hands toward the padre.

"Help me! Please, pray for my soul," he whimpered.

Fray Angelico barely acknowledged him. Instead, he fixed his gaze on the kachina impersonator and the other, similarly costumed clan members who'd joined him.

She should tell the Spanish that the Hopi were harmless so they'd lower the weapons they'd raised, but before she could decide on the wisdom of that, New Corn whimpered; Angelico's knife had nicked the child's flesh.

"Padre, careful!"

"Make them stop! Make them stop! Otherwise—" Angelico fixed his gaze on Morning Butterfly—"I *will* kill her."

"You are a man of peace."

If he heard her, he gave no sign, and from the way his eyes bulged and his jaw muscles twitched, she wasn't sure he knew what he was doing. The Bear Clan members had stopped chanting before emerging from their kiva, but although the hollow reverberations had lessened in volume, what remained continued to flow around, through, and over her.

"This is a place of peace," she told the padre. "We are the Peaceful Ones, and if you harm this child—"

"Shut up!"

Fear for New Corn had made her forget everyone except

Fray Angelico, and she jumped at Captain Lopez's order. His long-barreled musket represented deadly strength and for too long commanded her attention.

"Shut up, Morning Butterfly," Lopez repeated. "I do not know what's going on here, but it is going to stop, now!"

So this was what it felt like to have a Spanish weapon pointed at her. She'd recently seen blood flow from Drums No More's wound and knew what a musket was capable of.

"I say to you what I said to the padre," she told him. "What we hear does not come from Hopi throats, and I have no control over it."

Lopez shook his head much as the padre had done a few moments earlier, and even Gregorio no longer looked as if he owned the land his feet stood on. However, she had no time for the changes in the two men because the padre was backing away from the kachina singers, and his knife hadn't left New Corn's throat.

"Padre." She started after him. "Padre, I beg you—"

"Leave him!" Lopez ordered, his voice like thunder. "Get back here, now!"

Captain Lopez might be afraid, Cougar thought, but fear hadn't destroyed the soldier in him. The musket aimed at Morning Butterfly didn't tremble and his hard eyes and clenched jaw said he wanted her dead. Morning Butterfly's concern continued to be for the girl the padre held, which meant she might not be attuned to the captain's mood.

Letting his body say what he didn't have the Spanish words for, Cougar stepped out of the shadows. He'd already fixed an arrow in his bow, and if he released it, it would bury itself in the captain's chest. Nothing mattered except seeing the captain turn from Morning Butterfly to him, the hatred in his eyes. Morning Butterfly, too, now stared at him, her eyes filled with emotion.

When Lopez spoke, each word was a low thunderclap. "He says," Morning Butterfly translated, "that if you shoot him, you will die."

"So be it."

"Cougar, do you not understand? He has ordered his men to kill you."

He started to tell her that his life was only one and worth sacrificing as long as she lived, when it hit him that his life was as vital to her as hers was to him.

Fray Angelico said something, but the words all ran together and barely earned a glance from Morning Butterfly. "He is praying," she said. "At least I think he is; his words are so strange, tangled together. Cougar, you are one Navajo among many Spanish."

"Maybe it is enough."

He hadn't taken his eyes off Lopez, which enabled him to see something both desperate and determined in the captain. He couldn't say how many Hopi were watching, but he felt their strength, absorbed it, and fed off it.

If he lived through the day, he would find a way to tell his people about what he'd experienced—not just the confrontation and danger, but what wasn't of this world. Energy and light.

"Kachinas," he said to Morning Butterfly. "Kachinas and other things Hopi are with us, speaking to us and telling the outsiders of their existence."

"Yes. I do not understand it, but my heart is full."

He'd been wrong to think he was ready to face death. Now he realized that not enough had flowed between him and the young Hopi woman, that what he was now hearing, feeling, and experiencing would take a lifetime to understand.

First Man, Changing Woman, Hastseyalti, I give myself to you. If my time to walk this land is over, so be it, but I pray for many more seasons so I may learn—

protect
love.

Captain Lopez's eyes were still telling Cougar about hatred and determination. Lopez might never understand what was happening on Oraibi but he was a soldier and wanted to do what soldiers have always done.

They walked toward each other, arrow and musket at the ready, Navajo feet silent, Spanish boots thudding almost in time with the chants. Fray Angelico had stopped praying and, like the soldiers and the Hopi, simply watched. Cougar's head was full, not of what he had to do to stay alive, but a Hopi song.

The song resounds back from our Creator with joy, it said. *And we of the earth repeat it to our Creator at the appearing of the yellow light, repeats and repeats again the joyful echo, sounds and resounds for times to come.*

"With beauty before me, may I walk," he chanted in Navajo. "With beauty behind me, may I walk. With beauty above me, may I walk. With beauty below me, may I walk. With beauty all around me, may I walk. Wandering on a trail of beauty, lively, I walk."

A growl escaped the captain's throat followed by something from Fray Angelico, but Cougar held onto the song of the Dineh and made it part of the Hopi Creation song, the two coming together inside him, warming and strengthening him.

Only vaguely aware of what he was doing, he let his bow and arrows drop to the earth. Captain Lopez continued to study him with his predator's eyes, but that was all right because one predator understands another—only Cougar was more than that, more than a Navajo warrior today.

Slowly, gracefully, Cougar lowered himself so he now squatted close to the ground and placed his hands flat against it. His eyes challenged the captain to do the same, and although he looked confused, Lopez handed his musket to the nearest soldier and followed suit—except that his hands hovered over the earth instead of making contact with it.

Captain Lopez de Leiva wanted to do what the savage had done, to prove he was equal to whatever insane show of strength Cougar had in mind, but he felt a rumbling through his boots, and his legs were both hot and cold. When he looked at Cougar's hands, it seemed to him that they'd grown larger; instead of remaining separate from the ground, the two flowed together, threatened to merge.

In an effort to free himself of this insanity, he looked for his father-in-law, but what he read in Gregorio's stare weakened him.

"You do not understand," he told the older man defiantly. "You will never understand."

"Because there is no comprehending," Gregorio retorted, but maybe he was talking about more than Lopez's behavior.

A few moments ago, Cougar had been chanting something, but he was silent now and although the savage should be watching his enemy's every move, he didn't seem to care about anything except what he was doing. Lopez tried to concentrate on the earth; although it was an insane thought, he could swear it had come to life.

Something was down there—a humming, a rumbling, a breathing—no! Not breathing! How could the earth breathe?

"What is he doing?" Lopez demanded of Morning Butterfly. Although his throat felt rough, his voice held at a whisper.

"Speaking to Mother Earth."

The world grew darker, and if he'd been able to concentrate, Lopez would have looked up to see the size of the cloud that blocked out the sun. When he breathed, he inhaled the scents of dirt and rock, Hopi cooking—and something wild as if the air itself had a smell. His vision narrowed until he thought he might be going blind, and yet he could still see Cougar's features, feel the savage's challenge.

Touch Mother Earth, Cougar said without words.

Finally, because he had no choice, he did.

Heat. No, cold. Something beating. Lopez's head screamed and he was afraid he would fly apart. He told himself—tried to, anyway—that this wasn't happening and if he could only fix his mind on—

Yes, that was what he would do. Force away the shadows and concentrate—

Oh, God, no!

"What is that?" He pointed at what had caught his attention.

"Tell me, Captain, what is it to you?" Morning Butterfly asked.

"You see it, do you not?" he demanded of Gregorio and Fray Angelico. "Tell her! Tell her!"

Although both men stared at where he'd indicated, neither spoke. Still squatting, his calves and thighs burning, Lopez stared at the gray creature standing at the edge of the mesa.

"A wolf," he mouthed more than spoke.

"Not a wolf," Morning Butterfly said. *"Chindi."*

Something clamped around his throat and he couldn't breathe. He felt himself rising, but how could that be, when an instant ago he'd lacked the strength to move. The dark shape had simply materialized, but that—like so much—was impossible. A wolf wouldn't venture into the middle of a Hopi village.

Fray Angelico must be seeing the same thing, because the padre had released the girl he'd been holding and his arms hung limp at his side. He'd dropped the knife, his mouth was open, his eyes bulged, and maybe he was crying. Lopez tried to step toward him, but before he could think his way through the incredible task of making his legs work, Gregorio started running toward the ladder.

The wolf was walking toward Lopez, its steps clean and weightless, teeth bared, and yellow eyes unblinking. The infernal chanting continued, part of the air and the earth.

He screamed, trying to silence the sound, but the chant swallowed his voice.

And when he started running, it was because the *chindi*-wolf was howling and the howl had found its way into his soul and he couldn't stand it.

Someone was already on the ladder. Bellowing at the living hindrance to his escape, he thrust the man away and began scrambling down.

He didn't hear Gregorio's scream as his father-in-law hurtled through space; nor did he feel the hands that guided him down to the desert floor.

* * *

"You are all right?"

"Yes."

Relief poured through Cougar and he clutched his grandfather to him. He still hadn't fully come to grips with the fact that he was no longer on Oraibi. Indeed, he might spend the rest of his life trying to make sense of everything that had happened up there, but because he hadn't died today, he would have that time.

Although the sun was just now setting, the soldiers huddled around their camp had already built a fire and showed no inclination to leave it. They spoke little, and when they did, their voices didn't carry. A few Hopi might still be on the mesa but most had followed the soldiers down after Gregorio de Barreto had fallen—or been pushed—to his death.

Singer Of Songs had guided Captain Lopez to his tent. The Spaniard hadn't said anything for a long, long time, not even to acknowledge her presence. After settling him on his bed, Singer Of Songs had turned her back on the captain and walked to her parents, who'd welcomed her with loving embraces.

Left alone, Lopez had first fortified himself with a healthy dose of whiskey and then started going through his father-in-law's belongings. His hands shook and he kept dropping things. He muttered to himself while continually and apprehensively glancing at his surroundings. When his gaze lit on his troops, he looked at them only briefly. For their part, they stared relentlessly back at him.

"What is he saying?" Cougar asked Morning Butterfly.

"That he is leaving here and does not care what anyone else does. He says the same words over and over again. I think his mind is no longer his."

Satisfied with that explanation, Cougar turned his attention to Drums No More. Singer Of Songs was taking care of him now. An elderly Hopi man stood nearby, his attention never leaving Drums No More's wounded side, his single hand holding the healing herbs.

"It is right that my grandfather and One Hand meet," Cougar told Morning Butterfly.

Nodding, she whispered that she believed the same thing. Although she was trembling, he was afraid to touch her.

"The time will come when we will speak of what happened today," she said, "but I am not ready for it."

"Neither am I."

He swept his arm in an arch indicating not just the still-muttering Lopez but Fray Angelico and the soldiers as well. As he watched, one of the soldiers separated himself from the others and, head down, trudged over to the pile of rocks that covered Pablo's body. Kneeling, he placed something on the mound and remained there for several moments before standing and walking back to his companions. Cougar recognized Madariaga, but he seemed much older than he had when Cougar had first seen the young soldier. He wondered if the soldier had prayed over his friend's body or if prayers had failed him.

"Tonight they are the deer and we, Navajo and Hopi, are wolves and cougars," Cougar said.

"But we are not predators who seek to kill."

There were enough Navajo and Hopi that if the newcomers put up a fight, they couldn't win. Still, he was glad the Spaniards had put down their weapons. Sometimes when a wolf or cougar is full, he sleeps near a deer herd and the deer continue to feed because they know they aren't in danger. It was like that tonight.

"The men of my village will soon meet," Morning Butterfly told him. "They want the padre to leave when the others do and must talk of how that is to be done."

When they'd first returned to the desert floor, Fray Angelico had paced here and there like a trapped animal, but now the padre was standing in the doorway of his church, his shoulders slumped and his head hanging. He'd made no attempt to get anyone to join him or to walk over to where the soldiers were; it was as if they lived in separate worlds.

"Is he praying?"

"I do not think so," Morning Butterfly told him. "Maybe, after what happened at Oraibi today, he has forgotten how."

"Maybe by morning he will have remembered."

"Perhaps, but it will not be the same as before for any of them. I believe that when the other Spanish leave, he will willingly go with them; no one will have to tell him he does not belong here."

Morning Butterfly knew more about Fray Angelico than anyone, maybe more than the padre himself did, which made it easy for Cougar to accept what she'd just told him. He and his fellow warriors had brought food with them and he spotted Navajo adding their supply to what the Hopi were preparing for dinner. This peace, like what existed between Indian and Spanish, might be gone before morning, but he had no need to look beyond tonight.

"Did we see a *chindi?*" Morning Butterfly asked. "If we did, then what is Navajo came to Hopi land."

"I have asked myself the same thing, but what else could it be?"

Staring up at him, she began shaking her head. It might only be the dying sun, but he thought he saw something in her eyes that had never been there before. The way she gazed at him—the same look had been in Sweet Water's eyes the night their bodies came together for the first time.

"Cougar?"

"What?"

"You risked your life for me," she whispered. "You did not have to, and yet—why?"

"I do not know," he started to say, but a man who has faced his enemy's weapon doesn't hide from a woman's question. "If you died," he told her, "I did not want to go on living."

"When Captain Lopez aimed his musket at you, that was how I felt. Without you, without you . . ."

A tear trickled down her cheek, and he brushed it away with a finger that wanted to stay on her flesh.

"I think—" She swallowed and started again. "I believe that we are no longer Hopi and Navajo but two people who have come from Mother Earth and are touched by her love."

"What you feel," he told her with newfound wisdom, "is not just Mother Earth's love but what I have for you."

It didn't matter which of them reached for the other first because when they embraced, they ceased to be two halves and flowed into a whole.

As they did, two maimed old men looked at each other and smiled.

Postscript

Fray Angelico, Captain Lopez, and the soldiers did indeed leave Oraibi the next day. The padre returned to Santa Fe and the Franciscan mission there, which provided shelter for the broken man. He never spoke of what had happened on the mesa. Captain Lopez went to the de Barreto land holdings where he made a feeble attempt to take up the reins of ownership, but his wife soon left him and he eventually drank himself to death. Unfortunately, they were far from the last Spanish to come to what is now Arizona.

History records that attempts to Christianize the Hopi and Navajo were less than successful. The Navajo lifestyle kept them at a distance from missionaries and the military, and the Hopi held their traditional beliefs to their hearts while outwardly accepting what was imposed on them.

Although a mission—the Hopi called it the slave church—was eventually constructed at Oraibi, it was destroyed during the Pueblo Indian revolt of 1680 and no piece of it remains. Today Oraibi, which may be the oldest continuously occupied community in the United States, belongs to the Peaceful Ones and is part of the Hopi nation, a pocket of land surrounded by the larger Navajo nation. These days Highway 264 provides access through land virtually unchanged since the first Hopi and Navajo settled in it, bringing past and present together.